Betrayal

By the same author in the *Empire* series

Wounds of Honour
Arrows of Fury
Fortress of Spears
The Leopard Sword
The Wolf's Gold
The Eagle's Vengeance
The Emperor's Knives
Thunder of the Gods
Altar of Blood

Betrayal

The Centurions: Volume I

ANTHONY RICHES

First published in Great Britain in 2017 by Hodder & Stoughton
An Hachette UK company

1

A CIP catalogue record for this title is
available from the British Library

Hardback ISBN 978 1 473 62871 7
Ebook ISBN 978 1 473 62873 1

Typeset in Plantin Light by Palimpsest Book Production Limited,
Falkirk, Stirlingshire

Printed and bound by Clays Ltd, St Ives plc

Hodder & Stoughton policy is to use papers that are natural, renewable
and recyclable products and made from wood grown in sustainable forests.
The logging and manufacturing processes are expected to conform to the
environmental regulations of the country of origin.

Hodder & Stoughton Ltd
Carmelite House
50 Victoria Embankment
London EC4Y 0DZ

www.hodder.co.uk

For Helen

ACKNOWLEDGEMENTS

The process of writing a novel is never a smooth one. Much time is spent looking out of the window (or even worse, the big electronic window on the world of interesting stuff). As ever, I am indebted to the patience of my editor Carolyn and the smooth facilitation of her assistant Abby, and the constant encouragement – only occasionally backed up with the use of force – of my wife Helen. My thanks to all of you who pushed me to get my backside in gear and deliver a readable book.

Taking a leaf out of a highly successful colleague's playbook, and for the first time ever, I've used an external consultant to advise me as to the accuracy of what's known as I've used it, and the probability of what's speculated where I've written fiction. Jona Lendering, owner of the fantastic Livius website (*livius.org*) very kindly agreed to cast an eye over the manuscript and point out any gross errors. This kindness paid dividends when he drew my attention to at least one major issue from a historical perspective, and thereby turned an ambush in the woods (in the next book) into something quite different because, as he pointed out, the pollen record pretty much proves that there were no trees in the place I'd written about! Thank you, Jona.

And lastly, thanks to you, the reader, for continuing to read these stories. Without getting all misty-eyed and gushing, it's a simple truth that without your imaginations as the seedbed for my imaginings none of this would ever have seen the light of day. So please keep reading. We're only taking a temporary break from the *Empire* series, by the way, and once this story of the Batavian revolt as seen through the eyes of the men I've imagined fighting on both sides is done Marcus and his familia will return.

Thanks everyone!

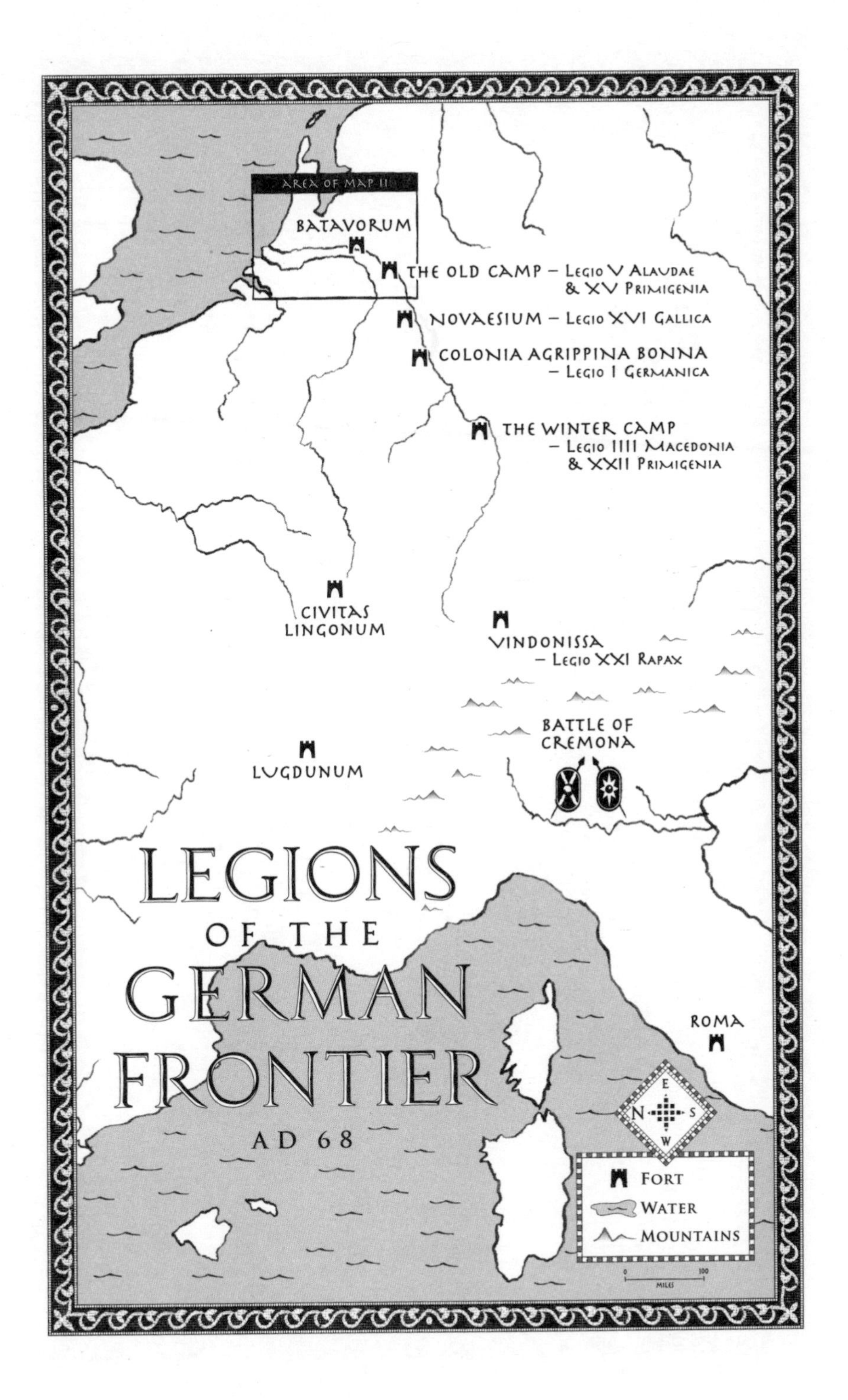
AREA OF MAP II
BATAVORUM
THE OLD CAMP – Legio V Alaudae & XV Primigenia
NOVAESIUM – Legio XVI Gallica
COLONIA AGRIPPINA BONNA – Legio I Germanica
THE WINTER CAMP – Legio IIII Macedonia & XXII Primigenia
CIVITAS LINGONUM
VINDONISSA – Legio XXI Rapax
BATTLE OF CREMONA
LUGDUNUM
LEGIONS OF THE GERMAN FRONTIER
AD 68
ROMA
N
E
S
W
Fort
Water
Mountains

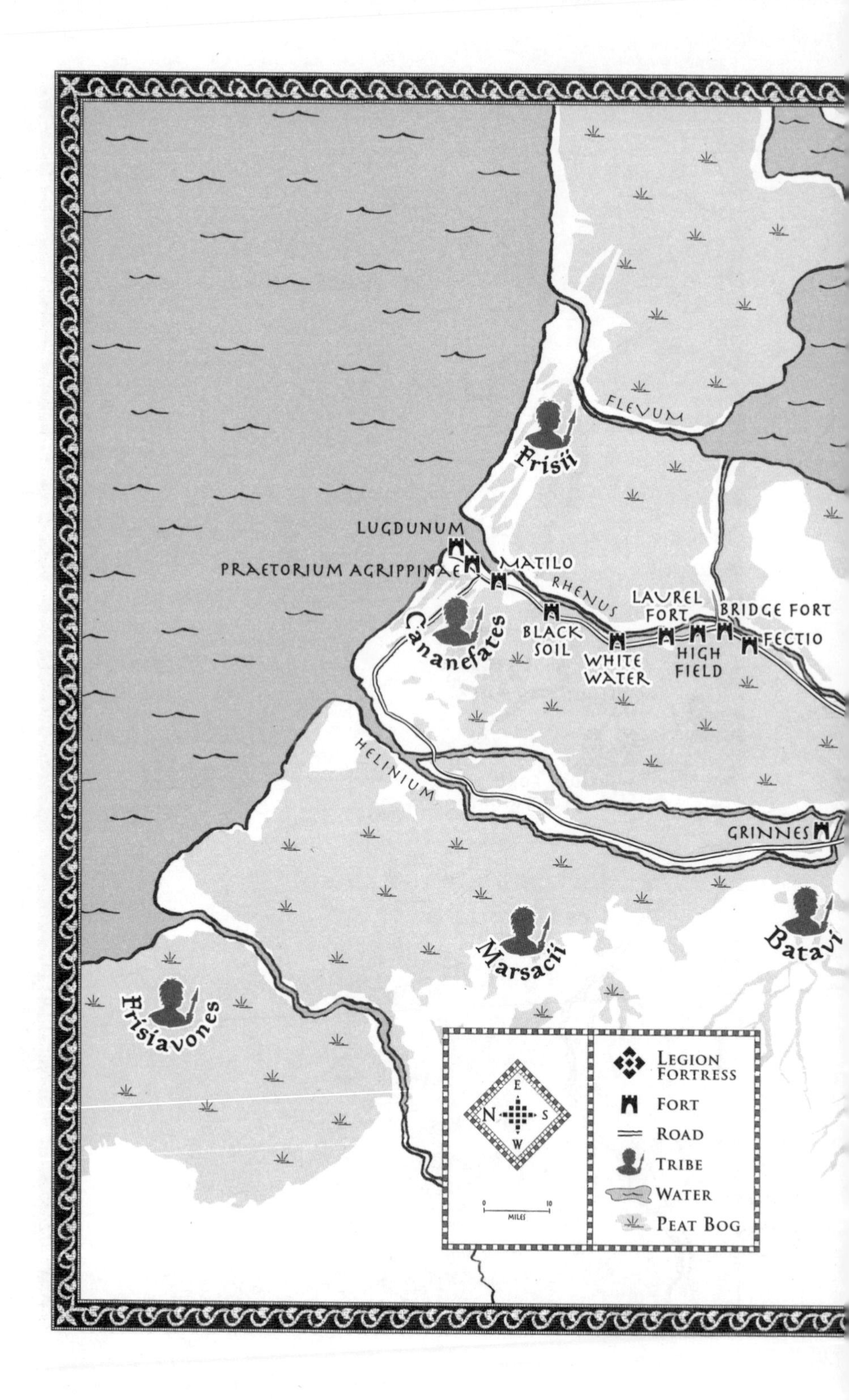
FLEVUM
Frisii
LUGDUNUM
PRAETORIUM AGRIPPINAE
MATILO
RHENUS
LAUREL FORT
BRIDGE FORT
BLACK SOIL
WHITE WATER
HIGH FIELD
FECTIO
Cananefates
HELINIUM
GRINNES
Marsacii
Batavi
Frisiavones
LEGION FORTRESS
FORT
ROAD
TRIBE
WATER
PEAT BOG
E
N
S
W
0
10
MILES

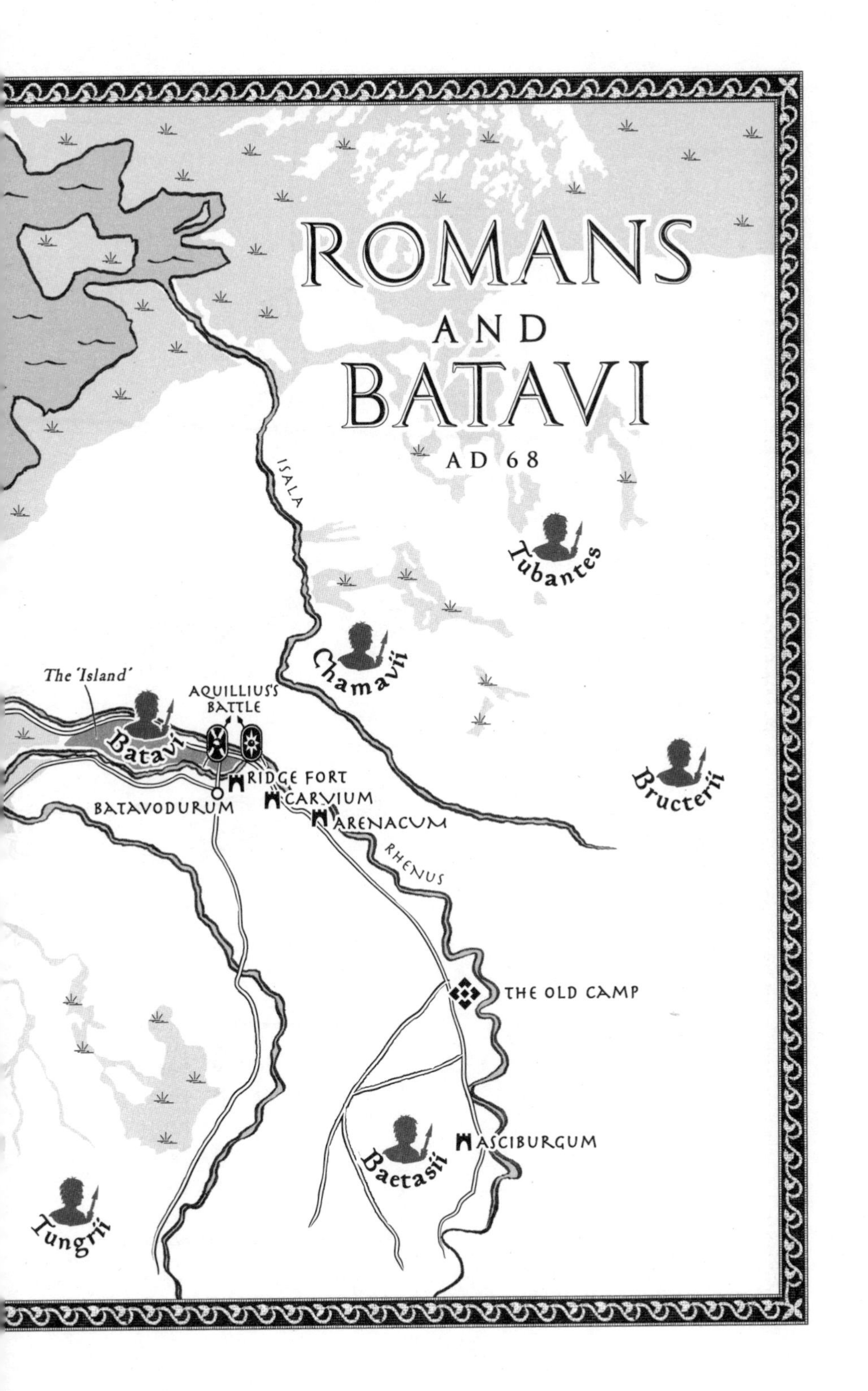
ROMANS
AND
BATAVI
AD 68
ISALA
Tubantes
Chamavii
The 'Island'
AQUILLIUS'S BATTLE
Batavi
RIDGE FORT
CARVIUM
BATAVODURUM
ARENACUM
Bructerii
RHENUS
THE OLD CAMP
Baetasii
ASCIBURGUM
Tungrii

Preface

In the year AD 68 an era ended. From Gaius Julius Caesar's usurpation of the republic's power, Augustus's brilliant seizure of the throne as 'first citizen', Tiberius's descent into depravity, Caligula's apparent insanity, Claudius's pragmatism and re-stabilisation of power, and Nero's deeply flawed and latterly egomaniacal reign, the same family had ruled the empire for almost a century – but the end of the line had finally been reached. A general fatigue with the extravagances, insecurities, indignities and sheer unsuitability of Nero's rule came to a head when the governor of Gallia Lugdunensis (modern day north and eastern France), Gaius Julius Vindex, a noble of the Aquitani tribe and a Roman senator to boot, declared a revolt against the emperor and in support of the man he believed should be emperor, the governor of Hispania Tarraconensis (the Mediterranean coast of modern Spain along with the central plateau), Servius Sulpicius Galba. But in failing either to secure powerful allies among those of his senatorial colleagues who commanded legions and armies, or to raise an army of his own to defend his uprising, this ill-judged rebellion simply sealed his own doom. The legions of Germania Superior (Upper Germany) swiftly marched south into Gallia Lugdunensis to challenge his light auxiliary force, and despite their commander, Lucius Verginius Rufus, agreeing a truce with Vindex, his legions then attacked anyway, routing the meagre rebel army at the battle of Vesontio (Besancon in France) in May AD 68. Defeated, Vindex committed suicide.

From Nero's perspective, however, the damage was already done. Verginius Rufus's legionaries attempted to name their general as emperor, and, while he wisely refused to accept, Galba remained a focus of discontent in the senate. Nero committed suicide in early June, in the mistaken belief that he had been declared a public enemy by the senate. Galba, promptly declared emperor by a relieved aristocracy, began his march from Hispania to Rome to take the throne. It seemed that a relatively peaceful transfer of power had been achieved, and a disastrous civil war averted. The new emperor, a man old enough to have met Augustus as a child, was widely expected to provide some linkage with an age of strength and stability and thereby to re-establish the Pax Romana, name a suitable heir and either cede the throne or simply die at a suitable time. A new era apparently beckoned, promising the restoration of a state based on the virtues of Roman dignity and service to the empire, with an end to the excesses of the past century. But it was not to be . . .

Prologue

Britannia June AD 43

'It comes down to this then. All that hard marching from Germania Superior to the coast, coaxing the men to risk Neptune's wrath despite their terror of the open sea, all the marching and manoeuvring since we landed . . .' The speaker paused, staring down across the mist-shrouded valley, its contours delicately shaded by the faint purple light in the eastern sky behind him. 'It all boils down to this. A river, and an army of vicious savages determined not to let us get across it.'

Gnaeus Hosidius Geta looked down from the hill's summit at the legions waiting in the positions they had taken up along the river before dark the previous evening, almost invisible in the pre-dawn murk, then raised his gaze to stare across the river that snaked across the flood plain at the foot of the slope, and the dark mass of tribesmen on the far side, clustered around the pinprick points of light that were their smoking camp fires. Although still remarkably young for a legionary legatus at twenty-three, he was already a veteran of a successful military campaign in Africa the previous year, and had lobbied hard to join the long-awaited mission to conquer the island of Britannia despite already having done enough to earn the highest position on the *cursus honorum* for a man of senatorial rank, that of consul. The sole arbiter of every meaningful decision that would be made with regard to the conduct and disposition of Legio Fourteenth Gemina's five and a half thousand men and their supporting Batavian auxiliaries, as long as he operated within the plan that had been agreed the previous evening in the general's command tent, he clearly expected his men to see combat before the sun set on the field of battle laid out before them.

'Indeed . . .'

His companion nodded, not taking his eyes off the vast army gathered on the river's far side, the fighting strength of at least half a dozen British tribes gathered in numbers that threatened a difficult day for both Geta's Fourteenth Legion and his own Second Augustan, unless the plan in whose formulation they had both played a leading role worked as intended. When he replied the words were uncharacteristically quiet for a usually bluff man, betraying his nervousness of the coming day.

'Indeed. It all comes down to this. On the far side of the river there are a hundred and fifty thousand blue-faced barbarians, while on this side we have less than a third of their strength. More experienced, better armed, better disciplined and with a plan to make the best of those advantages . . . but what plan ever lived long beyond the moment when the first spear was thrown?'

Geta grinned at him wolfishly in the half-light.

'Nervous, Flavius Vespasianus? You, the steadiest of all of us?'

The older man shook his head.

'Just the musings of a man who knows his entire career turns on this day, colleague. All you're thinking about is how soon you can get your blade wet, and how much glory you can earn in a single day's fighting, whereas all I can see before me is the myriad ways in which I can throw this one last chance to prove myself into that river, and end up with the same feeling I had the day Caligula shoved a handful of horse shit into my toga for not keeping the streets clean. Or just end up dead. And dead might well be preferable, given Rome's attitude to defeat. The prospect wouldn't bother me quite so much if it didn't also imply letting down the close friend who worked so hard to get me this position.'

The younger man laughed softly at his frown, waving a hand at the mass of Britons crowded into the land behind the river's opposite bank.

'Look at them, colleague. Every warrior in this desolate waste-land of a country, gathered from hundreds of miles around to oppose our march on their settlements. Some of those men haven't seen their own lands for months, but still they've held firm in their opposition to our advance. Their priests have told them the stories of how we treated the tribes we defeated in Gaul, how we deal with any people that resists us. They know that if they had chosen to join us of their own free will we would have spared them the horrors that follow any battle where Rome triumphs, the slaughter, the enslavements and the despoilment of their womanhood. They know that their resistance means that everything they hold dear will be torn down when they lose, and yet still they choose to fight. Gods below, Titus, they seethe with the urge to fight us! Indeed, they might already have overrun us, if we hadn't advanced with such care to prevent any chance of an ambush. Their chieftains know just how bloody a straight fight would be for their people, were they to turn their warriors loose to rail at our shields while we cut them to ribbons, and so they lurk behind a river they believe we cannot cross in the teeth of their spears, offering us a battle they expect not to have to fight. Look at them. Does that really look like an army readying itself for battle?'

Both men stared across the river at the British camp, a stark contrast to the ordered precision with which the four legions and their auxiliary cohorts facing them waited in their agreed start positions, close to the river. Geta pointed at the dark mass of their enemy, his voice rich with scorn.

'They call us cowards, for not fighting man to man in their style, and yet they hide behind a narrow ditch full of water because they imagine themselves protected from our iron. Today, my friend, is the day that they will learn just how it was that we came to conquer most of the world.'

He turned to Vespasianus with a hard smile.

'My father tried to stop me from joining this expedition. He asked me if Africa wasn't enough victory for me, if the capture of the chief of the Mauri hadn't already brought an adequate fresh measure of glory to our name. I just pointed to the death masks of our family's forefathers, staring down at us from the walls and daring me to give any less for my people than they did. Given the chance, I will show this ragged collection of hunters and farmers how a Roman gentleman conducts himself when the stink of blood and death is in the air.'

He nodded at the older man.

'And you, Flavius Vespasianus, I know that you will do the same. You may not come from an old established family, but there is iron in your blood nevertheless. You and your brother both serve the emperor with the same dedication as men with ten times your family's history.'

'Thank you, Hosidius Geta. That's high praise from a man of your exalted station.'

The young aristocrat turned to find another officer standing behind them, and he dipped his head in salute at the newcomer's rank.

'Greetings, Flavius Sabinus. Has the legatus augusti sent you to make sure your brother and I do our duty once battle is joined?'

Sabinus, a legatus on the general's command staff rather than a legion commander, shook his head in evident amusement.

'Far from it. The general has every confidence in both of your abilities to enact the plan we discussed. In truth he was far keener for me to remain at his side in order to be ready for the transmission of the order to exploit your legions' success. I persuaded him that an engagement of the sort of ferocity we're likely to see today often places an intolerable strain on our command structure, and suggested that I should accompany your forces forward to the riverbank in case either of you should by some mischance be incapacitated. After all, it only takes one well-aimed arrow to spoil a man's day in an instant.'

The legion commanders shared a swift glance, then Geta's face creased in a slow smile.

'I don't know about your brother, Flavius Sabinus, but I have no intention of being any man's pin cushion! The warrior who comes for my life will need to look into my eyes as he makes the attempt!'

Both brothers smiled at the younger man with genuine fondness before Flavius Vespasianus turned back to the battlefield below them.

'My brother Sabinus has come to play the vulture, and swoop down on the feast of our success, should one of us be unlucky enough to fall in the coming battle.'

His older sibling shook his head in mock disgust.

'Your brother Sabinus has, in point of fact, come to see Hosidius Geta's German auxiliaries show us all just why it is that the legatus of the Fourteenth Legion is forever singing their praises. So Geta, tell me, what is it that you have in mind for your armoured savages that had you argue for them to be placed in the front line today?'

Geta nodded, looking out across the river with the hard eyes of a man who understood only too well the damage that could be done to his command were it wielded by a man without an appreciation of its strengths and weaknesses.

'A timely question. And in answering it, allow me the liberty of asking one of my own. Tell me, Flavius Sabinus, what's the greatest threat the Britons present to us today?'

The senior officer answered without hesitation.

'Their chariots, that's their greatest strength. The Britons might be one hundred and fifty thousand strong, but they're farmers and woodsmen for the most part, some brave, some not, but very few of them as well trained or conditioned as our men. Their greatest fighting capability is concentrated in each king's companion warriors, the bravest and the best men chosen to accompany their chieftain into battle. They number just a few hundred men, but they've been trained to fight from childhood; they're well-armed and superbly motivated by their priests, and they fear dishonour in the eyes of their gods far more than death itself. Combine those men with the two hundred chariots our scouts have reported and the enemy commander has the means to deliver a pair of their best warriors with each one, as fast as a galloping horse, to any point on the battlefield where they can have the optimum impact.'

Geta nodded solemnly.

'Exactly. Several hundred picked men descending on one point of the battlefield as fast as a charging cavalryman, delivered to the place where they can do the most damage almost as soon as that weakness becomes apparent. If a legion falters in crossing the river under the rain of their arrows, then those warriors will pounce on us like wild animals as we try to get ashore. Who knows how many men they might kill under such a circumstance, perhaps cut down an aquilifer, or even a legatus? They could blunt or even break an attempt to get across before we could put enough men on the far bank to hold it. But if we destroy those chariots . . .'

He waited in silence while the brothers considered his words.

'But their chariot park is protected by the mass of their army. How can we hope to . . . ?'

Vespasianus fell silent at the look on his colleague's face, and after a moment Geta pointed down at the Roman forces marshalling on the river's eastern bank in the dawn murk.

'Your Second Legion will be crossing that river soon enough, Flavius Vespasianus, under whatever missile attack the Britons can muster, pushing across to form a bridgehead for my Fourteenth to exploit. But if we don't do something to prevent it, then just as your leading ranks step out of the water, they're very likely to find themselves face-to-face with a cohort strength attack from the best swordsmen they've ever faced, almost certainly before they've had the time to reform any coherent line. Unless, of course, we can destroy those men's ability to cross the ground quickly enough to be there when your men reach the far bank. An objective in which we are assisted by the fact that they've tethered the horses a sufficient distance from the main force to prevent any harm coming to them in the night, given the number of hungry tribesmen there must be over there.'

Sabinus's eyes narrowed and he stared down at the deploying legions and their auxiliary cohorts with fresh insight.

'You've ordered the Batavians to attack before the Second moves forward, haven't you?'

'Once there's just enough light for them to see what they're doing, yes. You are indeed about to find out just what my armoured savages are capable of.'

★

'Centurions! On me!'

With his cohorts in place as directed, drawn up in their distinctly non-standard formation in the gap between the left flank of the Ninth Legion and the right flank of the Second Augusta, Prefect Gaius Julius Draco waited. His officers converged on his position behind the first row of three centuries, each one drawn up in their usual unorthodox battle formation of three ranks of eight horsemen and sixteen soldiers, with two infantrymen standing on either side of each beast. In the normal run of things he would now have been standing out in front of his men, looking for any signs of fear or weakness, and dealing with any such manifestation in his usual robust manner, but in the pre-dawn murk he had instead positioned himself in the cover of his eight-cohort-strong command, calling his officers together where they could be safe from the risk of a sharp-eyed tribesman spotting the obvious signs of something out of the ordinary. They gathered close about him, their faces fixed in the tense expressions of men who knew that they would shortly be across the river and spilling the blood of the empire's enemies.

'The Romans would usually be delivering speeches at this point, boasting of their superiority to those barbarians over there . . .' His officers grinned back at him, knowing from long experience what was coming. 'Yes, the same old Draco, eh? You all know what comes next, since it's the same thing I say before every battle. About how we don't waste any time telling each other how superior we are to those barbarians over there, because if you strip off all this iron the Romans give us to fight in, we *are* those barbarians over there.' He paused, playing a hard stare across their ranks. 'Only more dangerous. Much more dangerous. We are the Batavi!'

He allowed a long silence to play out, just as he always did, giving time for his words to sink in and letting the growing legend of their ferocity take muscular possession of each and every one of them as it always did. Knowing that his challenge to them would take the weapon that had been wrought by their Romanisation, their appetite for war made yet more deadly by the addition of the empire's lavish iron armour and weapons, and would rough-sharpen it back to the ragged edge that was what had attracted Rome to the Batavi and their client tribes in the first place.

'So why do I say the same thing once again, eh?'

'Because this will be just like every other battle we've fought for Rome? A bloody-handed slaughter?'

The speaker was a young man known as Gaius Julius Civilis to the Romans, but named Kivilaz within the tribe, tall, muscular and impatient in both his words and bearing, forever on the verge of fighting, or so it seemed to Draco, who viewed him with the critical eye of a man who knew he might well be looking at his successor as the tribe's military leader. Loved by his men for his pugnacity and constant urge to compete, Kivilaz was regarded with amused tolerance by the tribe's older officers and with wary deference by the more junior men among his peer group, who knew only too well that their apparent equality within the tribe's military tribute to Rome was a polite fiction. Kivilaz was a tribal prince, a man whose line would have been kings with the power of demi-gods a century before, but whose members now occupied more finely nuanced positions within the tribe. Under Roman rule the men of the last king's line were respected for their blood, and granted membership of the emperor's extended *familia*, and while they possessed no more official power than any other man present, now that the tribe's lands were governed by a magistrate appointed by vote, their effective control of that magistrate's appointment made them almost as good as kings. Draco cocked a wry eyebrow at the younger man, echoing the smiles of his other officers.

'I say the same thing once again, *Centurion*, simply because it is true. It's time for your chance to cut off your hair, if you've killed for the tribe when we've been across that river and back.'

He waited for the good-natured laughs at the younger man's expense to die away, one of Kivilaz's closer friends nudging him with a grin and reaching out to tug his plaited mane, grown long and dyed red in the tribe's traditional mark of a man yet to spill an enemy's blood for his people.

'So the Romans have, as usual, managed to stir up the nest until every single wasp has come out to fight. See them?'

Draco turned to gesture to the mass of tribal warriors camped on the opposite bank, their positions mainly defined by the glowing sparks of their camp fires.

'There are enough men there to meet any attempt to cross this river and throw it back into the water broken and defeated, leaving the riverbank thick with the corpses of Rome's legionaries, if the battle goes the way they expect. Except that isn't going to happen. Because these Britons have no idea who it is they face. They expect no more than that which they have seen from the Romans until now: ordered ranks, tactical caution and a slow, disciplined approach once the sun is high enough to light up the battlefield. They do not, my brothers, expect the Batavi at their throats like a pack of wild dogs in the half-darkness, while most of them are still thinking of their women and stroking their pricks. In time this land will tremble at the mention of our name, but for now we are nothing to them and they do not fear us. They do not guard against us, because they do not know what we are capable of doing to them, and by the time they know that danger it will be too late.'

He looked around them.

'We attack now, as soon as you've had time to ready your men. Tell them that we will cross the river in silence. No shouting, no calling of insults to the enemy, no singing of the paean. They are not to suspect our presence on their side of the water until we're in among them. Once the first man has an enemy's blood on his face they can make all the noise they like, but until then I'll have the back off any man who disobeys this command. And remind them that we're going across the river to do just one thing, but do it so well that from this day the Britons will shiver whenever they hear our name. It might be distasteful to men like us, but since it has to be done we'll do it the way we always do, quickly and violently. Like warriors. And now, a prayer before we attack.'

He beckoned to the man waiting behind him, a senior centurion who was upstanding and erect in his bearing as he stepped forward to address them, carrying himself with the confidence of a warrior who understood both his place in the tribe and his supreme ability to deliver against his responsibilities. In the place of the usual centurion's crest across his helmet, a black wolf's head was tied across the iron bowl's surface, the skin of its lips pulled back in a perpetual snarl that exposed the long yellow teeth, the mark of the tribe's priests who fought alongside the cohort's warriors with equal ferocity in battle and tended to their spiritual needs in addition to their military roles.

'As your priest, my task is much the same as that of our brother Draco. Nothing that either of us can tell you now will make you better warriors, or more efficient in your harvest of our unsuspecting enemy. Draco's role at this time is to assure you that you are the finest fighters in the empire, straining at your ropes to be released on these unsuspecting children . . .' He waved a hand across the darkened river. 'Whereas mine is to remind you that Our Lord Hercules is watching us at all times, but above all at *this* time, eager for our zealous sacrifice to his name. So when you kill, my brothers, kill with his name on your lips, and if today is your day to die for the tribe's honour, then die in a blaze of glory, shouting his praise as you take as many of them with you as can be reaped by a single man. And if you are to die, then make your death a sacrifice to him, and send enough of the enemy before you to earn your welcome into his company.'

Draco nodded.

'Wise words, which are being shared with your centuries by each of your priests even now. But remember, nobody here is to go looking for their glorious death. What I need most is live centurions for a difficult summer of fighting, not more lines in the song of the fallen, so any man I see risking his life unnecessarily will have me to deal with after the battle, if he survives.'

He waved a dismissive hand, sending them back to their centuries.

'Enough. Go and tell your men that it is time to be Batavi once again.'

*

'They're on the move.'

Vespasianus stared down into the gloom, barely able to make out the men of the Batavian cohorts as they advanced out of the long line of legion and auxiliary forces that had formed a wall of iron along the length of the Medui's twisting course across the battlefield. Staring across the river, he strained his ears for any cries of alarm from the men who must surely be watching the river, but the only sound that he could hear was the bellowing of centurions and their optios along the legions' line as they chivvied their men into battle order.

'How is it that they're not seen?'

Geta smiled, his teeth a bright line in the near darkness.

'Simple. The Britons do not expect an attack, and therefore they do not look for one. The fires that have kept them warm and on which they plan to cook their breakfast serve only to destroy their ability to see in the darkness. And now, colleague, watch the impossible.'

The Germans' first cohort had reached the river's eastern bank, and without any apparent pause had advanced into the water with their determination unhindered by the fact that it was reportedly too deep for a man's feet to touch the bottom at that point, especially with low tide still an hour away. Vespasianus shook his head in amazement.

'They're swimming? In armour? Gods below, I heard the stories but I wasn't sure I could believe them.'

'Until now?' Geta grinned at the brothers. 'Believe. But that's only half of what they can do.'

Swimming alongside the leading horse, the mount of the decurion who commanded his first century's squadron of twenty-six horsemen, Draco looked back at the dimly illuminated scene on the riverbank behind them, nodding to himself at the speed with which each succeeding wave of men was quickly and silently entering the water. Two fully armed and armoured soldiers were swimming alongside every horse, each man using one hand to grip onto its saddle and the other to hold his spear and shield underneath him for the slight buoyancy they afforded, kicking with his legs to swim alongside the beast while the rider used its bridle to keep himself afloat. Both men and horses swam in silence, the only noise the beasts' heavy breathing as they worked to swim with the weight of three armed men to support, filling him with the same fierce pride he felt every time the tribe practised the manoeuvre, or employed it to cross an unfordable river and turn an enemy's flank with their deadly, unexpected presence. The far bank loomed out of the murk, and the horse beside him lurched as its hoofs touched the bottom, dragging him forward as its feet gripped the river mud. Feeling his boots sinking into the soft surface he pumped his legs furiously to keep pace with the beast, its rider now wading alongside his mount's head as it forged forward, restraining its eagerness to be out of the water.

Releasing his hold on the saddle, he waved a hand forward at his chosen man.

'Two hundred paces up the slope and hold,' Draco whispered. 'Form ranks for the advance and then wait for me. *Quietly*.'

Both the chosen man and decurion nodded, vanishing into the gloom while Draco turned back to the river, as his body recovered from the exertions of swimming under the dead weight of so much iron and sodden wool. He waited as the rest of the first three centuries followed the leading horses, their spacing so close that all of the seventy-odd beasts were past him in barely twenty panting breaths. The cohort's remaining three centuries were hard on their heels, Kivilaz nodding his respect as he passed Draco at the head of his men with a look of determination that made his face almost comically grim, the cohort's rear rank passing him with the front rank men of the second cohort close up behind them. Their senior centurion waded ashore, water pouring from his soaked clothing, saluting as he panted for breath, and Draco returned the gesture as he turned away, having passed responsibility for the river's bank to the man whose soldiers were now surging ashore. Hurrying back up the slope, he found the front rank of his own cohort formed and ready to move, a compact mass of muscle, bone and iron with the Batavi soldiers standing alongside their horses, any uncertainty they might once have felt at the beasts' looming physical presence long since trained out of them, just as the animals were equally well used to the presence of armoured men on either flank.

'Any sign of life out there?'

His chosen man's response was no louder than a whisper.

'It's all quiet. Want some scouts out while we form up?'

'Yes. But quietly.'

He turned back to the river and walked down the slope past the waiting cohorts, heartened to see that his command's incessant stream of men and beasts was almost invisible despite the slowly lightening shade of grey in the sky above them. Hurrying up the slope, they packed in close behind the leading cohorts, men squeezing water from their tunics and upending scabbards to empty them of any remaining water as they readied themselves to fight, rubbing their limbs to massage some heat back into them. The closest of them looked at Draco questioningly, eager to be on the move. Draco shook his head, his words loud enough to reach only a few of his men.

'Not yet. But soon enough.'

A waterlogged figure squelched up to him, and Draco saluted as he recognised the tribune who had been given permission by his legatus to accompany them across the river in order to provide the army's commanders with an account of the raid.

'Tribune Lupercus.'

The Roman took a handful of his tunic, squeezing out the water, and looked about him.

'Well now, Prefect Draco, are we ready to attack? The fact that you've allowed me across the river must mean you've got your entire command between my delicate body and the Britons.'

Draco grinned back at him, having warmed to the young Roman in the days since Legatus Geta had appointed him to accompany the powerful cohorts fielded by the Batavi and their allies. While the Roman was only attached to the tribe as an observer, with no formal command responsibility given that the tribe provided their own officers, the man's eagerness to fight was as transparent as that of his own men, and there was little that the tribe respected more than a man born with the urge to fight.

'We're ready, Tribune. Just stay close to me and don't do anything stupid. I've no desire to win this battle and then find myself in the shit for letting a young gentleman get himself run through with a spear.'

'Or trip up and fall on his own sword?' The Roman grinned at him in the half-darkness. 'Have a little faith, Draco. My father didn't invest in ten years of tuition in the finer arts of swordsmanship to see me end up face down in the mud of a tawdry little battlefield like this. If I'm going to die for Rome I expect the time and place to be a good deal more auspicious!'

'Where are they now?'

The last of the eight Batavian cohorts was across the river and had disappeared into the gloom, invisible to the men watching from the hillside.

'I gave orders for them not to attack until they had their entire strength across the Medui.'

Geta was staring across the river at the encamped Britons.

'And then to strike fast and hard. We'll know when that happens, I expect, by the sound of screaming, if those Germans can be trusted to do as they've been instructed . . .'

Draco nodded with satisfaction as the last of his men trotted up the slope still panting for breath from their swim, clapping a hand on the eighth cohort's leading centurion's shoulder.

'So far, so good. I'll give your men a short while to get their wind back, then we move. Coming, Tribune?'

At the column's head, the scouts had returned from their brief foray into the spectrally lit countryside, saluting as he completed his swift march up the column's length with Lupercus close behind.

'What did you find?'

'Open ground for a quarter of a mile to the east. Sounds of men and horses to the south.'

'Any sounds of alarm? Any shouting or noises of horses moving?'

'No, sir.'

He turned to the three centurions of his front rank centuries. 'Ready your men. We move on my command.'

Waving a hand, he led them forward at the walk, knowing that each successive rank would follow on behind the leading centuries, leaving his sword in its scabbard in a calculated gesture of confidence as they climbed the shallow slope in a stealthy movement that would hopefully take them past the left-hand end of the unsuspecting Britons' line. After counting off two hundred paces' progress, he stepped out ahead of the front rank and hissed a command at his leading centurions, sweeping his right arm out in an exaggerated gesture and staying in position to direct the second three centuries to follow the front rank as they wheeled the column through a quarter-turn, changing their path from one past the enemy line's end to a direction that would take them directly into the Britons' rear, if his estimate of the distances involved was correct. Passing the task of marshalling the oncoming centuries to the second cohort's senior centurion, he hurried to catch his own front rank, silently ordering a halt with both hands outstretched. After a moment, the leading men and horses of the second cohort took their place on the first's right, their deployment from the marching column into a two-century-deep line one they had practised time and time again, until the transition from march to line of battle was second nature. Waiting until the eighth cohort had taken their place in a long line of horsemen and soldiers, he stepped into the front rank, positioning himself alongside his decurion's horse once more and raising his right hand to his lips in readiness to give the signal his men were waiting for.

A gust whipped away the curtain of mist that was shielding them from the unsuspecting Britons for a moment, and with an exultant leap of his heart, Draco saw the disorganised sprawl of the enemy camp barely two hundred paces from where they stood, their horses tethered to stakes across the back of the tribes' rough line of campfires and tents, while the chariots they were intended to pull in the coming battle were scattered among them in a seemingly random manner. The mist closed in again with no indication that they had been sighted by the unwary tribesmen, and with a savage grin he took hold of the big horse's saddle and stuck two fingers into his mouth to whistle once, a piercing note that would be heard along his force's line, telling his men that the time to fight was upon them. Vaulting into the saddle, his decurion spurred the beast to a trot, Draco increasing his pace to a long striding run to keep up with the animal, using his grip on the saddle to drag him along faster than any unaided man could run carrying so much weight.

Suddenly the mist parted, and the Batavi line swept out into the clear morning air moving fast and still undetected, closing the gap by five paces with every heartbeat. A tribesman walking sentry duty on the tethered horses let out a scream of terror at the thundering line of horsemen bearing down on him and was gone, speared by one of the leading riders and dropped into the meat grinder of the charging cohorts' boots and hoofs. A few dozen of the more alert Britons ran through the tethered horses in a suicidally brave attempt to defend the precious animals, but they had barely cleared the chariots' obstruction as the Batavi line raced to meet them, soldiers releasing their grip on the horse's saddles as their riders reined them in and using their shields to smash into the Britons' pitiful defence with the momentum of their headlong charge, making short work of the few defenders as their flickering spears reaped the lives of those men who were resolute enough to stand against them.

'First rank centuries! Push through and form a line!'

The leading centurions along the line's length recognised their leader's gruff bellow and led their men forward through the enemy's horses, ignoring the tethered beasts in their haste to do as they were bidden. Erecting a wall of shields three men deep and reinforced by their comrades who had left their horses under the control of a few riders while they strode to join the fight, they set their spears ready to fight off the tribesmen who were now rapidly waking up to the fact that they were under attack. A hubbub was growing among the tribal encampment as men rolled out of their blankets and climbed out of tents, reaching for weapons and shrugging on mail if they were wealthy enough to possess such a small fortune in iron, girding themselves to meet the unexpected attack. Draco turned back to the second row of centuries where they stood awaiting his command, roaring the order that so pained him despite its necessity.

'Second rank! Hamstring the horses!'

The waiting Batavi stabbed their spears into the ground and drew their swords, advancing into the chariot park with grim-faced purpose, hacking and stabbing at the tethered animals with devastating effect, severing muscles and tendons to leave the beasts lame and screaming in their unexpected agony. The Fourteenth Legion's young legatus had been insistent on this tactic when he made his orders clear the previous evening.

'A horse that has been crippled has to be put out of its misery by some poor bastard, and in the meantime may well pull its tether and cause chaos in their lines. And it's quicker than making sure the beasts are dead. I want you and your men in and out with the minimum casualties, Prefect, as I suspect I'm going to need your strength at my back later in the day.'

Draco looked over the line of his men's shields at the Britons facing them, growing rapidly in strength as they turned away from the expected direction of the Roman attack and re-oriented themselves to face the hard-faced auxiliary soldiers who stood waiting for their attack. Shaggy-haired warriors were striding forward up the hill's shallow slope towards their attackers, some running, recognising from the horse's screams what was happening behind the line of oval shields, the initial trickle of men swiftly becoming a flood. Exchanging glances with Tribune Lupercus, he nodded decisively at the Roman's questioning look.

'Better to be the men doing the attacking, if we want to be away from here clean.'

Raising his voice to be heard over the growing cacophony of agonised equine screams, as his soldiers rendered one horse after another incapable of ever running again, he shouted the command that his men were waiting for.

'Form ranks for battle! Front rank! Advance!'

Along the eight-cohort-strong line of soldiers the command was repeated by each centurion, their barked orders sending the Batavi down the slope towards the oncoming Britons at a steady walk and in a neat, unbroken formation, shields up and spears held ready to fight. The Britons, seeing their enemy come forward, increased their own pace, eager to get at the invaders, loping forward with their weapons raised.

'Into them!"

The Batavi line stepped into the advancing Britons and took the leading runners down hard, punching with their shields and following through with spear blades, halting the enemy charge in an instant and reaping the enemy warriors with swift, clinical strikes that opened throats, bellies and thighs, killing their targets with the efficiency of long, hard practice, and then stepping forward again to repeat the slaughter on those who followed. The Britons railed at their shields, occasionally finding a way past the wall of wood and iron to take a life or leave a man bleeding on the turf, but they died in their hundreds as German ferocity married with Roman discipline drove the Batavi forward one step at a time, their weapons carving a bloody path.

'Change!'

At their centurions' command each century's second rank men released their grip of the front rank's collars, stepping forward and sliding their shields around the leading men's left sides to protect their comrades as they fell back, breathing hard from their exertions and the sheer thrill of the fight, taking their places and renewing the ferocity of the Batavis' grinding advance into the tribal warriors opposing them.

From the knots of men facing the first century, a handful of warriors stepped forward to face the attackers' line, half a dozen hard-faced men carrying long swords and small shields, moving as one as they stalked towards their enemy, each of them scrutinising their enemy in search of a weakness to exploit. The man who seemed to be their leader pointed and barked a command, and their walk accelerated to a run as they came on in silence, picking a point where the Batavi line had been thinned by the natural chaos of the battle and bursting through the shields raised against them with brute force. Scything their way into the soldiers to either side of the rupture, their assault sent the Batavi soldiers skipping back with shields raised, while the biggest of them killed the only man between himself and Lupercus, levelled his sword at the Roman and stepped in to attack without breaking step, flashing the blade in at head height with a bellow of anger in an attack so fast that the tribune could do no more than raise a weak parry to block the blow. He staggered back as the flat of his own blade smashed into his helmet, momentarily scattering his wits and leaving him open to the death blow. Draco threw himself forward and lunged with his gladius, but the Briton side-stepped with sinuous ease and shifted smoothly from defence to attack, stepping forward to put all his strength behind his colourfully decorated shield's hard bronze boss and sending the prefect flying with the force of the blow. Turning back to the tottering Roman, the Briton pulled his sword back, bellowing in his victim's face as he swung the long blade at Lupercus's head with lethal intent.

'That's what I was waiting for!'

The initial screams of maimed horses from the far side of the river were now underlaid by the sounds of battle, iron clashing against iron and the shouts and imprecations of men fighting at close quarters. Geta pointed down at the waiting legionaries whose front ranks were barely a hundred paces from the wide bend in the river, which the invasion force's scouts had reported as the best place to mount a legion-strength attack across the Medui's natural barrier, the water slower through the bend's curve and shallow enough to be waded, with a narrow mud-bank island in the middle of the stream to provide some firmer footing for their men.

'Now is the time, Flavius Vespasianus! Time for your men to make their attack across the river and take a bridgehead, while the enemy are concentrating on the threat to their rear!'

The older man looked down for a moment longer and then nodded his agreement.

'Have your men ready to follow up, but concentrate your force to either side of my legion. Once we're across I expect they'll throw every last man down that slope at us, and I'll be happier knowing you have my flanks if the worst happens.'

He turned away and hurried down the hill's slope with a pair of auxiliary cohort prefects following in his wake, while his brother and Geta stared out into the slowly clearing mist and tried to discern the course of the battle in the enemy's rear.

Dazed, and unable to defend himself, the tribune stepped unsteadily back out of the blade's slashing path, feeling the wind of the sword's passage past his face and a sting of pain as the point scored a deep nick into his cheek below his left eye. His attacker was still advancing, rolling his wrist over and leading with the point, spearing it down at the Roman so fast that he barely had time to get his own blade up to meet the thrust, flinching as the sharp iron skated down his sword's length and hammered into its hand guard, smashing the weapon from his numb fingers. Stepping shakily backwards on legs still reluctant to obey, he found himself unable to put any distance between himself and the remorseless Briton as the warrior stepped forward again with his long blade held overhand, teeth bared as he aimed the weapon's point at the helpless Roman's neck.

As he stepped in to make the kill something stole his attention for an instant, and then, faster than the dazed tribune could comprehend, he was gone, fighting in turn for his own life as a mail-clad man with a centurion's crest assailed him furiously from his left, bulling through his defence with a combination of brawn and speed the equal of that which the Briton had used to defeat Lupercus a moment before, his sword the shining tongue of a viper as it flickered in the iron-grey dawn. Turning the newcomer's blade aside with his own, the Briton punched out with his shield, but the Batavi officer who had saved Lupercus's life met the punch with the boss of his own shield, sparks flying with the resounding bang of their impact. Before the warrior could strike again, Draco was upon him from behind, hamstringing the Briton with a sweep of his sword and dropping him to his knees with his back arched in agony and his sword pointing uselessly at the grey sky. His other assailant stepped forward and put the point of his gladius into the gap between the man's mail shirt and his helmet, plunging it deep and then tearing the blade free in a fountain of blood as the dying warrior tottered and then sprawled headlong, his eyes dimming as the life left his body. Turning away from the dead man's corpse, the tribesman's killer wiped the blood from his lips and then, as matter-of-factly as if he were adjusting the fit of his armour, pulled off his helmet and took hold of the rope of dyed red hair that hung down to the square of his back, putting the bloodied blade to it and slicing through the plait with a sawing stroke of the sword. Draco walked forward and offered the tribune his hand, pulling him to his feet and picking up his gladius. He turned to look at their saviour, who was retying the leather thong that secured his helmet's cheek guards.

'Kivilaz.'

The younger man knotted the leather cord and kicked the dyed red rope of his discarded hair aside, then saluted.

'Draco.'

'You're supposed to be maiming horses, Centurion.'

The prince shrugged.

'Other men might be content with maiming horses, but I am not one of their number.'

He might have said more, but from the mist that still shrouded the river a mournful blare of horns began to sound, first one, then another, and then a chorus of sonorous notes that presaged an attack in force by the legions on the far side. Draco shook his head, still winded by the shield punch that had momentarily floored him.

'We will speak of this later. Return to your century and prepare to fall back.' Kivilaz nodded brusquely, saluted again and turned away, stopping as his superior spoke again. 'But on my behalf and that of Tribune Lupercus, thank you.'

Nodding again, the younger man walked away to rejoin his century, leaving Draco staring at his back for a long moment before turning to give the order for the retreat to the river.

I

The Palace of Tiberius, Palatine Hill, Rome, September AD 68

A clank of iron against iron as the cell's door was unlocked announced a break in the usual routine, and it was all that Kivilaz could do to stop himself turning his one-eyed gaze from the window slit through which he had been staring north across the city from the Palatine Hill's elevated position. He had determined weeks before that he would never show any sign to his jailers that the sheer loneliness and crushing boredom of his imprisonment was anything more than an inconvenience, but the unexpected contact with another person, even one of the impassive men who watched over him wordlessly for the most part, was still enough to set his heart racing.

'There is a visitor for the prisoner Civilis.'

He composed himself and turned away from the window to find one of his jailers standing at the open door with another man, a stranger dressed in the formal toga of a Roman gentleman and with the gold ring of a senator on his finger. He stared at the newcomer for a moment in perplexity, knowing that he recognised the man's air of alert watchfulness from somewhere, but was unable to place him. The jailer stared at him for a moment with obvious irritation before speaking again.

'Does the prisoner Civilis *wish* to receive the visitor?'

Jumping to his feet, and pushing away his chair so hard that it toppled to the hard stone floor with a loud clatter, Kivilaz nodded eagerly.

'I would be happy to receive the visitor.'

Standing aside, the jailer gestured to the man waiting behind him.

'You may enter the prisoner Civilis's cell, Senator.'

Kivilaz frowned at the man quizzically as he turned away in apparent disinterest.

'That's all? Shouldn't you stay to ensure that nothing treasonous is said between us? Or to stop this man from giving me—'

'The visitor has been authorised for the prisoner Civilis by Praetorian Prefect Tigellinus. And he is a Roman gentleman.'

With nothing more to be said on the subject he walked away, leaving Kivilaz staring at the man in front of him for a moment before coming to his senses.

'Where are my manners? I must appear every inch the barbarian. Please come in.'

The Roman bowed, but remained where he was.

'I should introduce myself before accepting your invitation. When you know my name you may not be quite as eager to welcome me.' He sighed. 'I have become something of an outcast among the men of my class. The jailer tells me that you are reading the *Iliad*?'

Kivilaz nodded with a slight smile.

'I asked him to find me a copy in Greek, rather than the bastardisation of a translation into Latin, just to make the point that not all northern barbarians are completely uneducated.'

The newcomer nodded, raising a hand to declaim from Homer's epic poem.

'No man or woman born, coward or brave, can shun their destiny.'

He looked over at Kivilaz with a wry smile.

'My destiny, so far at least, has been to play the bold role of the bravest of commanders, and yet to end up being regarded with no better sentiment among my peers than the rankest of cowards.'

He waited for Kivilaz to respond, and after a moment the prisoner nodded his head slowly.

'I know who you are. It's . . . *Cerialis*? Is that right?'

'Yes. My name is Quintus Petillius Cerialis. You remember me as legatus of the Ninth Hispania in Britannia ten years ago, at the time of the revolt of the Iceni, whose full strength I was unfortunate enough to encounter as I marched to relieve their siege of Camulodunum with two and a half thousand of my men. Having already sacked the city, and drunk with victory, they simply mobbed us without any regard for their own lives, numbering perhaps three times our strength. They overran us in minutes, as I'm sure you remember, killing every last legionary and chasing myself and the legion's cavalry away to the nearest fort . . .'

He paused, shaking his head at the memory.

'Where they kept us bottled up until Suetonius Paulinus defeated them and relieved us. I was recalled to Rome, of course, and it would probably have been less embarrassing for all concerned if I had fallen on my sword like that poor fool Posthumus, but at least I answered the call to duty and didn't hide in my fortress like that coward did when he became convinced that Boudicca already had the province in the palm of her hand. In any case, I wasn't ready to throw my life away over a battle that no man in Rome could have won, and so I declined the suggestion of an honourable death and left the province with my head up, ignoring those men who weren't there and had no right to an opinion. Although, as I discovered soon enough, a man who loses a battle that badly does tend to find himself ostracised, shunned by those of his peers who have never suffered such ill-fortune, which is of course most of them.' He shrugged, a wan smile betraying the lingering wound that his defeat had inflicted on his pride and sense of self-worth. 'So, now that you know both my name and my crime in the eyes of polite society, are you still willing to receive my visit, Prince of the Batavians?'

Kivilaz smiled slowly.

'You could be considered the very lowest man in Rome and it would make little odds with me.' He lowered his voice so as not to be heard by any unseen listener. 'Between you and me, I would still seize upon your visit with the eagerness of a drowning sailor thrown a rope. Join me.' He beckoned to the other man, picking up the chair and turning it to accommodate his visitor. 'Please, be seated. I spend so much of my day sitting at that window and staring out over the rooftops of Rome that some time on my feet will be no hardship whatsoever. And perhaps I'll manage to persuade you to call my people by the name we call ourselves. We are the Batavi, a tribe of which I am prince only in name.'

Cerialis inclined his head in acknowledgment of the correction. 'Your point is taken. We Romans will insist on renaming everything we come across to suit our view of the world.' He took his seat, looking up to find Kivilaz leaning against the cell's open door with a calculating expression. 'You're wondering what brings a Roman senator to visit a man accused of treason and imprisoned to await the emperor's judgement, aren't you, Civilis?'

The Batavi shrugged.

'I care little, to be honest, the opportunity to speak with anyone other than my jailers being so rare. But since you mention the question . . .'

The other man smiled wryly.

'I must confess that when I heard you had been brought to Rome to stand trial for treason, I was at once curious to know how it was that you came to be accused. The last time I saw you was when your cohort was part of the relieving force that rescued what little remained of my legion from the fort at Camulodunum ten years ago. My abiding memory was that while the gentleman officers of the Fourteenth Gemina were all sympathy to my face, doubtless traducing me behind my back, you looked at me with the openly curious disdain of a man to whom I was already irrelevant. You evidently weren't given to either tact or diplomacy then, and I doubt that's changed, and so it seems clear to me that if I want to know the truth of the matter with regard to this whole Vindex thing for which it seems you're imprisoned, I am best served speaking directly to you. You're accused of having collaborated with the rebellious senator himself, if I have the right of it?'

Civilis leaned back against the wall, looked down at his visitor and crossed his arms.

'There's little to tell. My brother and I were accused of allying our tribe with Gaius Julius Vindex, after the defeat of his short-lived revolt in Gallia Lugdunensis, back in the month of Maius. Since it had been action taken by the legatus augusti commanding the legions of Germania Superior that put Vindex down, while the forces in Germania Inferior had little chance to join in, their legatus Fonteius Capito decided that he needed to be seen to be taking some form of action as a means of bolstering his protestations of loyalty to the throne. After all, Nero had something of a habit of ordering even his best soldiers to commit suicide, so what hope for a man whose legions could have been accused of sitting on their hands while their neighbours dealt with Vindex in such a brutal manner?'

Both men were silent for a moment, remembering the ruthlessness with which the recently deceased emperor had ordered his most gifted general, Gnaeus Domitius Corbulo, to commit suicide two years before in order to remove a perceived threat to his own position, and the soldier's laconic response – the single Greek word '*Axios!*' – which Kivilaz's educated Roman friends had told him best translated as 'worthy', before he had fallen on his own sword. It was an act of selfless loyalty in the face of Nero's paranoid jealousy, which still had the power to stop conversation when the men of Rome's ruling class met to discuss such matters.

'And so, short of any other means of disassociating himself from Vindex, Legatus Augustine Capito accused my younger brother and me of treason, alleging the crime of our having plotted against Rome with Vindex based purely on the grounds that I had visited the senator before the battle that resulted in his suicide. My brother was still two years short of his twenty-five years' service, a fact which Capito used to argue that he was therefore not yet a citizen despite the fact that we had both inherited citizenship from our father. He was executed the same day that we were arrested, after the briefest possible trial, but as I was already a time-served citizen of the empire he had no legal choice but to send me here, in the not unreasonable expectation that Nero would have me put to death and praise him for having rooted out such a canker.'

'I see.' Cerialis nodded his understanding. 'In that case it might please you to know that Capito is dead, murdered on the orders, it seems, of a rather brutally minded legionary legatus called Valens, in hopes of gaining the favour of the man who has succeeded Nero. These are troubled times, and the more ruthlessly ambitious among us seize their opportunities as they see them arise. When Capito made some hard-faced jest to a man accused of treason that he had no need to demand his right to trial by Caesar, because Caesar was already before him, he offered the perfect reason for his own death. Death by centurion, apparently, an officer apparently so enraged by the implied treason that he took his pugio to the legatus the same day.'

Kivilaz nodded, his face remaining inscrutable.

'I'm grateful for the news. I hear next to nothing in this place, since my jailers are trained to share nothing of the outside world with the prisoners.'

The Roman shook his head.

'But even shut away here in the palace, surely the fact that Nero was already dead by his own hand by the time you reached Rome cannot have escaped your ears? The very man Vindex was purporting to support in his ill-fated rebellion is now marching from his province of Hispania to Rome at the head of a newly formed legion, and with an escort of praetorians shipped out specifically to give him the appropriate gravitas, now that he's been voted as emperor by the senate. Surely Galba won't have you executed, given the fact that you have waited all this time in a prison cell to face the charge of supporting his friend, the man who revolted against Nero on his behalf?'

'That much I did know, but as to how Galba will treat me, who can tell? I shall face the new emperor with no more expectation of mercy than I would have done with his predecessor. That way I shan't be dismayed if he decides to punish me for the disloyalty to the throne of which I was accused by my brother's murderer. And as to my imprisonment, the conditions here in this part of the palace are comfortable enough, for a prisoner. The food's better than most of what I ate on campaign in Britannia, the accommodation is adequate enough, and the jailers are respectful for the most part.'

His visitor smiled.

'Like any imperial servants in these troubled days, they know all too well that they might be out of work soon enough if Galba chooses to sweep the palace clean, which might make them somewhat vulnerable to an act of revenge when he undoubtedly frees you. But you approach captivity in this somewhat strange situation wisely, I would say. My father-in-law will be interested to hear tell of it, and impressed, I expect, by your stoicism in the face of such harsh adversity and grave personal loss.'

'Your father-in-law?'

'A legatus augusti in the east, sent to put down yet another revolt in Judea. His name is Titus Flavius Vespasianus.'

Camp of the Germani Corporis Custodes, Rome, October AD 68

'He's here, Hramn.'

The officer set to watch the road that led to the gate of the German Bodyguard's camp hooked a thumb over his shoulder at the brick-built barracks' entrance. The man for whom his warning had been intended nodded dourly and turned to his second in command with a knowing look. A big man, even among a cohort chosen for their size and physical presence as much as for their battle experience, he straightened his ceremonial belt and checked that his tunic's hem was perfectly straight just above his knees.

'If they take their iron to me, kill every fucking one of them.'

His fellow officer laughed, his harsh accent giving the Latin words an edge of belligerence.

'If they take their iron to you, *you* kill every fucking one of them. They're praetorians, Hramn, not proper soldiers.'

Following the soldier back to the wooden gate, he stepped through the doorway to find a magnificently armoured figure waiting for him in front of a century of men whose white tunics, the same colour that Hramn's men wore, immediately identified them as the expected praetorians. The soldiers were also armoured, their equipment shining even if there was nothing to compete with their prefect's gleaming bronze breast plate, beautifully engraved and polished to perfection, and Hramn saluted the man whose soldiers protected the city of Rome and the Palatine Hill's imperial palaces.

'Prefect.'

'Decurion.'

The praetorian prefect's voice was soft, but Hramn had heard the stories that circulated among the palace staff about his cruelty and licentiousness. As a close associate of the emperor Nero, he was reputed to have used the weight of his office to behave in ways that would, under a different ruler, have seen him stripped of his position and quite possibly of his equestrian rank as well, and both male and female slaves in the emperor's household had learned not to catch his eye, or even to fall under his gaze if it could be avoided.

'Prefect Tigellinus.'

'Your men are gathered?'

'They are.'

Hramn nodded, and Tigellinus moved towards the gate only to stop short as the German, rather than stepping out of his path as he would have expected, remained motionless, with one hand resting on the pommel of his sword while the other, holding the vine stick that was the badge of his office, hung easily at his side.

'I have come to address your men, *Decurion*, not to stand here waiting for you to get out of my way!'

The German nodded again, telling himself not to rise to the man's insulting tone. Today, as he had pointed out to his brother officers an hour before, was a day for calm heads.

'And address them you will, Prefect. However, given the rumours that have been circulating in advance of this address, I think it would be wise for you to brief me first, and for me to explain the situation to my men before you speak to them directly. We Germans are, as I'm sure you know, a hot-tempered and barbaric people, and were my men to be insulted by your words, given the news you bear, events might not run to the smooth path I believe you and I would both desire for a matter as difficult as this.'

The prefect shook his head in amazement.

'I am your superior, Decurion. Stand aside, so that I can tell your barbarians what it is that the emp—'

Hramn's voice hardened, cutting across the other mans' words with whiplash strength.

'In point of fact, Prefect, while I am bound by my oath to respect your position, which of course I will, I am not required to follow your orders. The terms of our enlistment are to provide the emperor with a bodyguard, and to obey only his instructions or those that are communicated to us with his authority. This is intended to prevent any repeat of the incident when the *praetorian guard* murdered Caligula, and until the emperor himself rescinds those instructions, I am still the master of this camp. And whilst I am perfectly willing to allow you to address my men, I wish to prevent any unnecessary provocation of their dignity, given that they have already been told what your message is by certain loose-mouthed members of your cohorts. So I suggest we first discuss the way in which you intend to deliver the emperor's order, unless of course you wish to go straight in and deliver it to five hundred very unhappy guardsmen in some unwise fashion that might make the bubbling pot of their anger boil over?'

Tigellinus blinked, and then nodded.

'Very well, Decurion. Your authority here will be at an end very shortly in any case.' He lifted a scroll from his side, holding it up for Hramn to see. 'These are orders from the emperor, which means that you cannot argue with them. With Nero dead by his own hand, the last member of the dynasty founded by the blessed Julius has gone. A new empire will be constructed, with none of the ills of the last few years . . .' He smirked at Hramn's wooden-faced disgust with the blatant hypocrisy in his words. 'My praetorians are to be the guardians of the emperor's person, and you Germans are dismissed to your homelands. Perhaps Galba, a man who has lived through every event in this city since before the divine Augustus went to meet his ancestors, is more concerned with the example of your unit's failure to protect Caligula from his assassins, and the widespread slaughter you Germans inflicted on both the guilty and the innocent in the wake of his death, than with the actions of the few rogue praetorians who assassinated him. Henceforth, he tells me, he has decided to have his person protected by *professionals*.'

Hramn stared at him for a moment, ignoring the barb.

'The rumours were true then. We're being . . . disbanded.'

The praetorian sneered at him, shaking his head in contradiction.

'Disbanded? You're being packed off home as unfit for purpose. Galba doesn't trust you people, he wants good Roman iron around himself and his family. And not before time. From now on *I* will be the man who safeguards the first citizen from the ill will of the unworthy, while you Germans walk home to your mud huts and leave your equipment and horses to—'

Hramn shook his head brusquely.

'I think you need to read those orders again, Prefect, and remind yourself that they specifically permit us to depart with what little honour is left to us, as a formed military unit, armed, equipped and mounted, to join the army of Germania Inferior. We still have friends in the palace, Prefect, and the wording of the emperor's order was known to me before the ink was dry. We will march back to our tribal lands *with* our weapons, *with* our equipment and mounted on *our* horses, as allowed in the emperor's final orders to his loyal bodyguard. Although we clearly leave the shreds of our dignity as servants of the empire behind us for *you people* to trample as you see fit.'

Tigellinus looked at him for a moment, then shrugged.

'Take what you wish, but you *will* leave this fort within seven days. Where you go after that is no concern of mine, but if you remain in the city you will surrender your arms and equipment to my men at midnight of the seventh day, or else risk action to remove you as a potential threat to the order and stability of Rome.'

Hramn shook his head, feeling the last vestiges of his already tenuous grasp on his temper slipping.

'Stay? Why should we want to *stay*? This city, Prefect, is dirty, dishonoured by its emperor having been hounded to suicide, and no longer safe for simple men like us. I want for nothing more than to breathe the clean air of my homeland again, and walk around without an itch between my shoulder blades. Come, tell your story to my men and then leave us to mourn our lost pride.'

Hramn turned away, and a fuming Tigellinus followed him into the camp, the two men walking out in front of the waiting guardsmen. Opening the scroll, the prefect took a breath to proclaim the German Bodyguard's death knell, only to find that Hramn's deep voice was already booming out.

'My brothers!' The decurion spoke swiftly, not allowing the prefect the chance to launch into a proclamation of the order held in his hands, switching to his native language and addressing his men in his booming parade-ground voice. 'It is as we feared! This hypocritical pederast carries orders for our disbandment, and clearly hopes to witness signs of your distress with which to regale his men! So listen in silence, and give him *nothing*! Not one word! Keep your faces straight and your mouths shut! We will march from this place with what is left of our dignity intact, and none of you will bring shame to our peoples' name today, or give them the reason they so clearly desire, *any* reason, to torch this camp and put us all to the sword!'

He turned back to Tigellinus, who was waiting with his scroll unfurled. Shaking his head in disgust, the praetorian prefect began speaking in a triumphant tone.

'Men of the German Bodyguard! By the order of the emperor, Servius Sulpicius Galba Caesar Augustus, you are hereby dismissed from imperial service. Your duties will be assumed by the praetorian guard at the end of the current century's turn of duty in one hour, and you are hereby granted seven days' notice to quit this facility, after which it will be occupied by men of the guard. You are no longer authorised to carry weapons inside the city of Rome, and any attempt to do so will be treated as a capital crime. The emperor thanks you for your service, and has recommissioned you as a five-hundred-man cavalry wing in the army of Germania Inferior. You are to report to your new posting at the Old Camp in Germania Inferior on the first day of the new year. That is all.'

He rolled up the scroll, nodding curtly to Hramn with a face pale with anger.

'I may not speak German, but I understand enough of it to have a fairly good idea of what you called me a moment ago. Don't let my men catch you in the city, Decurion, or you may discover the price of insulting a Roman gentleman quite so openly.'

The German looked him up and down, then stared briefly over Tigellinus's shoulders as if searching for something, shaking his head slowly as the last traces of control over his utter disgust for the man vanished.

'When I see a gentleman, Prefect, I'll be sure to give him all the respect he deserves, but all I see here is you, a degraded husk of a man, hanging onto your position through bribery and flattery, and terrified that your new master will see through you at any moment and have you dealt with in the manner you deserve. A day which, if this man Galba is as straight a stick as he sounds, surely cannot be very distant. And I'll be sure to write to the emperor and wish him the very best of luck before I leave the city, because with you and your men standing at his back, I have the feeling that he's going to need it.'

The Palace of Tiberius, Palatine Hill, Rome, November AD 68

'Bring the next prisoner forward!'

Kivilaz felt a push in the square of his back from the praetorian standing behind him, and started a slow, carefully paced approach to the imperial throne on which Rome's new emperor was seated between a pair of men similarly armed and equipped to the guard behind him. He frowned, surprised to see that the bodyguards were clean-shaven rather than bearded in the usual fashion, but quickly focused his attention on the man who would decide whether he was to live or die. Galba looked up at him from the scroll in his hands, flicking another glance down to double check the details of the case against the man before him. The soldier tugged at his charge's formal toga, and the German immediately stopped walking and squared his shoulders, determined to meet his fate like a Batavi prince rather than showing the men gathered to witness the emperor's judgement any sign of fear.

A freedman stepped forward and started reading the charge that had been levelled at him by the now deceased legatus augusti, Capito, and which had seen him transported to Rome to receive the justice of an emperor who, by the time of his arrival in Rome, had already taken his own life in the face of overwhelming public and senatorial hostility, to be replaced by the man sitting before him.

'The accused, Gaius Julius Civilis, Emperor! The accused is charged by Legatus Augusti Gaius Fonteius Capito, commander of the imperial army of Germania Inferior, that in the month of Maius of this year he did collude with the Governor of Gallia Lugdenensis, Gaius Julius Vindex, to overthrow the imperial family and seek the restoration of a second Roman republic! Before his own unfortunate demise, Legatus Augusti Fonteius requested that the emperor should administer the death sentence to the traitor Civilis, and was pleased to report that the prisoner's brother, being peregrinus and therefore not having the privilege of demanding an imperial hearing, had already been executed for the same crime!'

Galba looked at Kivilaz for a moment before speaking, and when he did the German noted that his voice quavered slightly, with a hint of his advanced age that was impossible to miss. The emperor looked all of his seventy years of age, perhaps bowed slightly under the weight of his new responsibilities, his eyes dark with fatigue and the skin on his bald head sallower than might have been expected of a man who had recently made the long journey from Hispania. Rome's new emperor was, as the rumour mongers were already broadcasting far and wide, an old man, cruelly robbed by his years of the vitality for which he had previously been famed just at the moment when both he and Rome had the most need of it. And perhaps, Kivilaz mused, the responsibilities of Galba's new position were already grinding down upon him with incessant pressure that would have been hard enough for a man still in his prime.

'Gaius Julius Civilis, you are brought before me charged with treason. How do you answer these charges? Did you indeed conspire with Gaius Julius Vindex against the throne?'

Kivilaz had thought of little else in the period between his trial date being announced and this moment. How best to answer the inevitable question that Galba had no choice but to ask? Were he to answer in the affirmative, that he and Vindex, both men of high birth in their tribes, had indeed conspired against Nero in support of Galba's claim to the throne, would the old man praise him for his support or take a more old-fashioned view of self-declared treason, as seemed quite likely given the man's reputation for being a stickler for Roman law?

'Caesar . . .'

He was on safe ground in his use of the title, he knew, given that Galba had already allowed himself to be acclaimed in public as Imperator Servius Sulpicius Galba Caesar Augustus, and he paused as if composing himself to answer, although in truth he had never felt calmer in all his life, waiting to see if the emperor would offer any subtle clue as to his likely reactions. If there were any such signals, they were imperceptible to the German, and so he proceeded with his chosen route of argument.

'Caesar, it is indeed true that I travelled to Vesontio in order to meet with former Governor Vindex. And I did indeed have one such meeting with the man, in the course of which I advised him that I shared his dismay . . .' He stressed the word, carefully chosen to position himself on the side of the Roman senators who had censured Nero and brought about his suicide without implying any predisposition towards violent action, and paused fractionally to allow it to hang in the air between them. 'Indeed I spoke to him of my own *utter* dismay at the turn of events that had led him to feel constrained to rise up against the throne. My purpose in speaking with the man, I should hasten to add, was to counsel him from a position of some shared ground, given that while I did not share his senatorial rank I am, as was he, the prince of a tribe that has long been the happy and willing partner of the empire. I told him that while I understood his deep unhappiness with the situation in Rome, the mother of the empire we both loved as loyal and willing servants, that I felt his actions were perhaps . . .' He paused again, weighing the word before using it. 'Hasty.'

Hours of thought had gone into the choice of the last word. 'Intemperate' would have implied that Vindex's revolt, avowedly in support of Galba, was poorly motivated and lacking in justification. 'Treasonous', while factually correct, would have been open to being construed as opposing Galba's assumption of the throne. These and half a dozen other words had been considered, weighed and rejected, leaving him with an adjective whose use told Galba that while he believed Vindex's cause was noble, his decision to revolt militarily had been taken precipitately and without consideration of the realities he faced. After a brief pause he added, as though an afterthought, the counterbalancing point that would imply his loyalty to the man with the power of life and death.

'Although of course I am forced to note that it was his noble and selfless action in declaring for you, Caesar, that resulted in your accession to the throne, even if he did not live to see that happy result.'

Galba nodded slowly, seeing the path that Kivilaz had cleared for him.

'I see. And how did you counsel him as to that *hastiness*?'

The German held his hands out, palms upward, opening his argument to the emperor's scrutiny.

'I told him that while I could understand his dismay at the state of affairs that so troubled the empire, and his desire to see a better man take the throne and restore Rome to its full glory, I could not in all conscience condone his taking to the field against Roman legions, which were, of course, bound by their oaths of loyalty. Untroubled by any real knowledge of how matters were deteriorating in Rome itself, they would therefore be forced to offer him battle, a battle he could never win, given that the balance of forces was so much against him, and which could only result in the deaths of thousands of innocent men on both sides. I urged him to meet with Lucius Verginius Rufus, who I knew to be marching south with the best part of three legions, and to make peace with him, a pact between two men of honour to respect the writ of Roman law.'

Galba nodded again.

'Advice he seems to have taken to heart, even if the German legions ignored the agreement Vindex and Rufus formed between them, and fell on the rebel forces despite their orders to stand down. Clearly Rufus may have been, as you say, an honourable man, but I would be happier today if he had held a stronger grip of his legions' collars.'

Kivilaz gave a slight nod of agreement, knowing from his visits from Cerialis that Rufus's legions had not only failed to follow his instructions to allow Vindex's army to surrender in an orderly manner, but had then tried to persuade their general to accept the imperial purple, and set himself up in opposition to Galba's rule.

'But, given that he is clearly a wise man, I have invited him to join me as one of my trusted advisors, and replaced him with a fresh legatus augusti whose control over the legions of Germania Superior will hopefully be tighter.' Galba smiled tightly at the man before him, and Kivilaz tensed for whatever it was that he was about to say. 'It is the time for new commanders in Germania, as I have also been required to replace the man who executed your brother and sent you here for trial. Fonteius Capito, as I expect you already know, is dead, murdered by one of his centurions, it seems, after taking liberties with the title "Caesar" in front of his men.' He watched the German closely for any sign of a reaction. 'Nothing to say on the subject of his death, Julius Civilis? Do you not take pleasure in the demise of the man who had your brother executed, and who sent you here to stand before an emperor he had every expectation would order you to a similar fate? Not to mention the brutality you endured at the hands of his men. I hear the effects had not entirely worn off when you arrived here several weeks later?'

Kivilaz nodded.

'It is true, Caesar. His officers went out of their way to make me suffer, and I was still in some pain when I reached my cell in the palace, but the injury was dealt not by Capito but by his centurions, a class of men well known to be a law unto themselves when they feel the occasion merits their intervention. As a centurion myself I too have, on occasion, ignored the orders of older and wiser men in the pursuit of Rome's glory, so I can hardly complain when a similar crime is committed against me with honourable intentions. And as for my brother, Caesar, what choice did Fonteius Capito have? An accusation was made, with evidence that could be construed to damn us both, and he believed he had the power to execute one of us. What was he to do, given his men's zealous desire to see us dead? Would he have been wise to risk their censure and his possible removal from his post by an outraged Nero?' He shook his head. 'I have no urge to revenge, Caesar, only to return to my homeland and live quietly.'

Galba frowned.

'You expect me to believe that you're willing to dismiss any desire for revenge on the men who beat you, and who drove their general to have your brother killed, illegally given his inherited citizenship, with a statement that amounts to little more than "boys will be boys"?'

He stared intently at Kivilaz, but the German simply opened his arms wide in a gesture of his innocence.

'It seems to me, Caesar, that when a man places his hand into a wasp's nest he can expect to be stung a few times. If you choose to pardon my foolishness in ever going to meet Julius Vindex, even if it was with innocent intentions, I shall repay your trust by withdrawing from imperial service, and further by keeping my own counsel for the rest of my life, providing no further provocation to the men of the German legions.'

The emperor nodded magisterially, having apparently heard enough to reassure himself that the man before him represented no threat to the state.

'I see. Very well, Gaius Julius Civilis, I have reached a judgment in your case.' The praetorian standing behind Kivilaz reached out a hand and took a firm grip of his toga, although whether this was for the purposes of restraint or support in the event of the emperor's decision going against him was not clear. 'I find you guilty, as you state so clearly, only of naivety in travelling to speak with Julius Vindex, naivety which cost your brother his life, even if the execution was not legally correct. I find that your common cause with the misguided senator was both understandable under the circumstances and pursued in the interests of a non-violent solution to the matter, and not intended to further the revolt, as is proven by Vindex's resulting actions in suing for peace. I find you not guilty of treason, as you clearly counselled him to desist from his plan to meet the German legions in the field, a battle which events later proved to be unwinnable for his auxiliary forces in the face of overwhelming strength. You are therefore freed to leave Rome and to journey back to your home.' The hand released his garment. 'However, I am unable to release you from your oath of service to the empire as you request. Rome has continued need of the bravest and the best, as your people have long been known to us, and I will not deprive the empire of your proven martial skills. I have in the last few days released my German bodyguard from their duties, and issued them with orders to march north and join the army of Germania Inferior under their new legatus augusti, Aulus Vitellius, and I have further decided that you will be restored to the rank of prefect and placed in command of these guardsmen in order to assist them with their adjustment to military service. Your lack of self-interest in the matters we have discussed today will provide them with a salutary example of how a soldier should approach life, and it is to be hoped that they will gain from your leadership. You are hereby freed to leave the court, and instructed to return to the palace tomorrow to receive your formal orders.'

The hand tugged at his toga, pulling him away, and with a deep bow he did as he was bidden, backing away until the appropriate distance had been covered and he could turn to walk from the chamber. At the door he turned back for a last look, seeing that the next man in line was already standing before the emperor with another praetorian at his back, one hand on the dagger at his belt in readiness to draw it and strike at the slightest provocation.

'Well now, Julius Civilis, here you are, not only exonerated but given an elite unit of your own people to command. I'd imagine that if you were to fall asleep on a bed of dung you'd wake up smelling of roses.'

He recognised the man standing before him with a beaming smile, a pair of heavily built men with the look of former soldiers standing behind him and eyeballing anyone who so much as looked at their master.

'Quintus Petillius Cerialis.'

Cerialis took his hand and clasped it, shaking it vigorously.

'Well done, Gaius Julius Civilis, very well done indeed! Your performance in front of the emperor was little short of masterly, a delicate circumlocution of several tricky issues to do with the need to admit your visit to that poor doomed fool Vindex, and the fact that his revolt was a bad thing whilst still being necessary and indeed, in the end, positive in terms of its outcome. I'm surprised Galba didn't appoint you to his diplomatic service, but then once a soldier, always a soldier, eh? How I long for another chance to prove that I'm more than the man who lost half a legion to Boudicca's screaming blue painted maniacs, and so I wish you all the joy possible with your new command. I wouldn't wait too long to take it up though, your men are at something of a loss as to what they should do next, when the answer is in truth staring them right in the face and no more complicated than quitting their barracks and riding north. Perhaps as their new prefect, you can make the decision simpler for them to understand. Anyway, enough of that, I've sent a messenger to them with news of your acquittal and appointment to command them, and tonight you must stay in my house and enjoy the company of those few men who have chosen to defy convention and remain my friends despite the fact that I'm something of a social pariah. We'll dine in fine style, and tomorrow I'll walk you over to the camp of the German Bodyguard to meet your men.'

He grinned at the German's nonplussed reaction.

'Mark my words, Civilis! It isn't every day that a citizen condemned with treason faces the emperor and talks his way out from under the charge while at the same time managing not to offend Caesar, despite Caesar's rather obvious vulnerability to being offended on the subject of his friend Vindex's somewhat ill-timed revolt. Let's face it, you might well have been a cooling corpse by now, instead of which you'll spend this evening being toasted in the best Falernian red that money can buy! Exhilarating, isn't it, to dodge death, as we can both attest?! So let's make the most of it!

'Oh, and don't worry about these two . . .' He waved a hand at the unsmiling thugs standing behind him. 'They're colleagues of mine from that unfortunate day in Britannia who I've taken into my familia. I pay them a decent wage and in return they make sure that anyone who thinks it might be clever to abuse a defeated legatus sees the painful error of their ways.'

Later that evening, reclining on a couch and listening to one of Cerialis's friends recite poetry, Kivilaz reflected that of all the outcomes he'd expected for the day, this was not one he had considered. Catching the German's wry smile, his neighbour smiled back.

'Oh, I don't think the poetry is quite *that* bad. Although the writer seems to have enjoyed something of a leg fetish, to judge from his frequent references to his young male friend's finely turned ankles and calves.'

Kivilaz grinned, troubled by the feeling he'd had all the way through dinner that he knew the man, although he knew it was unlikely.

'Forgive me. My grimace was not intended as literary criticism, but more as a comment on my own day.'

The other man bowed slightly, a respectful tone entering his voice.

'Ah. Your apparently miraculous escape from the executioner this afternoon. Nothing less than you deserved from where I was sitting. I'm a lawyer by trade, you see, and I listened to your explanation of the circumstances by which you came to be standing before dear old Galba with a significant degree of admiration, given that you were trained for war and not for the courts. Allow me to introduce myself, I'm Gaius Plinius Secundus, one of Quintus Petillius Cerialis's closest friends. I was a soldier for a while, and indeed I ended up commanding the cavalry wing at the Old Camp, quite close to your homeland, but for the last ten years or so I've confined myself to practising the law. That and writing books on grammar and rhetoric so unbelievably tedious that not even Nero could take exception to them and have my life prematurely terminated because he disagreed with some conclusion or other, or simply failed to understand it. It wasn't always that way, of course. I once wrote a book on the use of spears on horseback by mounted soldiers, and a twenty-volume work on the German wars, but for a few years now it's been safer not to attract the emperor's attention for any reason whatsoever, and so now I write about such tedious subjects as how a student should go about his studies. We'll have to hope that Galba's ascension to the throne has brought with it an end to that terror, and the re-establishment of something more like normality.'

Kivilaz nodded.

'It was kind of our host to invite me to this party. Three months in a cell can leave a man desperate for company, and yet surprisingly uncertain as to how he might go about finding someone to talk to who'll understand the reasons why he might be a little unsure of himself.'

Plinius nodded earnestly.

'He's a good man. Although he'd be the first to admit an ulterior motive. He collects friends, do you see? Having been ridiculed by all and sundry when he was sent home from Britannia with the disgrace of his defeat hanging around his neck like a lead weight, he's slowly but surely built up a group of men who know better than to castigate a man for being caught on the wrong side of an unwinnable fight. Men who know that, but for the grace of the gods, they could just as easily have found themselves in the same position. Clearly he's taken a liking to you, and any friend of his is a man I would be pleased to consider a friend of my own.'

Kivilaz put out a hand and the two men clasped.

'And now, Gaius Julius Civilis, known to his countrymen as Kivilaz, join me in another cup of wine. Our mutual friend Cerialis is known for parties that do not end until the dawn, when he greets his clients and then goes about his day's business with a cheery whistle while the rest of us crawl away to our beds. The man will be the death of me, and quite possibly you too, unless you truly do have the blood of a barbarian prince in your veins as it is rumoured!'

Kivilaz grinned, taking a mouthful of his drink.

'I believe that there's more wine than blood in my body at this point in time, Plinius Secundus. So yes, perhaps our mutual friend will be the death of me, too. But then having served, you'll know the old saying: What does not kill us only serves to make us stronger.'

Germania Inferior, December AD 68

'Batavodurum. That's not a sight I expected to see this year.'

The man riding alongside Hramn stared across the open landscape for a long moment before replying, his cloak's hood raised against the east wind's biting grip.

'Nor I, Decurion.'

Turning in his saddle the Bodyguard's commander looked back down the long line of his men, raising a hand to signal a halt.

'Officers, to me!'

At his shouted command the other five decurions trotted their mounts up the column, dismounting to stand round their leader. Hramn tipped his head in the direction taken by the road's arrow-straight path, directing their attention to the thin fingers of smoke that reached skywards from the huddled buildings that were visible on the horizon.

'Batavodurum. Home. Your men have already seen it, and they're delighted and terrified in the same measures. Delighted at the thought of seeing home, those of them who weren't already effectively married to Roman widows . . .'

He paused for the obligatory chuckles. It was an article of faith among his men that nothing loosened the morals of Roman ladies of a particular class like the sight of a well-built, six-foot-tall tribesman in full armour, and every man in the Bodyguard seemed to have a dubious tale or two to tell about his off-duty escapades.

'And they'll be terrified of what our people are going to say when they see us ride into the city with nothing more than a mule and the weight it can carry in equipment. So go back to your men and tell them that when we ride in past the cavalry fort I want them to carry themselves as if the Bodyguard had never been sent home. Tell them that I *expect* them to look like the biggest, the nastiest, the smartest and the deadliest men on this frontier, and that I *demand* that they carry themselves like heroes coming home from battle: eyes front, spears upright and no emotion. Tell them they're on parade, and that the audience is a good deal more knowledgeable than the Romans ever were, so any man that makes *my* Bodyguard look bad will be having a short and unpleasant discussion with me before the sun's beneath the horizon. Got that?'

His officers nodded and dispersed back to their centuries, leaving him to stare up the road at the city of his birth with pursed lips.

'What? You just warned your decurions not to let anyone pull the sad face when you ride in, and there's you looking like a man who's woken up to discover that his dream of a foot-long prick was ten inches more generous than the reality. You do know the elders will be out to greet us, don't you? You of all people are going to need to be wearing your bravest face.'

Hramn looked at the distant city for a moment longer before replying to his companion's jibe.

'I can tell my men to ride in there like they've got balls big enough to play harpastum with. I can put on a face so hard that you could break your knuckles on it, but I can't give these men the future they were depending on . . .'

'And so what?'

The decurion shook his head in amazement.

'And so what? Our tribe's honoured place at the heart of Roman power is torn away from us, spat on by those praetorian arseholes and then trampled underfoot? We're forced to endure the spectacle of a cohort of the bastards waiting to take over our fort while we ride out, all of them grinning and shouting insults after us. And you say "And so what?"?

The other man shrugged, pulling his cloak about him a little more tightly.

'Didn't you take a good long shit on your bed before you led the cohort out that last morning? I know they all did . . .' He gestured to the men of Hramn's command, gathered around their officers to hear his commands. 'Because they've told me so. And to be frank with you, I'm amazed that we lasted as long as we did in the role. The Bodyguard could have been disbanded after Arminius and his horde of maniacs ripped three legions to pieces back in the days of the first emperor. And what about the blood our idiots spilled after Caligula's death, eh, taking out their rage at having failed to protect the lunatic by slaughtering anyone that got in their way with equal lunacy? Hardly our finest hour.'

He looked at the decurion for a moment.

'For everything, Hramn, there is a time. Nothing lasts for ever. Every man dies, no matter how good a life he leads, and everything comes to an end. Even empires fall, eventually. So, shall we get mounted, now that your men know you expect them to put on a show for the people of Batavodurum that could put a smile on the statue of Hercules in the forum? Not to mention giving Claudius Labeo something to gnash his teeth on, now that he's no longer the only Batavi commanding a crack cavalry cohort.'

Hramn looked round in surprise.

'Labeo? *He's* commanding the First Batavian Horse? How did

that happen, I thought command of the Horse was usually given to the Julii?'

'It was. But the times are changing, Hramn, and the days when the men of the Julii and the Augustii clans ruled the tribe are slipping away from us. The families that gained the citizenship under Claudius and Nero are flexing their muscles and demanding their share of the tribe's honour, and Labeo took command of the Horse last year after my cousin Ansugaizas left the service. Shall we go? Your men are looking suitably bad tempered.'

Hramn led his men up the road towards the city four horses abreast, looking back to find their formation immaculate and their faces locked into immobility. Ignoring the smirks of his companion, he stared hard at the walls of the First Batavian Horse's wooden palisade, but beyond the fort's expected sentries there was no sign of the Bodyguard's sister unit's presence. Another half-mile brought them to Batavodurum's massive east gate, where a gathering of the tribe's elders effectively barred their way into the city. Raising a hand he halted the column and dismounted, waiting in grave silence as a single man stepped forward, supporting his weight on a thick staff of polished wood.

'Travellers from the south, what is your purpose in seeking to enter the Oppidum Batavorum?'

Hramn took a pace forward, raising his hand in a crisp salute.

'The men of the Emperor's Bodyguard humbly request our elders' permission to enter our tribe's city, and to travel onward from here to our homes, many and various, both within our tribe's lands and that of our allies.'

The elderly man smiled and extended a hand to direct them in through the gate.

'The city's elders have considered this request in advance, being forewarned of your arrival, and naturally we welcome the men of the Bodyguard back to their homeland.'

Unable to contain himself any longer, former Prefect Draco strode forward and embraced Hramn warmly.

'Decurion, you and your men are welcome in your home whenever you wish to visit.' He waited for the other man to take the hand. 'Although as we are both painfully aware, this is not a visit. When all five hundred of the Emperor's German Bodyguard come home, every man with his horse and a mule for his possessions, then it seems that the evil tidings from the south were correct. It's true that the Bodyguard has been dismissed from the emperor's service?'

Hramn nodded, flicking a stray lock of his fair hair away from his face, his piercing blue eyes still staring hard at the veteran's lined face.

'It is true. I will speak more of it when my men are billeted and their horses stabled, but until then a leader of the Bodyguard still has duties to perform. But the news I bring is not all bad. Here is the man the emperor has appointed to command the Bodyguard, now that we will serve in the army of Germania Inferior. Prefect?'

He gestured to the man who had ridden to the city's gates beside him, and the rider dismounted and flicked his cloak's hood back to reveal the familiar shock of black hair, now shot through with grey, his disconcerting one-eyed stare for once creased into a grin.

'*Kivilaz!*'

The newcomer strode to meet the veteran, taking the proffered hand and grasping it with both of his own.

'Well met, Draco! Not a greeting I ever dared to hope I would make again in this life, but strange times sometimes throw up fortunate outcomes.'

'How is it that you return to us without any forewarning? You were freed by the new emperor, I presume?'

His former centurion nodded dourly.

'After making me wait four months for a judgement, it took the man less time than you or I could use to peel and eat an apple to free me without further charge or censure. The emperor regretted the illegal execution of my brother, and noted that the man responsible for his death had been murdered, apparently by a disaffected centurion, which would perhaps give me some small cause for satisfaction, although I was careful to hide my joy at the bastard's death and my regret that I wasn't the man to send him across the river. I was pardoned, and further to that given command of the "Bodyguard" cavalry wing, with, as Hramn correctly stated, the rank of prefect. And with that I was ushered away, a free citizen of Rome and no longer invited to stay within the palace walls, but fortunately I was already in receipt of an invitation to enjoy the hospitality of a Roman we last met at the end of the war with the Iceni. An unlucky former legatus by the name of Cerialis. Remember him?'

Draco nodded.

'I recall the stories that circulated during my last days in Rome, before I passed command of the Guard to our brother Furistaz. Your host was indeed an unfortunate man in that he ran head on into several times his own strength of wild-eyed Britons on the march, but lucky enough to get away with his skin, even if his reputation was shredded beyond repair. But what made him take any interest in the doings of a Batavi prince, even one so infamously mistreated?'

Kivilaz smiled knowingly.

'The man might have been unlucky ten years ago, but he's no fool. It seems his father-in-law is a legatus augusti by the name of Vespasianus, currently battering the Jews back into submission in Judea. You'll remember him, it was his Second Augusta that forced the crossing of the Medui after we'd hamstrung the Britons' chariot horses, and then helped us rescue that young idiot Geta from the trap he'd driven his legion into. And this man Vespasianus is well thought of, it seems, a proper soldier with little time for the niceties of the court and apparently barely tolerated by Nero despite having been highly successful during the invasion of Britannia.'

Draco stared at him for a moment.

'Have you been playing at politics again, Kivilaz?'

The prince looked back at him with an amused expression.

'Straight to the point as ever, Prefect. And politics? *Me?* How is it political to accept the hospitality of a man whose family feel some connection to our tribe? I stayed at Cerialis's house for a few days, until the Guard were ready to leave, then quietly joined them as an anonymous horseman, identically equipped, and rode out of the city completely unremarked. It was my opinion that the less visible I could be in returning to the Island the better, given that there are still men of the legions at the Old Camp who still very much want my head on a spike above their main gate. And besides, surely today is about our brothers-in-arms here, and how badly they've been treated by the empire?'

Draco nodded slowly, then turned back to his fellow elders.

'It is. Elders of the tribe, I suggest that we allow these men some time to attend to their horses and bathe away the dust and grime of the road. We will gather again later to discuss the events that have led them here.'

The Bodyguard's officers congregated in the city's meeting hall after dark, once their horses had been stabled, and those of their eight hundred men whose families lived in the city's environs had been reunited with parents and siblings. Those men whose homes were too far from Batavodurum to make the remainder of their journey home in daylight, and their Ubii comrades whose homeland was several days' march upriver, had been housed overnight in a temporary barracks in the city's forum. The tribe's elders took their seats to hear Hramn's version of the events that had led to his command being relieved of their role as the emperor's most intimate guard, while the other five centurions sat in stone-faced silence behind him. Hramn noted the presence of Claudius Labeo, the Batavian cavalry wing's prefect, among the elders, his right as the commander of the tribe's most prestigious unit.

'So there was no warning? No obvious cause?'

The younger man shook his head dourly at Draco's question.

'None at all. But you have to understand events in the capital to see how it came about.'

Kivilaz leaned back in his chair, seated among the elders as was his right as a prince of the tribe.

'I might have a view on that.'

Hramn looked at him in surprise.

'A view from a prison cell? How much could you see from there?'

'More than you might think, Decurion. Cerialis was happy enough to share the gossip of the day when he came to visit me, more as an equal than a barbarian prisoner. It might amuse you to know that he and his friends considered me something of a gentleman.'

Hramn smiled despite himself.

'It might take you a while to shrug *that* off. As to why we've been dismissed by the new emperor, that's simple enough, he made it very clear to me through the praetorian prefect. Galba doesn't trust anyone who was loyal to Nero, and we men of the guard were scrupulously loyal him until he committed suicide. Of course, we offered Galba our service when he entered Rome, but the praetorians had already been in his ear, telling him that our sympathies were still with Nero, and that we might well look to take revenge for his suicide. Throwing them the bone of their men replacing us in the palace must have seemed like a good idea to him.'

Draco shook his head.

'The man's a fool. Since the days of Augustus the emperors have kept faith with the idea that they need their Germans to keep them safe from the potential plots involving the praetorians, and if Galba thinks that coming to power on the back of Vindex's revolt makes him secure enough to do away with our men's services, then I suspect he'll soon enough realise that he might as well have invited a viper into his bed. But that will be a painful lesson that he'll doubtless learn in his own time. So you were disbanded without any proper warning?'

Hramn nodded grimly.

'We were told to parade for a briefing from the praetorian prefect, without any hint as to what it might be. Fortunately, we have enough friends in the palace to have known what was planned for us, but it was still done without any regard for our pride, or, more importantly, that of the Batavi people. We're to join the army of Germania Inferior and act as ordinary cavalrymen, even if we are to retain the name of the Bodyguard.'

'And the emperor's traditional end of service donative, the gift bestowed for years of service in a foreign land? Surely—'

'Not a word. Men with twenty years and more of service have been tossed aside, their years of commitment to Rome rewarded with a fist to the balls and a cheery wave goodbye.'

'And these were the emperor's orders?'

'Not as such. One of his freedmen came to us discreetly, and told me that his master would seek to make restitution for the way we had been treated by the praetorian prefect, given time to stabilise his rule, but that he would be unable to do so for some months, to avoid further irritating the praetorians. He'd already decided not to pay them the donative that they were promised by his representatives in Rome, when they were busy convincing the city that he was the right man to succeed Nero, and they weren't all that happy with the retraction.'

Draco shrugged.

'You'll never see a bronze coin of that promise, and Galba won't last until the end of the year if he goes breaking promises made to the praetorians. Your men will have to be happy with the pay of regular cavalrymen, I suspect. Your new prefect can sort it out with the legatus augusti in Colonia Agrippina when he goes to present his respects.' He glanced at Kivilaz. 'You do plan to visit the new man in command of the army on the lower Rhenus, I presume?'

The prince nodded.

'My command of the Bodyguard formally takes effect on the first day of next year. In the meantime, I plan to write to him and make sure he knows that he's got a new cavalry wing as of that date. Doubtless he'll summon me to let me know what his plans for us are once we've got Saturnalia out of the way.'

He looked at Draco questioningly.

'Speaking of which, I'd be grateful for any news of our cohorts. I had the impression from my friends in Rome that they've been regarded as something of an oddity since they were split away from the Fourteenth Legion to stop our boys and theirs from fighting like rats in a barrel whenever they're in the same place. Do we have any idea where the poor bastards are now?'

Labeo spoke up crisply, his voice authoritative.

'The last time I heard any news of our cohorts, they were camped at Andematunum, keeping a close eye on the Lingones, and close enough to Vesontio to make sure the Sequani don't get any ideas about re-starting Vindex's revolt. They're not needed there, or course, but someone in Rome has clearly decided that a show of force should be made, so our men get to spend the winter in the middle of Gallia Lugdenensis while the legions all go home to their barracks on the Rhenus for the feast. We've so few men of military age on the Island that the traditional game of harpastum against the Fifth Alaudae at Vetera looks unlikely to be played this year.'

Hramn looked up sharply.

'Harpastum?'

2

Civitas Lingonum, Gallia Lugdunensis, December AD 68

'Look at them. Wide-eyed and innocent to a man . . . well, to a boy, I should have said.'

Alcaeus stood with his hands on his hips staring at the twenty new recruits for a moment before answering his friend's wry observation. Lean and well-muscled, with black hair and brown eyes that hinted at Roman blood somewhere in his past, he was a good half-head taller than the speaker, whose sandy blond hair and beard and piercing blue eyes would have made him the model of a tribal warrior of the Batavi from before the Roman conquest of Germania, were it not for the fact that, like Alcaeus, his hair was cropped short and his tunic's hem was held above his knees by a leather belt decorated with ornate silver plates, immediately identifying him as a man in the military service of Rome.

'I remember a young man with eyes as wide as a cow's standing on a parade ground just like this one in Britannia not all that long ago, with a dyed red plait just like they've all got, straight off the boat from the Island and determined to seem as tough and knowing as the best of us. He ended up having to be taken down a peg or two by his tent mates, as I recall? What was his name now . . . ?' His companion affected to ignore the question. 'Ah yes, it was Banon, wasn't it? Fresh from the Island, had never been any further from home than the forum at Batavodurum and then suddenly there he was, shipped across the sea and dumped on the Second Century without our having any say in the matter, as we had last pick that time round and he had a bit of a difficult look to him. A capable enough soldier, proved himself against the Britons well enough, but those first few weeks . . .' He grinned at his comrade. 'It was like having a new puppy in the house, pissing on the floor and having to be shown the right way to do everything.'

His chosen man pulled a sour face and gestured to the waiting recruits.

'Alright, Centurion, you've made your point. Let's go and have the choice of the litter, shall we?'

The two men strolled across to where the recruits were waiting under the watchful eye of a chosen man from the cohort's first century, who clasped hands with Banon and acknowledged Alcaeus's status as his colleague's superior with a salute.

'Here you go then, Centurion, you get first pick.'

Alcaeus looked up and down the line of young men, all of whom were standing to attention and staring at the wooden fortress wall with attempted expressions of composure, pointing with his vine stick to the men of his choice.

'I need four men for the Second, so I'll have that one with the muscles, the one with the red hair, him, the big lad, and . . .' he looked up and down the line of men once more and then nodded to himself as he caught one of them looking at him rather than fixing his gaze to his front. 'And you, the curious one. Yes, *you*, don't look so surprised. Get fell out, the four of you and follow me.'

He walked away and ceded his place in front of the remaining recruits to the next centurion in turn, taking his new men twenty paces from the scene before holding up a hand to halt them.

'Form a line here and look at me, so I know you're listening.' The recruits flashed him nervous glances, and the Batavi officer laughed softly at them. 'It's alright, forget what your daddy told you about not making eye contact with the officers and just look at me.'

He waited until he had the attention of all four of the recruits before speaking again.

'My name is Alcaeus, and apart from my other role, I am your new centurion. This man . . .' he gestured to Banon, 'is my chosen man, my deputy. I command the Second Century of the First

Batavi cohort, the best century in the best cohort in the army, which means that you've struck lucky in being chosen by me and not one of those other arseholes with crests and vine sticks. And now, given that this is a decent century, unlike some I could name, I'm going to teach you three quick lessons in how to survive in the army. Firstly, there are three men whose word is the law in the Second Century: me, Banon here, and my watch officer Hludovig. Banon's called a chosen man because he's been selected to be my deputy. In the legions his role would be to stand behind the century pushing men into place, but in the Batavi cohorts he doesn't need to do that because for one thing every man already knows his place, and for another there's not one of us that needs encouraging to do his duty. And Hludovig's called a watch officer because he's responsible for organising our men's turns at whatever duties need to be carried out. When you know us better, when you've spilled blood for the cohort and won honour for the tribe, then you can call us by our names when we're off duty, although I wouldn't advise you to try it on with Hludovig, not unless you're keen to wear some lumps for a day or two, he's a bit old-fashioned in that way. In the event that Banon and I get killed in action, then Hludovig will be the man telling you what to do, and on that day you'll have to hope that Hercules has mercy, because you can be sure that Hludovig won't!'

'As well as Banon, Hludovig and me, every tent party – which is a group of eight men who share a tent on campaign and a barrack when we're pretending to be civilised – has a leading man. It's an unofficial title, and it tends to be given to the man who combines the ability to batter the shit out of any two of his tent mates in a straight fight with the ability to read and write, and so help out the watch officer with his duties if required, and with discipline in their absence. They keep order, mostly by taking the piss out of their mates until the poor bastards get bored and beg for mercy, occasionally by taking them behind the tent for one-to-one tuition. Whichever tent party you join will have a man like that, charged with keeping order and making sure that the men are always properly equipped and ready to fight at all times.

Do not, whatever you do, get on the wrong side of your leading man. Be respectful of his position, suffer his jibes and insults with a smile, and obey each and every command he gives you as quickly as if it was me telling you what to do. Because if you don't, your first warning will be a slap and there probably won't be a second warning. Have you all got that?'

He waited until the four new men had mumbled their agreement, shaking his head sadly.

'Lesson number two. When I ask you if you understand something, then I want you to tell me that you do understand it, and I want you to tell me in a voice loud enough to be heard a mile away. When I ask you if you understand, you will respond, "Yes, Centurion!" loud enough to make a child's ears bleed. Got that?'

'Yes, Centurion!'

The response was a decent attempt at complying with his instructions, the curious recruit in particular roaring his reply, but Banon smirked knowingly as his superior looked at them in apparent disgust.

'Do you think that was loud enough, Chosen Man?'

His answer was a roar loud enough to have been heard on the far side of the camp.

'*No, Centurion! I could barely hear them!*'

Alcaeus nodded his agreement.

'Lesson three – and let me make this simple for you – shit *always* flows downhill. So, let's try that shouting thing again. Recruits, did you understand what I just told you?'

'*Yes, Centurion!*'

'Better. Keep working on that, because your leading men will expect us to have properly educated you as to the right ways to acknowledge orders, and if I hear you're making the two of us look bad, I'll be expecting Banon to have a word with you in private. Which should make my last lesson for you obvious. I know this is all very exciting, and rather a lot for you to take in, so I'm keeping it simple today. The last lesson is that when someone tells you to do something, as long as that person has more experience than you, then you will do it, quickly, without asking questions and as well as you can. If you fail to do so, and get a slap from a tent mate as a result, when your leading man finds out, he's liable to give you a slap too, just to make sure the lesson's sunk in. Every man in this cohort other than you four and the virgins you shipped in with is a better soldier than you; many of them have fought and killed for the tribe and therefore, coincidentally, for the Romans, and they all know what they're doing a good deal better than you. And if Banon has to "have a quiet word" with you, then you can be sure that your leading man is going to want to show you how embarrassed he is at the chosen man having to get involved in your education, so you'll get the same lesson twice. And if I have to give you a tap with this . . .'

He raised the vine stick again.

'Then you can be sure that both Banon *and* your leading man will want to reinforce whatever small lesson it was that I was teaching you. Like I said, shit always flows downhill and until you've made your first kills and cut off those red plaits the men at the bottom of the hill will always be you. So watch yourselves, do what you're told and stay out of trouble, and eventually you'll be of some value to our century rather than just being the ration thieves that you so clearly are now. Got that?'

'*Yes, Centurion!*'

'Good lads. You . . .' He pointed to the curious recruit. 'You look like you're about to shit yourself with the urge to ask me something. What's your problem?' He held up a hand to forestall a shouted response. 'No need to shout it, just ask.'

The recruit took a deep breath, squaring his shoulders before speaking again.

'You said that you have two roles, Centurion?'

Alcaeus shared an amused glance with his chosen man.

'So I did. And would you care to guess what that other role is? Anyone?'

'Are you also a Wolf Priest, Centurion?'

Alcaeus nodded, looking at the man with slightly narrowed eyes.

'Yes, I am.'

He stepped closer to the recruit, sweeping a glance up and down him, taking in his perfect stance and obvious comfort with the heavy equipment that had been issued to the new men upon their arrival in the Batavi camp.

'So, what's your name and whose son are you?'

'Egilhard, Chosen Man, son of Lataz.'

'Which means that your uncle is Frijaz, right?'

'Yes, Chosen Man.'

The older man looked at Egilhard for a moment, then pointed to the sword at his waist.

'And if you're Frijaz's nephew then that must be Lightning, if I'm not mistaken. May I?'

He waited while the recruit drew the sword, inclining his head in respect as Egilhard offered him the weapon's hilt. Hefting the weapon with an expert hand he held it up to look down the blade.

'Beautiful. I always wondered how it was that a piss head like Frijaz ended up with something of such quality, given that he always spent everything he had on beer and women. He never told me, no matter how hard I badgered him. Won it in a game of knuckle bones in some tavern or other, that was my usual guess, but he just used to look at me and smile, the smug bastard.'

He stepped away from the recruit before making a series of practice cuts with the sword, nodding approval as he returned the weapon to its owner.

'You've got something special there. Let's hope you can take advantage of it when the time comes to spill blood for the tribe, eh? Although Lataz and his brother were both warriors in their own quiet way. If they've prepared you for service then you are indeed a lucky man. And yes, I am a Wolf Priest. In battle I wear a wolf's head over my helmet rather than a crest, and I am expected to provide every man of my century with an example of service to Hercules, and to help any man who asks to devote themselves to his service, as do I. And after battle . . .' He looked at the recruits for a moment in silence. 'You'll find that out in due course.'

Alcaeus looked at the curious recruit questioningly.

'Do you have any more questions for us, Egilhard, son of Lataz and brother son of Frijaz?'

'*No, Centurion!*'

'Good. There are limits to even my patience. Very well then Banon, deliver them to the tent parties we discussed earlier, their leading men can take their pick as they see fit except for the curious one. I think he'd be best placed in Grimmaz's tent party. He's either inquisitive and keen to do his best for the tribe or an idiot who doesn't know when to keep his eyes to himself. Or both. Either way Grimmaz can have the fun of finding out which it is, and either encourage the one until he's a proper soldier or punish the latter until he's a proper soldier. Or both. And until we know which it is, his tent party name will be Nosey, given his apparently insatiable curiosity. Off you go Nosey, go and meet your new best friends.'

'*Yes, Centurion!*'

'Good boy. See, Banon, they *are* capable of learning quickly when managed the right way.'

Banon marched the recruits across the Batavi cohorts' camp, commentating as they passed row after row of wooden barrack blocks.

'See this? This is the point of the Batavi spear, us and our allies. Eight full cohorts of men: four of our own, two from our strongest allies, the Frisavones and one each from the Cananefates and the Marsaci. Our full fighting strength is two and a half thousand soldiers and half as many cavalry, the best soldiers in the empire. We've been fighting for Rome for getting on for a hundred years, ever since they conquered Gaul, and in all those years we've never faced an enemy we couldn't send home with their tails between their legs, which means that you have a lot to learn in a short time. Here we are then.'

He stopped in front of a long wooden building with a row of eight doors granting access to rooms with just enough space for eight men and their equipment, choosing a door and ushering the red-headed recruit through it.

'This is your new home, carrot top. In you go.'

When the other three recruits had been handed over to their leading men, the Chosen Man paused for a moment, playing a serious stare over the last of them.

'So did Lataz and Frijaz teach you to fight?'

'*Yes, Chosen Man!*'

Banon raised a hand.

'You can relax a little now. You still have to call me by my title, but you only have to shout your answers when you're being given an order or asked if you understand. The rest of the time you can speak normally, with me at least. Just make sure you show the appropriate respect to anyone you don't know. So, Soldier Egilhard, those two nasty old bastards raised you for the cohorts, right?'

'Yes, Chosen Man.'

'They trained to fight with a sword and shield?'

'Yes, Chosen Man, they did their best to make me ready.'

'Good. It's always a lot easier when recruits have some idea of what's happening. So you know that when I introduce you to your tent mates they're going to want to have some fun with you? Just like the older men did with them in their time.'

'Yes, Chosen Man.'

'And what are you going to do when they find some new and novel means of making you look both uneducated and foolish?'

'Smile, Chosen Man?'

Banon nodded.

'Excellent. You're clearly better prepared for your first few days in the army than I was. I ended up punching my leading man in the face, although that was the only punch I landed on him and in return he beat me halfway to death. Didn't do me too much harm though, given I'm now his deputy. Some of us just have to learn the hard way. And what did your father say about intimidation?'

'He told me that if any man tried to steal from me or fuck me then I was to hit them, as hard as I could, and to keep hitting them until they stopped trying to do whatever it was that made me hit them.'

The chosen man nodded again.

'Sound advice. But it won't happen in my century, because my men all know that we don't tolerate that sort of thing. So, here we are . . .'

He opened the barrack door, ushering Egilhard in through the opening and walking in behind him.

'*Tent party, stand to attention!*'

The soldiers sprang to their feet and dropped from the bunk beds, coming to attention with commendable speed.

'This is Egilhard, your new tent mate, fresh from the Island and clearly a curious young type, which is why we're going to call him Nosey until a more appropriate name occurs to us. And these, Nosey, are your tent mates. Apart from Grimmaz, who goes by the title "Happy" due to the fact that he very rarely is, your other comrades are Andreios and Andronicus, who we call "the First One" and "the Other One" – they're twin brothers if you haven't already guessed – Levonhard, or "Ugly", Lanzo, "Dancer" and that big beast at the back goes by the name of Wigbrand, although when you get to know him he may let you call him by his nickname. Which is "Tiny". Welcome to your new family.'

He paused, looking at the expression on the recruit's face.

'What is it now? Come on, I know you have a question, you frown every time something occurs to you. Ah . . .' Understanding twisted his face into a smile. 'You'd like to know what my nickname is, wouldn't you, but you don't want to ask in case it's something I don't like. You really are a bright boy, aren't you Nosey? What's my name, Lanzo?'

The soldier spoke quickly, clearly ready for the question.

'Kneecaps, Chosen Man!'

Banon turned back to face Egilhard with a grin.

'There you are. My tent party name is "Kneecaps". And now you're wondering why, with that little frown back on your face. But you only get to find that out when you've fought for the tribe, so for the time being all that curiosity would be better employed in working out just how to avoid pissing any of these men off, wouldn't it?'

Centurions' Mess, Legio IV Macedonica, The Winter Camp, Mogontiacum, Germania Superior, December AD 68

'Well, you can all swear allegiance to the bastard if you want, but I'm not fucking having any of it!'

The speaker swallowed his wine down with a swift tip of his wrist, smashing the cup down on the scarred wooden table in front of him, belched loudly and clenched a big fist, looking unsteadily round at his comrades in search of any dissenting opinion.

'This new fucking Legatus Caecina can kiss my arse if he tries to make me promise to serve that cocksucker Galba, and that's the end of it! It was us soldiers who put down the rebel Vindex, under the command of Verginius Rufus, a proper Roman general, to protect the emperor from his fucking sedition, but the next thing you know, Vindex's mate Galba's on the throne, and throwing his weight around like a bull with its fucking tail on fire.'

The man sitting next to him raised a hand to indicate that he was speaking too loudly, but the drunken officer wasn't willing to be calmed.

'Don't tell me to be quiet, I couldn't give a *fuck* who hears me! Make no mistake about it, we're the ones being screwed here! This fucking Galba has our general, the best man in the whole fucking empire, replaced with that fat gouty cunt Flaccus, and then he has Legatus Augusti Capito, the only other proper gentleman on the length of the frontier, killed just so he can't pose any threat to his grip on the throne!' He pointed to a steward, lurking uneasily in the corner with a jug of wine as instructed, then stabbed the finger down at his cup. 'You, more wine!'

He stared sweaty-faced as the man rushed forward to refill his cup, allowing a gap in his stream of invective for one of his drinking companions to interject.

'But is it for the likes of us to challenge them, Quintus? They're the gentlemen, we're just the bulls who make what they want to happen come about.'

Several of the men around the table shook their heads, dark-faced with disagreement.

'Bullshit!' The drunk was on his feet, waving an angry hand to dismiss his colleague's opinion, swaying unsteadily. 'If it weren't for us, the sixty proud centurions who give this legion leadership, there wouldn't be no fucking legion, no fucking frontier and no fucking empire! All those toga-wearing pricks would be no better than the rest of us, instead of which they float around like a bunch of faggots thinking they can be telling us what to do, when the truth is they don't have a fucking clue! "Indeed, Centurion". "Quite so, Centurion". "As you suggest, Centurion". All code for "I haven't got a fucking clue, Centurion"!'

He subsided back into his chair, his eyes starting to roll up as the effect of the copious quantities of wine he'd thrown down his neck since coming off duty hit him with the force of a lead-weighted cosh, but even as he stared around the table, his eyes struggling to focus, he continued to spout the hatred that the long drinking session had freed from any restraint.

'Mark my fucking words boys, because you'll find I'm right when this has all played out. When this legion goes on parade on New Year's Day, there won't be a man in the Fourth willing to swear allegiance to Galba, and that's the truth of it. I know what *my* lads are saying, and I know what *your* lads are saying, and there ain't one of them that thinks that wrinkled old prick Galba should have been allowed to drive poor old Nero to kill himself. And if the scum that inhabit that cesspit Rome didn't have the sense to stand up against the bastard, *we* do! He can replace a proper general with a fat useless slug if he wants, and murder another good man to make sure he's got no rivals, but it ain't the generals that command the German legions, and it ain't the gentlemen legati and tribunes either. It's. Fucking. *Us*.' He belched and stared around the table, his eyes unfocused. 'Think on . . .'

Looking around the table one last time, he put a hand on the wooden surface and pushed himself upright, waved a dismissive hand at the men staring at him and staggered away. The oldest man at the table, the legion's seam-faced veteran senior centurion, a man who should by rights have retired three years before but whose appetite for soldiering was a strong as ever, pointed to another man and then at the shambling drunk.

'Go and keep an eye on him, young Marcus, and make sure he gets to his own bed without getting himself into trouble shouting his mouth off in the camp. You can wake up his optio too, and tell him to watch our brother in the night and make sure he doesn't choke on his own puke. Junior man's duty, there'll be a new boy doing the same for you one day. We'll have a cup of the good stuff waiting for you when you get back, eh?'

The youngest centurion at the table nodded solemnly and followed the drunk out of the mess, leaving his audience to exchange variously bemused and amused glances. The veteran looked about him with a hard face, having hardly sipped at his wine all evening.

'Well then, he said what we're all thinking. He might be pissed up, but he has the right of it, more or less. The German legions are the best in the empire, stands to reason given we stand between Rome and a horde of envious tribesmen who'd be across the river to burn everything that doesn't move and fuck everything that does in a heartbeat, if we weren't here to scare the shit out of them.'

The men around the table nodded at the truth of his words.

'And Galba might be a former soldier, and a hard man too for all that he's an old bastard.' He looked around the table with a wry smile, recognising his own advancing years. 'But it's just not right. It was our man Verginius Rufus who put Vindex down, and for his loyalty to the throne he gets promoted to where he can't be any danger to Galba and replaced by Hordeonius Flaccus, a man unfit to command, with no value other than the fact he also poses no threat to our new emperor. And now he's had Fonteius Capito murdered in Germania Inferior, to remove another competitor, and replaced him with this man Vitellius. He thinks he can control the German legions by putting his own men in to command the armies on the Rhenus, but he's forgetting one thing.

If he can make himself emperor with just one soft legion from Hispania, think what a better man could do with seven bone-hard legions from the northern frontier.'

He looked around the table.

'Think about it, boys. Seven legions. Better than that, seven battle-ready veteran legions, *and* all their auxiliaries. Fifth Alaudae and Fifteenth Primigenia at the Old Camp. Sixteenth Gallica at Novaesium. First Germanica at Bonna. Then there's us, Fourth Macedonica and our comrades of the Twenty-Second Primigenia here in the Winter Camp, and nastiest of all, those evil-minded pricks of the Twenty-First Rapax at Vindonissa. Seven veteran legions, boys, enough fighting power to tear the guts out of any other army in the empire. And the three legions in Britannia would be on our side too, and them with the most battle experience of all of us, if we had the right man in command. The right *emperor*. And if one legion can give a man the title *caesar*, why can't seven legions take it off him and put their own man on the throne, eh?'

The officers around the table were nodding at the justness of his argument, looking at each other with sober expressions as they realised the weight of what he was proposing. The veteran leaned in, speaking quietly, and they all listened, keenly interested in what Secundus had to say now that he had decided to state a view.

'And nothing we've discussed tonight is anything more or less than our legionaries are saying, so even if we weren't minded to do something about this state of affairs, it'd soon be out of our hands. But for the time being this hard-on needs to stay out of sight under the blankets. Not a word to the tribunes, not even the one or two we've got some time for. And get a grip of your men, let's have no soldiers shouting out comments on parade that'll get us into hot water for not being in control of our centuries before the time comes. Crack down hard on the loud mouths, but quietly let your boys know we're not going to stand for this. Tell them that Secundus wants the word to go round that we're the German legions, and we're not going to tolerate being punished for our loyalty to Nero. If Rome wants a new emperor, then Rome can have a new emperor. Just not the one they've think they've chosen.'

The Old Camp, Germania Inferior, December AD 68

'Io Saturnalia!'

The men of Legio Fifth Alaudae didn't need telling twice, opening their throats to bellow a reply to senior centurion Decimus's shouted challenge.

'IO SATURNALIA!'

Drawing another deep breath, he filled the silence that followed their first response with another salutation that was louder than the first.

'Io Saturnalia!'

His men, knowing the game that he was playing, and keen to enter into the spirit of the feast, hurled the words back at him with sufficient volume to cause his lips to twitch in a slight smile.

'IO SATURNALIA!'

'*Io Saturnalia!*'

The third time was different, as it always was, pitched an octave higher than the first two in that gravel-throated roar that was an imprecation in and of itself, its tone a deliberate affront to his men's manhood and their right to wear the military belt so precious to legionaries, reminding them that they were soldiers of the finest legion in the empire that ruled the known world and challenging them to shout themselves hoarse in reply.

'*IO SATURNALIA!*'

Nodding in satisfaction he raised his vine stick to signal to his centurions.

'Light the torches!'

Within the ranks of the waiting centuries, single flames swiftly multiplied to become dozens of points of light, as each legionary lit his torch from the man to his left and then turned to the man on his right. The previously dimly lit parade ground swiftly transformed into a blaze of light, until every one of the five thousand soldiers held a burning brand, their flames flickering in the slight evening breeze. Stalking across the flat expanse, Decimus saluted his legatus, who bowed gravely in return and then signalled to the local magistrate that he might begin the ceremony, sharing a grimace with his most senior soldier at the civilian's usual long-winded approach to the ritual that, while important religiously, was the only thing standing between them and an evening's debauchery whose prospect already had half the legion shuffling its feet with impatience to be away. After a good deal longer than was strictly necessary, the ceremonial bonds tied about the effigy of Saturn's ankles were cut away and the festival declared to be in effect, and with an undisguised sigh of relief, the legatus turned and saluted Decimus, a reversal of military etiquette entirely in the spirit of the feast. The older man returned his superior's salute with the grave seriousness of a veteran, acutely aware that, while all things might be permissible at Saturnalia, when masters could enjoy the novelty of serving meals already cooked by their servants, who in turn faced the distinctly unnerving experience of becoming masters for a day, the essential truth was that a master slighted was a dangerous man, no matter what the circumstances. Wise servants made sure that the festival's drunken merry making did not become a domestic casus belli for an unwinnable war, and wise centurions simply ignored all but the unavoidable formalities of the feast when dealing with Roman gentlemen, whose skins were notoriously thin when it came to slights both real and imagined. Breathing a sigh of relief, he turned and bellowed the order for his first cohort to lead the legion off the parade ground, and thereby to commence the twenty-four hours of eating, drinking and whoring that was the deeper meaning of the festival for the average legionary, smiling at the thought of his nice warm quarters, a jug of rather good wine and an accommodating woman of quite prodigious sexual appetite to whom he'd taken the precaution of offering his money months before. His centurions could spend the next day watching their men walk the fine line between festive abandon that could safely be forgotten by all involved and behaviour requiring a violent encounter with a vine stick the day after; he would be keeping himself to himself for the next day or so.

Well back down the column's length, in a cohort whose place in the legion's order of battle traditionally reflected poorly on the readiness for war of its members, centurion Marius, deliberately named after one of Rome's greatest men by a father determined to see his son follow him into the service, and who therefore went by the nickname of 'the mule' whenever his men thought he wasn't listening, marched alongside his century with the look of a man resigned to taking his part in the festivities.

'Cheer up, Centurion! We don't want no sour faces while you're pouring our beer!'

Marius nodded at the men marching beside him, acknowledging their grins with a hard smile while at the same time looking hard for any sign of malice behind their cheeriness. Saturnalia was always a difficult time for any legion's less confident officers, among whose number he secretly considered himself, even though any such public admission would have ended his career in a heartbeat. The Fifth was not a legion that tolerated any sign of weakness in any man, with the long cherished belief among its centurionate that even one step backwards was tantamount to a defeat. Men settled their differences with their fists for the most part, and officers were expected to show no mercy to any man who offered them even the slightest challenge, and so, certain as he was that he would never master the apparently effortless swagger that he so envied in those of his colleagues who seemed born to lead men, he had long since learned to mask his insecurities with a show of stone-faced confidence that seemed to convince the men under his command that while fair minded, he was not to be trifled with. In truth, he mused, once a man was carrying the vine stick, blessed with a brutally efficient chosen man and a well-chosen watch officer to dispense his discipline and make sure that the century's unofficial spine of leaders, the eight men who ruled its tent parties, followed the rules and presented their comrades in good order and ready to fight, the show of brazen self-confidence that he had needed to present to the world on his way up through the ranks was no longer quite so necessary. He was a centurion, and therefore the voice of the vengeful and jealous spirit that resided in the legion's eagle as far as the eighty men who sweated and suffered at his command, and who might one day live or die with him on the battlefield in the unlikely event of the legion being commanded to take to the field against an enemy worthy of the name, were concerned.

Breaking off the line of march, the legion headed for their section of the huge camp that housed both the Fifth and their sister legion the Fifteenth Primigenia, with Decimus at their head barking out the marching pace and looking for any sign of deviation from the discipline that was still expected of every man until they were formally dismissed, Marius stalked alongside his eighty men with his vine stick held ready to chastise any man who was unwise enough to break step while they were still on such public display.

'Smile, Centurion! You know the rules! *Io Saturnalia!*'

He favoured the man in question with a hard grin as the entire century roared out an echoing cry, knowing full well that from the moment the priest had cut Saturn's bonds a different code had applied to the carefully regulated discipline that ruled the century's collective life for the other three hundred and sixty-four days of the year.

'Just make sure you've got a full gut before you start pouring beer into it, eh Legionary Julius? It'd be a shame to waste all that anticipation by being as pissed as a rat before the fun starts.'

He slowed, dropping down his century's length while the soldier reassured him that the centurion wasn't to worry about his ability to consume beer just as fast as his officers could bring it to him. It was an assertion Marius had both reason and experience to suspect would be correct until, with depressing rapidity, the man in question went from happy drunk to incoherent incontinent, and had to be laid out on the grass outside his barrack to lie in his own filth until the effects of drink wore off to leave him sore-headed and rueful.

'It'll be a long night.'

He grinned at his colleague in command of the cohort's fourth century, a man with whom he had joined the legion on the same day seventeen years before. Having sweated, cursed, eaten, drunk, fought and whored in each other's company as members of the same tent party for several years, before both had been selected for promotion to watch officer, Gaius knew him as well as any man could, even to the point of keeping his friend's insecurities as closely guarded a secret as if they were his own. He grinned at the observation, falling into step with his brother officer.

'It's always a long night at Saturnalia. First they all need to be fed, but at least they're not staggering about threatening to puke while they're eating. Then they get pissed up and the whores start earning their coin, and for a few hours all we'll hear is songs about where the centurion can put his vine stick and the occasional scream as they commit some indignity or other on the ladies . . .'

Gaius laughed.

'Remember that lad of yours last year? The one who chased one of the girls three times round the barrack block, naked and sporting a stick of red celery that a mule would have been proud to claim ownership of, while she kept on shouting he was coming nowhere near her with that thing.'

Marius nodded, rubbing his chin at the memory.

'I remember having to tickle him with the night officer's best friend to calm him down a little. And I remember what he said when he woke up . . .'

Gaius smirked.

'So do I! He rubbed the back of his head and muttered "What the *fuck* was I drinking last night?"' He looked at his friend for a moment before speaking again. 'It's only a few hours. Every year they swear they'll greet the sun together, and every year sunrise finds them unconscious, covered in vomit and with their purses empty and their pricks worn to the bone. So grin at them the way you always do, all jutting chin and hard eyes, and they'll know not to get on your wrong side. And besides, you can always threaten them with being picked for the usual harpastum game with the Batavians.'

The two men stopped and watched as their optios chivvied the soldiers good-naturedly into their barracks, with a remarkable lack of the usual shouting and prodding with their brass-knobbed staffs.

'Harpastum?'

Gaius nodded, raising an eyebrow.

'Yes, harpastum. You know, two teams, one ball, violence and sudden physical damage? A game beloved of those men whose brains have already been knocked about so many times they can't feel the damage being done to them any more?'

His friend poked him with the tip of his vine stick.

'No, I was referring to the Batavians. And my question was, "*What Batavians?*". They're standing guard duty on the Gauls to the best of my knowledge, all eight cohorts, so how they're going to muster a harpastum team with any chance of standing up to our lunatics is beyond me.'

Gaius grinned back at him.

'Stop poking me with that fucking stick or I'll have to give your lot something real to sing about. And all I know is what that old bastard Decimus told us at the dawn meeting today, which you'd have known if you hadn't been guard centurion and therefore busy shouting at sleepy sentries. Seems the Batavians have managed to scrape up a team from somewhere. Old men and children, I'd imagine.'

The Old Camp, Germania Inferior, December AD 68

'What a collection of animals.'

Marius nodded his agreement, watching with an expert eye as the Fifth legion's harpastum team stood waiting for their Batavian opposition to arrive under the watchful eye of the legion's senior centurion.

'Decimus knows how to choose a team, you have to give him

that. Big solid lumps to form a pack around the ball, a few fast wiry types to move it quickly when we tear it away from the other side . . .'

'And his speciality, the dead-eyed bastards who go in to get it.'

'Given that he did exactly that for twenty years, it's no surprise he knows how to pick them, eh? And tell me, brother officer, where exactly do I fit into this *collection of animals*?'

Gaius laughed.

'Oh, he can pick them alright. You're perfect material for a harpastum team captain, and he spotted you quickly enough. You're just hard enough to earn the men's respect without being such a bastard that they feel they have to make an example of you.'

It was true. Where most centurions took the opportunity of their promotion to give up the game, on the grounds that being manhandled by the troops was hardly conducive to discipline, and knowing full well that an officer made a tempting target on the pitch that few men would be able to resist, Marius had played with a greater intensity after being awarded his vine stick, meeting those opponents who chose to single him out head on, and showing them why it was that he had a crest across his helmet and they didn't. After the first few broken ribs and concussions inflicted on opposing players who tried to test the new centurion's mettle, usually just in the run of play but occasionally with a more calculated savagery he had deemed necessary for his own survival, the legion's men had learned to treat him with cautious respect when he was anywhere near the sacred turf. Fifth Alaudae had been playing the man's game ever since its founding back in the days of the divine Julius, when the republic's last dictator had raised them from the conquered natives of Gallia Transalpina to fight his battles alongside the Italian legions, and the spring tournaments, with every century putting up a team to contest their cohort's championship and the winners fighting it out for dominance of the entire legion, had long been an essential part of training after the relatively inactive days of winter.

'And where are these Batavians you promised me then?'

Gaius looked about himself with feigned concern, then laughed softly.

'Who cares? With their men away making sure the Gauls don't decide to go for another attempt at the Vindex revolt, there's no way they're going to able to muster a proper team, so it might be better for all concerned if they didn't show. After some of the epics we're seen over the years, it would be an insult to their reputation for our lads to walk over some poor collection of weak sisters. And you know Decimus won't let you go easy on them.'

Marius nodded.

'Life's just like harpastum, boys.' His voice had taken on their First Spear's characteristic rasp. 'Just when you think you've got the ball over the line, some ugly bastard comes out of nowhere and smacks you in the face while the arbiter isn't looking, and the next thing you know you're on your back spitting teeth and counting stars while he runs off with the ball, fucking laughing!' He paused the obligatory moment before delivering the usual punch line. 'Well you won't find me fucking laughing!'

Gaius laughed, attempting the same mimicry with their superior's best-known catchphrase.

'So fucking do it to him first, eh?'

They laughed at the collected wisdom of their commander, then Marius raised a hand and pointed at the road that ran alongside the pitch to the fortress's main gate.

'There they are. Showing off their bloody horses as per usual.'

The Batavian team traditionally arrived for the game on horseback, emphasising what they saw as their superiority over the legions that were almost completely infantry based, whereas one man in every three in a Batavian cohort rode one of their famed beasts, trained to swim rivers with a rider and two fully armoured infantrymen men hanging off them to deliver fighting troops to the most unexpected parts of a battle. The two men frowned, staring at the newcomers in incomprehension, Gaius shaking his head in puzzlement.

'How are *they* Batavians? Their tunics are the wrong colour for a start. The Batavian cohorts wear red, whereas these boys are all dressed in white.'

The opposition team dismounted as they watched, and Marius whistled at their size.

'Old men and children, you promised me.'

His friend shrugged with the insouciance of a man who would be watching rather than participating in the forthcoming violence.

'What's your problem? You're supposed to be the hardest men in the legion, or so you keep telling the rest of us. Come on, let's go and have a closer look.'

When they reached the spot where the opposition had dismounted, they found that Decimus had beaten them to it and was far from sharing their bemusement. Embracing the Batavian team's leader with the familiarity of an old friend, he turned back to greet his officers with a broad grin.

'Now I *know* we're going to get a real game! This man . . .' he turned to gesture at the German he had greeted a moment before, '. . . is Hramn. He's an old friend from games we've played in the past, a decurion from the Batavian cohorts who was a titan of the game, before he was selected to lead the emperor's German Bodyguard in Rome and was promoted to the exalted rank of decurion. Now that Galba has sent him and his men back home to join the army of Germania Inferior, they have nothing better to do than come and match their wits and muscle against our own. Did you get much harpastum in Rome, Hramn?'

The German laughed softly, his blue eyes alive with amusement.

'We taught the praetorians to play the game, but only to give us someone to practise on. I'm expecting that you'll find us slow, like men with rusty swords and broken shields after so many years without proper opponents.'

Decimus cocked his head to one side.

'Oh, you think so? I'm away to give my lads a talking to, so I suggest you get your animals suitably warmed up and we'll see you on the pitch. I'll judge one half and you can take the other, if that suits?'

Gathering the two centurions to him, Decimus walked towards his waiting men, a tone of genuine excitement in his voice.

'This should be a proper game, not like beating those women of the Fifteenth when there's no one better to take on. Right, you ugly collection of half-wits!' The Fifth's team looked back at their leader with expressions that combined inquisitive curiosity with their usual aggressive confidence as to who it was that they were facing. 'Those men aren't just any Batavians, they're the men who until a few months ago were the emperor's personal bodyguard. That's right, the poor bastards who got sent home by that arsehole Galba when Nero decided to kill himself. I remember Hramn from the old days, when we used to play games that would make you children go white with the violence that was on offer, and then we'd sweat out the mud in the bathhouse like old comrades and get pissed on that dog-rough beer they drink. So be warned, my lads, these men know the game. You'll be on the back foot from the moment I blow my whistle unless you get stuck in like the men you keep telling each other you are.'

After completing their ritual preparations for the game, the two teams took to the pitch, twenty-five men to a side, and the two judges paced out the all-important line between the two, while both sides stood and stared at the other in the usual silent attempt to convince the opposition that they were only there to make up the numbers. Drawing the line into the pitch's soft mud with a spear blade, the two judges clasped arms and tossed a coin for first possession, which was promptly awarded to the men of the Fifth. They parted after another clasp, Hramn walking to the sidelines while Decimus stood with one foot either side of the newly inscribed line and addressed both sides in a loud voice.

'The Fifth has possession!' He tossed a hard leather ball the size of a pomegranate to Marius, whose team promptly assumed a defensive formation around him ready to resist the inevitable Batavi onslaught. 'Each half of the game will last for a half-hour sand glass, which will be timed by my centurion here!' He pointed to Gaius. 'At the half-time point my friend and former colleague

Hramn will assume the duties of judge and the teams will change sides of the pitch! The team with the most successful carries over the line will be judged to be the winner! And the rules . . .'

Marius and Gaius shared an amused glance, knowing Decimus's often-stated opinion that in harpastum, as in life, the rules mainly existed to be broken, and that the only measure of success was not to be caught in the act of gaining an unfair advantage.

'The rules are these: *no* biting, *no* eye gouging, no *deliberate* bone injuries and *no* stamping once a man is on the floor! Any man of either side who breaks these rules while I am judge will receive a swift and harsh punishment!' He raised a heavy leather cosh loaded with small lead balls, a means of enforcing discipline that the Fifth had long used to ensure that a pitch judge had the means of quickly calming any situation where tempers had got sufficiently out of hand for his whistle to have become ineffective. 'Although if I have to use it . . .' He raised a clenched fist that had become famed as his usual means of dishing out swift punishment on the pitch. 'Then you'll already have got to know this!' The men of the Fifth laughed softly at the old joke, but Marius noticed that the Germans were stone-faced, clearly intent on their game. 'And, as is usual in these *friendly* games . . .' He paused again for effect, a small smile creasing his lips, but not even his own men laughed this time. 'There will be no punching or kicking tolerated unless in a direct attempt to get to the ball. So no private fights on the side, gentlemen, not unless you want to wake up feeling like it's the morning after Saturnalia all over again!'

He turned to the Batavians.

'Ready?'

The German captain set his body, ready to run at the Fifth's pack and with his eyes locked on Marius in his position behind the Fifth's line.

'*Ready!*'

Decimus looked over at his own men, nodded at their determined faces.

'Ready?'

The twenty-five men barked an answer in unison, slapping big hands down onto their muscular thighs as they set themselves to resist the Germans' rush.

'*READY!*'

Blowing a long note on his whistle, the senior centurion pointed at the Germans and then gestured them forward over the line, stepping smartly back to avoid being overrun by the charge to contact that he knew was coming.

'Play!'

Holding the ball in the centre of the Fifth's pack, Marius had little to do other than wait and watch for his moment to come, as the charging Germans hammered into the legion team's defensive line, their entire focus on getting through the bodies that were protecting the game's objective and taking possession of the ball. Their attack was swift and brutal, each man knowing his role in taking a member of the opposing team and dealing with him swiftly and efficiently, tackling him to the ground where their struggle for dominance of the wrestling match that resulted ensured that the legionary was unable to resume his place in the line between the Germans and Gaius. With the first line of defence stripped away the Batavian pack bored in hard, the bigger men crashing into the legion team's defence with a collective grunt of expelled breath followed by a hectic struggle as the two forces fought for supremacy toe to toe, punches being traded with no signal from Decimus in his role of judge other than to nod approvingly as one of his men rocked a Batavian back with a jab that broke the German's nose with an audible pop, then snarl his approval as the other came back with a countering jab and hook that dropped the legionary in question to his knees, shaking his head in confusion.

'*Elephants!*'

Barking the legion's battle cry the last men between Marius and the attacking Germans stepped in to fight, but the Batavian drive forward had been too fierce, taking too many of the defenders out of the fight for possession, and their superior numbers swiftly told, one huge man simply wrapping a pair of legionaries up in his ape-like arms and taking them to the ground with his weight holding them down, laughing as they rained punches onto the top of his head to little effect. Realising that the time for a static defence was gone, Marius backed away from the protection of the crumbling line in front of him, watching in horror as the rampaging attackers dismantled the last vestiges of his defenders with brutal efficiency. Turning to his right, looking for a gap in the Batavian attack, he saw a knot of legion men who had gained superiority over three Germans whose only aim had been to temporarily take them out of the game, and darted towards them with the ball under his left arm and the other hand clenched into a fist. Shoulder-charging an unprepared German out of his way, he covered another half-dozen steps towards the sanctuary of his comrades' reforming line before going down under a tide of German bodies, a swift punch to the back of his head turning his fingers to jelly and allowing the ball to be stripped from his grasp by the man whom Decimus had called Hramn with no more resistance than a small child might have offered. Lying on his back, momentarily dazed, he watched in disgust as the German pack fought their way back over the line to their own territory with equally brutal speed and power, a dozen men gathered around their captain and literally punching their way back into their own territory. Decimus blew his whistle to announce the point won, and Marius allowed his head to sink back onto the cold mud, wincing at the bruise that was still making his head ring. Opening his eyes he saw the senior centurion standing over him with a hand outstretched, his eyes alive with the delight of the game.

'On your feet Marius! Your turn to attack.'

Shaking his head, he exchanged a wry glance with Gaius, then barked an order to his team to reform for the restart, his eyes roaming over the Batavian defence for any sign of a weakness to be exploited as he bellowed a challenge at his team.

'Are you still sleeping?! Wake up your ideas, you bastards! Make them pay for that point in blood! For the honour of the Fifth! *Elephants!*'

An hour later, with the Fifth having lost the match by seven points to five, the two teams stood panting and bloodied in ankle-deep mud that their boots had chewed into foaming ruin, a miniature replica of a battlefield apart from the lack of blood, urine and liquid excreta pooling in their bootprints, while Decimus addressed them in glowing terms and reluctantly admitted that the game ranked with the finest he had played.

'That was harpastum to rank with the best! There was no honour lost there by either side, and you can all be proud of the way you played! The men in the infirmary will get beer and food, once they've been treated, the rest of you follow me to the bath house. You've earned a sweat and a drink, and the Fifth Legion always lays on a good meal for our Batavian brothers-in-arms on this occasion!'

Marius's legs were weak to the point of near collapse, and the lump on the back of his head was now the size of an egg, rendering him slightly dizzy, but having washed the blood from his face with a bucket of warm water, he lowered himself onto a bench in the warm room and took a mug of beer from one of the stewards detailed to serve both teams in a bath house that had been cleared for their exclusive use. A Batavian sank heavily onto the bench beside him, taking a beer and offering his hand to be clasped. It was the man who had taken the ball from him the first time by dint of inflicting the bruise on his head that was still throbbing sickeningly.

'I'm Hramn. That was a good game, Captain.'

'Marius. That was a *hard* game. Harder than most I've played in.'

The German shrugged with a lopsided grin, one of his eyes almost closed as the result of a punch that Marius had dealt him a few minutes after losing the ball for the first time, a punch the German had greeted with the smile of a man truly at home on the battered turf of a harpastum pitch.

'A hard game is a good game. And we needed a hard game.'

Marius nodded, recognising the slight note of apology in the man's voice.

'You've been treated harshly. If the Fifth were dealt such a blow I know plenty of men who would be spitting blood and eager to find some way to avenge themselves on the men who denied them what they had earned.'

The other man raised his mug of beer.

'We are a patient people when we need to be, the Batavi until the time for patience is at an end. For now we can wait, to see if the emperor changes his mind given enough time, play harpastum and drink good beer with the new friends we have the opportunity to make while we have nothing better to do.'

Marius leaned closer, lowering his voice.

'You may not have to wait long. The talk in our centurion's mess is that legions all along the Rhenus are hostile to Galba, given the murder of our own legatus augusti, and the replacement of the man who rules Germania Superior with a man whom his legions despise.'

Hramn nodded with a hard glint in his one good eye.

'I pray daily for another man to take the throne, restore my men's lost honour and give back some meaning to my years of service. For that I would risk more than a bruised face. Much more . . .'

3

Colonia Agrippina, Germania Inferior, December AD 68

'Gentlemen. May I first say what a pleasure it is to finally get the chance to speak to you all together.'

The gathered legionary legati of the army of Germania Inferior and their senior centurions looked back at their new legatus augusti as he greeted them into his palatial office. Decimus shot a surreptitious glance to either side, quietly amused at the stances of the men around him. The four legati were looking at their new general with obvious interest, while their senior centurions, including, he mused, himself, stood to their superiors' rear, their stiff and awkward stances a reflection of the novelty of this unexpected situation. It was one thing for an army commander to exchange pleasantries with his centurions if the occasion demanded it, or even a little rough humour if he was that sort of a military man, but for such an august man to invite his legions' most senior professional soldiers to join him and his legati in the commanding general's praetorium was almost unheard of. Vitellius gestured to the steward moving among them with a tray of wine in glass cups, an unimaginable luxury to men used to taking their drink from metal cups.

'Please do help yourselves to a glass cup of wine and take a seat. You'll find them stronger than they look, so there's no need to worry about breaking them unless you manage to drop one!'

Decimus took a glass and held it carefully between his fingers, marvelling at the subtle shade of blue in its impossibly thin, transparent walls, then turned his attention to the newly appointed commander of the four legions that comprised his army. Tall and overweight, he stood slightly crookedly, the result, it was rumoured, of a chariot accident caused by the emperor Caligula over thirty years before, when he had occupied the somewhat risky position of one of the deranged young emperor's favourites. The Old Camp's two legati had been equally gloomy on the subject of the man's competency during their ride south, the Fifteenth Legion's commander, Munius Lupercus, venturing an opinion that had his colleague Fabius Fabullus's head nodding in agreement.

'He was an unexpected appointment to the role, and that's no secret. The collective opinion is that Galba has put a pair of nonentities in command on the Rhenus in order to neuter the threat from the German legions. Neither Hordeonius Flaccus in Germania Superior nor this man Vitellius on the lower half of the river have the military record or the dynamism to muster much support from the troops, strictly between us.'

The legatus augusti took his own seat behind the massive slab of oak that was the office's defining feature, clearing his throat, and Decimus was careful to show the right degree of attentiveness, noting in the corner of his eye his brother centurions assuming similarly alert positions.

'Well now, comrades.' Vitellius raised his glass. 'Let's drink to the success of our army and the destruction of our enemies!'

They repeated his words, each man sipping at his wine and watching their new commander over the rims of their glasses, waiting expectantly for whatever it was that he intended to say next. Shifting in his chair a little awkwardly, as if in reflection of his thoughts, he paused for a moment before speaking again, a note of regret entering his voice.

'I only knew my predecessor Gaius Fonteius Capito a little, gentlemen, but he always struck me as an upstanding man. A principled man, and not easily diverted from a course of action if he believed it to be the right thing for the empire. So if you're wondering how I feel about assuming command of your legions at this time, after his murder, my feelings on the subject are mixed, to say the least. I am delighted to have the opportunity to work with such a fine selection of Rome's gentlemen, not to mention some of the very best soldiers in the empire. The reputation of the German legions as the finest army in the world is well known.'

Heads nodded, and Decimus found himself joining with the reaction to their general's words. The man was only stating what they knew to be the truth, but his sincerity was evident.

'And at the same time I find myself downcast, gentlemen, horrified at the depths to which the empire has fallen in the past few years, and the way in which any hint of military genius has been snuffed out with brutality that smacks of simple dictatorship. First came the enforced suicide of the finest general the world has seen since the Divine Julius . . .' The legati were nodding now, each of them musing on what might have been if Gnaeus Domitius Corbulo had not been ordered to fall on his own sword by Nero two years before. 'It was my fondest hope that the accession to power of Servius Sulpicius Galba would at least result in a more rational rule, but it seems the new emperor has taken up the reins where the old one dropped them. You may or may not know that he had the First Classica, a legion of marines who had been recruited into the army by Nero, cleared from his path by cavalry and then decimated with significant loss of life, when he arrived at the gates of Rome in his triumphant march from Hispania. Decimated, gentlemen, a punishment from the early republic, when Rome was literally fighting for her life and discipline was unavoidably harsh, a penalty so brutal that in these enlightened days no emperor since the divine Augustus has resorted to it! And Galba, gentlemen, is no Augustus, with neither the stature nor the justification for such a desperate measure. Consider it! A legion guilty of no more than petitioning the man they consider to be their emperor for the chance to continue in his service, ready to bend their knees and swear loyalty to him and him alone, found themselves under the cavalry's lances. And worse, as the penalty for their understandable disquiet at being dismissed with their petition unheard, Galba ordered their decimation!' His audience looked at each other in shock, this being news to them. 'It was suppressed, of course, and not made general knowledge, but I have the right of it when I tell you that on his order one man in ten was pulled from their ranks, and the remaining nine ordered to beat him to death with their bare hands, guaranteeing the brutal deaths of many not responsible for the mild protest their comrades had voiced! I saw their corpses with my own eyes, so that's no rumour but the absolute truth. And the murder of my predecessor, apparently without motive, hints at a similar lack of scruple when it comes to dealing with the men of his own class. It seems that Rome has exchanged a paranoid tyrant for a tyrant of an entirely different sort: cold and calculating where Nero was irrational and bestial. I find myself uncertain as to which of them represents the greater threat to the empire.'

He paused for a moment, shaking his head slightly in evident disgust.

'I am dismayed, brothers, heartbroken that the man we were told would bring a new honesty and vigour to the throne only represents more of the same, just more rational in his brutality although, it seems, even more paranoid and afraid of the threat he perceives in his own military leaders. But enough of my concerns.' He flashed a hard smile at them. 'Let us talk about your commands. Tell me what you need and I will make it available to you. After all, there can be no greater priority than the defence of the empire's frontier, even if there are drawn swords at our backs. And tell me, since I'm quite sure your men will be in need of some cheering up in the wake of Legatus Augusti Capito's murder, what is the one thing I can do now, today, that will prove to them that their general understands their worries and is determined to do the right thing for the empire and for them?'

In the moment of silence that followed, Decimus found himself musing that he knew exactly what the men of his Fifth Legion wanted when Vitellius spoke again, staring straight at him.

'You have the look of a man who knows exactly what would make his men a deal more content with their lot. Would you perhaps care to share it with us, First Spear?'

Standing reflexively, literally jumping to attention and saluting, Decimus dithered for a split second under the general's keen gaze before half a lifetime of indoctrination to the fact that the legionary centurion was the most superior form of life in the world overrode any qualms he might felt at being asked a direct question by such a lofty personage.

'My name is Decimus, Legatus. And it's an easy enough question to answer, sir. There's a local man who your predecessor accused of treason and participation in a revolt of the Gauls, with evidence so strong that he had this man's brother executed without a single man doubting that his death was deserved. He sent the traitor to Rome to face imperial justice, only for him to be freed by the new emperor a few weeks ago.' He paused for a brief moment before delivering the point that would see just how closely tied this new commander was to the man who had elevated him to his new office. 'The same emperor who had stood to gain the most from this man's treason, Legatus.'

Vitellius sat back in his chair with a thoughtful look.

'And your men still believe that Gaius Fonteius Capito should have had this man executed?'

Decimus shook his head with a small smile.

'Such a thing wasn't within his powers, more's the pity, sir. It seems the man in question is a citizen of the empire as he has served twenty-five years with the auxiliary forces, whereas his brother was still short of having served his term and was therefore subject to a different legal code that allowed for his execution. As an honourable man Legatus Augusti Capito was obliged to send the older brother to Rome for an imperial judgement, and by the time he got there, the emperor who would have condemned him to death without hesitation had killed himself and been replaced.'

'By Galba, whose rise to power was brought about, eventually, by the ripples and echoes of the very revolt I presume you're talking about. You mean that this traitor was deemed guilty of participating in Vindex's attempt to put Gaul behind Galba's cause, I presume?'

Decimus nodded, knowing that the moment of greatest danger had been reached. Vitellius stared at him for a moment before speaking again, his tone thoughtful.

'So you offer me a way to gain the confidence of my men, all twenty thousand of them, while at the same time risking loss of favour from the man who appointed me to this post and who, with a single sentence to the right person, can have me removed from it, by one means or another. And he won't hesitate to do it, I've known this new emperor long enough to be in no doubt about that. Servius Sulpicius Galba, as I am well placed to be able to relate as a fellow senator, is an original, a throwback to an age that we lost a long time ago, that may only ever have truly existed in the body and mind of the man who founded this empire we serve. Who he is old enough to have known personally, by the way. Only as a child mind you, but it's a well-known fact that the Emperor Augustus himself pinched his cheek when Galba was a small child, and some measure of the man's appetite for war must have communicated itself to the boy, because he grew up to quite the soldier. As a legion legatus he went on manoeuvres with Caligula when he was two years past his fortieth birthday, and the emperor later confided to me that Galba had trotted alongside his chariot at the double march, carrying a shield, mind you, for the best part of twenty miles. He was as hard as oak then, and he's lost little of that inner fortitude as he's grown older, I can assure you of that. When Caligula was murdered by the praetorians, and his friends all urged him to take the throne over Claudius, he'd have none of it. As honest as a vestal's virginity. So when he called on me to take command of this army I was of course flattered . . . at first. Until the whispering started, the gossip that I was to command the four legions of the army of Germania Inferior simply because Galba believed I was too fat and comfortable to pose him any threat. I was to be classed with my colleague Marcus Hordeoneius Flaccus as a commander who is considered unfit for command, and therefore given this command to remove the threat posed by these legions in the wrong hands. He knew the stories would get back to me, he's nobody's fool, but when I went to receive my orders from him in person I smiled to his face and told him how honoured I was. I told him that I wouldn't let him down, and that the army of

Germania Inferior would be as loyal to him as it was to his predecessor under Capito.'

He looked around the gathering, a half-smile creasing his lips.

'And so, Centurion Decimus, you offer me a difficult choice. On the one hand, the emperor may look askance at my re-arresting a man he has already pardoned for the same crime, which means that his reaction to my having him executed might well be . . . severe. He might with good cause consider such an act an affront to his authority, and few emperors take such things lightly. On the other hand, it seems that you propose a means of putting the men of four legions on my side with no greater effort than my telling you to arrest this man . . .'

'Civilis, Legatus. His name is Gaius Julius Civilis.'

'Civilis. I see . . .'

Vitellius fell silent for a moment, and Decimus looked around at his colleagues to find them intent on the man's face, each of them clearly eager for his answer, as were their legati for the most part, only the Fifteenth's commander, Munius Lupercus, apparently perturbed by the discussion's unexpected direction. At length the legatus augusti nodded decisively.

'Under the circumstances, gentlemen, it seems to me that there can only be one appropriate course of action with regard to this Gaius Julius Civilis.'

Civitas Lingonum, Gallia Lugdunensis, December AD 68

The tent party was more or less ready to go on parade when Alcaeus walked in through the barrack door.

'*Centurion!*'

The soldiers snapped to attention, drawing a satisfied nod from Alcaeus to their leading man.

'Nice and taut, Grimmaz, you've been doing your job for a change, I see?'

If the statement had an undertone of relaxed humour, the subject of its enquiry took no risks in his response.

'*Yes, Centurion!*'

'Good man. We'll make a watch officer out of you yet, if we can just get you to smile every now and then.'

Alcaeus dispensed the compliment with his look of wry amusement, turning to look at the tent party's newest member.

'Well now Egilhard, let's have a look at you before we get on parade. At the command "stand to attention", show me what you can do.' He drew breath, shooting Grimmaz a swift conspiratorial glance. 'Stand to atten-*tion!*'

While most of the command had been delivered in a tone not much louder than a normal conversational tone, the final syllable was barked so loudly and high pitched that it could have been the enraged scream of a man suffering an unexpected physical violation. The recruit snapped smartly into the required posture, head up, chest out, shield and spear held neatly upright and boots clamped together.

'Not bad. You've been coaching him, Grimmaz?'

The leading man shrugged.

'Yes, Centurion! I wasn't going to have one of my boys look bad on parade and get the rest of us into trouble. Besides, his father and uncle seem to have done most of the hard work for us. He knew all of the tricks we tried to play on him, he knows how to wear his equipment, his boots already have a better shine than half of this lot—'

'Oh, so you like to polish leather, do you, sonny?'

Egilhard kept his gaze fixed rigidly on a point over Alcaeus's shoulder, barking his reply in the expected manner.

'*Yes, Centurion!*'

'Excellent! I've got two pairs in need of some attention. I'm sure Grimmaz can spare you for an hour or two while you exercise your strong right wrist and make them gleam for me.'

'*Yes, Centurion!*'

'Good boy. After all, what would the world be coming to if the new recruits didn't have to pay some sort of price for entry into this, the finest of all places that a man could be?'

He turned to Grimmaz with a satisfied nod.

'Good work, he even looks a bit like a warrior. Very well, let's get you all on parade before Scar starts blowing his whistle and getting all bad tempered.'

Marching through the rows of wooden huts that had been built on their arrival at the city, as part of a semi-permanent camp intended to demonstrate to the previously restive Lingones that Gaul was as much a part of the empire as ever, and that the empire fully intended to keep the relationship exactly as the divine Julius had defined it over a century before, Alcaeus stood aside as Grimmaz led his tent party out onto the parade ground. A cold north wind stirred the hairs on the white wolf's head that was mounted atop the iron bowl of his helmet to denote his priestly status. Banon walked over to join him.

'They all look tidy enough, Centurion. That new boy in the sixth tent party, the one with the muscles, he had to be given a couple of clips around the ear for the state of his boots, but he seems to have responded to encouragement.'

The centurion nodded, looking across the freshly constructed parade ground to where the cohorts' senior centurion stood waiting for his men to take their positions. The wide expanse had been hacked out of the flattest piece of ground available into which drainage channels had been cut and filled with shingle, then covered in tons of gravel broken by labour conscripted from the defeated Gaulish tribe on whom the cohorts had been posted to ensure peace, all to provide enough room for the eight Batavi cohorts to parade together.

'And now that Scar's got a parade ground big enough to take all eight cohorts, what game do you think he'll have us playing today?'

Alcaeus grinned at his subordinate's question.

'I prayed to Hercules for help to see that future last night, but all he could show me in my dreams was battle drill. Hour after hour of battle drill, led by a bad-tempered Prefect looking a good deal like our own beloved leader, until our boys were puking with exhaustion.'

Men were streaming onto the open surface from the adjoining

camp, called by the braying of the trumpeters who were standing alongside each of the eight senior centurions who led the cohorts, organised chaos quickly resolving itself into the expected ordered ranks as centurions, optios and watch officers bellowed orders and hurried along latecomers, the slower soldiers and anyone they simply didn't like with casual acts of physical encouragement. When every man was in his appointed place, with the cohorts paraded eight deep to pack their numbers into the available space, the man who ruled their world and led them into battle stepped forward and looked up and down the line of centuries. Scar's hair riffled gently in the cold wind as his hard gaze swept across his command, the facial disfiguration that had earned him his nickname, a thick ropey line of scar tissue from his left eyebrow to the corner of his mouth, visible even at fifty paces since the senior officer had eschewed the use of his helmet for the morning's parade. Taking one last look along the line of his cohorts he spoke, his voice a harsh crack of the whip that unconsciously straightened men's backs and stiffened their stances.

'I trust you all enjoyed Saturnalia!'

He started pacing down the line, looking at individual soldiers as he spoke.

'Some men had a more hectic time of it than others! More than a few of you found your way to my disciplinary table and took the risk that I might have erected the whipping posts this morning! You are fortunate that I have decided to avoid ending the year in such an inauspicious manner, despite the temptation to demonstrate to our new intake of recruits the standards that we expect of you all, and what happens when you fail to meet them! Instead of inflicting the usual punishment, I have decided to replace the usual sentences for your various misdemeanours with two disciplinary measures! Firstly, I have kept a record of your names and crimes, and will apply the necessary punishment on top of any future sentence if you appear before me again at any point in the next year! And secondly, you have sentenced the cohorts to an additional session of battle practice! Doubtless your comrades will express their disappointment with this extra exercise in their usual robust manner!'

A chorus of muttered imprecations rippled across the cohorts, and Scar's face creased into a hard grin.

'Yes, I thought that might please you all! Centurions, prepare for battle practice!'

Alcaeus turned to face his men.

'You know how it works! Those of you that are new, watch the men in front of you and learn fast! You leading men, help them along! No man fails in this century unless and until *I* decide he's no use to me!'

He walked to the front of Grimmaz's tent party and then down the file until his eyes found Egilhard, tucking himself into the line of men behind the new recruit.

'Let's see what you have for me, Egilhard son of Lataz and brother-son of Frijaz. If those two old soldiers have done right by you then you might be halfway decent on the dance floor.'

He raised his voice to be heard over the hubbub of centurions and watch officers readying their men for the drill.

'The same as ever! On the command "advance with spears" we go forward, spear stabbing with your right leg and butt spiking with your left. Every man will keep contact with the man in front of him as you've been trained! It's easy now, but wait until you're doing this in the dust that twenty thousand men's feet can raise in the summer and you'll know why you need to grab your mate by the collar, because you won't be able to see your hand in front of your face! Ten paces forward, and the man at the front rolls out to the right, while the man behind him brings his shield in around him from the left and protects them both. Listen for the whistle! And I'll say it again, you new men, watch the soldiers around you and try not to fuck it up! Ready!'

The century barked their response as one, abruptly more than a collection of disparate individuals.

'READY!'

Taking a grip of the collar of Egilhard's mail, the centurion pitched his voice just loud enough for his new recruit to hear.

'Shield and spear in your left, then take a nice firm grip on the man in front with your right. Let him know you've got him.'

He nodded with approval as Egilhard reached up to grasp the same spot on Lanzo's armour, tensing himself for the command to advance.

'Right leg first. Let's not fuck up first time out, eh? We've had recruits shit themselves with nerves at this point in the past, so if you can avoid that, the rest's easy.'

Egilhard nodded grimly, clearly tensing himself for the drill to commence. Silence fell over the parade ground, as each cohort and century readied themselves for the order to advance. Scar looked up and down the line of his men with a grin.

'And I think we'll do this singing, shall we? Batavi! *Advance! With! Spears!*'

As the leading men of every file stamped forward, stabbing out with their spears in the underhanded grip that exposed as little of their bodies to potential retaliation as possible, he bellowed the first line of their battle hymn.

'*Batavi! Swim the seas!*'

The spearmen stepped forward again, front rankers swinging their spears up to point at the sky, punching with their shields as they stepped forward with their left legs and then stabbing down with the spears' butt spikes at the point where an opposing warrior's feet would be in combat, the paean's uncompromising roar of martial sentiment forcing a shiver though the recruit's body that raised the hairs on his arms and legs, power abruptly seeming to fizz in his blood with the song's collective purpose and energy.

'Batavi! Swim the seas!
Worship mighty Hercules!
Swords and spears!
Take your ears!
Never showing mercy!'

The advance continued, spears alternately stabbing out and butt spiking as the soldiers stepped forward one pace at a time.

With a flurry of movement Grimmaz rolled to his right out of his place at the head of the tent party's file, Levonhard smoothly swinging his shield around the leading man's body as he did so, taking the leading man's place with the seamless skill of long hours of practice and stepping into the stabbing stroke with easy grace.

> '*Batavi! Break your shield!*
> *Gut you even if you yield!*
> *Slash and hack!*
> *Stab your back!*
> *Never showing mercy!*'

Levonhard stepped away to his right as Banon took his place, his crested helmet ducking and bobbing with the violence of his exertions, and the advance continued unabated as Scar walked backwards in front of them, casting critical glances at those men whose errors or hesitations disturbed the perfection of his men's warcraft.

> '*Batavi! German spears!*
> *Best and bravest many years!*
> *Nail your balls!*
> *To our walls!*
> *Never showing mercy!*'

Banon stepped aside and Lanzo took his place with the same deadly fluidity of movement, his assumption of the lead flowing into his first spear attack so smoothly that Egilhard almost neglected to match his forward step, so much was he in awe of the movement's simple beauty, but Alcaeus's firm grasp propelled him into the stride to the point where his training took him forward. Scar, less than ten paces from the tent party's place in the line, smirked momentarily before bellowing the hymn's first line again. As the soldiers roared out words intended to strike mortal fear into their enemies' hearts the centurion counted

Lanzo's paces, readying himself for the moment when he would push the recruit forward into the front rank. Egilhard's tent mate strode forward once more, his spear flickering out and back to open an imagined enemy's throat, then again, punching with his shield to disrupt an attack, and throw his opponent back in disorder, stabbing down with the butt spike to impale a carelessly exposed foot. Again, the spear lower this time, aimed at the soft wall of a man's gut. Again, lower still, aimed at the thigh where a well-aimed strike would leave an enemy bleeding out before his killer's eyes, unable to do anything but fall to the ground beneath a remorseless wave of stamping boots and punching spikes.

'*Ready . . .*'

Alcaeus's soft growl was combined with a tightening of the grip on the recruit's mail, ready to propel him forward even as Egilhard released his hold on the man in front of him and took his spear in the freed hand, and as Raginmund stabbed and spiked for the last time, the centurion pushed him smoothly forward into place, knowing only too well what Scar would do next and that he would be powerless to assist the young soldier to pass the test. The recruit looked down reflexively to check the positioning of his feet, and in the moment of his distraction the prefect stepped in close with his shield raised and spear held ready to strike, close enough to see the amusement in his eyes, his stare fixed on Lanzo as the soldier started his rotation to the right in readiness to fall back. Alcaeus barked a command, even as Egilhard responded to the challenge, his limbs seemingly no longer his own as conscious thought surrendered to the lightning-fast reactions of instinct and long conditioning.

'*Shield!*'

As the recruit swung his shield round Raginmund's body, Alcaeus heard the thud of iron on wood as Scar struck with the blade of his spear, expertly tapping the wooden board hard enough to make his point before dancing backwards.

'*Strike!*'

Stepping forward at his centurion's urging, Egilhard stabbed out with his own spear, twisting his wrist at the moment of maximum extension, the point where the blade would be slicing into an enemy's body. The weapon's point just barely reached Scar's shield, but even as the recruit marvelled at the veteran officer's nimble footwork, Alcaeus barked another command, pushing at his mail's collar to drive him forward.

'*Shield! Punch!*'

Egilhard's body was jarred by the fearsome impact as Scar stepped in to meet him with his own shield raised, sparks flying as the bosses met with a violent clang of iron colliding with iron. The centurion close behind him recognised the deeply ingrained reflexes gifted to the recruit by the long afternoons spent training with his father, conditioning which brought the spear upright without conscious thought. He pushed at the collar again, driving the younger man through the drill, his voice insistent in Egilhard's ear.

'*Spike!*'

Stepping forward with his right foot, the young soldier hammered his spear's butt spike down at the retreating prefect's feet, its iron point finding only gravel as Scar stepped smartly backwards again. Nodding satisfaction, Scar turned away and walked off down the advancing line, leaving a dazed Egilhard acting on instinct and Alcaeus's barked commands, his mind clearly still reeling from the shock of finding himself shield to shield with the man his father had described with such evident reverence.

'*Rotate!*'

Alcaeus tapped the recruit's armoured right shoulder and then swung his shield smoothly round to cover his retreat, smiling to himself as, in the corner of his vision, he saw the boy's tent mates reaching out to pull the dazed soldier back to his place at the rear of their file, each man patting the recruit's back as he passed down the line of men and muttering unexpected praise. As the eighth man completed his ten attacks, Scar raised his voice to bellow another order over the din.

'*Halt!*'

They stood in sudden silence, breathing hard from their exertions, some men softly cursing at their own mistakes and missteps, others more vehemently pointing out those made by their comrades.

'Take a moment to get your breath back! Talk to each other!'

Banon nodded to Grimmaz, who looked at his tent mates with a grin.

'That was rusty, boys, no other way to put it. Not bad, but not good either.' Egilhard stiffened as the leading man winked at him. 'Not so bad, Nosey, even if you did have a centurion at your back telling you what to do! Not everyone manages to keep their nerve when Scar comes knocking on their shield. At least one man I know practically shat himself, and ended up with a spear point at his throat. Didn't he, Lanzo?'

The soldier who had displayed such intensity and purpose a moment before nodded with raised eyebrows, taking his superior's ribbing with the good humour that seemed to embody Grimmaz's relationship with his men.

'This is true. Although I've never actually tripped over my own feet and broken my nose on my shield's rim, have I?'

Grimmaz nodded his acceptance of the counter.

'I think you'll find I fell over somebody else's feet, but that's enough criticism for the time being. Get ready to do it again, because Scar's got the look of a man who has a long morning planned.' He turned to address Alcaeus, who had walked out of the line and was looking at his other tent parties for his next pupil. 'And this time you can go and baby another recruit, Centurion sir, because ours seems to have his shit in a fairly tidy pile.'

The Old Camp, Germania Inferior, December AD 68

'Centurion sir.'

Marius turned from his inspection of one of his men's boots, having just drawn breath to launch into a tirade on the subject of wax and a brush, to find an unfamiliar legionary standing behind him wearing the sort of apologetic expression that a wise man would adopt when interrupting an officer.

'First Spear Decimus's regards, Centurion. He sent me to ask you to attend him in the principia, sir.'

Marius nodded, and was in the act of turning back to his victim when the messenger continued.

'Begging your pardon, Centurion, but he was most insistent that I should tell you that the summons is urgent.'

The centurion smiled. Everything was always urgent to his superior, but he had no desire either to get the legionary into trouble or attract his superior's ire by being seen not to respond with the appropriate degree of respect.

'Very well, soldier, please run back and tell the First Spear that I'm on my way at once.' He gestured for his optio to come forward, which the man did by pushing his way through the ranks of men in between them. 'It seems my presence is required in the headquarters building as a matter of the greatest importance. Take over for me.'

He glared at the offending footwear again for effect, then turned and walked swiftly away in the running soldier's wake. Walking in through the guarded doorway of the principia, he was greeted by his unusually cheerful-looking superior, who returned his crisp salute with a swift nod before drawing him away into a corner to speak without being overheard by the legionaries on guard duty.

'Good news, Marius! The legatus augusti has informed our legatus that he wants the traitor Civilis bringing to justice. The legatus has in turn ordered me to organise the man's arrest, and I've decided to allow you the honour of being the man that brings him in.'

Marius looked at him for a moment before replying.

'I thought that he'd been pardoned by Galba?'

'Don't say that name too loudly around here, Centurion.' Decimus's face had darkened at the mention of the man who was increasingly viewed as a usurper by the legion's officers. 'As far as the German legions are concerned, that man has got away with the most blatant act of robbery in history, and this traitor Civilis stands accused and convicted of being his accomplice in the whole dirty affair. Legatus Augusti Capito's interrogations of the prisoners we took after we'd crushed the Vindex revolt provided conclusive proof that Civilis and Vindex were to be rewarded with their own kingdoms, once Galba had power. When he was pardoned by the usurper, we put men on the road from Rome, hoping to quietly cut his throat and put him away for good, but he was bright enough to ride back in the company of the men of the German Bodyguard who'd been dismissed from the service, and our boys couldn't get near him. So now you're to go and get him, bring him back here to rot in a legion cell for a while and consider the error of his ways until the new legatus gets round to having him executed. Him and his men have been riding the high horse with us for long enough, and now it's time for them to be put back in their place.'

'But I thought they were—'

Decimus laughed softly at his puzzlement.

'Our dearest allies? Once upon a time, perhaps, when they were happy to fight alongside us and understood their place in the empire. But they've come to see themselves as better than us. They swagger round the fortresses they're posted to like they own them, full of piss and vinegar and spoiling for a fight half the time. The Fourteenth Legion got tired of them years ago, or why else would they have left the barbarian bastards behind in Britannia when they were posted east, eh? They think they're better than us, and that the empire has no place ruling them, and this man Civilis is the pushiest of the lot of them. He fancies himself as their king and wants nothing more than to put a sword into our back and watch us bleed. A game of harpastum against an old friend and a few of his big lads is one thing, but having to tolerate their bullshit any longer is out of the question. It's time they learned their place in the natural order of things.'

He stared at Marius levelly.

'I know you made some friends with their guardsmen on the pitch, but there are no scruples to be exercised when there's treason involved. So you take your century, you march to that shithole collection of hovels they call their city, and you bring this man Civilis back with you, preferably alive so that he can sweat a while as he waits for Rome's justice to stop his wind. But you bring him back dead, if necessary. As it happens, the new legatus augusti wants him alive, so if you bring him back breathing there's probably a promotion in it for you. Bring him back dead and every officer in this camp will slap you on the back and buy you a drink. Either way you can't lose.'

'He's planning to revolt?'

Decimus nodded.

'He must be, or why else would he have met with Vindex to plot their joint treason? It's pretty much clear that he sees himself as the tribe's king, loyal to nobody, and that's not something we can tolerate. Even if he's got as much chance of making it happen as I do of becoming emperor, a revolt would see a lot of good men dead, if he managed to get the Batavians fired up. Why else do you think their cohorts would have been left to guard the cities in Gaul that supported Vindex rather being brought home, but to keep them away from their homeland? Not that four legions couldn't deal with them easily enough, but together they're more or less the same size as a legion, and too much of a risk under the wrong commander. So, get your boys moving, march to that dung heap Batavodurum, and bring me back a Batavi prince, living or dead. Just don't come back without him.'

Walking briskly until he was outside the fortress walls, Marius slowed to a more leisurely pace once he was sure Decimus wouldn't see, and mistake his need for some thinking time for a lack of resolve, and strolled back to the parade ground deep in thought. When his optio saw him returning, he snapped out a command to one of his two watch officers to keep their men working at their sword drill and walked across to meet his centurion before Marius could get within range of the century's eager ears.

'What was it then? A recruiting trip across the river? I could do with a week or two of looking down my nose at the local boys and down the length of my prick at—'

'We're ordered to make an arrest.'

The other man's jocular tone turned professional in a heartbeat.

'Arrest? Who?'

'A Batavian prince by the name of Civilis. He's been fomenting rebellion, so we're ordered to take the century to their capital and bring him back here so that the legatus augusti can apply some old-fashioned Roman justice to him.'

The optio whistled softly.

'Eighty men against a town full of those maniacs? You know they could rip us a new one if he decides that he's not going with us willingly? And you can never tell with those Germans, can you? Sometimes they'll go for their iron just because they feel like it. Wouldn't it be better to go and get this Civilis in cohort strength?'

Marius shook his head briskly.

'Quite possibly, but I wasn't consulted and I certainly wasn't going to make myself look like a cry baby by telling Decimus that my century isn't up to the task of marching from here to the Island, collecting one man and then marching back again. So get them fully kitted up, two spears apiece like we were marching away to battle, swords sharpened, and daggers too, and let's go and get him, shall we?' He leaned closer, speaking so quietly that his comrade had to bend closer to hear him. 'I'm told there's a promotion in it for me if we bring him back with a pulse, but not much more than a lot of slaps on the back and a cup of wine or two if he's a stiff. And if there's something in it for me, there might well be something in it for you. I'll recommend you for Centurion, if I get moved up to lead the cohort, but unless we bring this Civilis back alive, that'll just be a nice dream that I wake up from to find the beautiful girl whose legs I thought I was going to get between is actually old enough to be my mother. And looks like your mother.'

His optio nodded solemnly.

'You're not going to have to worry about him getting killed, because nobody with any brains is going to kill the man. Because if we do end up with him as a prisoner, he might well be the only thing stopping the Batavians from lopping our ears off and decorating their roof beams with our severed pricks.'

Oppidum Batavorum, The Island, December AD 68

Hramn was eating his morning meal, sitting at the table in Draco's house and still groggy from a troubled night's sleep, plagued by dreams in which he relived the gut-wrenching moment when his guardsmen had been dismissed from their service. Chewing disconsolately on a piece of bread, he shook his head at the memory of the self-important runt of a freedman who had first revealed to him the emperor's decision to disband the unit, which had guarded the rulers of Rome for almost a century, doing it in such a matter-of-fact tone that he could have been reading a list of goods to be purchased from the market, rather than destroying the lives of five hundred men. Tearing off another piece from the loaf, he considered his options for what felt like the hundredth time since he and his men had returned from Rome.

'What would you do if you were me, Draco? The men of the Bodyguard are starting to get restive, now that Saturnalia has been and gone, and we've no more information to share with them than we had on the day we left Rome.'

The older man looked at him over the rim of his water cup.

'There's still no word from the legatus augusti at Colonia Agrippina?'

'No.' Hramn shook his head dismissively. 'Kivilaz's letter to him got no response at all. I had a word with Decimus, the Fifth Legion's senior centurion, when we played their harpastum team, and he promised to take our case up with his legatus. He suggested that we might be recruited to their service as a mounted cohort to support them in the field, but he also told me not to hold my breath, and I sensed a distance between us that was never previously the case. This matter with Kivilaz seems to have turned the legions against us, and made our men little better than outcasts as long as he commands us. The most galling thing about it is that I don't even know whether their enmity is justified.'

Draco sipped from his beaker of water before responding.

'You're asking me if Kivilaz and his brother Paulus were in collusion with this man Vindex? I can't say. Kivilaz certainly travelled to Lugdunum to meet with him, once the fool had rebelled and started stamping Nero's coinage with the letters SPQR, but by Kivilaz's own account, his only intention in going to meet with him was to counsel the idiot, not to attempt an armed revolt. If he was plotting to support Vindex and Galba in return for the restoration of the Batavi kingdom, with himself as the natural king, then he's not saying. And Vindex took the truth of it with him when he fell on his sword after being defeated by the legions from Germania Superior. But I'd have to say that they probably had a lot of common ground, given the fact that they might well both have been kings of their people if Rome hadn't conquered the Batavi and the Aquitani, and might have been restored to those positions by a grateful emperor had Vindex's revolt paid off. Who's to say that Galba hadn't quietly promised Vindex a kingdom within the empire, and if he could have been made the offer, then why not Kivilaz?'

Hramn nodded.

'And now he's been made prefect again by the new emperor, in what must look suspiciously like a reward for services he would have rendered if he had had the chance. This senator Vindex must have written to Galba frequently, given he'd raised Gaul in support of the man's first bid for the throne, and if he thought he'd reached an agreement with the Batavi tribe, surely he'd have told his friend so before he died? I can't see how else Kivilaz went to Rome condemned as a traitor and came back with a new command. And since it was the legions at the Old Camp that arrested him and his brother, killed Paulus and sent Kivilaz south to Nero, then surely they must still harbour a grudge? What if we end up in the field together? How could they even trust us, if they believe Kivilaz to be a traitor?'

Draco shrugged.

'It's of little importance what we think, or what the legions at the Old Camp make of it for that matter. All we have to worry about, and them too, is fulfilling our oaths to the emperor. Whatever Galba decrees is the law for us all, so now that he's restored Kivilaz to the rank of prefect I doubt anyone's going to trouble him, given he's so favoured by—'

The door burst open, and one of Hramn's men blurted out the news he had been sent to deliver.

'Roman legionaries approaching from the east!'

The two men hurried to the city's main gate, from where the wooden fort inside which Tiberius Claudius Labeo's auxiliary cohort was based could be seen, perched on the escarpment that commanded the landscape around the city. By the time they reached it the unexpected visitors were within two hundred paces, and Hramn stopped to appraise the oncoming soldiers for a moment. Marching at the standard pace, they looked like nothing more than a legion century on a training march, but Hramn's trained eye was quick to spot the differences as they drew nearer.

'Two spears apiece. That's a war load. And they're holding their shields ready to use, rather than having them slung over their shoulders, and look at their faces . . .'

Draco followed his gaze, and immediately recognised what it was that the younger man could see in the oncoming legionaries.

'Some of them look shit scared. And some of them look ready to fight. See how pale they are?'

Hramn nodded.

'Ready to air their iron and lay about themselves.' He turned to the guardsman who had fetched them to the gate. 'Gather as many of our men as can be found, and order them to arm themselves and be ready to defend the city, but to keep out of sight unless it comes to blows.'

Draco was clearly gathering himself to walk out and greet the Romans, but the younger man put a hand on his sleeve.

'Leave this to me. I think I recognise that centurion.'

Walking forward with the easy gait of a man supremely confident in himself, he raised a hand in greeting and waited impassively as the marching century came on with a grinding of hobnails on the road's cobbled surface, and the perpetual jingle and rattle of equipment that accompanied the Roman soldier on the march. The centurion marching at the column's head barked an order, and the men halted with impressive precision, stamping their booted feet in perfect unison and grounding their shields and spears at a second command. Nodding his satisfaction, the officer turned back to Hramn with a nod of recognition but without any smile of greeting, his facial expression betraying the stress he was feeling.

'Good morning. Hramn, isn't it?'

The Batavi smiled tightly.

'Well remembered, Centurion Marius. And greetings. Welcome to Batavodurum. Your head has recovered from the game, I presume?'

The Roman inclined his head in recognition of the point.

'I no longer see two of everything. And your eye seems to have reopened.'

Hramn grinned despite the tension of the moment.

'You punch like the kick of an irritated mule, Centurion. I couldn't see out of it properly for the best part of a week.'

The two men shared a moment of mutual appraisal, Marius breaking the silence.

'I'm here in an official capacity.'

Hramn nodded.

'So I have gathered. It was not hard to deduce that you are not here for a rematch.'

He gestured to the armed men waiting in their ordered ranks, and the Roman nodded.

'I could wish it were not so, but I have been issued with an order that I have no choice but to see through. I am to take a member of your tribe into custody and return to the Old Camp with him, where he will face trial for treason. The prisoner's name is . . .' He made a show of consulting his tablet. 'Civilis. Gaius Julius Civilis. Perhaps it would better if my men and I were to wait here, and give you the time to find this man Civilis and bring him to us, rather than make an already sensitive situation worse by entering your city on such business.'

Hramn looked at him for a moment, weighing his words, before speaking.

'Kivilaz . . . Civilis will be with his family. His farm is not far from here, but it will take a good while for me to get a message to him, and for him to come here.'

Marius looked at him levelly.

'I'd guessed he wouldn't be waiting at the gate. But what guarantee do I have that he'll surrender himself that easily?'

Hramn shrugged.

'That's down to the man himself. But given he's been pardoned once already, and by an emperor, then unless you've got some fresh evidence of his crime perhaps he'll consider this no more than an administrative error. Doubtless any failure on his part to obey this summons will result in . . . repercussions?'

He stared hard at the Roman, and Marius looked down at his boots for a moment before nodding unhappily.

'For both of us.'

'Say no more, Centurion. I see the position in which you've been placed. I suggest you settle your men down for something of a wait.'

He turned back to the gate where Draco was waiting impatiently.

'What do they want?'

'What do you think?'

They found Kivilaz waiting for them in the great hall, alerted to the presence of the Romans by one of Hramn's men.

'They've come for me then. I was half expecting it. After all, they have a new general who'll be keen to show his men he means business, and to have a little of whatever was left of Fonteius Capito's popularity with his men rub off on him.'

Hramn took a seat opposite him.

'They clearly believe you to be guilty of this treachery they are so persistent in levelling at you. So tell me Kivilaz, before we discuss whether you should surrender to these men and allow yourself to be marched away to a legion cell in the Old Camp, is their accusation justified?'

He fixed his superior with a hard stare, and Kivilaz met his gaze for a moment before replying.

'The specific charge against me, Hramn, is that I colluded with Gaius Julius Vindex, Roman senator and prince of the Aquitani people, to restore the independence of both his own people and the Batavi from the Romans. It seems that this was the agreement Vindex had reached with Galba, to be allowed to rule his people as a kingdom, rather than an administrative district within the province of Gallia Lugdunensis, and I seem to have been white-washed with the same brush. Fonteius Capito was convinced of the truth of this alleged treason, so much so that he had my brother killed without his even being allowed to make a statement in his own defence. And while the bastard was unable to order my own death, I was beaten so badly that it took more than a week for me to be able to mount a horse again, and even then the pain in my ribs was excruciating.'

The big decurion nodded tersely.

'I have heard this story before. I lament the death of your brother, and I sympathise with your tribulations. And I still want to hear you answer my question – did you commit an act of treason in your dealings with Vindex?'

Kivilaz smiled at him, unperturbed by his subordinate's evident irritation.

'Would it matter? Not to this new Roman general Vitellius, it seems. He knows his men want my head on a sharpened post, and he is determined to give them what they want, whether I am guilty or not.'

Draco opened his mouth to speak, but Kivilaz raised a hand to forestall him.

'Very well, since neither of you seem inclined to give me the benefit of the doubt, let me be absolutely clear. Did I visit Gaius Julius Vindex, before he confronted the army of Germania Superior and lost his gamble for power? Yes. I did. And why shouldn't I have met with him? He was a respected Roman senator, indeed more Roman than Aquitani, and his aims seemed honour-able enough in seeking the end of a thoroughly corrupted dynasty and its replacement with someone more suitable, with heirs to be named by the broad consent of the senate rather than simply inheriting power no matter what their faults might be. But did I offer him our support?'

He slapped an emphatic hand down on the table.

'No! How could I have done so, when our cohorts were all deployed in Britannia at the time? So there's the answer to your first question. Now you'll want to know if I ever discussed the potential for Vindex's ally Galba to re-establish the Batavi as a kingdom, presumably with myself as the king, in order to provide him with a set of eyes and ears in the north, and powerful allies in this part of the world to counterbalance the legions if they were to turn on him? Of course not!'

He shook his head in exasperation.

'Of *course* I didn't! You may not be aware of it, but Galba is widely known to be old-fashioned in the extreme, and not likely to give up control of a tribe that Caesar conquered. So no, I didn't offer Vindex my support, much less that of the tribe, and no, I didn't collude with him in any other way either.'

Hramn stared at him levelly.

'So why did you bother going all that way? What more was there to discuss?'

Kivilaz raised his open hands in a gesture of innocence.

'I simply wanted to talk with the man. To understand why he had chosen to take such a huge gamble. After all, he was already minting his own coins proclaiming that he was the saviour of humanity, so he was either going to be rewarded with a seat next to Galba's throne or an unmarked grave. And do you know what I found?'

'Surprise me.'

Ignoring the younger man's acerbic tone Kivilaz leaned forward and whispered his answer.

'*I went looking for a man who might just be a leader we could get behind. But what I found—*'

'But you said—'

The prince slapped the table again with a sudden crack.

'Fucking well *listen*! I said I didn't discuss those things! And I *didn't*! I went looking for the leader of a revolt, but what I found was nothing more impressive than a dreamer! Vindex? The man was hopeless. Anyone with an ounce of calculation would have made sure that Galba's legion was marching to join his auxiliaries before declaring for the man. Instead of which he was more interested in putting his head on the fucking coinage! I spoke to him for long enough to realise that any hint of an alliance with him would have been a fatal mistake, told him to make peace with Rome before it was too late, and left as quickly as I could. Gods below, even Rufus Verginius didn't want to fight him, despite the fact that his three legions were facing nothing more threatening than a ragbag force of auxiliaries, because he knew Vindex was harmless! It was his centurions who settled the matter by taking their iron to the Gauls despite the talk of a negotiated surrender, the bastards. But they were right.'

He leaned forward, stabbing a finger into the table for emphasis.

'When you have a position of strength you play it for all it's worth!'

Hramn sat back.

'So you *would* have talked treason if Vindex had been worthy of your expectations. But you didn't, because he wasn't. And now the Romans have come for you for the second time, because they know all too well that you met with Vindex, and they can't believe that you didn't discuss the things you're accused of. By meeting him at all you've laid yourself open to their charges, and it's no mistake that they've sent the centurion we were playing harpastum against only a few days ago to come and dig you out. It's a message to us that while we might be allies, they will do their duty to the empire. And why do you suppose they've sent a small unit of foot soldiers to fetch you back to the Old Camp, when they know we have five hundred guardsmen sitting around waiting for something to do?'

Kivilaz waved a dismissive hand.

'That's easy. To show us that they know they're our masters. If my guardsmen resist my arrest they'll send the Old Camp legions to teach us a lesson, slaughter anyone that puts up a fight, burn the place to the ground and do whatever else they think would teach us a lesson. Those legionaries out there will have one eye to their rear all the way back to Vetera, terrified that the tribe might decide to rise and liberate me, but we all know that would be stupidity of the highest order. I'll just have to go with them, and hope that this man Vitellius isn't simply planning to slap his buttocks at Rome and have me killed to bolster his popularity with the legions.' He stood, stretching his powerful frame. 'No, this isn't the right time to be standing up to Rome. I'll just have to hope that I live long enough to see a time that is.'

Marius looked back down the road behind his century, drawing an amused glance from the prisoner walking easily beside him. He had agreed that there was no need to restrain Civilis, given the peaceable way that the Batavi prince had surrendered himself to their custody and Batavi had easily kept up with the century's marching pace for the whole of the previous day's twenty-mile march. The men posted to watch him, with dire warnings as to what would befall them if he were to slip away under cover of darkness, had nothing more to report at dawn than that the prisoner had enjoyed an apparently untroubled sleep, which was more than Marius could say for himself.

'Still wondering if my people are going to realise what a travesty of justice you're committing here, and hunt you down, are you, Centurion?'

The Roman looked at him levelly for a moment before speaking, evidently deciding what degree of openness to share with the Batavi noble.

'I didn't think your people would accept this as easily as seems to be the case.'

Civilis shrugged equably.

'My people are a loyal part of the empire. We have a legion's strength serving with you, men your own generals have called the best and bravest of your allies. We conquered Britannia for you, and we defeated the Iceni tribe for you. We can swim rivers in full armour, and deal a battlefield death blow where no fight is expected, as we did at the Medui river in the reign of the emperor Claudius. And as for me, I fought at the Medui when I was not much older than these men behind us. I gave twenty-five years of my life to Rome.'

Marius inclined his head in respect, waiting for the Batavi to continue, and Kivilaz looked at him with a questioning expression.

'And yet the loyalty in this relationship all seems to be going in one direction, that's what you're thinking now, isn't it? Devoted service, wounds, watching friends die for the empire, all for nothing now I'm arrested once again, to be imprisoned and face the same tired old charges that neither side can prove or disprove. To find my fate once again hanging on the opinion of a single man at whose whim I can either be freed or sent to my death. So how do I remain so good-tempered?'

He walked in silence for a moment, waiting for Marius to respond, and after a moment the Roman pointed at his face.

'How did you lose the eye?'

Kivilaz smiled, putting a finger to the empty socket.

'This? This was the price I paid for fighting in the battle that consigned that mad bitch Boudicca to history. That was a day to have lived through, Centurion, a battle that they'll still be talking about a hundred years from now, a single day that saw the Iceni tribe beaten to their knees by a force a tenth of their size. They dared us to attack them, once we had them run to earth, taking up a position between two forests and arraying themselves in depth with their women behind them. Idiots. Anyone with the smallest military experience could have told them that they had effectively cut off all of their routes of retreat and denied most of their men the opportunity to fight.'

Marius nodded.

'It sounds like it. Any army that had to retreat into a forest will come out the other side of the trees as a collection of individuals, no longer an army. What was their frontage?'

Kivilaz looked up for a moment, recalling the memory.

'Four hundred paces.'

The Roman winced.

'Just wide enough for a legion strength unit to deploy ten deep, rotating the front rank to present fresh spear arms while the barbarians would have been too tightly packed to fight back effectively. It was a slaughter, I presume?'

Kivilaz nodded.

'It was. I lost the eye in the aftermath, when one of their women came out from beneath the cart she was hiding under, got inside my sword's length and went for me like a wild cat. Fair exchange, I suppose, my eye for her life, she got her claws into me just as I put my dagger into her. So that's how I lost the eye, Centurion. And you're right, of course, by rights I should be furious to once again find myself the prisoner of men determined to see me dead for a crime that no man can prove I committed. But . . .'

He fell silent, and Marius waited for a moment before prompting him.

'But?'

Kivilaz grinned.

'Nobody lives for ever, Centurion. Not you, not me. So if your masters in the Old Camp choke me to death this evening, half an hour after we reach the fortress, I'll be no more dead than if I die in my bed thirty years from now, ringed by my family when I finally go to meet my ancestors. It's a matter of when, and how, but not if. So let's go and play this game of yours, and see where all our whens and hows end up, shall we?'

4

The Winter Camp, Germania Superior, January AD 69

'*Fourth Legion!*'

An instant later the other senior centurion standing out in front of the two legions paraded in the chilly dawn of a New Year's Day, the morning sullen and overcast beneath an iron-grey sky, barked out his own challenge to the ranks of men stretching out into the mist before him.

'*Twenty-Second Legion!*'

Their voices cracked out across the parade ground as one in a whiplash command that echoed back an instant later from the walls of the fortress where both legions were garrisoned.

'Atten-*tion!*'

Ten thousand legionaries snapped into the brace position, their precision enough to warm the heart of the hardest-eyed centurion, standing perfectly still in the cold silence that followed. Centurion Secundus, standing before his senior centurion along with the legion's other eight cohort commanders, nodded his head in approval of the rigid discipline being observed by the men paraded behind him, respectful of the warning he had issued to his brother officers that what they were about to do required them to be on otherwise perfect behaviour. Where usually the occasional man would have coughed, or broken wind, perhaps muttered an insult or greeting to another within earshot of a harsh whisper, the silence was total, palpably expectant to a man who knew what to listen for.

Secundus was arrayed in his ceremonial finery, as was every officer on parade for this most affirming day of the year for an empire whose very foundations were sunk deep into the bedrock of the legions that guarded every frontier. Each one subtly different in tradition and make-up, all were charged with being perpetually vigilant, and totally loyal to one man above all others, their princeps, the man who ordered the Roman world and made the decisions on which their futures hung. Across the empire's far-flung expanse men like them would be standing to attention on parade grounds separated by distances that might take half a year's march to traverse, but whose intent and ceremonies were identical, carefully choreographed over years of planning and practice so that nothing could go wrong in this defining moment of an imperial year.

At dawn on New Year's Day, 821 years after the founding of the city of Rome, the moment had come for the empire's legions to swear the sacramentum, the oath of undying loyalty to emperor and empire, to promise to follow and obey him, to protect Rome against threats from either within or without, and if need be to lay down their lives in defence of the sprawling edifice that he ruled in their name. But today would be different. Where their sister legion the Twenty-Second was at best indifferent and at worst hostile to Galba's seizure of power, the officers and men of the Fourth Macedonica were seething with fury on the subject, and the lid was about to come off that bubbling pot of rage.

From his place at the front of the legion Secundus could see the army's new legatus augusti, Hordeonius Flaccus and his two legion legati looking out across the ranks of soldiers from their elevated position on the raised wooden tribunal, which had been erected the day before to enable them to look over the veritable hedge of the two formations' standards that were paraded between them and the soldiers, positioned so that when a man swore loyalty to the emperor he also pledged his fealty to the standards that he would fight for in battle. Before them stood the two legions' standard bearers, the cold wind that was blowing across the parade ground ruffling their fur capes. Soldiers selected for their imposing size and martial prowess, who knew that they were expected to fight and die for the gold and gilt images and symbols they carried, bearskins complete with the animals' heads were affixed to their helmets to make them even taller and give them some of the same elemental terror that the tribes across the river used to their advantage on the field of battle. A pair of gold eagles took pride of place in the thicket of standards in the firm grips of the aquilifers, each with an image of the emperor presented to their right on a standard carried by an imaginifer alongside them, gold-plated masks that had been hurriedly fashioned in Galba's image and rushed to the empire's frontier fortresses to replace those of Nero. On each eagle's left a vexillarius proudly carried the lovingly embroidered square banner that would take the place of the eagle when, as frequently happened, a vexillation of several cohorts was detached under the command of a senior officer to perform a task that did not require the legion's full strength, their bright red backgrounds decorated with capricorns and, in the Fourth's case, as a legion founded by Julius Caesar, a bull. Clustered around them were the standards of each legion's sixty centuries, topped by the image of an open hand that symbolised the oath the legionaries were about to swear, the signifers who bore them all similarly clad in heavy bearskins and shieldless, depending on the men of their centuries to protect them in battle with their lives if need be. The final detail was an imposing life-sized bust of the new emperor, standing on a tall stone plinth to raise the head and shoulders to the same height that would have been the case were Galba present to witness the ceremony.

Secundus watched and waited as Flaccus nodded his satisfaction with their commands' taut discipline to the legion commanders who flanked him, pitching his voice to be heard by the standard bearers in the certain knowledge that every word would be reported back to the soldiers with whom they lived.

'A fine turn out, gentlemen, you and your officers are to be congratulated! We will proceed with the sacramentum and then go for a well-earned breakfast!'

A few men tittered at the statement, loudly enough for the portly senior officer to have caught the trailing edge of their cruel humour, and for a moment he stared out across the ranks of men, then shook his head to dismiss the idea of his being shown any disrespect on such an auspicious day. He stepped forward to the platform's edge, raising a scroll whose wording he knew by rote but which nevertheless had to be displayed to the men of the fortress as an essential part of the ceremony. In the event of any one of them being deemed to be in breach of the oath, the scroll could thereby be opened in front of him and the accusation made that he was in breach of the solemn promise he had made under the eyes of the gods on the first day of the year. But as he opened his mouth to start the ceremony, a single voice shouted one word from the mass of men standing before him, a word that froze him to the spot and left his jaw hanging open. Secundus closed his eyes for a moment as his colleague Julius bellowed the one word that had been agreed would be the signal that would start their resistance to the pretender Galba's rule.

'*No!*'

An awestruck silence hung over the parade ground for a moment, as ten thousand legionaries and their officers considered the unthinkable heresy, when another officer's voice was raised in agreement.

'*We're not swearing loyalty to the usurper Galba! Give us Verginius Rufus!*'

The reference to the army's former commander could hardly have come as a surprise to Flaccus, given that the men of the Winter Camp had done their very best to persuade Verginius Rufus to declare himself emperor on the news of Nero's death. Their acclamations had been rebuffed by the man's steadfast and, to Secundus's mind, entirely honourable refusal to accept the accolade, a denial of their attempts to make him emperor that had only made the legions' centurions desire for his rule that much stronger, turning away their protestations of his suitability to rule with the blunt statement that it was for the senate to make an emperor, and not a matter for a mere legatus, no matter how august he might seem. But the carefully planned outbursts had rocked the ordered world in which they all lived to its very foundations. Looking to his two legion commanders, Flaccus gestured wordlessly for them to do something to restore discipline and return the ceremony to normality. But as they stepped up alongside him, drawing breath to shout commands to their senior centurions, the ten senior centurions who led the Fourth Legion's cohorts marched forward half a dozen paces from where they stood before their men and stamped back to attention, their raised voices, trained by years of issuing commands intended to be heard by every man under their command, ringing out across the parade ground in what was clearly a carefully rehearsed statement of the facts as they saw them.

'*Legatus augusti and legati legionaris! The men of our two legions have agreed that they cannot swear loyalty to an emperor whose claim to the throne is no stronger than that of Verginius Rufus, a man of honour who refused to accept the throne when we offered it to him! We demand that our wishes in this matter be conveyed to the senate and the people of Rome, and that an emperor be chosen who we can accept!*'

Shooting a glance to his right as he joined their chorus, Secundus saw that, as agreed the previous evening, the Twenty-Second Legion's senior centurion was standing stock still, his eyes deliberately turned to ignore the outraged gestures his legatus was making at him to do something. If the Fourth Macedonica, an old legion founded by Caesar himself, was willing to take part in an act as vulgar as a parade ground mutiny, the Twenty-Second's senior centurions were hardly likely to oppose an action intended to display the senior legion's sense of outrage.

Flaccus gaped at the spectacle of two whole imperial legions defying him, knowing that his career was circling the plughole unless he could take a grip of the situation. But even as he dithered, the Fourth's senior centurion gestured to the nine men gathered behind him, all cohort commanders, Secundus at their head, and they hurried forward towards the podium. Stepping back involuntarily, fearing that he was about to be the subject of an assassination, Flaccus watched in horror as they toppled the bust of Galba that had been set on a plinth before them to land with a crack on the gravelled surface. Secundus and his colleagues stepped into the tight pack of standard bearers, each of them ripping away the portrait medallions bearing the new emperor's image that dangled from their crossbars, dashing them to the ground to lie discarded and trodden upon. A sudden hubbub behind Secundus made him turn, to discover that a handful of the Twenty-Second's officers, men he assumed had been carefully excluded from the conspiracy to prevent their loyalty to the throne from alerting Flaccus to what was to come, were fighting with his colleagues for control of their own legion's standards.

'*The Twenty-Second Legion is loyal to the emp—*'

The centurion protesting went down with a fist in his face, and Secundus winced at the blow's unexpected ferocity, shooting a glance at the other legion's ranks as the counter-protest was swiftly snuffed out and the four men hustled away to temporary confinement by more of the Fourth's centurions. Not a legionary had moved, and he breathed a sigh of relief that two fully armed and armoured legions were not about to take their iron to each other in the cold grey dawn. Their carefully calculated act of mutiny complete, the legion's centurions looked up at the men on the podium, Secundus holding his breath as he waited to see how they would respond.

'Gentlemen . . .'

Flaccus was looking down at the scene with a calculating expression, while behind him the gentlemen legati and their tribunes looked helpless in the face of such a show of obduracy. Such things were hardly unknown in Roman history, but most mutinies came from a legion's rank and file, open to swift and vicious displays of the army's savage disciplinary code, whereas there was little official guidance as to how to deal with a revolt led by a legion's centurionate and where the object was not, at least on the face of things, based on self-interest. The general looked round at the men behind him only to find them equally nonplussed.

'So I am to take it as a given that you are unwilling to swear your loyalty to the emperor?'

Secundus frowned, finding Flaccus's tone of voice different to what he had imagined. Where the expectation of a weak-willed glutton of a man had been inspired by discussions in the mess, the reality was that the senator sounded a good deal more resolute than had been predicted. He stared down at the centurions with an expression the centurion found almost predatory.

'No sir, we won't swear loyalty to a man who's stolen the empire, and punished good men who fought to defeat a traitor only to find that traitor's friend on the throne. We want Verginius Rufus!'

The other officers nodded their agreement with their First Spear's aggrieved statement of what they saw as the immutable truth of the matter.

'I see.' Flaccus turned to look at the other side of the parade ground. 'And where does the Twenty-Second Legion stand in all this, First Spear? Surely you cannot ally yourselves with such . . . *precipitate* action, no matter how honourable it might be in its motivation, and no matter that the legion conducting this . . .' He paused for a moment, searching for the right word. 'Well, perhaps I have no choice but to call it a mutiny? No matter that the Fourth Legion is such an old and well-respected part of the army?'

The Twenty-Second's senior centurion answered in a calm voice.

'To be very clear with you, sir, the Twenty-Second Legion lost a number of men dealing with the traitor Vindex, and to find ourselves punished for our loyalty by the removal of a good and honourable leader is hard to bear, never mind finding the man Vindex was fighting for on the throne. It is an insult to our dead, and to the empire itself, and we too wish for the senate to choose a successor to Nero of whom we can approve.'

Flaccus looked at him for a moment, and Secundus could have sworn he was fighting an urge not to smile.

'Your commitment to the senate and people of Rome are noted, First Spear. And please accept my compliments on your devotion to the empire's best interests. Your views are much the same as those I've heard expressed by some members of the senatorial class . . .' He turned and looked at the Fourth's legatus with a piercing expression. 'So, if you're not willing to swear loyalty to the emperor, will you at least declare that you remain devoted to the service of Rome? Failure to do so will, I am afraid, be interpreted as an outright mutiny, and will leave me with no option but to summon assistance from the neighbouring fortresses to put down this revolt.'

And the best of luck with that, mused Secundus, knowing full well that informal contacts between the Winter Camp's legions, First Germanica at Bonna, 100 miles downriver, and the famed Twenty-First Rapax 250 miles to the south at Vindonissa, had already revealed that they shared the strong disaffection felt so deeply by their comrades of the Fourth and Twenty-Second, with whom they had jointly crushed the Vindex revolt in support of Galba to such good effect the previous year. The Fourth's legatus stepped forward, a man by the name of Caecina Alienus, who mess gossip said was tarnished by his previous association with Galba in Hispania and was obviously the reason why he had been appointed to command the legion. The commonly held opinion was that he was not a man who could be trusted under the circumstances, and the rebellious centurions looked up at him dubiously.

'I'm sure that such an irrevocable step won't be required, Legatus Augusti. After all, I am myself, as every man here knows, a recent appointment to command the illustrious Fourth legion, approved in my post by Galba himself. If any man here has a reason to declare these two legions as in revolt it should be me. And yet I can see the justice in what they say. Perhaps we should compromise, as you suggest, and ask our comrades to swear allegiance to senate and people, and then seek a resolution to this matter under less pressured circumstances?'

Secundus turned to look at the legion's senior centurion, who in turn looked to his colleague from the Twenty-Second. They nodded, and turned back to face the senior officers.

'We will. Our loyalty to the empire burns as fiercely as ever, and we yield to no man in our love for Roman ideals.'

Caecina smiled beatifically and gestured to Flaccus, who was looking at him with the expression of a man who had trodden in dog's faeces after taking his boots off.

'In which case . . .'

Flaccus stared at him for a moment longer and then raised the scroll that had hung loosely in his hand.

'Very well, and my fulsome thanks to Legatus Caecina Alienus for stating what we were all thinking with such insightful perception. Return to your units, centurions, and we'll proceed. Oh, and can someone pick that bust of the emperor up and place it where it cannot be seen? I'm sure you'll agree that it would be disrespectful in the extreme for us to continue with such an august personage staring up at us all from the mud into which he has been so unceremoniously been deposited?'

The Old Camp, Germania Inferior, January AD 69

'Why is that the one day we have to get them all out onto the parade ground to swear their loyalty to the emperor is always freezing cold or blowing a gale? Do the gods know something we don't?'

Marius smiled at his friend's complaint, guessing from the looks on some of his men's faces as they marched out onto the Old Camp's parade ground that more than a few of them had misjudged the weather and failed to pad out the space between armour and flesh with their spare tunics. He himself was wearing three garments beneath his heaviest subarmalis, and even with the thick padded arming jacket to retain his body heat the wind seemed to be cutting straight through him. Gaius shivered and pinched his nose to clear it, flicking the mucus from his fingers.

'Let's hope the legatus hasn't wrapped up warmly enough, that'll make the ceremony nice and quick and we can all get back inside for something hot to celebrate another year of service to the empire. My nose is running like a bloody fountain.'

Marius shot him a jaundiced look.

'Celebrate? Have you heard the grumbling that this lot have been doing in the last week?'

His friend shrugged, sniffing loudly.

'Of course. The legions upriver are in a state of ferment, or so the rumours say, pissed off to the hilt with the way they've been treated by Galba despite, or perhaps *because of* their loyalty to the throne in dealing with Vindex and his Gauls. None of which, I hear, has been helped by the fact that the Gauls in question seem to have got off very lightly for a bunch of rebellious barbarians, not punished in any meaningful way and even rewarded by the emperor, according to some of the stories I've heard. Not that our boys are very much happier. And not that I care. They'll swear their loyalty to the emperor because the alternative is unthinkable.'

Marius nodded.

'They don't have to be happy, they just have to get it done.'

But when the legion was paraded, and he walked out in front of his cohort, the expressions on the faces staring back at him were even more sour than he had expected. Strolling back towards them, he stopped by one of his officers, lowering his voice so as not to be overheard.

'What the fuck is going on? They look like they're ready to throw their rattles out of the cot.'

The other man shook his head, clearly sharing Marius's bafflement.

'I don't know. I've heard nothing from my officers, and they're usually pretty close to what's going on in those tiny minds, but they're sullen alright. All I've had out of them all morning is yes and no, all respectful like, but there's something that's got to them, that's for sure.'

Marius nodded and turned away to find Decimus pacing towards him.

'Well then, Centurion, perhaps you can illuminate this strange state of affairs for me. This lot look like they've lost a gold aureus and found a clipped copper as.'

'We don't know, First Spear. But I could hazard a guess.'

The senior centurion nodded.

'So could I. They think their legatus augusti was assassinated on Galba's orders. And they're probably right. They think they've been put under the command of a man who'll offer no threat to Galba's hold on power, where the last legatus augusti was an emperor in waiting. And they're probably right. And they hear the stories about how the Gauls are taking the piss out of the legions further up the Rhenus, flaunting the fact that Galba's let them off any punishment for rising in support of Vindex while our lads find themselves in the doghouse for having put down the new emperor's best mate, so they draw the conclusion that the German legions are being handed the shitty end of the stick. And they're probably right.'

He looked out across the two legions, waiting in silence for their orders, then turned to make sure that the senior officers of both were in their places on the raised dais.

'This could all go very wrong very quickly. We've all heard the stories of what happens when a legion mutinies, and it doesn't often end well, especially without anyone with enough seniority to nip this in the bud. In the old days there'd have been an imperial prince or even an emperor up there to calm it all down, but whether or not they're decent soldiers, that pair are going to be as much use as tits on a bull if this lot take it into their heads not to swear the oath. Come with me.'

Gathering the senior centurions of all the Fifth Legion's cohorts, he marched back to the dais where the two legion's aquilifers and their attendant signifers and imaginifers were gathered, stolidly waiting for the ceremony to begin. His opposite number from the Fifteenth Legion had followed his example, and the two groups of officers met in front of the clustered standards to which the soldiers would shortly swear their loyalty. Decimus gestured to the standards, then tapped the hilt of his sword as he issued his instructions to the small group of officers.

'Get lined up in front of the standards, and be ready to use these if any man steps out of line. Better one man dead than the mayhem that will result if we let them riot.'

The two men conferred briefly, and then Decimus turned to the dais, his words pitched loudly enough for every man on parade to hear them.

'With your permission, gentlemen, I would like to say a few words before we swear the sacramentum?'

Legatus Lupercus looked to his colleague Fabulus and then nodded their joint assent. The First Spear turned to face the ten thousand men paraded before them, raising his voice to its usual parade ground bellow.

'Men of the Fifth and Fifteenth Legions! Before we proceed with the swearing of the oath of loyalty to your emperor and your legion's standards, I have something for you to consider. It is apparent to your officers that you are unhappy with the current state of affairs following the defeat of the revolt in Gaul. We share your disappointment that the men who revolted against the legitimate emperor have not been more soundly punished, while our comrades who put down their rebellion find themselves without imperial favour! But let us be very clear, men of the Fifth and Fifteenth Legions, we are first and foremost servants of the Roman republic to which we pledge our allegiance when we swear the sacramentum! So join me, comrades, in committing myself wholeheartedly to the service of Rome for another year, as we repeat the solemn promises we made before our legions' eagles when first we entered the service!' He turned back to the dais. 'Please carry on, Legatus!'

Lupercus, the more senior of the two on the grounds of his greater age, drew breath to administer the oath, and Decimus muttered something under his breath that Marius was just able to discern.

'And make it sound like you've got a pair.' He looked to the centurions on either side of him. 'As loudly as you like, gentlemen, let's make it clear where we stand in all this.'

The legatus's voice rang out over the silent soldiers, and Decimus breathed a sigh of relief at the note of command in his voice.

'Soldiers of the Fifth and Fifteenth Legions! We are gathered to renew our sacramentum, our oath of loyalty to the republic and the man who commands it! So repeat after me!'

He paused for a moment, taking a breath.

'I swear that I shall faithfully execute all that the emperor commands!'

The gathered senior centurions repeated the legatus's words as loudly as they were able without actually shouting, but the soldiers' response was lukewarm at best, and to Marius's eye few men beyond the front rank were actually repeating the oath's words.

'I swear that I will never desert the service of Rome!'

He glanced sideways at Decimus, but his superior's face was a blank mask as he repeated his vow.

'And I swear—'

From somewhere towards the rear of the gathered ranks of soldiers a stone flew, fast and low over the heads of the legionaries, to strike the bust of the emperor that had been set on a plinth in front of the raised dais. With an audible crack the statue's nose sheared away, projectile and debris falling to the ground. Decimus started forward, apoplectic with rage at the defiant act.

'*Find that man!*'

After a moment's silence the truth dawned on Marius, that with the entire legion's attention locked on the two legati administering the oath, nobody with any incentive to report the stone thrower had actually seen the act, while the men around him probably shared his sentiment. He turned to his superior, speaking quickly and quietly.

'I couldn't say where that stone came from, not even which legion.'

Decimus nodded furiously.

'Watch your cohorts! If that happens again I want the culprit out here!' He turned to his colleague, who issued a similar order, then returned his attention to the ranks of legionaries, and if he realised that the two legions were only one provocation away from rioting, the knowledge didn't appear to trouble him. 'Whoever threw that stone seems to have got away with it! Your feelings on the matter of the emperor's right to the throne have been noted. But if there's one more act of defiance this morning then I'll have my entire legion on punishment duties for the rest of the year, and so will my colleague here!' He gestured to the Fifteenth Legion's senior centurion, who nodded with an equally angry expression. 'And if you cunts want to find out exactly how serious I am then go ahead and find out! And just in case you think it was clever to throw that stone, let me assure you all that you're lucky the fool that threw it had a steady hand. Because if that stone had hit my eagle I'd have found out who threw it by flogging one man in ten in every bloody century until the culprit was identified, and then I'd have had the bastard crucified, and both legions kept on parade until he choked out his dying breath!'

The hush that greeted his threat was so profound that even the birds in the trees that surrounded the parade ground seemed to have fallen silent.

'You think that's an empty threat? Then I fucking dare you, any one of you cunts, to throw one more fucking stone and find out just how vindictive I can be when I'm provoked!' He stared out across his command with his chin jutting out, pugnacity radiating from the set of his body and the white-knuckled grip on his vine stick. 'Nobody? Good! Perhaps now we can get on with swearing our loyalty to the fucking empire!'

He turned, gesturing to the two legati to continue with the sacramentum, and after a moment Lupercus raised the scroll again.

'And I swear that I will not seek to avoid death in the service of the Roman republic!'

The soldiers' repetition of the sacred vow was now barely audible, and at its conclusion Decimus turned to his officers with an expression little less furious than before.

'Get them off parade as quickly as you can! The sooner they're back in their hutches the happier I'll be! We can worry about preventing this turning into a mutiny once the risk of a riot has been avoided!' He nodded to his opposite number from the Fifteenth and raised his voice to roar the command his soldiers were waiting for.

'The Fifth Legion is dismissed!

The Winter Camp, Germania Superior, January AD 69

'Aquilifer Volpeius!'

A swift knock on the door of the eagle bearer's room reinforced the urgency of whoever was trying to attract his attention, and

Volpeius sprang to his feet, crossed the room in three paces and flung it open, ready to remonstrate vigorously with whoever it was who had disturbed his usual and well-known routine after coming off parade. Opening his mouth to issue a tirade of abuse, he closed it again at the sight of the legion's senior centurion.

'I know. You've only just managed to polish the paw marks of half a dozen centurions off the eagle, and you probably haven't even had time to offer your usual prayer to Mars, never mind get your head around what just happened.'

Volpeius nodded brusquely, still seething at the way his standard had been manhandled by the legion's senior centurions less than an hour before. The eagle was now safe in the chapel of the standards, under the watchful eyes of soldiers he had warned would pay with their hides if he found so much as a single finger mark on its gold surface when he returned to clean it again, once he had communed with his god. A big man among his peers in more than one way, in a profession that favoured soldiers who could physically and mentally dominate their men to ensure their instant compliance with any order, he was half a head taller than the man addressing him and, in the opinion of many of the legion's centurions, would have been a natural leader of men if he'd not been chosen to carry the Fourth's eagle instead. As if recognising his aquilifer's effortless and yet always dominating presence, the man standing before him was always appropriately respectful to his eagle bearer, and often went out of his way to include him in command meetings at which his attendance was not strictly required.

'It's been a disturbing morning, First Spear. I was praying.'

The senior centurion nodded.

'I know. You're lucky to have had the time. I've spent the last hour with my colleague from the Twenty-Second, our legati and the legatus augusti. Caecina wants to see you.'

Volpeius shook his head in bafflement.

'The legatus? Wants to see *me*?'

The other man nodded with a grim smile.

'You heard me. So blow out the candles, put on a clean tunic and your best belt and boots, and get yourself over to the praetorium. Now.'

He turned and walked away, leaving the baffled aquilifer to hurriedly change and comb his hair before walking quickly across the fortress to the commanding officer's residence and presenting himself to the guards on duty, to find himself ushered swiftly inside with the respect due to such a pivotal figure in their world and into the presence of the legion's commander himself. Stamping to attention, he saluted and awaited his commanding officer's requirements of him.

'Ah, Aquilifer Volpeius. Thank you for attending upon my request so swiftly. Do take a seat.'

Blinking in surprise at such a breach of formality, he did as he was told, sitting bolt upright in anticipation of the legatus's orders.

'I have decided, Aquilifer, to take matters into my own hands. A conference with Legatus Augusti Flaccus, my fellow legatus and our senior centurions has ended without agreement. I favour declaring in support of the absolute need for a new emperor, someone more fitting and better supported than Galba, whereas the Twenty-Second Legion's legatus is of the opposite opinion, quite at odds with that of his men, and has declared himself loyal to the emperor who has been acclaimed by the senate, no matter who that man is. After the best part of an hour's discussion we could agree on nothing better than to consider our positions prior to another meeting later today. I believe that this refusal by *both* of our legions to swear loyalty to Galba means that we need to act now, and make common cause with the legions of Germania Inferior. He, on the other hand, is more cautious. I am convinced that his fear of the emperor's revenge will prevent him from taking the sort of decisive action that is needed, and I don't intend sitting on my hands while the men of my legion agitate for a new man on the throne.'

Volpeius stared at him in amazement, momentarily forgetting who it was he was talking to.

'You mean that you . . . ?'

Caecina laughed tersely.

'Of course not, man! I'm too young, and too junior, to be a credible candidate to rule the empire. Added to that, there's some talk about Galba having ordered an investigation of my dealings in my previous role as finance secretary of Hispania as well, which would probably disqualify me in the eyes of the senate. No, I'm thinking of another man, older and with a good deal more credibility than I could muster. I need to get a message to him, and let him know what has happened here today so that he can take some time to consider his first reaction. Perhaps Hordeonius Flaccus will get around to telling him what's happened here at some point, but the man didn't seem to know what it was he wanted when we parted, and I expect him to dither for the rest of the day before taking any action. So . . .'

He stood up and Volpeius jumped to his feet as the legatus came around his desk with a message container in his hand.

'My First Spear tells me you can ride?'

The aquilifer nodded. His previous disdain for the legion's cavalry had been put aside on his assuming his lofty position, with a brusque instruction from the previous senior centurion to master horsemanship.

'If the legion stands alone in a sea of the enemy, and I have a choice between some dirty-arsed barbarian getting his paws on the eagle or my aquilifer riding away in the company of the last of our horsemen, to ensure that it comes back at the head of an army to witness the bastards' destruction, then I'll take the option that sees my legion's spirit live to fight another day. Learn to ride, Volpeius, or you're no use to that eagle and therefore no use to me.'

As with every other military skill he'd ever learned, his mastery of horsemanship had been swift and effortless, prompting envious comments from the cavalrymen who'd been detailed to train him, and who had greeted him to their lines with much joking about teaching a mule to ride a horse but soon enough been forced to eat their words.

'I have that ability, Legatus.'

'Good.' Caecina put the waxed leather tube in his hand. 'This message is for the eyes of Legatus Augusti Vitellius, and for his eyes *only*. You are to defend its contents to the death. To your death if need be, but preferably that of anyone who tries to take it from you by force, in that unlikely event. You look like a man who's not to be trifled with . . .' He nodded decisively. 'Take a horse from the messenger stables, with my authority if your own won't suffice but keep my name out of it if you can. Ride for Colonia Agrippina, as fast and as hard as you can, changing horses at every station of the cursus publicus. My seal is on the container, use it to convince any man who attempts to get in your way that they should accede to your demands. And carry a spear. Do what you have to do, but get that message to Legatus Augusti Vitellius, into his hands and no one else's, and before the end of the day. Time is the one thing that I don't have enough of. Go, and speak to nobody of this.'

Saluting, Volpeius strode from the praetorium and walked swiftly to his quarters, equipping himself with armour and weapons before making his way to the cavalry barracks where he had learned to ride the previous year. He was greeted by the senior decurion with a grin, the man seemingly untroubled by the morning's events.

'If it isn't the mule that can ride! What can we do for you, Volpeius? Got bored with marching, have you? Decided to come and be a horse's second arsehole like you foot-slogging cunts are always singing about?'

Taking the man aside, the aquilifer decided to trust him with as much of the truth as would be required to gain his assistance.

'This is an urgent dispatch for the legatus augusti at Colonia Agrippina. Our new legatus wants to know how the men of the First Germania reacted to being told to swear their allegiance to the emperor before he decides what to do about this morning, and he wants the legatus augusti to know the state of matters here.'

The horseman shrugged.

'That ain't going to come as too much of a surprise, I reckon. There's been mutterings up and down the frontier for months, from what I've heard. So what's that got to do with me?'

'I need a horse, and without any awkward questions being asked. A fast horse. And I need you to ride with me to the first cursus publicus stable on the road north, and help convince them to give me a mount.'

'Why not just go to the cursus stables here?' The decurion laughed knowingly as the reason for Volpeius's request dawned on him. 'I see. This being by way of a *secret* message that the legatus doesn't want to get to the ears of that lard-bucket Flaccus, right? And if you demand a horse from the fortress stables then Legatus Augusti Flaccus will hear about it in no time. Whereas this way you can throw your weight around with the man in charge at the next stable up the road and make sure he keeps his mouth shut about a messenger riding north. Especially if you're with me when you get there, given the fact they all know me. Come on then, it's a nice enough day for a ride!'

Taking a spear from the armoury for Volpeius, he led the aquilifer to the legion's stables, picking out a horse for the big man.

'Ordinarily I'd warn you that he's a right bad-tempered bastard, but what with you having the magic touch with beasts you'll doubtless have him on his back asking to have his belly rubbed soon enough.'

The horse, whose name was Volcanus, was indeed restive, but soon settled down to a canter alongside the decurion's mount, the two men riding north in silence once the inevitable exchange of ribaldry with the gate guards was done with, the two men making out that they'd agreed a New Year's Day ride out during the Saturnalia feast.

'I'll wait to come back through the gate until the guard's been changed, so that hopefully nobody will comment on the fact that you're not on the horse. You can ride on to Colonia Agrippina . . . or wherever it is that you're going.'

At the eight-mile marker on the road to the north they reached the first of the cursus publicus stables, the points where horses were kept ready for official messengers riding up and down the road that followed the frontier through a succession of fortresses and auxiliary forts. Dismounting from their sweating beasts, they called for the stable's ostler, the decurion taking the lead with a man he clearly knew well, exactly as Volpeius had hoped.

'Let's have these horses rubbed down, eh, before the chill gets to them? And my mate here needs a fresh mount, he's carrying a message from the legatus augusti!'

The man whose responsibility it was to issue fresh horses, and to care for the spent beasts until they were ready to run again, shook his head with a disapproving expression.

'You know the rules as well as I do. No horse will be issued without an official permit, not to nobody. If your mate here wants a mount he'll need to—'

'Come on, I know fine well you've broken the rules before. And all he's going to do is ride north for a while and then turn round and ride the same horses back south again. You'll have the beast back in its stall inside a day, and that's a promise.'

The ostler looked doubtful.

'And what if he don't come back? I'm down a horse which I can't explain. I'd be flogged if I were lucky, or just killed out of hand for the crime of selling imperial property.'

The decurion leaned closer to him, and lowered his voice.

'The two legions in the Winter Camp want this message to go north as quickly as possible. Those two legions want that a *lot*. And if it doesn't happen quickly enough, those legions are going to be very, very unhappy, and mostly with *you*. So what's worse, some official who won't be along to check your inventory for at least a week, or ten thousand men who live less than ten miles away? And besides, he'll need a horse to ride back to the Winter Camp, so you can keep Volcanus here until he gets back, can't you? Just don't approach the bastard from behind, he kicks like a bolt thrower.'

Reluctantly allowing Volpeius to take one of his mounts, the ostler watched with hard eyes as the aquilifer rode away to the north at a pace the beast would struggle to maintain all the way to the next cursus stable a further ten miles up the road.

'So where's he going that's so important that he has to risk my bloody horse falling and breaking a leg, eh?'

The decurion followed his gaze, watching as the distant figure vanished over a rise in the ground before answering.

'Given the message I *think* he's carrying, and the person I *think* he's taking it to, my suggestion is that we'd both be wise to forget all about the whole thing. That way if anyone comes asking questions, you'll be able to deny any involvement in whatever it is he's involved in. Won't you?'

The aquilifer went north at the best speed of each successive horse for which he exchanged his spent mounts, his equipment, his no-nonsense attitude and the fact that he was riding horses bearing the cursus brand ensured that nobody asked him for his permit to be using the public messenger service's horses, but simply assumed that he had every right to be doing so. By late afternoon he had passed all of the major fortresses on the road to the headquarters of the army of Germania Inferior, and as the sun was setting he rode up to the gates of the castrum that housed the First Germanica and the headquarters for the army of Germania Inferior, dismounting and handing the fortress's cursus ostler the reins of a horse that was visibly exhausted, trembling with the effort of staying on its feet having been galloped most of the way from the last stables.

'What have you done to this poor fucking animal, you bastard?'

Volpeius wasn't listening, but was instead striding towards the gate guards with a determined expression. Seeing a man well over six feet tall, bareheaded, dressed in armour of a quality well above the usual and bearing a cavalry lance, the soldiers did the only wise thing under the circumstances and called for their centurion, who took one look down his nose at the unknown soldier and shook his head in blunt rejection of his peremptory demand to be taken to the general.

'Not a fucking chance. Legatus Augusti Vitellius is entertaining guests for a New Year dinner. We admitted them to the fortress less than an hour ago, and he won't want his evening to be spoiled by the likes of you. You can wait in the—'

He fell silent as the aquilifer allowed the point of his lance to drop from the upright position to point squarely at his face.

'My name is Volpeius, Aquilifer, Fourth Macedonica. I carry a message from Legatus Caecina, my legion's commander, for Legatus Augusti Vitellius. I've ridden from the Winter Camp today, leaving a trail of exhausted horses behind me, as a means of following my orders to get this message into the legatus's hands *tonight*. If you won't take me to him then get out of my fucking way, Centurion. And if you won't get out of my way, then get ready for—'

'What's all this?'

The senior centurion of the guard was walking towards them, and his officer snapped to attention and saluted.

'First Spear! This man claims to have a message from a legatus in the Winter Camp for Legatus Augusti Vitellius!'

The newcomer, equally as tall and imposing as Volpeius, looked at the aquilifer with interest.

'Does he now? Very well Centurion, dismissed. I'll take this from here.'

Waiting until a visibly relieved centurion had marched stiffly out of earshot, he looked Volpeius up and down.

'Aquilifer?'

'How did you know?'

The other man smiled thinly.

'For one thing, you're in armour but you're bareheaded. And for another, I don't know many men below the rank of legion First Spear who'd have the stones to face down a legion centurion on his own ground, much less offer to stick a spear up his nose. So you've ridden from the Winter Camp in a day, you say?'

Volpeius pointed back to where his mount was being rubbed down by the indignant ostler, pointed comments reaching their ears in the cold evening air as the stable hand calmed the trembling animal.

'See that beast? I've left a dozen more in just the same state, because my orders were to get here today without fail, and to hand this . . .' He raised the message container. 'To this man Vitellius and to nobody else. And trust me, this is one message where any delay in delivery could result in demotion of the men responsible, including me. And you, Centurion,'

The senior centurion nodded decisively.

'I can't take you to Vitellius himself, but I can get you an audience with the man who commands my legion. And as fate would have it, Legatus Valens is currently at dinner with the very man you're looking for. So your message will be in Vitellius's hands soon enough that you'll be able to say you did your duty and go to get a feed and a cup of wine with a clear conscience. Let's just hope that whatever news it contains is important enough to disturb their dinner, eh?'

The Old Camp, Germania Inferior, January AD 69

'You wanted to see me, First Spear? I was requested to report to the principia.'

Decimus looked up at Marius from his desk in the heart of the Fifth Alaudae's headquarters building. The principia's corridors and offices were bustling with activity, as had been the case since the momentous announcement from Colonia Agrippina a few days before, as the two legion's commanders and their staff struggled to keep up with the swift changes that Legatus Augusti Vitellius's acceptance of the imperial purple had brought upon the army of Germania Inferior.

'Yes, Centurion. Come in and close the door.' He gestured to a chair facing his desk, and Marius took off his helmet before taking a seat. 'I expect that you share my surprise and pride at the events of the last few days.'

Marius nodded his agreement.

'Indeed, First Spear. Although to say that what's happened has been a surprise would perhaps be an understatement?'

'An understatement? I couldn't argue with that. And within the confines of this office we're Marius and Decimus, so you can save all that centurion and First Spear stuff for the parade ground, eh?' The older man looked down at the tablet on the desk in front of him before speaking again. 'If it's any consolation, you're not the only one who's still wondering if this is all really happening.

I'm finding it hard to believe that less than a week ago we were all loyal subjects of the emperor in Rome, freshly sworn in for another year and with nothing more troubling than the spring training schedule to exercise our minds. And now . . .' Marius waited for him to continue, knowing from experience that his silence was not an invitation for discussion. 'And now we find ourselves serving a new emperor, a man who was widely thought to be nothing more than a placeholder who has shown us his true ambitions almost overnight. One of our own, from a distinguished family, a man whose father was an imperial governor. A man who will listen to the voice of his legions, as he's already proved by rearresting the traitor Civilis and showing every sign of being ready to have him executed. The men are falling over to prove their loyalty to him, and when they voted to donate the contents of their burial clubs to his cause I felt we had no alternative but to follow suit . . .'

He gestured to his medal harness, hanging on a hook at the office door, the leather straps devoid of their phalerae, the gilded silver discs that denoted his status, and Marius looked down at his own sword belt whose decorative silver plates had also been donated to the new emperor's cause. Any item of equipment with a precious metal content had been collected and melted down, along with the substantial amount of coin in the legions' savings chests, and was in the process of being converted into a new coinage which, it was rumoured, would hail the new emperor as 'Germanicus' rather than the term the soldiers would have preferred to see him adopt, that of 'Caesar'. As long as they received a donative based on the new coins, he doubted any of them would be troubled by their new emperor's caution.

'It's amazing how quickly it all happened. Two legions two hundred miles up the Rhenus refuse to swear loyalty to the emperor in Rome, and within a week every man on the river has acclaimed *our* legatus augusti as Caesar, and is straining at the ropes to be set loose to march on Rome. Speaking of which . . .'

Decimus looked down at the tablet again, and Marius leaned forward expectantly.

'We have our marching orders. The army of Germania Inferior is to commit more than half of its strength to unseating the usurper Galba, and will move south under the command of Fabius Valens, the First Germanica's legatus. Apparently it's his reward for being the man who persuaded Vitellius to accept the acclamation of his legion as emperor, once he'd been made aware of the ferment further south by his colleague Caecina. The informed opinion is that we'll make sure the Gauls know their place before crossing the Alps by one of the western passes, and meet up with the army of Germania Superior somewhere in northern Italy. After that the combined army will be strong enough to crush whatever opposition Galba can put forward, and take Rome. And you, Marius, have your own very particular orders to carry out.'

The centurion leaned forward expectantly.

'Legatus Fabullus will lead the Fifth on the advance south into Gaul, along with four cohorts drawn from the Fifteenth and further vexillations from the First Germanica and the Sixteenth Gallica to form a double strength legion fit for battle against Galba's men. But two cohorts of the Fifth will *not* march south when the rest of the legion leaves, and yours is one of them. The Fifteenth's legatus will assume overall command of the remaining men of his own legion and those two cohorts, and the resulting force will stay here and watch the frontier until such time as the emperor is ready to ride south, at which time it is expected that you will accompany him. The cohorts that will stay here in the Old Camp will be the seventh and the ninth. It's to be expected, they're the weakest men we have and still in need of further training and conditioning.'

Marius closed his eyes in silent comment, and Decimus looked up at him with a sympathetic expression.

'It's not what you wanted to hear, I can understand that. Most of your brother officers are heading off to war against an enemy who they expect will stand little chance of offering any genuine resistance, and will fight for the empire on the side of right, while you stay here to babysit two cohorts of raw recruits. But it's not all bad news, or at least not for you, Marius. You're the best centurion in the two cohorts we're leaving behind, so I'm temporarily appointing you as First Spear to command those two cohorts in my absence. And if you think that sounds like a meaningless promotion then I suggest you think again. Our new emperor Vitellius has ordered the recruitment and training of as many men as can be squeezed out of the local area, and he's temporarily suspended the citizenship qualification.'

He nodded at Marius's look of surprise.

'I know. More than one of the senior centurions has complained to their legati that their legions will be diluted unnecessarily, but I have to say that I don't hold with that view. A man who's not a citizen is no worse a soldier than a man whose father served, and this is a good chance to get some fresh blood into the legion, so I want you to grasp this opportunity with both hands. It means that you can recruit on both sides of the Rhenus, and you're going to have get about it smartly, because the emperor's instruction was for us to at least double the size of the forces that remain behind, and to do so by the time whatever army Galba can put into the field has been destroyed. So get recruiting, Marius, and when you've gathered all the men that can be found, ride them like slaves until they're hard enough to stand alongside the rest of the legion. I'm counting on you to have a decent-sized pool of trained replacements ready when you march to join us, because the fight to put Galba's men away isn't going to be as easy as the hotheads would like to think.'

He leaned forward and lowered his voice conspiratorially.

'And while you're busy recruiting and training the men I'll need to replace my battle losses I want you to keep one more thing in mind. Something I want more than anything else.'

Marius nodded, saying the name he guessed was on his superior's mind.

'Civilis?'

'Civilis. I want that bastard traitor dead. So you make sure that Legatus Lupercus doesn't have an attack of guilt and exercise his power to free the man, right? And when he's dead I want his body taken back to his people. Dress it up as Rome honourably allowing them the chance to bury him if you like, but I want them to *see* that he's dead. That's the best way to break their will, I'd say. Remember that, Centurion – and don't let me down.'

Marius stood, pulled his helmet back on and saluted. The word 'Centurion' told him that the informal part of the interview was over. Only unhesitating acceptance remained.

'I won't let you down, First Spear! We will do what is ordered and at every command we will be ready!'

Outside the headquarters building he found Gaius waiting on the steps, watching the organised chaos that was the two legions' preparation for war.

'Your orders were as you expected, I gather, from the unhappy expression you're wearing?'

Marius shook his head in disgust.

'The Seventh and the Ninth get to stay here and learn how to tie their own shoelaces, while you and I recruit and train as many barbarians as can be dug out of the tribes on both sides of the river. We *might* escort Vitellius south, once the army's torn the arms and legs off anything sent to block their path to Rome and beaten whatever's left to death with the wet ends, but in the meantime we're to do nothing of any more value than persuade the local boys to join up and then break it to them that they've just made the worst decision of their lives. Oh, and he also expects me to ensure that Civilis is executed, and take the body back to Batavodurum to make sure the Batavians know what's happened. Nothing more challenging than that.'

His friend fell in alongside him as Marius started walking.

'Look on the bright side, Marius. With over half the fortress emptied out, the local whores are going to be a good deal keener to please than is usually the case. And the price of wine will come down too, because there won't be enough mouths drinking the stuff for the innkeepers to keep on charging their usual extortionate prices.'

The newly promoted senior centurion shook his head in negation of the argument.

'What you're forgetting in your eagerness to cheer me up is

that I'm specifically charged with recruiting and training at least two more cohorts of men, if not double that, once the rest of the legion has buggered off and left us sitting with a double-sized fortress full of empty barracks. Which I'll be trying to do in the face of a dozen taverns offering cut-price beer and a population of whores who, if they weren't bright enough to go with the boys that march south, will be desperate for coin and only too capable of bribing their way in here with their cunts and then using those empty barracks for an alternative purpose to sleep. Any suggestions you might have as to how to keep the recruits' attention on sword practice that doesn't involve their cucumbers would be much appreciated.'

'Marius! *Centurion Marius!*'

Both men turned to see who it was that had called out to them, snapping to attention as they realised that they had been followed from the principia by an officer wearing the instantly recognisable tunic of a man with senatorial rank, a thick purple stripe over one shoulder, and with a gold ring on his right hand. Legatus Lupercus was in his mid-forties, old for a legion commander, a man with the reputation of being a man for whom military service was his calling rather than a step on the cursus honorum. His experience, it was said, included time as a legion tribune in Britannia, spells as an auxiliary prefect in both Syria and Dacia, a return to Britannia as a cavalry tribune and finally, after a tour of duty commanding a legion intended for Nero's aborted campaign in the east, his appointment the previous year to lead the Fifteenth, one of the empire's younger legions and clearly in need of an experienced leader to develop their skills and reputation. Grey at the temples, lean of face, and with a thick white scar cut into his left cheek just below the eye as evidence of his combat experience, he was a good deal fitter than his colleague Fabulus despite being ten years older, the result of punishing daily exercise with the men of his bodyguard. The gladius that hung at his left hip was an old and well-used weapon, the very obvious dent in its handguard the evidence, it was rumoured, of his time with the famed Fourteenth Legion during the conquest of

Britannia, and his legion's opinion of him had swiftly mellowed from the usual disdain for yet another senator with little clue about warfare to a healthy respect for a man who clearly knew which end of his sword to use on an enemy and, more importantly, how.

'My apologies for hailing you on the street, Centurion, I intended speaking to you in the principia but missed you as a result of a discussion with my camp prefect. The blasted man will insist on choosing the worst moments to discuss matters of supply. You *are* Centurion Marius? First Spear of the 5th Alaudae's seventh cohort?'

Marius saluted, Gaius following his example an instant later.

'Yes, Legatus. This is Centurion Gaius, one of my officers.'

'And I'm Quintus Munius Lupercus, legatus commanding the Fifteenth Primigenia. I believe that you'll be reporting to me, once my colleague Fabius Fabullus has led the Fifth and most of my own legion south. Legatus Augusti Valens has charged me with bringing the Fifteenth back up to full fighting strength and capability as quickly as possible, in order to be able to resist any further challenge that might arise to Vitellius's power once we have dealt with the pretender Galba. Since my own First Spear will be marching south with our vexillium behind your legion's eagle, I'm going to be depending on you to help me recruit and train four cohorts to replace those I'm releasing to Valens's command.'

Marius nodded confidently, repeating the standard response to any command, no matter how unwelcome.

'Yes, Legatus! We will do what is ordered and at every command we will be ready!'

Lupercus nodded briskly.

'Thank you, Centurion. I can see that we're going to have an excellent relationship. Once the legions have marched south, I plan to hold a dinner party for the officers who are left behind, a morale-building celebration of the fact that we're trusted with the defence of the frontier at a time like this. And who knows, the emperor himself may find the time to be present and to favour us with his wisdom.' Marius could have sworn the legatus was smirking, but the expression was fleeting. 'Perhaps you'll be able to spare the time from what are bound to be onerous duties to attend?'

Marius nodded again, his face's long ingrained immobility masking the incredulity seething beneath its imperturbable surface.

'It would be an honour and a pleasure, Legatus!'

Lupercus's lips twitched in the smallest intimation of a smile. 'Excellent. I'll inform you of the details in due course. And now, if you'll excuse me . . .'

He nodded and turned away, leaving the two centurions staring after him as he strode away towards the headquarters building.

'Fuck. *Me.*' Gaius stared after the legatus in unfeigned amazement. 'Did that really just happen? Did you really just get invited to go and lie on a couch and drink wine with the rich people? You? A man who didn't even own a pair of shoes until you joined up.'

Marius stared after the legatus for a moment before answering. 'I know. And I'm buggered if I have a clue what they get up to at these dinners, or even what they wear. But it won't be scale armour and army boots, no matter how well they're polished.'

A thought occurred to him, and he closed his eyes in disgust at the realisation that he had just become the servant of two masters.

'What's wrong now? You've just been invited to hobnob with the rich and idle and you're pulling a face like a recruit who's paid for the full hour and stained his tunic at the first touch.'

Marius turned on his friend with a tight smile.

'What it is, brother, is that when I saw the real First Spear just now he charged me with recruiting and training as many men as possible to act as casualty replacements for the Fifth, when we rejoin. He reckons that there's going to be a battle for the throne at some point, and the fact that all the other legions are only sending vexillia to follow our eagle is going to put the Fifth right in the middle of the fight. And now Legatus Lupercus tells me that he wants to replace the four cohorts he's detaching to join the march south – four *bloody* cohorts, Gaius – in order to be ready for any challenge to Vitellius's power. So I reckon I'm fucked all ends up, brother. *That's* what's wrong with me.'

His friend shrugged.

'Well that's easy enough. Just get Decimus to ask Legatus Fabullus to issue you with an order to recruit and train as many men as you can get your hands on, for the Fifth Legion. Let him and Lupercus argue it out once whatever we can scrape up and batter into shape is ready to serve, eh? I think you've got a bigger problem than who gets the recruits, or even what to wear to a legatus's dinner party.'

Marius shook his head.

'I defy you to show me something worse than either of those little questions.'

Gaius looked at him with a look that spoke volumes.

'Your problem, old son, isn't your wardrobe, and it's not the allocation of soldiers between legions. Money will solve the one, and the legati can dispute the other between themselves. Your problem, brother, is that the moment the Fifth marches out of the gates with half the Fifteenth along for the ride, and the same all down the river, I expect, the local tribes are going to tell their boys that haven't already volunteered to find somewhere to hide when the recruiting centurions come calling. They'll know that we'll be desperate for new blood, and they'll know that we're not always all that choosy as to who we bring back with us, volunteers or forced men. The problem won't be dividing the new boys up, it'll be having any new boys to worry about at all.'

5

The Old Camp, Germania Inferior, January AD 69

'I didn't think it was going to feel this bad.'

Gaius nodded gloomily at his friend's sentiment.

'Nor did I. Look at them.'

They stared emptily at the powerful force paraded before them, the available space barely sufficient to contain its massive strength. Eight cohorts of their own Fifth legion provided the leadership and the eagle beneath which another four cohorts each of the Fifteenth Primigenia, Sixteenth Gallica and the First Germanica would fight, between them forming a double strength legion numbering ten thousand men, fully equipped and ready for war, with a long line of horse drawn wagons carrying tents, equipment and food waiting behind them for the order to move out. The legion's centurions were making their final inspections before declaring their centuries and cohorts ready to march, the occasional raised voice and commotion marking those men who were being found wanting in their preparedness. The two men both smiled at one particularly loud scream of anger from deep in the body of waiting soldiers.

'That should have been us. They're going to march south, gather up all the glory and leave us here nursemaiding whatever recruits we can scrape up from the tribes.'

Gaius nodded again.

'Who'll know only too well that we'll be coming and will make sure there's nobody available except the elderly, the lame and the idiot. Look, here comes the new legatus augusti.'

Walking out in the middle of an ostentatious bodyguard of a

dozen picked soldiers, Fabius Valens had come to take command of his army. The man who had persuaded Vitellius to take the purple, he had been rewarded with command of the force that was to march south to the capital of Gallia Lugdunensis, and there add the famed First Italica to its strength before crossing the maritime Alps into northern Italy.

'Doesn't he love himself?'

Marius laughed softly at his comrade.

'Don't they all?' His mouth twisted in a bitter line. 'And besides, he's leading the best part of two legions to war. By the time he's collected the First Italica at Lugdunum and all the auxiliaries that have been ordered to join up, he'll have at least twenty-five thousand men at his back, and he's invading Italy. He probably thinks he's the divine Julius come again, off to cross the Rubicon at the head of an unstoppable army. Ah, here comes the *real* man of the hour.'

Senior centurion Decimus was walking out in the new legatus augusti's wake, overlooked in the excitement of Valens's magnificent appearance but looking no less impressive in his own way.

'The sly bastard! Look, he's still got his phalerae!'

The gilded silver discs that had been removed from the older man's chest harness when Vitellius had made his appeal for gold and silver had been replaced, as, on closer inspection, had the torques that hung around his neck and the bracelets that decorated his wrists. Spotting the two men he walked across to them, putting both hands on his hips and laughing softly at the looks on their faces.

'Two sorrier specimens I have yet to see. Anyone would have thought that you'd been demoted, Marius, rather than having been given the opportunity to serve as a First Spear with your very own vexillation to command. Not to mention the fact that your new legatus is one of the very few who doesn't look as wet behind the ears as a dwarf in a pissing contest, unlike the half-wit I've been saddled with. All things considered, given we're off to war just now and likely to be facing Galba's legions somewhere in northern Italy a month or two from now, I'd say you've got the best part of the bargain.' He stood and waited for Marius to respond, his smile twisting wryly as his subordinate looked down at the ground. 'I might think that, of course, but you'd be hard pressed to agree, wouldn't you?'

The younger man looked up at him, his eyes heavy with disappointment.

'Congratulations on your appointment to be the First Spear of the army, Centurion. I wish you joy of your new command, and I will pray that you come back to us safely, with tales to tell of the legion's doings in the south.'

Decimus smiled knowingly.

'Thank you, Marius.' His gaze shifted to Gaius. 'Keep an eye on this one, Centurion. He's going to need chivvying along, I think you'll find, daydreaming of battles, and glory, and a victory parade through Rome behind a forest of captured eagles and standards. What he's not going to be thinking about is the strong possibility that this fucking idiot . . .' he nodded his head in the direction of Valens, 'is going to allow his apparent thirst for that self-same glory to dismiss the fact that his military experience could be written in a message tablet with a pugio for a stylus. What with him, and the other chinless fool that's been given command of the army of Germania Superior's march south, I suspect we might find ourselves hard pressed to fight our way out of a brothel bedchamber, never mind across the Alps, all the way down Italy and into Rome. Not if Galba has half a brain, and actually appoints someone who's fought a campaign to command his armies. The gods know the choice isn't exactly a thin one, what with all the wars that Rome's fought in the last twenty years.'

He turned to look over at Valens, who was staring impatiently about him with the air of a man who believed he ought to be elsewhere.

'And now, I believe, it's time for me to go and introduce the new legatus augusti to his equally new command. I'll wish the pair of you a good day, and remind you, Marius, that I'm going to need replacements when I bring the legion home. A lot of replacements. And I want them to be fucking gleaming, *First Spear.* So don't spend too long mooning after a battle you won't have to fight, eh?'

He thrust his hand out, and Marius clasped it with a nod.

'Go well, First Spear. Oh . . .'

Decimus stopped in the act of turning away from them.

'Oh?'

His subordinate shrugged, a sly smile creeping onto his face.

'I just meant to commend you on the smartness of your turn out, sir. I don't know how you do it.'

Decimus took one of the gilded phalerae between finger and thumb.

'These old things? I found them in the bottom of my campaign chest, which I'm sure you'll agree was fortunate.'

'More than fortunate, First Spear, that must have taken divine intervention.'

The senior centurion shrugged with a grin.

'Any fool can do things the hard way, Marius. Try to remember that, while I'm away.'

He walked away, saluting the general and speaking with the great man for a moment before turning away to take command of the army's preparations for the march.

'Want to stay and watch them leave?'

Marius shook his head.

'No. It'll take them the best part of an hour to get off the parade ground, and that's with all of their kit already loaded. I pity any decent-sized town on their route, because that lot are going to be the most unwelcome visitors anyone's had in a decade or more. And that's if they behave themselves. No, let's go and round up the legion's remaining centurions and start planning a recruiting drive. You heard the man, he expects to see shiny new cohorts of legionaries when he comes back.' He rolled his eyes and rasped an imitation of Decimus's harsh tones. 'And I want them to be gleaming. Fucking gleaming, *First Spear.*'

Gaius stared over at the senior centurion as he barked an order at one of his officers, pointing with his vine stick for emphasis before stamping away to find a fresh victim for his enthusiasm to be on the road.

'You think he'll come back?'

His friend laughed softly.

'Decimus? He's the gristle you can't be bothered to chew until your jaw aches to make it eatable. He's the harpastum ball that's been used too long, but which never gets thrown away because it's not burst or worn through. Decimus is that last mouthful of the wine that's just too disgusting to drink, even when you're really hammered, because of all the crap that's sunk to the bottom of the jar. He'll come back all right, because that leathery, objectionable old bastard is indestructible. And besides, he's right about the likelihood of there being casualties to replace. Neither our man or this Galba is very likely to step down and invite the other to take the throne, not while they've both got several legions of idiots like us champing at the bit. Look at that lot . . .' he gestured at the waiting troops. 'All of them desperate for the chance to take their iron to an enemy, and somewhere on the other side of the Alps there's an army that's probably just as eager. I can't see this whole thing getting settled without a good-sized river of blood being shed. So let's go and work out how to trick as many of the local idiots to join up as possible, shall we?'

Batavian encampment, Civitas Lingonum, Gallia Lugdunensis, January AD 69

'Centurion Alcaeus!'

Banon and Alcaeus turned away from their consideration of one of their men's armour to find a breathless soldier standing behind them.

'Prefect's compliments, Centurion, and will you join him in his office straight away.'

Alcaeus nodded, turning away with an aside to the soldier in question.

'You can consider that a lucky escape. If that armour's rust free by the time Scar's done with me you'll be only pulling one week of latrine duty. Banon, you're in charge. Do whatever you want with them as long as they're sweating like pigs on a spit when I get back, and make sure they know that "Rusty" here's the reason for their labours.'

He walked briskly into the Batavi camp, acknowledging the salutes of the men on guard duty with a wave of his vine stick and heading for the headquarters building. Outside the imposing wooden structure a horse was being rubbed down by a pair of cavalrymen, its mud-spattered legs and hoofs telling their own story.

'Ah, here he is . . .'

Scar gestured to a seat alongside the man already sitting facing him with a cup from which steam was rising, both hands wrapped around its surface.

'Decurion, this is Alcaeus, my deputy and the Batavian cohorts' chief priest. The decurion here, Centurion Alcaeus, is a messenger from the Winter Camp. He's carrying orders from the emperor. The *real* emperor, that is. I've already assured him that we were delighted to hear of Legatus Augusti Vitellius's acclamation as emperor by the German legions. Obviously no man in any of the Batavian cohorts was going to be anything other than happy to hear that the man who dismissed the German Bodyguard from Rome has been challenged by one of our own. But the decurion here is the bearer of more news in addition to those orders, and stranger tidings than I could have imagined.'

He gestured to the messenger to repeat the information he had already shared with the Batavi commander.

'I was telling Prefect Germanicus that the pretender Galba has been assassinated.'

Alcaeus shook his head slowly.

'*Assassinated…?*'

The decurion nodded, sipping at his drink.

'Murdered, it seems. The news reached Legatus Augusti Caecina yesterday, just as I was preparing to ride south with your orders for the advance south. Galba was killed by the praetorians . . .' Scar and Alcaeus shared a knowing glance. 'But the murder was instigated by one of his followers, a man by the name of Otho. It seems that Galba decided that since he was an old man and unlikely to enjoy a long reign, he ought to choose someone to be his heir. And as it turned out, the man he chose wasn't Otho, despite Otho himself having apparently harboured an expectation that it would be. Seems he then bribed a handful of praetorians to spontaneously rise up and attack the old man in the street. They murdered him and made sport with his severed head, then convinced enough of their fellow soldiers to stand behind Otho when he went to convince the Senate to do the sensible thing and elect him as consul that the Senate did exactly what they were being told. Apparently we should all now be grateful that the empire has been rescued from disaster by Otho's selflessness in taking the throne in the face of such chaos and lawlessness.'

Scar shook his head and turned to his deputy, switching momentarily to their native language.

'Gods below. When these Romans decide to make a mess of things they really do make a complete *fucking* mess of things, don't they?'

The messenger frowned.

'What?'

'I was just telling my centurion that we can only hope to have the chance to avenge the old man. He might have been an idiot, whose legacy to Rome is a homicidal pretender to the throne rather than a real emperor, but that's no reason not to show him the respect appropriate to a man who believed he was doing the best for the empire. And now, it seems to me, we clearly need the intervention of a man fit to carry the title *caesar*.'

The decurion nodded his fervent agreement.

'You've got that right, Prefect. Here . . .' He took a scroll wrapped in waxed paper from the message container that was secured to his belt. 'Your orders, from the Emperor Vitellius himself.'

Scar spilt the wax seal that held the orders tightly rolled, opening the message and reading in silence for a moment.

'We're ordered to divide into two four-cohort commands and march to join the emperor's army as it advances south along two routes, four cohorts to join the Fifth Alaudae marching via Lugdunum and then over the western Alps under Legatus Valens, and another four to join the Twenty-First Rapax and cross the northern Alps under Caecina.' He nodded decisively. 'You can tell the emperor and his legati that we will obey these orders with the appropriate urgency. We will do what is ordered and at every command we will be ready!'

The Old Camp, Germania Inferior, January AD 69

'He has to die! My men won't settle for anything less, and neither will any of yours!'

Marius looked across his quarter at Marcus, the most belligerent of the eleven other centurions who had gathered at his summons. He had called them to his personal rooms so that they could talk freely, unobserved by their men and without witnesses to whatever it was that they agreed to do in response to the news he had been given by Legatus Lupercus less than an hour before. Angered by the other man's vehemence in the face of a superior officer, he suppressed the urge to get to his feet and take his colleague by the throat, his face red with frustration at being the target of his officers' vehemence.

'Legatus Lupercus gave it to me straight, Centurion, and was very clear that his instructions come directly from the emperor. Vitellius is going to pardon Civilis today, with no ifs or buts, and he expects us to keep our mouths shut! He reckons he needs to keep the Batavians quiet until this war against Otho is done with. After that we can deal with them any way local command sees fit, but until then it's strictly hands *off*. Which means that if we're caught trying to kill him we'll be the ones facing execution for disobeying the decision of a fucking *emperor*!'

Marcus shrugged.

'So we can't get caught. Which means that none of us can do

it: our boys will be watching us like hawks for any sign that we're on their side. If they get as much as a hint that we moved on Civilis it'll be all over the fortress in an hour.'

Marius nodded vehemently.

'Too fucking right it will. And we'll be locked up to make an example of what happens to men who disobey the throne.'

Gaius laughed softly from his place between the two men.

'You're a good man, Marius, a man I'd stand alongside to the death, but you have one weakness.'

His friend shook his head in exasperation.

'Well, go on then. What's my "one weakness"?'

'Harpastum.'

'*Harpastum!*'

His brother centurion nodded knowingly.

'Harpastum. You're rock hard, Marius, but you play to the rules. On the harpastum field and in life.'

'The rules? In *harpastum*?'

'Yes, I know. On the face of it there might as well not be any rules. Kicking, punching, yes, I've seen men carried off the pitch with the idiot grins that come with having their wits punched out of them. And yes, there are usually three or four broken limbs each year and the occasional death or broken spine. But that's missing the point.'

Marius shook his head in disbelief.

'Which is *what*, exactly?'

Gaius smiled apologetically.

'Harpastum always stops short of really serious physical harm. The broken arms and legs are accidental, for the most part. You men batter the shit out of each other until the arbiter blows his whistle, then you go to the baths and get pissed together, swear undying brotherhood and walk away with the warm glow of having bonded with fellow men. Fuck, you even made friends with that man Hramn when we played the Batavians, and he's one of Civilis's officers.'

Seriously irritated, Marius raised a hand to point at his friend, but Gaius spoke quickly.

'Real life isn't like harpastum, Marius. Sometimes a man has to extend the hand of friendship with the other hand behind his back, ready to wield the blade he's about to put into the other bastard's guts. Do you see my point?'

The senior centurion nodded slowly.

'You think I'm conditioned by the game, too soft to make the hard decisions.'

His friend was silent for a moment before he spoke again.

'I think you're the best centurion I've ever served with.' The men gathered around the room nodded and muttered their agreement. 'You're certainly the best of us. But you're not the man to deal with this traitor Civilis. Not yet. So all we're asking is that you turn your back while we do what has to be done. I know a centurion in one of the Tungrian cohorts that have been moved into the fortress to keep up the appearance of numbers, a man who'll do any amount of dirty work for the right amount of gold, so I took the opportunity to drop him a heavy enough purse to buy his loyalty and his silence when the deed's done. They marched from their camp this morning, which means that they'll be waiting on the road between the Batavians sent to fetch the treacherous bastard after his acquittal and their dungheap village. The traitor Civilis and his friends will be found dead, a robbery that went wrong when they tried to fight back, but there'll clearly have been too many bandits for them to fight off. It'll make for a few days of excitement and extra patrols, but we'll be clean-handed and the traitor will be ash on the wind, and soon forgotten. That'll work for everyone, I would have thought.'

The Old Camp, Germania Inferior, January AD 69

'We are expected, legionary, and this is a pass from Tribune Cassius authorising us to enter your principia and attend the hearing of a legal case against one of our tribesmen, Gaius Julius Civilis.'

Hramn showed the soldier standing guard on the fortress's

headquarters building the wax tablet he had been given at the fortress's eastern gate upon presenting himself and Draco to the tribune of the guard. The two men had been selected to attend Civilis's trial by the tribe's council of elders, Hramn for his recent experience of Roman politics and the fact that he was Kivilaz's deputy, Draco for his excellent standing with Rome as a former commander of the Batavi cohorts during the war in Britannia and subsequent command of the guard in the later stages of Claudius's reign.

The soldier looked at the words scribed neatly into the flat wax surface with the blank eyes of a man without letters, but at the mention of Kivilaz's name he nodded.

'The trial of the traitor. Wait here.'

He ducked in through the door, leaving his comrade who, if it were possible, was even less prepossessing than himself, to watch the two men while he went to fetch an officer. Hramn shared a meaningful look with Draco and speaking quietly so as to avoid being overheard by the remaining sentry.

'The trial of the traitor. No bias there then. I wonder what odds one of our inveterate gamblers would give us on Kivilaz walking out from under this falling tree. After all, it's not the first time these legion bastards have tried to have him killed.'

Draco nodded, a smile pasted onto his face for the benefit of the remaining legionary.

'That's true, and *that's* why the elders wanted us here. In the event this new emperor finds our brother innocent, he's more than likely to end up in a ditch somewhere on the road back to Batavodurum with a centurion's dagger in his back. Now that most of the legions of Germania Inferior have gone south under Vitellius's legatus Valens, the roads are empty, and a man who has escaped their idea of Roman justice for a second time would make a tempting target for his accusers.'

'And if they find him guilty, where will that leave us?'

The older man grinned at him, chuckling gently.

'Smile, Hramn. Everyone dies, and in the event that these cocksuckers try to send me to join Kivilaz in Hades I'll take an honour guard of them with me to serve at table when I feast with my ancestors. And if you couldn't take a joke . . .'

'I shouldn't have joined? Is that your answer to everything?'

The soldier reappeared, closely followed by a blue-chinned centurion whose whole demeanour seemed to be one of disdain for everyone and everything.

'Come to watch the traitor Civilis being sentenced, have you?'

Hramn bowed his head fractionally.

'Greetings Centurion. Yes, we are indeed here to witness the proceedings of the imperial court, and to report back to our people the verdict that is reached by the emperor, may the gods reward his impartial justice with long life and fruitfulness.'

'Hmmm.' The officer looked them up and down. 'And you are?'

Hramn put a hand to his own chest.

'I, Centurion, am Hramn, formerly decurion in command of the emperor Nero's German Bodyguard in Rome, now relieved of my duties by Galba and sent north to serve with this army. And this man is Draco, former commander of the eight Batavi cohorts that serve with this army, and also a past commander of the emperor Claudius's Bodyguard. We have been selected to attend this trial as loyal subjects of Rome come to see Roman justice delivered in the case of our brother officer.'

The legion officer looked them both up and down, then held out a hand.

'Give me the pass.'

Hramn shook his head firmly.

'I cannot. The tribune who gave it to me was very specific that it was to be passed to no other man, for fear that an imposter might gain access to the presence of the emperor. He was insistent on this.'

The centurion stared at him in frustration for a moment and then stepped back, waving a hand for them both to enter the principia. Hramn waited until they were safely out of earshot before speaking again, a murmur that reflected his discomfort at finding himself in the very heart of the fortress's overt display of military power.

'Bastard. He would have taken the tablet, pushed us into a waiting room and left us there until after the trial.'

Draco snorted quiet laughter.

'Obviously. Although what such a desire to keep us from seeing a brother officer receive Roman justice says about the relationship between Rome and the Batavi, I hesitate to think.'

Taking their places in the principia's main hall, they stood quietly at the back of the room and spoke only to one another, ignoring the collected military officers and well-connected civilians who made up the bulk of the audience before whom the drama of their countryman's trial and that of another half-dozen men would shortly play out. Hramn looked around the room counting crests, stopping when he got to thirty, nodding at Marius when he saw the man in the midst of the Fifth legion's officers, standing next to a legatus with a scarred face.

'This must be every centurion in what's left of both legions. They're not taking any chances, are they?'

Draco shrugged.

'Vitellius is *their* emperor. They made him, and they're going to make very sure that no tribesman with a grudge gets within a mile of the man. Or any soldier who fancies collecting on the price that Otho has put on his—'

'Stand for the Emperor!'

The newest ruler of the civilised world swept into the room behind the formal escort of his lictors, clearly legion veterans who had been dressed for the occasion as a tacit reflection of his power base, while the legatus who had called them to attention continued speaking.

'Imperator Aulus Vitellius Germanicus, the one true ruler of the empire!'

'Germanicus?'

Draco nodded sagely at Hramn's whispered question.

'He's a cautious man, that much is clear. He won't take the title of Caesar until he feels secure enough to do so, for fear of upsetting the Senate, I expect. We'll just have to hope that his caution and calculation extends to our brother Kivilaz's case.'

The new emperor raised both hands to salute his men, clearly feeling himself to be among friends. A tall man dressed in a brilliantly white toga, florid and heavily built from a lifetime of indulgence, he limped heavily. Draco leaned closer to Hramn, whispering in his ear.

'The limp, they say, is the result of a chariot accident. Apparently Caligula took it into his head to—'

'My friends, please take your seats and allow me to lower these poor tired bones into a chair myself.'

'A nice touch.' Draco pursed his lips in amusement as a centurion carried forward a solidly constructed camp stool of the type used in the field for the emperor to perch upon. '*See, I am nothing more than a humble soldier forced to accept this position by the weight of opinion.*' He grinned at Hramn's grimace of disgust. 'Trust me, as the leader of Claudius's Bodyguard I saw many worse pieces of posturing. As I'm sure you did under Nero.'

A uniformed clerk had risen at the signal from his legatus, now that Vitellius had taken his seat, and was introducing the day's business.

'The emperor will now hear the cases against the following accused and will rule as to their fate!'

He nodded to a centurion.

'Bring out the prisoners as they are named!'

Consulting the list, he called out the first name.

'Pompeius Propinquus!'

A centurion opened the door behind him, beckoning to the first of the men who could be seen waiting in the shadows within. The prisoner walked blinking into the room's light, looking about himself with an expression that eloquently bespoke his terror at the circumstances in which he found himself. The centurion, having closed the door behind him, tapped him forcefully on the thigh with the vine stick in his right hand, barking an order at the cowed prisoner.

'Bow to your emperor!'

Waiting until the formality was complete, and had been received by Vitellius with nothing more welcoming than a cold stare, the clerk spoke again.

'Pompeius Propinquus, you stand accused that on the second day of Januarius, in your position as the imperial agent in the province of Gallia Belgica, you sent a messenger to Rome, to the usurper Galba, informing him that the legions of Germania were revolting and refusing to accept the authority of his illegal regime. Your communication was in direct contradiction of the will and direction of every legionary on the Rhenus frontier, a far larger and more legitimate constituency than the single Spanish legion with which the usurper seized Rome, committing the heinous crime of using his cavalry to scatter and murder innocent petitioners of legio First Classica from the gates of the city, blameless men recruited by his predecessor Nero from the fleet who were simply seeking reassurance as to their future enjoyment of imperial service. What do you have to say in your own defence?'

Propinquus looked around him, spreading his arms imploringly.

'I—'

'The accused will address the emperor!'

Swallowing, the accused man looked to Vitellius with a beseeching expression.

'Caesar, I only did what any good servant of the empire would have done in my place! My duty was to the man acclaimed emperor by the senate, although—'

Vitellius spoke over him, ignoring his entreaty.

'You fail to deny your crime, and are convicted of loyalty to the previous emperor, the usurper Galba, out of your own mouth.' He looked at the cringing Propinquus with hard eyes. 'You will be executed, today, as full and final punishment for your crime. Next.'

Leading the dumbstruck prisoner to another door, the centurion pushed him through it with a single word before turning away to fetch the next man to be tried.

'Execution!'

Hramn stared in amazement at the scene.

'An imperial agent, condemned to death just like that? *Gods below.*'

'*Keep your voice down, nod and look approving.*' Draco's reproach was so quiet as to be barely audible. '*If these men get so much as a hint that we don't agree with them we'll be the next to feel the noose closing our windpipes. That's better, and look a little more triumphant. I promised myself not to get killed unnecessarily today, and I'm keen to deliver on the oath.*'

'*I thought if you couldn't take a j—*'

'Bring out Julius Burdo!'

The next prisoner to be led out was dressed in a clean tunic, and after the obligatory bow to Vitellius his head was held high in the face of his accusers.

'Prefect Julius Burdo, you are accused that on the third day of Januarius, in your position as commander of the fleet upon the river Rhenus, you refused to swear loyalty to the one true emperor, Aulus Vitellius Germanicus, stating that you were loyal to the man appointed to the role by the people and the senate of Rome. Further, you are accused of having plotted against the emperor's predecessor as legatus augusti of Germania Inferior, Gaius Fonteius Capito, and with having conspired in his murder by the self-confessed assassin, the naval centurion Crispinus whose execution the emperor has already ordered.'

Draco breathed a comment into Hramn's ear.

'*An execution that prevents any evidence of Burdo's involvement emerging. I wonder if the prefect has any connection to the new emperor's circle of intimate friends?*'

Burdo turned to Vitellius and bowed deeply.

'Caesar, I can only entreat your mercy for a man who sadly misunderstood the circumstances of your timely and reluctant assumption of imperial authority, which I now know was motivated by no other urge than to save Rome from the depredations of a miserly, divisive man whose authority was based solely on the support of a single legion. A man who had spent most of the last decade sheltering from the vicissitudes of Nero's cruelty in Spain, while better men stayed in Rome and risked their lives for love of the city and the empire, which is the prime reason why the men of the seven German legions decided to declare their loyalty to you. Declarations of loyalty to which I will hopefully be allowed to add my own and that of the sailors I command. Further to that, I strenuously deny any connection with the actions of this man Crispinus who, whilst a part of my command, was not personally known to me.'

The emperor stared at him for long enough that the assembled officers leaned forward involuntarily, but at length he nodded his understanding.

'Prefect Burdo, the position you took was very clearly based on your loyalty not to the former emperor Galba, but rather to the empire, and misinformed to a degree that I know has left you personally embarrassed. You have offered to take your own life if required to do so, and while I laud your courage in making this offer, I cannot allow you to bring upon yourself the same honour enjoyed by Gnaeus Domitius Corbulo when the matter involved is so ambiguous. I could only be criticised by my colleagues in the senate for such a course of action, and with good reason . . .'

He paused as though further considering his verdict, and Draco leaned close to his friend.

'*Or to put it another way, while the soldiers want him dead for the alleged crime of plotting against the previous legatus augusti, Vitellius knows that executing him will turn the fleet against him, which is why this tidy little accommodation has been reached.*'

'And so I find you guilty of the charge, but with mitigating circumstances that require me to stay my hand from the ultimate sanction available to me. You will be imprisoned, treated fairly and given the leisure of time to regret your mistake, while the fleet you have previously commanded will now answer to your deputy, who I trust will ensure that no further acts of disloyalty occur.'

Burdo bowed again, and was led away by the obviously disapproving centurion.

Draco nudged his companion.

'*The legion would have cut his throat. It seems the emperor has put a saddle on a hungry lion.*'

'Bring out Julius Civilis!'

The two men exchanged glances, watching impassively under the scrutiny of the men closest to them as their fellow tribesman was led into the room. Dressed in a tunic that was almost as clean as that sported by Burdo, he had clearly been allowed the opportunity to prepare himself for the trial, his hair neatly cut and combed, his boots clean, and his expression almost serene. Draco nodded approvingly.

'*He might just get away with this, if he can be bothered to make the effort not to piss Vitellius off.*'

'Gaius Julius Civilis, known among the Batavian tribe as Kivilaz, you are accused that you have plotted against the empire. It is charged that you encouraged the rebel Gaius Julius Vindex in his revolt last spring, stating that you could deliver your tribe and its auxiliary cohorts to his support of the usurper Galba, and that you have additionally sought to inspire your countrymen to acts of disobedience against the rightful rule of Rome over your homeland. What do you have to say in your own defence?'

Looking around the room, Kivilaz shook his head in evident rejection of the charges laid before him. Draco shook his head in horror.

'*Oh gods, he's going to get himself killed.*'

Then, before Vitellius had any chance to react to his previous silent gesture of refusal to accept the clerk's assertion, Kivilaz made a deep and fulsome bow.

'Caesar, may I take this opportunity to offer you my congratulations on your well-deserved elevation to the throne? I would have made my declaration of loyalty earlier, and in person, but the officers of the Fifth and Fifteenth Legions I see gathered to witness your judgement have denied me that opportunity by means of my imprisonment incommunicado.'

Vitellius acknowledged the statement with a slight inclination of his head.

'I thank you for your informal declaration of loyalty, Civilis. You may yet have the chance to repeat it more formally, *if* I judge your imprisonment to have been without good cause. Now proceed with your defence.'

Kivilaz bowed again, turning to look around the room at his accusers.

'With the greatest of respect to the gathered officers of the two illustrious legions I see gathered here . . .'

'*Good start. At least he's trying.*'

'. . . I find myself outraged at the treatment that I have received at the hands of men I once considered to be my brothers-in-blood!'

'*Ah* . . .'

Vitellius raised a hand to forestall half a dozen centurions who had risen from their chairs with furious expressions.

'Much as I appreciate your prompt attempts to interject, gentlemen, the empire has a fine tradition of allowing an accused man to conduct his defence and at the very least receive a dignified hearing until he has concluded his words. Let us therefore allow Julius Civilis to state his case *before* we decide upon his guilt?'

Kivilaz bowed to the emperor once more.

'Thank you, Caesar. As I was about to add to my previous statement, perhaps "outraged" is the wrong choice of word. "Saddened" might have been more appropriate. Perhaps "mortified" would have better expressed my horror. "Bereft" would have served no worse. For I am all of these things in the face of having been imprisoned on charges that I know to be patently false, and which make light of my life of service to the empire.'

'You do rather seem to attract accusations, do you not, Civilis?'

Kivilaz nodded in respectful agreement.

'It seems I do, Caesar, although I find myself baffled as to how a man of my often demonstrated loyalty can be so traduced. I swam the river Medui to take my spear to the Britons' chariot horses, making it possible for the Second Augustan Legion to force the crossing by their outstanding bravery, untroubled by the enemy's best swordsmen. And I did this for Rome. I swam the ocean in the far west of that country to Mona, to take my iron to the tribal priests who encouraged their followers to resist our advance. For Rome. And I stood with the Fourteenth Gemina against ten times our number of the Iceni tribe, on the day of our glorious triumph over that murderous revolt, and gladly gave an eye to play a small part in that great victory. For Rome. In every battle the Fourteenth Legion fought, the Batavi were at their sides, myself no less than any other man, and I have the scars to prove it, not one of them in my back. All of them incurred in the service of Rome, and worn with pride as badges of my loyalty at any price to myself. Whereas my accusers have fought nothing more troublesome than a head cold since their brief trampling of the Frisii people thirty years ago.'

A growing murmur of outrage started to rise, but the emperor once more raised his hand.

'Silence! Nothing the accused has said so far has been anything other than factual! There is no hard evidence of the crime of which he has been accused, and his war record is indeed exemplary! If I find him guilty you can take out your frustrations on him for pointing out that neither of this fortress's legions have seen battle in thirty years to whatever degree you think justified and honourable – a flogging, perhaps, before an appropriately swift death – but until then I will have *silence*!'

An uneasy quiet descended on the room, and Vitellius raised a hand to indicate that Kivilaz should continue.

'Thank you, Caesar. I will keep the rest of my defence brief. There is indeed no evidence that I lack loyalty to the empire, and to the person of the emperor. No proof of these charges has ever been offered to me, only the accusations of men who are yet to make them to my face. I have already been sent to Rome for judgement in the matter of the Vindex revolt, while my brother was brutally sentenced to death by your predecessor as the legatus augusti of Lower Germania, Gaius Fonteius Capito, a man whose violent death last year is attributed by some to certain local senior military officers as an opportunist reaction to the apparent crime of refusing to join with Vindex and Galba against Nero . . .'

He paused to allow Vitellius to consider the implications of his words.

'As to my imprisonment in Rome, I was at length declared not guilty by the previous emperor, may the gods rest his spirit, for the lack of any proof that my visit to Senator Vindex was anything other than purely motivated, and solely intended to encourage him to make peace with Rome. As an innocent man whose brother has been murdered on the same hasty charges that saw me within a whisker of sharing his fate, to find myself accused once more is almost too much to bear. Only my continued faith in the scrupulous rule of Roman law in your own impartial hands gives me hope.'

He bowed to the emperor one last time, standing in silence to receive Vitellius's justice. The emperor stared at him for a long moment before speaking.

'It is true, Julius Civilis, that no man has produced any evidence of outright treason against you with any more strength than rumour and hearsay. And you have made it clear in private testimony that your meeting with Vindex was for the sole purpose of persuading him not to shed unnecessary blood by giving battle to the legions of Germania. It is also true that whatever evidence Gaius Fonteius Capito was in possession of with regard to your brother's apparent treason, he took it to his untimely grave, and so we shall never know whether that execution was merited. And finally it is true that you were released from captivity by the usurper Galba for lack of evidence, although in the eyes of some men here it seems as if he might well have released you as your reward for having abetted his supporter Vindex?'

He paused, allowed the muttered agreement with his last point to die down.

'I have never been inclined to have a good man executed on the grounds of gossip, no matter what the emotions behind such accusations might be. And you, Gaius Julius Civilis, are undoubtedly a true servant to the empire. You have fought for Rome all of your adult life, and provided us with an example of courage and determination to achieve victory over the empire's enemies that I would be proud to own. Therefore my judgement is this: you will be freed to return to your people, on the conditions that you resolve to live a quiet life, devoting yourself to the command of your cohort and encouraging continued loyal service to the empire by the men who serve in your cohorts. Do you accept these conditions?'

Germania Inferior, January AD 69

'You could have brought a dozen of my guardsmen with you, Hramn, if you're as nervous about getting back to Batavodurum as you seem to be? Or provided me with something a little more effective than this apple peeler?'

The decurion looked around him at the winter landscape to either side of the road's cobbled, arrow-straight line. The main marching route from the legion camp north to the Batavi island ran through farm land for the most part, but the hill they were slowly climbing was studded with boulders too large for economical removal, and had been left as straggling woodland, stripped bare of foliage by the season's cold. The prince had strapped on the belt that Hramn had carried with him from Batavodurum the moment that he had been freed, relishing the feel of a dagger on his right hip, but Hramn had agreed with Draco that they would neither provide him with a sword, nor even wear one themselves, on the grounds that they would be far less provocative to the men who had imprisoned their compatriot if they weren't obviously equipped to fight.

'Yes, we could, Kivilaz. But even with half their strength gone south to fight for the throne there are still a lot more legionaries in the Old Camp than there are men of fighting age left in our city. If I'd used our men to protect you on the way home, and dead Romans were the result, then it would be our entire tribe that would stand accused of treason by the centurions who seem determined to see your head on a stake, and not just yours. And that's not something the council of elders is willing to see happen.'

Kivilaz turned his head and fixed his one good eye on his subordinate.

'So you're still loyal to the empire even after all this, are you? Even after you were sent home in shame by an emperor not worthy of the title? Even after my brother was killed out of hand without a semblance of a trial? And even after I was beaten and sent to Rome to be judicially murdered, and when that failed was arrested again to allow a collection of power-crazed legion nobodies with the intention of pushing their toy emperor into killing me on their behalf? It's lucky for me that they didn't count on him deciding that he'd be better off maintaining friendly relations with the Batavi, rather than needlessly provoking the tribe, and decided to let me live, or they'd have done the job on me themselves while I was at their mercy in the fortress cells.

'The legatus commanding the Old Camp came to see me last night, late, when the visit was less likely to be noticed, I guess. His name is Lupercus, and it turns out I know him from a long time back, in Britannia, and that fight with the British tribes to get over the river Medui. I saved his life that day, as he was quick to remind me, and here he was repaying the favour. He told me he'd counselled Vitellius that my execution could destroy Rome's relationship with the Batavi for ever, and make it necessary for a campaign to bring the Island under direct military rule. A campaign that would require two or possibly three legions if it wasn't to end in an ignominious disaster.'

'Two or three legions they don't have.'

'Exactly. So the deal on offer was simple. My life would be spared if I were willing to return home and encourage the tribe to support Vitellius. Which, of course, I agreed. The big question now is what sort of lengths Lupercus's centurions might go to, once they come to the realisation that Vitellius isn't going to do them any favours in the matter, not now that he's wearing the purple and doesn't need their support quite as much as he did. Which is why, Decurion, I'd have been a good deal happier with an escort of my cohort's proudest and most bloodthirsty guardsmen than just you two.'

Hramn looked at him in surprise.

'You're going to continue calling us *guardsmen*?'

His new prefect nodded soberly.

'Yes, Hramn, I am. You were guardsmen in Rome, and you'll

still be guardsmen here in Germania. Galba may have dismissed you but there was no censure of any man involved, just an instruction that your service in Rome was terminated and you were to come north and serve under my command. And no alternative title was either offered or imposed. So guardsmen you were and guardsmen you will remain. *My* guardsmen, the Batavi Guard. You're still the cream of our people's manhood, the biggest and the fiercest men in all of the eight cohorts, and I will lead you with all the pride that your name inspires. We—'

His head whipped round, as Draco raised a hand to point.

'Well now, Kivilaz, do you think even a dozen of your guardsmen would have got us out of this?'

They had reached the hill's summit, with a clear view to the north, to see that the road was blocked by several tent parties of auxiliary troops, their dark-red shields identifying them to the three men's trained eyes, and the veteran laughed tersely.

'Tungrians. Trust those legion bastards not to do their own dirty work.'

Kivilaz reined his horse in, staring at the mail-armoured men waiting in a neat line across the road.

'How many do you see?'

Hramn's voice was flat with the realisation that their deaths were imminent.

'Forty.'

Draco spoke without taking his eyes off the waiting infantrymen.

'Enough to close the road off and deal with anyone that gets uppity, but not a full century. Which leaves another forty-odd men to close the road behind us and wait in the woods to either side, in case we try to ride out of their trap.'

Kivilaz nodded.

'Which means that if we try to run we'll be killed without any opportunity to reason with them. Looks to me as if our best option is to go and meet them. Just not on their terms.'

He dismounted, calling out at the silent trees that lined the road.

'Would one of you men come and hold my horse?' After a

moment's silence, a helmeted head appeared round the trunk of a fully grown oak, just for an instant, but enough for the Batavi prince's purposes. 'You! Yes, *you*! Behind the tree! Come on, I don't have all day!'

The Tungrian stepped out from his hiding place with a red face and walked forward with a hand on his sword's hilt. Kivilaz grinned broadly at him, holding out his horse's reins.

'You won't be needing the sword, I'm not in the mood for fighting. Today is a day for talking. Here, take these . . .'

He proffered the reins and smiled at the soldier's bafflement, as the hapless auxiliary obeyed his instincts and did as the officer told him. Hramn and Draco were equally puzzled, but passed their own reins to the man and looked at Kivilaz with the expressions of men who were completely out of their depth.

'You want to . . . *reason* . . . with them?'

Kivilaz grinned at the older man as if he had no care in all the world.

'If there's one thing I've learned over the last six months, Draco, it's that when you're in a situation where your sword, if you even still possess one, will be of no avail, then it's time to use a deadlier weapon. Shall we?'

He strode away down the road's gentle slope with Draco limping in his wake and Hramn walking backwards alongside the veteran, watching as men stepped out of the woods on either side and closed the trap around them.

'Well, it'll be a short fight if even *his* honeyed tongue can't ease him out of this one.'

Draco snorted, leaning on his staff as he followed their prince towards the waiting ranks of soldiers.

'A short fight followed by a long sleep somewhere beneath the leaves, with our people none the wiser as to where we lie, with no bodies to mourn over. Honourless bastards. At least I'll give one or two of them the last surprise of their lives.'

Kivilaz was calling out to the men waiting for them, his voice jovially at odds with the seriousness of their predicament.

'Greetings, brothers! It's been a long time since I stood alongside your tribe, back in Britannia when your cohorts and those of the Batavi won the war that bitch Boudicca started, tearing the Iceni to ribbons in the course of a single hour of bloodshed! Gods, but it was good to be alive on that day, even if it did cost me the sight of an eye! Batavi and Tungri, shoulder to shoulder and fighting like men possessed, as only *we* can!' He stopped in front of the century's officer who stood waiting for him in the middle of the road, looking along the short length of the Tungrian line with a smile at the blank-faced soldiers who were staring back at him with less enmity than had been the case only a moment before. 'Greetings Centurion! I'd ask what it is that I can do for you, but I think I can discern your purpose in being here. You've been given money to kill me, and these two blameless men, right? Blood gold, handed to you by a legion centurion?'

The Tungrian officer put a hand to the hilt of his sword, but Kivilaz was faster, stepping forward a pace and speaking so quietly that the men behind the centurion had to lean forward to hear him.

'Before you draw that weapon, take a moment to think this through. In return for a few gold coins, which I'd imagine none of these men behind you will ever see, you're not only going to murder a prince of the Batavi tribe, but you're going to dishonour two wholly innocent men, one a former leader of the emperor's German Bodyguard who is now a distinguished elder of my people, the other the man who was in command of the Bodyguard when it was so shamefully disbanded. The Bodyguard which has now been reduced in status to no more than a part of the army of Germania Inferior, when previously it was trusted to watch over the emperor's most intimate moments, and which still contains men of your own tribe, men the Batavi have accepted into their homes without a moment's hesitation. And when you've killed all three of us, men who will be sorely missed by our tribe, you're hoping that you'll be able to keep such a foul act of fratricide secret?'

His voice rose, pitched to indicate his incredulity.

'Do you *really* believe that not one of you is going to spill this dirty little story across a beer-stained table when he's in his cups? A tale that will be heard both by men who will delight in the tale, and at the same time by others whose faces will harden in disgust at the confirmation of something they already knew but could not prove until that moment.'

'And how will they know of it, if nobody here is stupid enough to open his mouth and betray his brothers?'

The voice belonged to a man in the Tungrian second rank.

'No denial then? No protestation that German brother could never turn on German brother? This really is a sad day . . .' Kivilaz shook his head, staring across the line of faces. 'A sad day for you, no less than for the Batavi people. When you kill me, you will at least grant me peace from the constant persecutions of the Romans, whereas *you* will spend the rest of your lives as hunted men, your century known to and hated by every man of my tribe. Each of you will spend a lifetime looking over his shoulder, waiting for the revenge of the Batavi to find you and leave you bleeding to death in the darkness, never to see your loved ones again. And you will be hated by your own no less than by the Batavi, because whenever your *two* cohorts and my tribe's *eight* cohorts camp together, you can be assured that my people will seek you out with only one thought, to avenge the wrong that you are about to do. And remember, brothers, that while the Romans conduct their murders in a civilised manner for the most part, with a man being allowed the chance to deny the charge put before him unless of course, like my brother, he is still peregrinus and therefore, like most of us here, not allowed such a luxury, the revenge of the Batavi will be taken with naked steel, and in dark places. How many of you will die in such a manner, and how many who were not here today, until your own brothers spit on you and disown you for the misery you have heaped upon them?'

The same man in the second rank shook his head in disbelief.

'That's balls! How will they know it was us?'

Kivilaz grinned, knowing that his argument was gaining ground from the looks of uncertainty on the soldiers' faces.

'How will they know?' He shook his head in apparent sadness.

'Gods below us, but there's the voice of a simple man! They will know, brother, because you are the only soldiers to have marched north from the Old Camp today. I asked the gate guards as we were leaving the fortress, and they told me, with a smirk and knowing wink to each other, that there were no other units on the road north other than a century of what they called Tungrians. So the only suspects will be the Tungri, and the matter of bribery will be quietly forgotten so that my death can be presented as a tribal matter, rather than the infamy it really is. It seems the men who really rule the Old Camp have made sure that there are no witnesses to this act of fratricide by cancelling the usual patrols, which means that they'll have disrupted their predictable routine and drawn the attention of every man in the Old Camp to your role in their design. The word will already have gone round that you're to do the deed that their very own emperor has forbidden his centurions, and put the prince of the Batavi in the dirt. Which means that by this time next week every man in my tribe's lands, and yours, will know that you . . .' he pointed at the man who had been so scornful a moment before, 'that *you* took part in the murder of a man whom Roman justice could not convict, and chose to betray your brothers-in-arms for the sake of . . . well, I wonder what? What have you promised these men, Centurion, that was enough to make them accept a lifetime of fear? It must have been something enticing! A gold coin apiece? A handful of silvers? Or was it just a few beers and your eternal favour? Whatever it was, I doubt it'll be enough.'

He met the officer's hard stare.

'Best you get it done, I'd say, and get on with the rest of your short, interesting lives.'

The other man nodded, putting the hand back on the hilt of his gladius and tensing to draw the blade.

'Wait!'

The officer turned, scanning the ranks behind him with fury, and for a moment his neck was lethally exposed to a swift dagger thrust. Kivilaz looked at it for a moment and then raised his hand from the handle of his pugio.

'I couldn't live with myself, if I were to strike a man whose guard was down.'

The centurion turned back to him, drawing the sword with a swift rasp of iron and raising the weapon's point towards Kivilaz's throat, the muscles of his arm tensing, and Kivilaz nodded his readiness for the death stroke. Beside him Draco's fingers tightened on the handle of his staff, but before he could act the Tungrian officer's eyes jerked wide open and he staggered forward a pace, almost falling. Turning his head slowly, he looked down at the handle of the foot-long dagger blade protruding from his right side, where the leather shirt to which his scale armour was attached was bound together with leather thongs that allowed him to remove it, leaving a gap in the protection it afforded him. Lifting his gaze he stared, aghast, at the man whose pugio had been thrust through the opening, as he wrenched the weapon free in a gush of blood.

'You . . . *fucking* . . .'

He pitched forward, his last conscious act an attempt to put the gladius into his intended victim, but Kivilaz had already stepped inside the sword's reach and caught him as he fell, lowering the dying man to the road's cobbled surface with a tenderness which belied the murderous intent that had confronted him only a moment before. Looking up at the line of soldiers before him he shook his head with what appeared to be genuine sympathy as the soldier with the bloodied dagger in his hand looked down pitilessly at his centurion. Rising to his full height Kivilaz nodded slowly, turning a slow circle to look at the soldiers gathered around him before speaking.

'A hard choice, and one you should not have had to make. Part of me is grateful that you chose to avoid the perpetual civil war between our peoples that would have resulted, had he followed through with his threat . . . and part of me mourns that a member of our brotherhood would choose to ally himself with men so hostile to our tribes. But I tell you this . . .' He pulled out his own dagger and drew the blade across his palm, opening a shallow but bloody cut. He then put the hand to the dying centurion's side and raised it to show them all, red with the stricken officer's blood while the centurion stared up at him with eyes almost sightless, his mouth opening and closed with the effort of breathing. 'I make this man my brother in blood. *Another* victim of Rome's duplicity! *Another* brother taken from me by their centurions' incessant efforts to see me dead! And I swear vengeance on those men, for my brother Paulus, and for this my new brother, in front of you all! The day will come when we will have our chance to exact that revenge on them, repayment for driving us to this, and when that day comes I will call upon the Tungri to exact that revenge alongside the Batavi! He will be avenged!'

They stared at him in silence, some still doubtless pondering the gold in the dying man's purse, and he pressed the bloody hand onto the front of his tunic to leave a splayed, bloody print.

'This is my promise to you! On the day that our vengeance on this cabal of murderers is at hand, I will appear to you once more, and I will be wearing this garment as a mark of this moment, to remind us all of the desperate things their malign influence has driven us to carry out. He will be avenged!'

This time they cheered, not all of them, but enough for the moment of danger to pass, and, pulling the sword from the centurion's scabbard with the bloodied hand, he raised it to point at the sky.

'*I swear it! In the name of Hercules Magusanus, he will be avenged!*'

This time the cheer was louder, as the thought of vengeance gathered weight, and he bellowed a fresh challenge at them.

'*Who will avenge him? The Batavi and the Tungri! We will avenge him!*'

Another, even louder cheer.

'*Who will avenge him?*'

They bellowed the response, fists clenched with anger.

'*We will avenge him!*'

'*Who will avenge him!?*'

'*WE WILL AVENGE HIM!*'

Hramn moved to stand beside him, looking round the circle of cheering soldiers with a look that combined relief and disbelief.

'If you fell into a lake of shit, I swear you'd climb out of it smelling of myrrh.'

Kivilaz looked at him levelly, sober despite the intoxicating energy of the moment.

'It's been said before, Decurion. And it's all a question of giving the men you're trying to convince what it is they want the most. Which in this case is a release from the guilt of killing their officer to save their own skins. It seems like a fair trade.'

He lifted the sword again.

'*Who will avenge him!?*'

6

The Old Camp, Germania Inferior, February AD 69

'Gods below, Gaius, but even by the standards we're got used to, this is a desperate crop of recruits.'

Marius's comrade affected to take a long hard look at the untidy century-sized formations of men that were being chivvied onto the parade ground by half a dozen centurions who already looked like they were at their wits' end keeping their charges in some semblance of a formation and moving in the right direction.

'I'd like to say I've seen worse. I'd really like to be able to say that.'

The senior centurion nodded grimly, taking a deep breath.

'Exactly. Decimus told me that he wanted at least two cohorts to replace the men he expects to lose in battle, and here we are with barely five hundred men where a thousand were the minimum he wanted.'

Gaius shrugged.

'If you'd seen the local reaction when we marched into the tribal villages you'd be surprised we managed to get this many. The Ubii were having nothing to do with it for the most part and the Batavi just laughed at us, still pissed off at the way their men in the German Bodyguard were dismissed, and the other tribes weren't much friendlier, not on either side of the river. What we have here is the arse end of what might have been available, men who were desperate, or starving, or just too stupid to know that this really isn't a good time to be joining up. After all, what good is the promise of citizenship twenty years from now if you're likely to be sent south to die in a place you've never even heard of, for a man you couldn't give a shit for?'

'So this is likely to be all we can find?'

'Truthfully? Unless we stop looking for volunteers and start demanding conscripts, yes. So I'd better go and give them the welcoming speech before we take them for their first walk in the countryside. Shit followed by honey, right?'

Marius nodded solemnly.

'Shit followed by honey.'

His deputy walked out in front of the newly equipped recruits, some of whom were still squaring their shoulders and trying to get used to the weight and awkward feeling of their new armour, hands grasping unfamiliar practice spears or touching the wooden swords tucked into their leather belts when they thought nobody was looking. Gaius stepped up alongside him, drawing breath and shouting over the buzz of conversation in German, his rough-edged roar cutting through their musings like a gladius through rotting meat.

'*Silence!*'

The hubbub died away to almost nothing, but a man in the front row made the mistake of muttering an inaudible comment to his neighbour, flinching as he realised that his new senior centurion was upon him, wielding his vine stick with real vigour to deliver a stinging blow to the miscreant's thigh.

'I said *SILENCE! And that means you, Goat Face!*' Spittle flew from his lips with the violence of his shout. 'The next man to open his mouth without being invited to speak can provide an example for the rest of you cunts as to what this . . .' he held out a hand to one of the other officers, who placed the handle of a short, thick leather whip onto his outstretched palm, '. . . feels like when it's delivering half a dozen swift blows to a man's bare back!'

He stared at the utterly silent ranks before him for a moment before speaking again.

'Good! None of you is rash enough to test me, which spares me a few moments of my life I'll never get back spent thrashing the hide off you, and spares one of you having your back opened up in six places! Because this nasty little fucker . . .' he raised the whip, '. . . will leave you marked for the rest of your days! But this is reserved for men we think might still make the grade, and earn the right to be considered as soldiers! Whereas for those of you who manage to fuck up badly enough, there's *this* . . .' He handed the whip back to his brother officer and accepted another instrument of punishment in return, shaking out its three tails for the recruits to see clearly, each of the heavy leather thongs studded with pieces of bronze, flailing it through the air inches from the soldier he'd reprimanded a moment before. 'This is the scourge, Goat Face, and this isn't designed to give you a gentle warning, or to leave you with a little reminder of what happens when you make me or any of my centurions unhappy. This little beauty is designed to take the flesh off a man's back, quickly, efficiently, but in no way quietly!'

He dangled the scourge in front of the hapless soldier for a moment, then walked along the front rank of recruits, holding it so that the men behind them would get a good look at it. The recruit he'd christened with a nickname that Marius suspected would stay with him for the rest of his military career looked close to either fainting or vomiting, his admittedly somewhat caprine features covered in sweat as he sucked in a long shaky breath, stiffening as Gaius walked back towards him.

'This is what we use when one of you – and trust me there will be at least one of you – makes such a big mistake that we want nothing more to do with him! Because all of you, at some point in the next few weeks, and you especially Goat Face, now that I'm looking out for you, are going to wish you'd never joined! And while it's too late to just walk away, because once my legion owns a man, even an ugly bastard like you, he stays owned for the rest of the twenty years he promised it, fucking up so badly that you get thrown out on your ear is going to look very, very good to you. Every last one of you is going to think about it, once we get to work on turning you from the dick-stroking ration thieves you are now into proper soldiers! So that. . .' he pointed to the whip being held up by his colleague, '. . . is for those little mistakes we'd rather you didn't make again! Three strokes for an accidental injury to one of your mates. Five strokes for getting caught with a woman in camp. Going over the wall for some unauthorised beer or cunt? That's dangerously close to deserting – so that's usually ten strokes for you and three apiece for your tent mates who, after all, allowed you to do it! We don't get many of those, but there's always someone stupid enough not to take me seriously when I say that we will lash you at the first opportunity, and we will double those penalties if you show the slightest sign of not simply taking your stripes and getting on with it! Or . . .' he cracked a hard grin at the sweating soldier, '. . . if I simply take a dislike to you! And be warned, dislike is my usual starting point with you animals, since none of you have as yet done a single thing to make me view you as anything other than useless cunts not fit to wax my boots!

'Whereas this . . .' he raised the scourge again. 'This, for those of you who *will* prove their determination to enjoy the experience at close quarters, is what we use when a man genuinely has no redeeming features, and no place in my legion! If I or any other of these officers charged with the thankless task of turning you into soldiers think you're not worth persevering with, then there's only one sentence! Thirty lashes with this little beauty, each blow stripping away the flesh from your back and ribs, and from your legs if I'm in the mood, until the blood runs down your legs like piss! I've seen men, the real hard cases, take a dozen with the whip and not make a sound! Grinning hard at the lashes, determined not to give us any sign of pain, not even a murmur! And I've seen the same men screaming and begging for mercy after their first two or three strokes with the scourge!'

He looked up and down the ranks before him, grinning again at the sudden solemnity that he saw on every man's face.

'Except there is no mercy! Because by the time you're bent double over the whipping post, we're not teaching you a lesson, or punishing you for the stupidity of a tent mate! No, when the scourge comes out all we're doing is ruining you, making your back a mess of scars and sending you away with a permanent reminder of just how big a mistake you made in pissing off your centurion so badly that we decided to stop trying to make you fit to serve! At least one of you, I guarantee, is going to make that mistake, and when you do, this *will* be waiting!'

He swung the scourge through the air before him, watching the closest soldiers' faces whiten at the thrumming note of the lashes.

'Oh, and desertion? That's simple, in case you were wondering! The sentence for desertion is death, immediate and without any right of appeal!'

He handed the whips back to his fellow officer and turned to his superior with a crisp salute.

'First Spear?'

'Thank you, Centurion.' Marius turned to face the sombre recruits. 'On the positive side, if you keep your nose clean, learn to soldier quickly and without making a mess of it, then you'll soon be members of a legion century entrusted with the defence of the empire's borders, well paid, fed three times a day and with the promise of citizenship at the end of your service, and citizenship for your children too! If you want to get a leg up the ladder of life, you've come to the right place!'

Shit followed by honey, that was the usual order of the day with new recruits. Scare them half to death with a centurion who was clearly deranged, then show them the way to avoid his clutches by explaining in reasonable terms what they would have to do to become soldiers.

'Over the next two months we're going to take you, and change you! We'll give you stamina, make you stronger, faster, train you with your weapons and teach you how to avoid getting wounded or killed by men with weapons just like them! You'll learn to ignore the weather, how to carry your pack and shield, how to dig out a marching camp, and a hundred other things that you'll need to know if you're going to serve in our army! You will learn to march, first twenty miles in five hours, and then forty miles in twelve hours, and once you can do that we'll go back to twenty miles a day but in your campaign kit, with a full pack and shield! You will practise every day twice a day with your wooden sword and shield which, as you may already have guessed, are a good deal heavier than the real thing! We give you wooden equipment for three reasons, firstly to avoid you killing each other in training, secondly because you will train in all weathers, in heavy rain or burning sun, and we don't want your kit getting needlessly rusty, and thirdly because when you get your hands on the real thing it'll feel so much lighter and easier to wield that you'll be thanking us for making you use wood for so long! You will learn how to throw a spear, and how to defend yourself against a thrown spear. You will learn how to kill an enemy with your sword quickly and efficiently, and you will practise with that sword so often that the strokes will become second nature. We will make you nimble, able to leap onto a vaulting horse with your sword drawn without either falling off the other side or stabbing yourself to death, and happy to climb a siege ladder while unpleasant men throw rocks and spears at you. Last of all, and the most fun of all – for your instructors, that is – you will learn the various formations and manoeuvres that we use to attack and defend in battle, first here, on the parade ground and then later out in the country, going forward, going backwards, going sideways, and through all this you will only ever have one objective, *if* you know what's good for you . . .'

He paused, smiling as the recruits leaned forward to hear his next words. Gaius handed him the whip, and he raised it above his head to reinforce the point.

'Your only concern will be not to be the slowest man to carry out your instructor's orders. Because the slowest man in the century will inevitably at some point become the man with the warmest back. Don't say I didn't warn you!'

He took his friend's salute and gestured for him to carry on, smiling to himself as he walked away, as a fresh tirade of abuse was unleashed on the hapless recruits. Shit, followed by honey, followed by a mountain of fresh shit. Seeing Legatus Lupercus waiting for him he cursed under his breath, adjusting his path to approach his commander and stamping to attention as he saluted the Roman.

'Legatus sir! The new recruits have commenced their training!'

'So I see. I presume that the air will be filled with the sound of swearing and casual violence for the next few weeks?'

The question was asked with a smile, and not for the first time Marius found himself warming to the man.

'Indeed it will, sir. They're no use to us until they can be divided up among our cohorts, and for that to happen they must at least be half-trained.'

'Indeed.' Lupercus looked at the recruits, still being lambasted by Gaius, then shifted his gaze to search the remainder of the parade ground. 'But surely that can't be all of them, First Spear? They can barely muster a cohort . . .'

Marius nodded.

'I'm afraid it is, Legatus. It seems that the local tribes have done much as we predicted, and held their young men back from joining up. It seems they fear that the remainder of the legions on the frontier will soon be dragged into the war against the pretender Otho.'

Lupercus nodded with his lips pursed.

'And who, strictly between you and I, First Spear, is to say that they're incorrect in that belief? The latest news from the south is that the legions on the Danube have declared for him, which means that our men marching over the Alps will find themselves opposed by not only the forces that he can muster from Italy but also several crack legions who will all too soon appear in their rear and threaten to cut off their line of retreat. Under those circumstances I would expect our new emperor to be away south with whatever force he can muster from Britannia, when the legion vexillations arrive from over the water, and whatever further men he believes it safe to remove from the garrisons along the river. And, worse than that, I've been warned by his army commander for Germania that we should be ready to host a visit in early March. Vitellius wishes to see the progress we've made in readying our new recruits for war.'

Marius stared at his superior in consternation.

'Their readiness for *war* . . . ?' He shook his head, barely able to believe what he was hearing. 'Legatus, they won't be ready for war in March. They won't even be ready to march a standard campaign distance with kit by then, never mind go to war.'

Lupercus nodded.

'I know. After close to thirty years' service to the empire I have a fairly shrewd idea of what it takes to produce a trained legionary who can be put into battle with some hope of success. But if our emperor decides that they're ready, then they'll just have to be ready, won't they?'

He raised a questioning eyebrow at Marius, who nodded reluctantly, clapping a hand on the big man's shoulder.

'I know. You will do what is ordered and at every command you will be ready. Carry on, First Spear.'

Northern Italy, March AD 69

'That water's going to be colder than the Rhenus in February.'

Banon nodded sleepily at Alcaeus's muttered opinion, watching the Po's dark water streaming past the riverbank by which they were squatting in front of the Second Century through half-closed eyes. The river had been swollen by snowmelt from the high mountain valleys of the Alps over which they had advanced into Italy only days before, and the water's fast-moving surface resembled a sheet of polished iron, such was the speed of its flow. The centurion looked across the river at the dark landscape beyond, straining his eyes for any sign that their enemy might be to hand, musing quietly on the task before them.

'We'll be awake by the time we reach the other side, and that's a fact. Let's hope that anyone keeping watch on the other side is still sleeping while we're staggering up the far bank blue with the cold.'

Scar had issued his orders as the sun had been setting the

previous evening, before sending the cohorts forward the last mile or so to the river's northern bank.

'Make your approaches to the river slow and quiet, with no shouting, cursing or loud farting to let anyone on the southern side know we're coming. If there are men watching the river they'll probably pull back to their camps overnight since it's still cold enough to freeze a bull's balls off once the sun's down, but let's not risk having their sentries getting curious as to what all the noise is. Each cohort has its own crossing point, which the scouts will lead you to, and when you reach the river get your men bedded down for the night and tell them to keep it quiet. I'll be wandering about and if I hear any of your men before I'm challenged there'll be unhappiness.'

He looked around at his officers.

'Our orders are for this to be a limited incursion into enemy territory. We get across, we cause as much damage as possible, and then we get back onto this side of the river. The aim is to put them off balance, get them wondering where we might pop up next, make them spread their forces out and open themselves up for attack. So once we're on the other side I want the cohorts scouting forward in force. Any enemy soldiers you bump into are to be captured if possible and killed if not, but under no circumstances are they to be allowed to get away and raise the alarm. Small enemy formations, if we encounter any, are to be overrun with speed and aggression. Anything up to a cohort is fair game, given our strength, so blow your horns and pile in, knowing that the cohorts on either side of you will be on them like hunting dogs soon enough.'

'What if we find a legion over there?'

The prefect had grinned hungrily at the question.

'That all depends on the legion we meet, I'd say. You cohort commanders will earn your corn if that happens, because you'll have to make a decision based on what you see. There are some legions on the other side which could be hard to handle – after all, our old friends of the "Fighting Fourteenth" are out there somewhere. If we run into them it could all get very warm very quickly.'

Alcaeus nudged the dozing Banon who, like many of the men of the Second Century, was sufficiently experienced to have fallen into a fitful sleep once the advance to the Po's northern bank was complete, untroubled by either the quiet grumbling of those soldiers unable to sleep or the contented chewing and snorting of horses being kept quiet by oat-filled nose bags.

'Did I tell you that Scar told us that if we find a legion on the far side we'll make the decision whether to fight or run once we can see who it is we're facing?'

Banon rubbed his face, momentarily groggy from the brief sleep.

'Scar could no more pull out of a straight fight with a legion – any legion, not just the soft touches – than young Egilhard over there will be capable of pulling his prick out the first time he gets it wet.'

Alcaeus smiled, leaning back and listening to the quiet voices of those of his soldiers who had been unable to sleep for the anticipation of the day to come, grinning at Grimmaz's muttered grumbling at anyone in his tent party who was listening.

'At last, the chance for some real soldiering. I've had a gut full of marching and scaring the shit out of civilians for no good reason. Once we're across this river we can get back to some real soldiering instead of having to watch the fucking Romans behaving like animals.'

He had a point, the centurion mused. The army's march from Civitas Lingonum, through the foothills of Helvetia and over the Alps, had been eventful, with the legionaries of the infamous Twenty-First Rapax picking one-sided fights with more than one of the tribes on their route, initially taking the chance to settle old scores and then, finding this dubious revenge to their taste, concocting new quarrels as the pretext for their brutality. The Batavi had watched in amazed disgust as city after city, terrified by the well-founded rumours that preceded the army's arrival, had opened their gates to Caecina's advancing army and offered up their wealth and, on occasion, even the honour of their women, as a means of appeasing soldiers who had swiftly become notorious for their barely provoked sack of the Helvetian countryside. Looting, rape and enslavement had all been inflicted wholesale on people who were supposed to be part of the empire.

Another voice reached Alcaeus's ears, that of the young recruit Egilhard.

'We're really going to swim *that*?'

The centurion smiled at the note of incredulity in the younger man's voice at the prospect of plunging into the Po's dark water, still barely visible in the dawn's first vague light, remembering the first time he had come face-to-face with the prospect of imminent combat after an exhausting swim.

'Of course.'

The throwaway tone in which Grimmaz answered his question clearly only served to increase the young soldier's sense of disbelief.

'Really? In armour?'

Alcaeus heard the rustle of mail as the leading man turned to face the newest of his tent mates, his amusement evident and his fatigue instantly forgotten.

'*Really*. In armour. You've run through the drills often enough, so you know what to do well enough.'

'But . . . what happens if I lose hold of the saddle halfway across the river?'

The older man chuckled softly.

'You drown. We all mourn your sad loss.' The men around them chuckled quietly, and in the half-light Alcaeus saw Grimmaz put a theatrical knuckle to his eye. 'Boohoo. Then we get on with killing anyone on the other side who thought they'd have nothing more difficult to do today than watch the river for any attempts at bridge building.'

He leaned closer and lowered his voice conspiratorially.

'Look, there is a secret to it, which we don't normally share with the new boys, to see if they can work it out for themselves. Since I can see you don't especially like the idea I can see that I'm going to have to let you in on it.'

Egilhard waited expectantly, and after a moment Grimmaz continued.

'The thing is, this whole swimming rivers thing is a bit overdone if you ask me. Sure, you get wet through, and it is genuinely useful if you can swim. You can swim, right?'

The younger man rolled his eyes, sufficiently confident of his place in the tent party to express his frustrations in a way he had learned from experience would be acceptable to the rough edged leading man, who expected a degree of give and take in his nevertheless firm control of the six other man who were his responsibility.

'You know I can swim. It's one of the recruitment tests.'

'Silly me, so it is. Anyway, there's a secret method to it that you either just master immediately or you never quite get the hang of. Come on, I'll show you. See this?'

He gestured to the horse waiting stolidly beside them, chewing happily on the contents of its feed bag, and Alcaeus guessed that he was pointing at the padded leather handle that had been stitched onto the beast's saddle.

'You're already familiar with this, but just to be sure let's go through it one more time. There's one on the other side just like it, for the other man who'll be swimming with the beast, which in this case is me, which is why you're on this side. I hate swimming with my spear and shield in my right hand, it just feels wrong. Anyway, this is your best friend in all the world my lad, a few inches of cowhide stuffed with horsehair and stitched on nice and strong, strong enough that a man can hang from it without the whole thing just tearing off. Take hold of it.'

Egilhard stepped closer to the beast, taking hold of the handle.

'Tighter. Squeeze it until your knuckles go white.'

Egilhard's scepticism was evident in his voice.

'And that's the secret? Holding onto the handle? That's it?'

Grimmaz milked the moment for all it was worth, knowing that their tent mates were listening to every word and waiting for the punch line.

'No lad, that's not it at all. Any fool can grab a handle and get towed across a river. No, the secret, the absolute essential if it isn't all to end in tears, ours, obviously since you'll already be dead, is this . . .' He leaned closer to Egilhard and lowered his voice almost to the point of inaudibility, his mates smirking and nudging each other at the old joke's inevitable pay-off. '*The secret is this.*' His voice was a whisper, as if the secret to life itself was about to be imparted. '*Whatever you do, no matter what urge comes over you . . . Just . . . don't . . . let . . . go.*'

Egilhard turned away in disgust while the men around them dissolved into stifled mirth. After a moment he shook his head wryly, seeing the funny side of the joke, and while he was still looking around in bemusement, Alcaeus stood up, the moonlight reflecting from his wolf's head and giving him an otherworldly appearance, a chimera of beast and man ready to bark at the moon or tear a man's throat out.

'We'll be crossing shortly, the light's just about good enough, so get ready. We're going across silently, or at least as quietly as two thousand men and six hundred horses can manage, just in case there's anyone on the other side we'd rather not have to meet on the far bank, which means no trumpets and no shouting either. Once we're on the far side our orders are for the leading centuries to scout forward in strength and overwhelm any light forces they might have out looking for us, not that they'll be expecting us on their side of the river this soon. And that means us, so once we're out of the water get formed up and be ready to move out.'

He looked at Egilhard appraisingly.

'Have they just done the old "don't let go" on you?'

The young soldier nodded.

'Fair play to your dad then, if he didn't warn you about that one. After all, where's the fun if you know all the answers, eh? Mind you . . .'

He put an arm around Egilhard's shoulders and lowered his voice in a conspiratorial tone.

'It's not entirely bad advice. I know men who are tempted to release their grip on the saddle every time they swim. Just imagine, a simple opening of your hand, a moment's struggle as the weight of your armour takes you under, and there you are with your ancestors. No pain, no blood, no long drawn-out agony from a death wound. I've even wondered about it myself, once or twice . . .'

He turned away from the young soldier and winked at his tent mates, who to a man lost themselves to the coffin humour of the moment, trying in vain to silence their mirth. Hearing them, Egilhard turned back with a retort on his lips only to be overridden by Scar's voice as the first touch of dawn light illuminated the eastern horizon.

'There's the sunrise! First cohort, on the move!'

The Po's water was bitterly cold, the river fed by snow melt from the mountains to the north, and after the first shock of immersing his body in the river's flow, the centurion could do no more than kick his legs and cling onto the horse's saddle and his equipment with a grim determination that made Banon, who was swimming on the beast's other side, grin even wider than before despite the icy water's effects, both men panting with the shock of the river's fierce grip on their bodies.

'Not long now . . . Then we get a . . . nice long run . . . to warm us up.'

The century staggered up the river's far bank like old men forced to rise from their death beds, the bitterly cold water sluicing from their sodden clothing and equipment, centurions and their deputies calling softly but urgently for them to move forward and make room for the next men crossing. Alcaeus hefted his shield and shook the water out of his boots, stepping forward and looking to either side at the ground before them.

'Form a line and follow me!'

Leading his century away from the water he pushed through a hedge and into a field of vines trained up wooden posts.

'Look alive! Spears and shields, ready to fight! And try not to do too much damage, this is some poor bastard's livelihood!'

Feeling the water's biting chill receding as his body heat started to permeate his tunic's sodden wool, he led his men forward up a gentle slope through the vines while the cavalry troop formed up behind them, readying themselves to ride deeper into enemy-held territory in the hope of neutralising any Othonian reconnaissance.

Cresting the shallow hill's ridge Alcaeus sniffed the air and pointed south, at a dimly visible farmhouse, half hidden behind a copse of trees two hundred paces from them, putting a finger to his lips and gesturing for his tent parties' leading men to gather round him.

'I smell wood smoke. You . . .' He pointed a soldier. 'Go back to the river, find Scar and tell him that we might be just about to contact the enemy, strength not yet known. The rest of you tell your boys to shut their mouths, and let's go for a quiet look.'

They moved forward through the vines towards the farm as swiftly and as quietly as they could, keeping low to avoid the dawn light casting their long shadows across the landscape, crossing the distance to the house in silence with only the harsh rasping of their breathing and the metallic rustle of their mail disturbing a silence that, as the riverbank's flurry of activity grew more distant, grew deeper and more profound. The smell of burning wood had strengthened, along with the tang of roasting meat. The centurion stopped and sank onto one knee, gesturing for them to gather round him.

'It's probably nothing more exciting than some old fart grilling sausage and bread for his breakfast, but just in case it isn't we're going in hard, spears ready and eyes open, right? And remember . . .' he looked around them, his eyes lingering on Egilhard, 'a girl with a kitchen knife can kill you just as dead as if an enemy legionary walked you onto his blade, if you let her get close enough. No mistakes. Stay quiet until you hear me, then you can be as noisy as you like.'

The farmhouse was deserted, windows and doors wide open, and the wreckage of the farmer's furniture and possessions strewn around the yard. The corpses of half a dozen men lay where they had been killed, one elderly, one middle-aged and four younger men between their early teens and mid-twenties, all with their throats cut.

'That's the mark of Otho's men alright. The women will be wishing they were dead too, I'd imagine.'

Rumours had already reached Caecina's army, whose own behaviour since entering Italy had been scrupulously fair, in stark contrast to what had gone before, that the enemy were waging the war as if against another nation rather than their own people, with all the looting and rape that such an attitude customarily entailed. Alcaeus looked around him with a suspicious frown, sniffing the air again before turning back to Banon and Hludovig, pointing at the latter.

'I reckon there's a good few of them on the other side of the building. Go back and tell the Prefect we need more men here, just in case we end up thigh-deep in the shit. And if he asks you how many men we need, just tell him everyone. That ought to get his attention.'

The watch officer nodded and was gone, leaving the soldiers looking at each other. Alcaeus laughed softly at their expressions.

'What's the matter? Were you expecting to live for ever?' His face hardened. 'With me.'

As the century advanced round the farmhouse, the sound of popping, crackling wood intensified, and for the first time they heard the sound of voices. Without warning a man came round the building's corner dressed in a blue military tunic and belt with a dagger on his hip, his feet shod in caligae, carrying a water skin and presumably heading for the river. He looked up and saw the Batavi soldiers coming out of the dawn's long shadows, and seemed momentarily rooted to the spot as his mouth gaped in surprise. As he drew breath to shout a warning Alcaeus was already in motion, taking a swift, grunting step forward and throwing his spear, the weapon spitting the hapless enemy soldier, then drawing his sword and waving his men forward past the dying man's writhing body. Bursting round the farm's side and into full view of the enemy encampment they froze momentarily, staring in amazement at the neatly ordered lines of tents that were laid out before them. A group of a dozen or so soldiers were walking towards them, deep in conversation, each man carrying a water skin and clearly intent on their discussion rather than having any expectation that they might be under attack. Behind them camp fires were burning, more tunic-clad soldiers busying themselves over cooking equipment while others stood around waiting for the food to be served, and the Batavi soldiers stood and stared incredulously at the scene.

'It's a fucking cohort!'

Alcaeus pointed at the ground before them, knowing that he had a precious moment in which to act while the enemy were caught so badly off balance.

'By twos! *Form! Line!*'

At his bellowed command every head in the enemy camp swung to stare at them, in a moment of dawning realisation that would have been hilarious under different circumstances. Then, while the century hurried to form a line two-men deep, chaos descended upon the neatly ordered scene before them, as men dropped whatever it was that they were doing and ran for their weapons, in a sudden cacophony of panicked shouts and roared orders that seemed to be utterly unheeded in each individual's need to seek the security of his own spear and shield.

'*Forward!*'

The century went forward at a slow, deliberate pace with their spears held ready and shields raised, advancing into the camp's confusion as individual unarmoured enemy soldiers came at them with whatever implements they had to hand and died, swiftly and uselessly. One of them ran at the line with a spade he had snatched up from beside his tent, only to have his desperate hacking stroke parried, and a pair of long spear blades stabbed deep into his body. He stood for a moment, almost hanging from the spears and staring helplessly straight at Egilhard, then crumpled as Andronicus and Levonhard tore their weapons free, falling to the trampled grass to stare lifelessly at the sky. As the number of blue-tunicked men facing the line increased, a dozen of them came at the line in a group, but while their attack halted the century's progress and even pushed the line back several paces by sheer determination, their unarmoured bodies were defenceless against their attackers' spears, and as they fell with savage rents torn in their bodies by the long blades, more of the men waiting behind them started backing away from the oncoming warriors. An older man pushed his way out of the throng of men, hastily armed but without either armour or a helmet, shouting at the men around him to rally to him. Alcaeus, recognising him for an officer by the thin purple line on his tunic, roared a single word at him.

'*Surrender!*'

The officer strode forward at the centurion's shout, pointing his sword at Alcaeus and snarling defiance back at them.

'To so few of you? Never!' He looked back at the men gathered behind him. 'We must overwhelm them! *With me!*'

More of his men who had managed to get themselves equipped were pushing their way through the crowd of soldiers, and with a sweep of his sword the bareheaded officer led them forward in menacing silence, making himself the head of the spear and pacing purposefully toward Alcaeus with his men on either side. They collided with the waiting Batavi in a clatter of shields, bursting through the line by sheer weight of numbers and plunging both sides into a confused melee. Going shield to shield with the enemy officer, Alcaeus stepped into the challenge, meeting his assailant's shield punch with one of his own that jarred both men's hands, but where the prefect stamped forward again, attempting to bull the centurion off his ground and onto the defensive, Alcaeus stepped quickly back and around to his left, allowing the power behind the unopposed lunge to put the other man off his balance. As the older man staggered forward, taken unawares by the move's simplicity, the centurion put out a booted foot and tripped him, then stepped forward and put the point of his sword to the prefect's throat as he sprawled onto the trampled grass.

'*Surrender!*'

The fallen officer snarled defiance back up at him, tensing his sword arm to hack at the centurion's legs.

'Fuck y—'

Alcaeus's lunge was pure reflex, pushing his sword's point down through the defiant prefect's throat in a bubbling gush of blood, then tore it free and hacked down with the blade to separate the dying man's head from his neck. Grabbing a spear from one of his men he stabbed its long blade deep into the severed head's bloody neck and then lifted it over his own head with a bellowed challenge.

'*Batavi!*'

The marines fighting around him, their gazes drawn to the spectacle by his furious roar, blanched as they realised what it was that he was holding aloft, staring in horror at their prefect's slack-jawed face, and even as the fight went out of them a tide of fresh men rounded the farmhouse behind the century and charged into the fight, while to either side horsemen were advancing around the embattled enemy's flanks, chasing down those men who had chosen to run rather than fight. A helmeted marine centurion stepped out of the mass of men that remained unengaged, looking about him with disgust as he threw down his sword and shouted for his men to stop fighting as the ring of spears tightened around them.

'Gods below, Alcaeus, but you'd give Kivilaz a run for his money if there was a competition for the bloodiest handed man in the tribe.'

Scar had pushed his way through the Batavi soldiers and clapped a hand on the gore-spattered centurion's shoulder.

'I'll take over now. See to your casualties and get your prisoners squared away.'

Alcaeus nodded gratefully at his superior, who had run from the riverbank, he discovered later, at the head of half a dozen centuries of men upon receiving the request for urgent reinforcement. Turning to his men he found Banon holding a terrified marine by the collar of his armour with his sword raised threateningly.

'It's too late to kill him now, they've given up.'

The disgusted chosen man kicked the legs out from under the man and then punched him hard in the side of his helmetless head, leaving him dazed and unable to resist.

'We're taking prisoners? How will we get them back over the river?'

Scar answered for Alcaeus.

'We are this time. Caecina wants the message to get back to the enemy generals that nowhere is safe from us, and leaving a big pile of corpses for them to find won't have quite the same effect as a cohort of disarmed men straggling into camp with their tunics hanging round their ankles. So get them disarmed and gather their weapons and armour, we'll keep the good stuff and put the rest in the river. And cut their belts, they don't deserve them.'

The centurion who had surrendered raised a hand in protest, but the prefect turned a stare on him that was hard enough to lower the hand simply by the force of the Batavi centurion's will.

'Don't try looking to me for sympathy, you fought like women so you'll have to get used to looking like them, until you find someone willing to issue you with fresh equipment. And I'll be expecting you all to pass under a yoke before we let you go, and swear to Mars not to take any further part in this campaign. It's that or we'll hamstring every last one of you. And if you break the oath then Mars's judgement on you will be of a lot less concern to you than mine, because if I ever see you on a battlefield I'll have your balls off before you die. Now drop your gear and get out of my sight.'

Alcaeus mustered his century, finding that the brief action had cost five dead and several others wounded to varying degrees, one of whom was hovering unconscious on the edge of death with a shattered skull inflicted by a vicious spade blow, while another looked unlikely to see the day out, frothing blood leaking from his spear-pierced chest. He knelt over the dying man for a moment, placing a hand on his head and commending his spirit to their god before moving on to the spear wound.

'I told you to keep your shield up, Wisaz.'

The casualty looked up at him, his face pale from blood loss, gasping for breath as he whispered his response.

'Killed two . . . of them . . . Tell my children . . . I died . . . like a man . . . Died cleanly . . . not . . . not . . .' A tear glistened in his eye. 'Not like this.'

Alcaeus nodded mutely.

'Your name will be remembered with pride.' Reaching out he placed the dying man's sword across his body, guiding his shaking hand to the blood-slicked hilt. 'And I'll make sure that Deathbringer will go to your oldest son. Now lie still and save your strength.'

He stood, turning to one of the dying soldier's tent mates.

'He'll fight for a while yet. Keep him comfortable, give him water and call me if he asks for the priest.'

Grimmaz's tent party had come through the fight unscathed, although Lanzo was sitting on the ground with the look of a man not entirely in command of his wits while a bandage carrier wound a strip of linen round his head to hold a thick wad of material cut from a dead marine's blue tunic to his injury. Egilhard was sitting beside him, his thoughts clearly elsewhere, and the centurion called their leading man over, gesturing to the battered soldier.

'What happened to him?'

'His helmet stopped a sword. Saved his life, but left him seeing stars. The bone doctor says there's no break in his skull, but reckons he'll be out of sorts for a day or two, sleepy mostly.'

The man in question raised a hand to stop the medic for a moment, turning away to vomit onto the grass beside him.

'Oh, and apparently it's common for men with a . . . what did he call it?'

Lanzo looked up at him with eyes that fought to focus.

'Concussion.'

'Oh yes. Men with concussion puke a lot, apparently. He's lucky though, he'd have been dead if not for the boy here, it seems. Egilhard killed two of them.'

The soldier shook his head, drawing a curse and a command to keep still from the men tending to his injury.

'Don't know about two, but he saved me alright. Without him I was food for the crows.'

'What happened?'

'I was on my knees and ready for the death stroke, looking up while the bastard who'd just smacked me on the head with his sword lifted it up to finish me off, when the boy here just turned and speared the fucker through his neck like he's been doing it all his life. If he needs a name then you can call him Achilles as far as I'm concerned, I was a dead man without him.'

'Hmmm. And the other one? What happened there?'

'I saw that.'

Alcaeus turned to find Banon beside him, his eyes on the young soldier.

'Go on then.'

'I was keeping an eye on him out of the corner of my eye while I played with that marine, the way you do with the new boys, to take the measure of them. When they rushed us one of them squared up to him, banged shields and stepped forward only to get Egilhard's butt spike through his foot, clean through mind you, boot sole and all, and that must have taken some effort. Then while the poor bastard was busy screaming and working out why his foot was suddenly on fire *Achilles* here stamped down on the foot to pull his spear free, stepped back a pace as cool as you like to get some room and then put the blade into his throat as neatly as a priest sacrificing a bull. In and out like a darning needle, almost too fast to follow, and his man went down with only the whites of his eyes showing. Dead, just like that.'

'And then he killed the man who'd put Lanzo down?'

'Without even pausing for breath, like it was just a dance step he'd done a thousand times before. Look, turn, stab, job done.'

Alcaeus looked down at the young soldier, nodding slowly.

'Well, that's one less thing to worry about.'

His chosen man looked at him questioningly.

'What, whether he can fight?'

The centurion guffawed.

'Oh he can clearly fight! No, I meant the question of what we ought to call him, now he's spilled blood for the tribe. Question asked and answered, I'd say. And you can cut that plait off, young Achilles, the days of you needing to prove yourself a man are now officially in your past!'

The Old Camp, Germania Inferior, March AD 69

'Fifth legion . . .'

Two hundred paces from where Marius stood, an answering command came from from the camp's other legion.

'Fifteenth Legion!'

Both men barked out their next words in perfect synchronisation.

'Atten-*tion*!'

Marius stared out across the ranks of his three cohorts as they obeyed the order, not with the expected crisp snap of thousands of boots hitting the floor at the same moment, but rather a ragged stutter that lasted for most of the time it took him to puff out a depressed gust of air, a final distant crunch of hobnails impacting on crushed rock incensing him beyond tolerance. Some fool had not only been half asleep, but had compounded the error by stamping to attention when all around him had finally fallen silent.

'*Take that man's name!*'

The senior centurion regarded his men bleakly for a moment longer before issuing his next command. Fifteen hundred men of legio Fifth Alaudae were paraded before their emperor: the seventh and ninth cohorts that had been left behind when the remainder of the legion had marched south in search of glory and the imperial throne, and the new cohort that had been allocated the number eleven, constituted in the main from raw recruits who had joined the army not much more than a month before, with a leavening of trained soldiers to show them how they were expected to behave.

'Five hundred men.' He had bemoaned their failure to attract men to the legion's service to Gaius the previous night in the officer's mess over several cups of red, shaking his head at the prospect of the following day's parade of the legion before their emperor. 'Decimus told me to provide him with at least another two cohorts, instead of which I've got half that number, most of them halfwits and men fit for nothing better than picking stones out of the fields and tossing themselves off behind trees when they think nobody's watching. And after tomorrow's shambles of a demonstration of their non-existent prowess I'll have a legatus, an army commander *and* an emperor up my arse. There's a meeting with important people in my very near future, Gaius, and nobody's going to be handing round the glass wine cups this time.'

In the cold light of a late March morning he was, if anything, more depressed than he'd been the previous night, with a sinking sensation in his gut that was only partially the result of having drunk more than was wise for a man whose legion would be on display to an emperor the next day.

'Form ranks for battle!'

He watched with his heart in his mouth as his three cohorts swung through ninety degrees, perhaps the hardest manoeuvre they would undertake that morning as one end of the line stayed motionless while the men at the other were almost running to swing their century through a wide arc to face the Fifteenth's cohorts who were performing the same manoeuvre. Closing his eyes in despair as he watched the more experienced soldiers literally dragging their freshly recruited comrades through the change of orientation. A man in the front rank of the leftmost century managed the seemingly impossible feat of tripping over the rim of his own shield and sprawling headlong to the parade ground's gravelled surface, and in the blink of an eye dozens of men were reeling in chaos as the succeeding ranks quite literally fell over him, in a chain of disaster that left a score of men struggling in a tangled mess of limbs and equipment. The century's centurion who was, Marius noted with a powerless sigh, one of the loudest and most brutal men in his cohort, waded into them with his vine stick thrashing out to left and right to deal out instant retribution, encouraging their efforts to rejoin the moving formation with kicks and punches. If the emperor had by some miracle missed the error and its resulting mayhem, there could be little doubt that he would be observing its aftermath with what Marius expected would be a distinct loss of his sense of humour.

Regaining their feet, the men who had fallen out of their century's formation literally ran to catch up with the cohort's stately progression through the arc that would bring them face-to-face with the Fifteenth, one man in such a panic at his officer's continuous stream of invective and violence that he left both his spears lying where they had fallen and sprinted for the safety of the first formed body of soldiers he saw which, unfortunately for him, happened to be the imperial bodyguard which had been formed from a cohort of the First Germanica as a short term expedient until the praetorian guards were to hand. Determined not to jeopardise their newfound status as by far the most impressive unit on parade, the result of not only their sudden rise to exalted status but also the fact that every other man on display was either apparently clueless or coping with the fact that the man next to him was completely overwhelmed by the novelty of the situation, they followed the simple but effective strategy of completely ignoring the stray, who roamed fruitlessly up and down their line in search of a friendly face.

'Dear gods below . . .'

Ignoring Lupercus's muttered imprecation, Marius watched with what under different circumstances might well have been dark amusement as the errant soldier, realising his error, dithered for a moment before realising that he was at severe risk of being charged with deserting his unit and, knowing only too well that he would at the very least be flogged for the transgression, turned and fled for the safety of his century, now a hundred paces distant. Intercepted by his centurion while still ten paces from safety, he covered the remaining distance under a rain of blows from the incensed officer's vine stick, throwing himself into the safety of the ranks while the centurion continued to stare at him meaningfully, his enmity and eventual further retribution clearly guaranteed.

'It seems that every pigeon will find its home in due course, Munius Lupercus. Even those that have attempted to join another flock!'

Marius waited stolidly for the emperor to follow up the seemingly mild comment with a curter rejoinder, but if Vitellius was angered by the hapless man's display he showed no sign, and as the two grossly understrength legions dressed their ranks facing one another, he turned to the legatus and saluted crisply.

'With your permission, Legatus?'

Lupercus nodded graciously.

'Do please carry on, First Spear. The emperor is keen to see how much training our Germans have managed to absorb in the short time since we recruited them.' He turned back to Vitellius as Marius turned away to march out onto the parade ground. 'You should have seen them on the day that we formed the new cohorts, Caesar. Perfect chaos, not a man with any idea as to what he should be doing, and our few veterans driven to distraction by the need to show them. Compared to that, this is like watching the praetorians changing the guard on the Palatine Hill.'

Both men laughed as Marius stalked away, his ire rising despite the fact that he knew his superior was only attempting to make light of the situation. Halting by the right-hand end of the Fifth's line, he raised a hand to his opposite number, the pre-agreed signal to indicate that his legion would take first turn at mounting an attack on the Fifteenth.

'Fifth Legion . . . are you ready for war?'

'Ready!'

The response, whilst audible, was disappointing to say the least, no better than a half-hearted rumble of voices rather than the stirring response that was supposed to answer his challenge. Looking up and down the line at his centurions, many of them newly promoted from the ranks of optios, he raised both his vine stick and his voice to redouble the call to action.

'*Are you ready for war?*'

'*Ready!*'

With their officers shouting threats and encouragement, the skeleton legion did better the second time, sounding more like soldiers ready to take their iron to an enemy and less like hapless men who had got themselves into something they neither understood nor desired. Waiting for a moment, he allowed his centurions the time to redouble their efforts to persuade the recruits that failure to impress the emperor was likely to result in a disinclination on his part to grant them a much hoped for afternoon off.

'*ARE YOU READY FOR WAR?*'

'*READY!*'

The last response was just about acceptable, a proper roar, and with a wave of his vine stick Marius signalled to his officers to lead their men in readying themselves for the attack that they would shortly make on the other legion. Their soldiers were swiftly organising themselves into a line of century-sized testudo formations, each century interlocking their shields to form a barrier that ought to be almost impenetrable to attack if carried out effectively. At his signal his officers began rapping their vine sticks against their greaves, the curved and sculpted metal plates that protected their lower legs, and in an instant the trained soldiers among his cohorts took up the rhythm with their spear shafts and shield rims, the pulsing sound rapping out across the parade ground and intensifying as the recruits quickly joined the more experienced men. Waiting while the Fifteenth's men dressed their formations in readiness for the assault, he relaxed into the moment, enjoying the rhythmic rattle of wood on metal. Judging that the moment was right he walked briskly out to one side of the legion's line and raised the stick again, then swung it down to point at the waiting men of the Fifteenth.

'Fifth legion . . .' he paused, allowing his officers to repeat his order for their own men's benefit, a chorus of gruff bellows instructing each century to be ready for the command to move. 'At the walk . . . *advance!*'

Long discussion had gone into what was planned to happen next, Marius and his colleague from the Fifteenth equally concerned both with the need to present their new recruits with the easiest possible challenge to meet in front of the emperor, whilst also exposing them to no more risk than was sensible under the circumstances.

'I know . . .' He'd sipped his wine once the two men and their senior centurions had agreed the routine to be followed, nodding with a hard smile at his colleague. 'If this follows form we'll lose a dozen men between us, half of them with recoverable injuries and half of them likely to be of no more use to us. One or two of them dead, quite possibly. Better now than on a battlefield though, where their mistakes won't just earn them a wooden javelin in the throat but might be the difference between victory and defeat. Better to weed out some of the dead wood now, I'd say, rather than having to suffer the consequences when we're face-to-face with Otho's legions.'

He counted the steps, knowing that a twenty-pace advance would bring them to the closest possible spear throw, and at fifteen paces shouted his penultimate order, inwardly cringing at what the result might look like.

'Spears . . . *ready!*'

The previous day when the legion's cohorts had practised the act of changing their grips on the one spear that they were carrying from the upright position to a throwing grip – Marius having been steadfastly opposed to risking the chaos that might result from his men having to juggle the usual two weapons while they were advancing – it had proven too much for more than a few of the new recruits. After the fiftieth dropped spear of the morning his patience had snapped, and the decision was made to minimise the risk of a repeat in front of the emperor by dint of the legionaries on both sides of the mock battle having been ordered to take to the parade ground with their spears pointing at the ground. With wooden training weapons there were no iron heads to give away the fact that the two legions were still too raw to be trusted to change their grips from the vertical carry to the throwing position without dropping them, and so the order for that position to be adopted passed almost without incident apart from the impact of one hapless recruit's dropped weapon tripping two men in the ranks behind him.

'Spears . . .'

Taking one last swift look at the Fifteenth's formation, reassuring himself that no fool was peering out of a surreptitiously opened gap between two shields that could just as easily admit a thrown spear as a view of the opposition, he took a swift breath and bellowed the fateful order.

'*Throw!*'

With a collective grunt that proved that some of them at least had been listening to their trainers when they insisted that a swift exhale would give their throws an extra five paces of distance, his men hurled their spears at the testudoes, not in one movement and with none of the graceful collective arcs that were the hallmark of the best trained cohorts, but all more or less in the same direction and at the same time. With a rattle of wood on leather-covered wood, their thrown weapons hammered into the Fifteenth's raised shields, which, for the most part, stopped them dead and dropped them to the ground. In a real battle the blades would have caught in the wood and dragged down an enemy's defences, but for Marius it was enough that the majority of the training spears had flown cleanly to their targets and that from the look of it there had been no worse casualties than a few men hopping around with bruised feet from failing to guard the bottoms of their legs against errant spears. And then, just when he'd breathed a sigh of relief that nothing had gone any more awry, a final spear arced out of his legion's line, thrown by a soldier who had stumbled at the crucial moment perhaps, regained his footing, gathered himself and thrown his weapon a good two heartbeats after his comrades and, critically, just as the Fifteenth's defensive formations inevitably started to crack open, with men eager to take their own turn with the spear. Where so many other men had hurled their missiles over the top or to either side of the target, or hammered them ignominiously into the ground in front of the closest testudo, his throw was clean, arcing through the air and whipping through an inopportunely opened gap in the raised shields. For a moment nothing happened, but just as Marius was breathing a fresh sigh of relief, the defensive formation burst open, men scattering from something among them that was evidently the cause of sudden horror. At least one of them bent over and puked his breakfast onto the parade ground, and as their bodies scattered away from whatever it was that had provoked such a reaction, the senior centurion closed his eyes momentarily in recognition of the fact that his morning had just gone from inauspicious to cursed in the blink of an eye.

That evening he attended the legatus's residence, freshly bathed and shaved, wearing his new best tunic and with his belt and boots waxed and polished to gleaming perfection, and feeling strangely naked without his vine stick and dagger. At the door the newly promoted soldiers from the First Germanica, dressed in gleaming white tunics, and ostentatiously armed with daggers and swords, and with their shields carefully stacked in a corner, searched him with a robust thoroughness verging on the unnecessary before waving him through into the house, where he was met by a steward bearing a tray of wine cups. Recalling Gaius's suggestion that senior officers probably didn't drink a cup of wine in one gulp, he sipped at the drink, finding its contents delicious compared to the usual fare on offer in the centurions' mess. Looking up, he started at the sight of the legatus augusti of the German legions limping towards him, and looked around for someone else who could be the senior officer's intended conversational victim. Finding himself the only possible objective for the older man's advance, he braced himself to be thoroughly upbraided for his many and various failings.

'First Spear Marius!' The man stuck out a meaty hand and Marius took it, finding his own calloused fingers engulfed in soft flesh. 'Greetings, Centurion, and well met.'

He took in Marius's nonplussed expression and laughed.

'I should formally introduce myself. I'm Legatus Augusti Marcus Hordeonius Flaccus, commander of—'

Marius had snapped to attention, and wine had splashed from the cup and soaked his hand, and quite possibly his new best tunic, but that was of small import when there were formalities to be observed. Flaccus shook his head good-naturedly.

'No need for formalities, First Spear, save that for the parade ground. Relax.' He waved to the man with the tray of wine. 'Here, steward, another cup of wine for my brother in arms!'

Looking down, Marius was gratified to discover that the spilled wine had missed his tunic, but when he looked up at Flaccus again he found that the man's face had adopted a disconcertingly conspiratorial expression.

'I have to say I enjoyed the demonstration today. Nicely done, First Spear, nicely done indeed.' Marius frowned, wondering for a moment whether the legatus was having fun with him. 'But seriously, there were some *truly* masterful touches! The soldier who managed to get himself lost, and who ended up trying to join the praetorians. And that incident right at the end, when one of your *recruits* . . .' he winked ostentatiously at Marius, 'hurled a spear clean through the front of a testudo and *killed* a man. I presume the casualty has made a swift recovery, and is even now enjoying the fruits of his role as a hapless corpse in some tavern or other . . .'

'Legatus Augusti Flaccus, I see you've already found my First Spear.' Both men turned to find Lupercus standing with a cup in his hand. 'And I see you've also both tasted the wine. It's rather good, if I do say so myself.'

Flaccus beamed at him, raising his own glass in salute.

'Quite excellent, Munius Lupercus, and from your family estate, I presume? And as I said to the centurion here not a moment ago, there need be no formalities between us soldiers. A straightforward "Hordeonius Flaccus" will suffice this evening. And while I'm on the subject of compliments, I was just extending my congratulations to Marius here. . .' he winked at the centurion again, 'on the conduct of his men this morning. Quite the most artful display of exaggerated incompetence I've ever seen, and trust me, I've watched some masters of the art display their wares.'

'Really?'

The older man nodded cheerfully.

'Oh yes, back when Nero was recruiting for his proposed campaign to take the Caspian Gates two years ago. I could name you at least two legion legati who quietly ordered their first spears to conceal their men's true abilities, in the hope that they would be deemed inappropriate for the task and allowed to stay where they were. The man in command of the Fourteenth Gemina made the mistake of taking pride in the skills they had built up in Britannia and got his command posted to the east, but then with Nero calling them his best legion after the way they dealt with Boudicca's tribal mob so easily he probably wouldn't have got away with it anyway. That's the price of being good at what one does, I suppose, to find one's betters will just expect you to keep doing it for them, eh? But yes, some men conspired to conceal their men's abilities and even their numbers, just as I suspect you did this morning, and as a result Nero took some rather drastic action, if you remember, such as commissioning a legion out of the fleet.'

He grinned at them both.

'And you'll get no argument from me, even if you are a pair of rascals. After all, my interests as supreme commander of the army of Germania aren't best served by having yet more troops stripped from my command. Just don't give Vitellius the slightest hint that this morning's little charade was anything but a demonstration of genuine incompetence by green troops, are we clear on that?'

He wafted away in search of a fresh cup of wine, and the two men exchanged glances.

'He really thinks—?'

'That all those errors today were stage managed? Yes. He told me as such earlier, on the podium. They weren't, were they Marius?'

The centurion shook his head with a rueful smile.

'No, sir. That was all their own work, and nothing to do with me. In fact, I did everything I could to disguise their inability.'

Lupercus nodded.

'As I thought, First Spear, much as I thought. Very well, let us humour our legatus augusti, shall we? And let's face it, being a little shamefaced if the emperor upbraids us for our men's display this morning won't be hard to simulate, will it?'

Northern Italy, March AD 69

'So, does it feel good to be a killer?'

Egilhard turned to find Alcaeus standing behind him, helmetless and without his armour in the evening chill, his grubby subarmalis unbuttoned to allow the air to his body. He moved to one side to allow his superior to get closer to the campfire's rekindled blaze that had been smouldering ever since their capture of the marine camp that morning.

'That's better.' The centurion warmed his hands for the moment before speaking again. 'It was a serious question. Do you feel like a better man now that you know what you can do in battle?'

With the men of the hapless marine cohorts disarmed, forced to swear an oath to their gods not to fight again and released to make their way back to their army's camp, Scar had ordered his first cohort to consolidate around the farmhouse for the day while the remaining Batavi forces put out scouting probes deep into the countryside beyond. Grimmaz's tent party, finding themselves cast as celebrities as part of the single century that had held off not one but two full cohorts of the enemy for the time needed for reinforcements to arrive from the river, had been unchallenged in their assertion that they were claiming one of the tents left standing in the marines' forlornly deserted camp. They had cooked their dinner over a fire in which a dying man had burned alive that morning, the stink of singed hair still haunting Egilhard's nostrils even if only as a horrific memory.

'Not especially, Cent—'

Alcaeus raised a hand.

'Forget the formalities, man, you're not a recruit any more. Off duty you can call me by the name all my warriors use, since you're one of them now, blooded and proven. So, tell me, why don't you feel like a better man? After all, you fought like a hero today. Lanzo's going to be singing your praises for a week of Saturnalias, once he gets over that knock on the head, and the whole century already knows what you did. Suddenly you're accepted. One of us. So why don't you feel better?'

The younger man stared into the fire for a moment, turning the question over in his mind.

'I . . .' His eyes narrowed as the reason for the centurion's question occurred to him. 'This is a priest thing, isn't it?'

Alcaeus grinned wolfishly in the fire light.

'I *knew* you were a smart one. Yes, this is a priest thing. Now answer the question before I have to remind you that I'm not only your priest but also *still* your superior, whether or not you're Achilles come back to grace us mortals with your divine skills.'

'Do I feel better?' Egilhard thought for a moment. 'No. Different, but not better.'

'And how is it that you feel different?'

'I feel . . . complete. I've seen battle and proved myself good enough to stand with my tent mates.'

Alcaeus snorted.

'Good enough? You're better than good enough. You wounded and then finished your first man just the way you've been taught, but even while you were giving him the death stroke, with your full attention focused on putting your spear through his neck, you were getting ready for your next move. You don't realise it, because it was all done without any need for thought.'

He paused, looking into the young soldier's uncomprehending face.

'And *that's* what makes you deadly. You turned on the man who was about to kill Lanzo without any pause to size up your target, or decide where to put the blade, because if you'd waited a heart-beat your tent mate would be dead now, rather than sleeping off a bang on his head. You just pulled your spear's blade free from the first man, even while he was tottering and not sure what had happened to him, you pivoted and you put it through the second man's throat so fast even Banon wasn't sure what he'd seen.'

The centurion shook his head slowly.

'You're a hero in the making, Egilhard. I won't treat you any differently, and neither will Banon, but your tent mates will. And the century will, as the story spreads. Men will nod to you when they pass you, little gestures of respect. They'll want to pat you on the shoulders and the back before our next fight, hoping for a little bit of you to wear off on them. At first you'll be confused, happy to have your skills recognised but wary of failing to live up to their expectations. But after a while you'll look back on that initial confusion as the happiest time of your life.'

Egilhard shook his head in bafflement.

'Why?'

Alcaeus smiled sadly.

'Why? Because when the confusion passes, when you realise

that you really are every bit as deadly as men say you are, a killer, you'll also see the truth of it – which is that you have no choice in the matter. I've known several killers in the last twenty years, men who fought as if their daemons were wrought of the deadliest rage, capable of facing two or three men at one time and defeating all three within a dozen heartbeats. The one constant in their lives was this . . .' He paused for a moment, looking at the young soldier with evident conviction. 'They all died before their time. All of them, without exception. Because the most gifted among us always end up being revered by their comrades, having nick-names like Achilles or Hector hung around their necks and being expected to perform feats of impossible skill whenever we met the enemy. Every such man I knew was ultimately driven to some act of suicidal bravery or other, in pursuit of what they came to see as their destiny, once they had fallen for their brothers' hero worship. And the problem with suicidal bravery is fairly obvious, when you think about it. It gets you *killed*, boy.'

He was silent for a moment, allowing the evident truth of his words to sink in.

'There is another path, of course. There's always an alternative, if you have the courage to choose the harder way and the grit to stick to it.'

He waited, and after a moment the younger man spoke.

'I would like to know where this other path might lead.'

Alcaeus nodded.

'The alternative path, if you have the strength to follow it, will lead you *away* from hubris and eventual self-destruction. What it will lead you towards is entirely your own choice. To follow this path, you must adopt a humble aspect with regard to your skills. Refuse to accept the role your brothers would have you adopt. Keep your head down, and accept the praise of the men around you when they tell you what a warrior you are humbly – no false modesty, mind you – but don't parade your skills to impress any man. Keep your sword work functional when sparring. Always beat whoever comes to test your skills, if you can, but avoid unnecessary showmanship as you do so. Use your spare time for more than practising better ways to kill your opponents. Develop another skill, one that you can take pride in, something which will bring some measure of relief from the weight of all the deaths which will be on your conscience. Because you're going to kill a lot of men in the next few months, I suspect. Right now there are only two of them on your conscience, but there are going to be more. A lot more. You'll see them at night, in your dreams, silent and uncomplaining. They won't torment you, because they have no interest in doing so, but they will come to you, to remind you of the cost they paid as the price for you to ply your skills. When that happens, if it troubles you, speak to me and nobody else. Now get to bed, we'll be on the move in the morning and I want you ready for anything.'

Egilhard nodded and turned away, then turned back with the questioning expression Alcaeus had come to recognise.

'You want to know why my tent name is "Seven", right?'

'How—?'

'Did I know that was your question? It wasn't that hard to guess. They all ask in the end, just like they all wonder why Banon's called "Kneecaps", except in his case it's a bit more obvious. You worked that one for yourself soon enough, I'd imagine?' The younger man nodded with a small smile at the memory. 'And now you want to know the reason for my tent name.' After a moment Egilhard nodded, and Alcaeus looked at him levelly for a moment before continuing. 'When a man is chosen to enter the priesthood of the wolf, because he displays the skills needed to help his brother warriors deal with their preparations to fight, and to live with the consequences of the fight when it's done and the field is strewn with the corpses of friend and foe, he is expected to pass several tests to prove his worthiness. And one of those tests, the one that really matters, is that he must go out into the forest in winter and kill the wolf that will become his badge of the priesthood, to prove his bravery beyond any doubt, to entitle him to voice an opinion as to the nature of men's courage. Some men do this by stealth and guile, setting traps to lure and ensnare an unwary beast which they must then kill with nothing more deadly than their pugio, and while no disapproval of such methods is ever voiced, these tend to be the younger and less impressive animals. Others seek to prove themselves by taking their prize with spear and sword, and that was the method I chose. I walked out into the forest one evening, a night with a full moon but still only fitfully lit as clouds hurried across the sky above me.'

He smiled at the memory.

'It was a poor choice. Snow fell overnight, making for hard going, and by late morning the next day I had been found by a pack of the bastards. They found me, you'll note, because I could have blundered around the woods for the next year and never known where they came from. They attacked as a pack, of course, two or three of them testing me face-to-face while the rest moved to take me from the flanks and rear just as we would, as all good hunters do, and I knew my only hope of survival was to take the fight to them with all my fury at my own stupidity, to strike and move, and not to allow them to overwhelm me. I didn't best fancy the thought of dying alone, failing in the sight of our Lord Hercules, but mainly I was terrified of being torn apart by the bastards, my bones scattered across the forest floor and only leaving my bloodied weapons to prove I had fought my best and lost that fight. That I had ever even existed.'

He stared into the fire for a moment.

'And what a fight. The bitches came at me first, evil creatures, while the dogs snarled and growled behind them, and I knew that to run would see me dead in no time, so I went for them with my spear. Two of them I killed in ten heartbeats, before they learned to be wary of my spear's reach, and I left them whimpering and bleeding out in the snow at my feet. After that the rest of them massed to mob me, and the moment of greatest danger was at hand. I didn't wait for them to come at me, but took the initiative, casting my spear at the biggest of the males to put him down, and Hercules was in my right arm that day because the cast was true, burying the blade deep in his chest and killing him instantly. My sword was in my hand by then, and I went at them in a kind of fury, not caring what happened as long as I was not ashamed before my god. My shield saved my life, allowing me to fend them off to my left, and punch at them hard enough to break one poor creature's jaw, while I took my iron to the others on my right, but even so I found myself on my back with the last two wolves worrying at me, one atop my shield and ravening for the meat of my face, the other boring in from the right seeking my sword arm. In desperation, and nothing better, I stabbed out with the sword and put it down his throat, either by chance or the favour of Hercules. Either could be true, although as a priest I naturally favour the latter.'

He grinned at Egilhard, reliving the blood joy of the moment.

'Which left one. The fiercest of them, the young male who would have supplanted the pack leader soon enough, pinning me down into the snow with his jaws inches from my face, snapping and snarling, and my strength suddenly ebbing like the river's tide, inevitable and unstoppable. My sword was stuck in the other beast's throat, with him coughing and spasming on the iron, and I could not pull it free, only drag his dying body closer to mine. My shield arm was weakening, losing the fight to keep the last of them from my throat by an inch at a time, the muscles burning with such pain that I was snarling back at him with that agony. I released my grip on the sword, freeing my right hand, and in that moment I knew there was a choice, to relieve the pain in my left by supporting the shield, and perhaps even throwing him off me, or to do something more subtle, and end the fight. The logical thing to do would have been to free myself from the creeping threat of his snapping teeth, only inches from my face, but before Hercules I knew what I had to do. I reached down under my shield and drew my pugio, lifted the blade to his throat and put the point against the place where his blood was just beneath the surface, holding back from making the kill for just a moment, with the iron pricking the skin beneath his fur. He didn't cease his attempts to get at me, of course, we were both too lost in the blood rage for any retreat, and so I allowed the shield to drop an inch, and pushed the pugio up an inch, no more, and opened his throat.'

He fell silent, and after a moment Egilhard felt compelled to speak.

'There were seven of them?'

'There were. The priests who were waiting for us novices to return were astounded when I carried seven heads back into their camp, covered in their blood and exhausted. I laid six of them on the altar to Hercules in thanks for his strength in my hour of need, and kept only the best of them for myself, not the biggest, but the last of them, to remind me that sometimes a man must retreat to attack, and that the greatest strength can only prevail so many times before guile and subtlety are required to bring about victory. And so I am "Seven".'

7

Cremona, Northern Italy, April AD 69

'Gladiators? Fucking *gladiators*? You're telling me that we're ordered to sit here and scratch our arses waiting for a few toy soldiers to turn up, while the real fight happens under our fucking noses but we're forbidden to take part with the grown-ups?'

Alcaeus watched from his place behind Scar as the man to whom the prefect had spoken shook his head at the vehemence of his subordinate's response to their orders, unmoved in the face of the German's malevolent reaction. Resplendent in a bronze cuirass, lovingly polished to a bright shine by his slave, and every inch the Roman gentleman at war, Alfenius Varus had been appointed to overall command of the Batavi cohorts less than a week before, and the two men were still adapting to the situation. Scar stared at him for a long moment, with the expression of a man about to say something deeply unwise, but he turned away, the only expression of his anger the rhythmic beating of his vine stick against one of his greaves. The Roman spoke to his back, his tone unchanged from the even but firm way he had dealt with his second in command since being appointed to command the empire's most warlike and challenging allied force. Clearly untroubled by the Batavis' reputation, he was apparently equally unawed by either his subordinate's evident military abilities or the facial wound incurred in Britannia that had gifted him his ferocious expression.

'You and your men are posted to this wing of the army, Prefect Germanicus, because the gentlemen who exercise the emperor Vitellius's power here do not entirely trust your men alongside their own. There have been too many fights in camp, too much recrimination between your soldiers and the men of the army's legions, for you to be accorded a place in the line. To be frank, there are doubts as to just how vigorously you will prosecute the fight against an enemy when the need to do so is at its most pressing.'

Varus had previously served as legatus augusti Valens's Camp Prefect, during the long march south to cross the Alps and rendezvous with the other half of the rightful emperor's army in northern Italy. Instrumental in quashing a mutiny during that march into the Roman homeland, in part triggered by the Batavi themselves, Varus had found himself appointed to command the troublesome auxiliaries once they had reunited with the four cohorts that had marched under Caecina, with orders to keep so tight a control over the Germans that no further provocation could be offered to legionaries who were clearly spoiling for a fight.

'Do I have to remind you, Prefect, that not only is this a direct contradiction of the treaty between Rome and my people, but that one of the few victories this army has won to date was achieved by my men, a single century capturing a cohort of enemy marines?'

Varus waited a moment to be sure that Scar had exhausted his ire before speaking again, addressing him by his Roman given name rather than that used by his tribal soldiers.

'And do I have to remind you, Prefect, that your men then spoiled their victory by strutting around the camp they shared with the Twenty-First Legion boasting about their victory, and pointing out that all the legion had managed to achieve was slaughtering the Helvetians. So there's no point in your looking so distressed, Prefect Germanicus, because your command has brought this punishment on its own head by its overbearing behaviour, and not just the four cohorts attached to the Twenty-First but those which accompanied us over the Alps by the south-western passes. Ever since your cohorts joined the army your men have been telling anyone stupid enough to listen to them that you Batavians had mastered your parent legion, long before the Fourteenth Gemina was sent to fight in the east, and that you are the match of any legion in the army. All of which needless posturing had the result that when Fabius Valens sent his four Batavian cohorts away on detached duty to ease the tension they were causing, the legions promptly mutinied at the loss of so potent a fighting force.' He laughed bitterly at the obvious irony. 'You know as well as I do that by making themselves thoroughly unpleasant with their posturing and boasting, your men also made themselves seem an essential part of the army, and their absence caused a horrendous uproar that almost saw the legatus augusti himself killed!'

Scar shrugged, staring across the battlefield that stretched away to their left from their position next to the river Po at the army's rightmost position.

'You dealt with that uprising quickly enough as I have heard the story, Prefect, and with the same ruthlessness with which you now hold us within this iron cage, forbidden to take a step forward without your permission.'

Varus nodded soberly at him.

'Which is exactly as it should be, Prefect. You Batavians have been riding the high horse for too long now, so a spell of doing what you're told will be good for your humility.' He shook his own head in amusement at the Batavi commander's obvious frustration. 'And who knows what the battle we're about to fight will bring, eh? You may yet get the chance to slake that well-known thirst for blood. So now, in the interests of a good working relationship, let us turn to more practical matters. Given that I may yet have cause to slip your collars and allow you into the fight, let us be clear what it is that we face, shall we?'

He pointed to each of the opposing force's formations in turn, naming one legion at a time from the enemy's left wing, directly opposite the Batavi cohorts, to the far end of the Othonian line over a mile distant to their left.

'In front of us I see a shiny new legion formed of blue tunicked marines who have yet to fight as a legion. To their right and our left are several cohorts of the very same praetorians who murdered the emperor Galba to put the usurper Otho on the throne, curse their treachery. And, if I squint hard enough to see the enemy's right wing, I can see what the scouts tell us is the Thirteenth Gemina, with a detachment of your former parent legion, the Fourteenth too. I fail to see how the Othonians think they can stand against the cream of the frontier legions with such a rag bag of inexperience and treacherous venality, even if the Thirteenth ought to give a good account of itself.'

He stared hard at the praetorians for a long moment, shaking his head in disgust.

'When the news of Galba's murder reached us, I sacrificed and prayed for the opportunity to look down the length of my bloody sword at the men who were self-serving enough to murder an emperor like a dog in the streets of Rome, no matter how insecure his reign might have become when the army refused to recognise his rule. So don't imagine that I'm happy being told to stand here and await the improbable attempt to turn the battle by an incursion across the river by a force of gladiators who may well have turned tail and fled by now.'

Scar turned to face him.

'You're not the only man on this battlefield with a score to settle against the palace guard, Prefect. We have our own reasons for wanting to get to a sword's length with them, and yet here we are, standing guard on a river that already protects our army's right flank. Our eight cohorts are indeed the match of any legion in this battle line, and yet here we sit, protecting the army against an attack by a cohort or two of men who are no better than slaves. Well-trained sword fighters, but with questionable military abilities and with no honour whatsoever. And no more than half our strength at their very best, by the scouts' estimate. Defeating any attempt they might make to gain this side of the river will bring us no glory at all, and any man who falls to their swords will be wasted for little purpose.'

'Little purpose, Germanicus?'

'You're right, Prefect, my words were poorly chosen. To no

purpose whatsoever.' The German turned to look at the legion being marshalled into position on their left, the words of a bellicose marching song drifting across the dusty farmland as the cohorts of veterans marched into their places in the Vitellian army's line. 'So while we stand and stare at an empty river, the Twenty-First Rapax is preparing for battle against *them* . . .' They turned to stare across the as yet unbloodied battlefield at the legion that faced the Batavi cohorts' new parent legion, their blue tunics making them a unique sight on a battlefield dominated by the more usual whites and reds of the established legions. 'First Classica. Soldiers from the fleet at Rome, you said?'

Varus nodded.

'Marines, recruited by Nero and treated rather badly by Galba when he took power after Nero's suicide. Ironic, isn't it? If he'd won them over to his cause they might well have protected him from the praetorians Otho bribed to kill the emperor and acclaim him as the man's successor. Instead, the men of the First Classica turned the men sent to seek their aid away at spearpoint. Although either course of action would still have put them right there, facing Twenty-First Rapax like lambs waiting for the slaughterman's blade.'

Both men stared at the legion standing opposite, their neat, ordered ranks gleaming in the afternoon's sun, every man in his place and standing in perfect, immobile silence, waiting for their opponents to complete their preparations to fight.

'The men of the Rapax will go through them like a knife through tunic wool. The Twenty-First isn't called the "Predator" without good cause.'

Scar shook his head slowly.

'I do not entirely share your optimism, Prefect.' Affronted, the Roman opened his mouth to issue a retort, but found his rebuke choked off by Scar's raised finger. 'In the interests of a good working relationship, it would be as well for you to be very clear that I am not given to overlooking opinions with which I am unable to agree, no matter what degree of mistrust my command might have sunk to in the eyes of the men who tell me where to go and fight. Or, as seems to be the case here, *not* to fight. It is not the way of the Batavi to hold back an opinion, and it is certainly not my way. It was one of the reasons that Julius, your first emperor in all but name, chose to ally our people with yours, but in truth we could not have changed that brutal honesty even if our very survival had depended upon it. So while I will ask for your forgiveness for contradicting you, I cannot apologise for the opinion. After the battle you may choose to put another man into my place – but then after the battle you or I may be dead, and the question of no more importance than what I had for breakfast this morning.'

Varus looked at him for a moment before replying.

'Why? How can you look at the Twenty-First Legion and see anything other than those marines' doom advancing on them? The Twenty-First has a hundred years of battle experience, a *hundred* years, and its eagle has seen victory in half a dozen provinces and more. That legion's centurions are the best in the army, fierce, proud and brutal, and not likely to be overly troubled by men whose cohorts were only formed a year or so ago, and who have never before taken to any field of battle. Are they?'

Scar scratched the skin beneath the flat plate of his helmet's neck guard, feeling the ridged line where an Iceni spear thrust had found the opening between mail and helmet, opening a six-inch-long gash that had soaked his back with blood, during the last battle of the revolt that had seen the rebellious tribes' warriors annihilated by legionaries and auxiliaries numbering little more than a tenth of the defeated Britons' strength.

'Battles don't always go with numerical superiority, Prefect, or with reputation for that matter. And yes, we know the Rapax well enough, a proud legion and nasty with it. Their centurions foster the belief that they are the best men in the army, savage in battle and careless of their lives when an enemy has the impudence to stand against them, much the same as ourselves. They are eager to fight and glory in the kill, painting their faces with the blood of the men they have slaughtered despite repeated orders not to do so. But I know fighting men, and what I see in those blue tunics is something equally dangerous.'

Varus snorted his disbelief.

'Dangerous? What could be any more dangerous than the Twenty-First Legion in full cry?'

The Batavi prefect smiled thinly as he stared at the stolid lines of marines.

'Discipline, Prefect. That legion over there may be new, but the cohorts and centuries that make it up look as ready for a fight as any veterans I ever fought beside in Britannia. Perhaps more so.' The Roman was shaking his head, but remained silent as the Batavi continued. 'We fought alongside our parent legion the Fourteenth Gemina often enough to see how you Romans face battle. And even in the ranks of the Fourteenth, named "victorious and blessed by Mars" after standing with us against ten times our own number to end the rebellion in Britannia, there were still men who had to be pushed into place with piss running down their legs. But that legion standing waiting for the Twenty-First to complete their preparations does so in complete silence, its ranks not wavering in the slightest. And see how well presented they are?'

Varus shook his head with a look of incredulity.

'Well presented? You're trying to tell me that a freshly polished pair of boots will win a fight with the most bloody-handed legion in the empire? Those men have *no* idea what's about to hit them, or they would be emptying more than their bladders at the prospect!'

Scar shrugged.

'There's more than one sort of courage, Prefect. The Twenty-First will be their usual wild selves, vying to be the first to get at their enemy, a warrior tribe of the sort that demands my respect. But those men facing us have one key attribute that might yet cancel out their ferocity . . .' He smiled tightly at the prefect's mystification. 'Their appearance tells us a great deal about their training, Prefect. Their armour and weapons gleam so brightly that it can only be the result of repeated cleaning and oiling. I doubt there's a single man in those ranks with his hair anything other than tightly cropped, and they've probably all shaved today as well, which means they have iron discipline, Prefect, unforgiving and harsh, with centurions who toil constantly to ensure that their men reach the highest possible standards. And men like that are unlikely to restrict their concerns to the closeness of a man's hair to his scalp.'

He grinned, raising a questioning eyebrow and tapping his purse meaningfully.

'But that's just my theory. Perhaps my Wolf Priest has an opinion?'

Varus dipped his head in a gesture of respect to Alcaeus, inviting him to join the discussion.

'The gentleman who captured a full cohort of marines is more than entitled to express his views. Centurion Alcaeus?'

Alcaeus had tried his best to remain a grey presence in the background from the moment that Varus had taken command, but his part in the previous month's victory had soon enough been revealed to the Roman, and the fact that Scar usually kept him close to hand as a second opinion had unavoidably exposed him to the prefect's curiosity. He stepped forward, looking across the battlefield at the marine's ordered ranks and then turning to look at the men of the Twenty-First Legion.

'Those marines will be desperate to recover their reputation from the disaster on the Po. They are well equipped, and they appear to be well led. Whereas our allies lack something vital to their success in such a fight.'

Varus raised an eyebrow.

'And what is it that they lack, Centurion?'

Alcaeus stared at the stationary ranks of soldiers for a moment longer.

'Their spirits are weak, Prefect.'

'Their . . . *spirits*?'

'They spent the march south terrorising the population, rather than preparing themselves for a fight to the death with men of conviction who clearly believe in their cause. There is no belief in them other than in their unassailable reputation as blood-soaked animals when battle is joined. What will they do when they come face-to-face with men who have no interest in their fame, and whose belief in their cause will make them equally stern in the iron storm?'

Varus considered his reply for long enough that Scar saw his opportunity and seized it.

'Would you care to venture a wager with me on the subject, Prefect? A gold aureus on the result of these two legions fighting it out?'

Varus smiled back at him, relieved that his deputy seemed to have dealt with the disgruntlement that had so taken him aback.

'Why not? Whoever's chosen legion wins the first clash of arms takes the coin. Although I'd say you're a brave man to wear your purse quite so brazenly on the battlefield.'

Scar shrugged.

'The man who can fight his way through my warriors and take it from my dead body will fully deserve the gold it contains.'

The Twenty-First was in position now, its legionaries still chanting their battle hymn with an underpinning rap of spears shafts on shield rims, a rhythm to stir the blood and get a man's neck hairs up as combat beckoned. With a blare of trumpets and shouted orders that rang out over the din, the legion lurched untidily into motion across the muddy farmland that separated them, advancing towards the waiting marines with evident purpose. Varus stared at them impatiently, clearly as frustrated with his cohorts' inaction as was Scar.

'Shall we go forward and watch at closer quarters, Prefect Germanicus?'

Scar nodded, happy to oblige his commander's evident eagerness for the fight, calling an order back to the decurion who led his century's horsemen, the tribe's best riders mounted on the finest horses that money could buy.

'We're going forward to watch the battle when these two legions meet, and you can come along with your squadron to make sure we're not interrupted by any rude men! Giftaz!' He pointed to the senior centurion of his second cohort. 'Watch the river! If you see any gladiators getting ready to cross the river have your trumpeter sound three long notes to get my attention!'

Cantering forward across the recently tilled farm land, easily overtaking the Rapax's front rank as the soldiers laboured across the soft earth, they reined in their mounts a hundred paces from the point where Scar estimated the two legions would clash. He nodded grimly as the Classica's marines readied their spears.

'Whichever one of us takes the aureus I can guarantee you one thing, Prefect. This is going to be *bloody*.'

As the oncoming ranks of legionaries advanced inside throwing range, a horn blew, loud enough to be heard over the cheers and shouted imprecations of the advancing Vitellians, and as one man the Classica's front line took a step forward and launched their spears at the oncoming soldiers, following up with another volley before drawing their swords and setting themselves to receive the oncoming legionaries' charge. Varus laughed out loud, grinning with delight.

'Hah! All they've done is get the men of the Twenty-First really angry! You're right Germanicus, this is indeed going to be bloody!'

Scar pursed his lips and kept his opinion to himself, counting the dozens of legionaries who were left inert on the trampled, bloody soil or struggling in agony to pull loose the barbed spear heads that were buried in their bodies, while their comrades stormed into the attack. With a collective bellow the attackers hurled their own spears into the waiting line of marines, to less effect, then closed the gap between them at the trot, eager to be at their enemies with sword and shield. The two lines met, men on both sides punching with their shields and stabbing at whatever targets presented themselves as the Classica's centre gave ground slowly, pressed backwards by the weight of their opponents' attack but in such good order that to Scar's eyes it looked more like a carefully controlled retreat than the result of their being out-muscled or out-fought.

'Look, see! The usurper's men are falling back! That aureus is mine already!'

Scar shook his head without taking his eyes off the fight.

'Only in the middle of their line, Prefect. I think I see their plan even if the Twenty-First's legatus can't.'

The Rapax's central cohorts pressed forward into the space that was opening up before them, hundreds of legionaries pouring forward with the legion's eagle close to the spearhead of their thrust as the leading cohorts drove savagely into the heart of the enemy's formation in an obvious effort to end the fight quickly by breaking the Classica's will to fight, and perhaps even to capture the enemy's standard and inflict the ultimate shame upon the inexperienced newcomers.

'Gods below, the *glory* of it! They'll cut their way through to the marines' aquilifer, tear the standard from his dead hands and show them what a real legion . . .'

Varus fell silent as another horn call rang out and the blue-clad soldiers who had been pulled out of the legion's centre, and who waited in cohort strength on either side of Rapax's fifty-pace incursion into their line, responded with a sudden driving counter-attack that rocked the legionaries facing them back on their heels. Feet pumping as they drove forward, they were seemingly intent on pushing back both of the Twenty-First legion's wings, fighting with a sudden shocking ferocity that dropped dozens of men on both sides into the churned, bloody mud but which, increasingly apparently, was driving both flanks of the Twenty-First Legion back from their central cohorts. Scar shook his head in evident admiration.

'The cheeky bastards are going for an encirclement! Their legatus must have deliberately weakened his centre to reinforce the wings in readiness.'

Varus shook his head in bafflement.

'But surely they can't . . .?'

It seemed that the Twenty-First legion's officers shared his bemusement, for as the marine cohorts to right and left forced back the men facing them, leaving the Rapax's leading units dangerously exposed to the risk of being separated from the main body of their legion, encircled and killed like penned-up beasts, no orders were being issued that might extricate them from the rapidly closing trap. Scar rose up in his saddle, bellowing at men too distant for his voice to stand any chance of being heard.

'*You're being encircled! Pull back!*'

They watched, as the flanking cohorts that had been pulled from the Classica's centre drove into either side of the Rapax's most advanced cohorts, every moment of indecision on the part of the Twenty-First's legatus deepening the trouble into which their headlong advance had taken them. A flurry of horn signals from behind the legion's line indicated that the men in command of the embattled Rapax had realised their predicament, but to Scar's practised eye it was already too late to stave off the disaster that was unfolding. He turned in his saddle and stared pointedly across the river to their right, still devoid of any sign of an attack across its channel.

'Just about now would have been a good time for eight cohorts of battle-hardened soldiers to have taken the enemy in their flank, don't you think?'

Varus didn't answer, his mouth hanging open in amazement, and when Scar turned back and craned his neck to look into the heart of the fight, he realised with a shock what it was that had so astounded the man.

'*Gods . . .*'

The Rapax's leading centuries were now surrounded in a sea of blue-tunicked soldiers, completely cut off from their comrades and under ferocious attack from all sides. Even as the two men watched in increasing disbelief, the legion's eagle, a golden flicker adrift in a sea of iron, lurched and sank into the melee, rising again a moment later to be shaken in triumph as the men of the Classica who had pulled it from the lifeless fingers of its bearer carried it away from the fight in triumph.

'We have to *act*!'

Varus shook his head grimly.

'I have my orders. To ignore them will make me little better than a traitor.'

The Twenty-First legion was rallying, centurions bellowing

orders as the cohorts that had been beaten away from the pitiful remnant of their isolated spearhead reformed their ranks and set themselves to attack again. Storming forward with the fury of men who faced the most ignominious disgrace imaginable unless they could redeem themselves by recapturing their lost eagle, they ripped into the Classica's line with a savagery Scar had rarely seen on the field of battle, men throwing their lives away for the chance to kill an enemy or simply to open a gap for their comrades to exploit, hurling themselves onto the marines' shields and pulling them down to open the men behind them to attack by the legionaries behind them. Still giddy with their victory, their foes were taken aback by the fresh onslaught, recoiling from the unexpected horror of facing an adversary whose collective sanity seemed to have absented itself in favour of a blood rage. Men who had moments before been reeling in defeat were transformed into raving beasts, crowding forward for the opportunity to take their revenge, and in the process driving those in front of them against the Classica's line in such numbers that the marines were unable to hold them. Killing and being killed in their turn by the men before them, themselves magnificently disciplined in refusing to panic in the face of such bestial rage, the Rapax's incensed soldiery tore great gaps in the enemy line and drove century-sized wedges into each one, hacking their way deep into the marines' formation and reaping a bloody harvest of the defenders without regard to their own losses. Varus pumped a fist in the air, shouting for the joy of what he was seeing.

'Look, they've taken the eagle back!'

Alcaeus cast an experienced eye over the group of soldiers carrying away a standard taken in the fight, the proud symbol of a cohort's pride, its silver finish black with the blood of uncounted men who had died in its defence and capture.

'That's not an eagle, Prefect. They won't take *that* back without tearing that entire legion to shreds in order to get to it.'

More standards were being passed back, but in none of these captures did there seem to be any recompense for the attackers, simply a grim pride in taking some small revenge upon the

Othonians. Even as the badges of the Classica's pride were being torn from dead men's hands, the marines were falling back under the command of their officers, reforming their shattered line and leaving the Rapax's exhausted legionaries to vent what remained of their fury on the dead and dying men who had fallen in their brief, incandescent assault, the rage that had fuelled their insane headlong charge burning out as they realised that the bloody fight was doomed to failure. The two sides drew apart, every man exhausted from the carnage that they had visited upon each other, leaving behind them a blood-soaked wasteland of deeply churned mud carpeted with the corpses and wounded of both sides. Some raised their arms to the heavens in supplication, others were still fighting and killing each other with whatever weapons were to hand despite being maimed or close to death, while those still standing leaned exhaustedly on their shields and eyed each other warily, lacking the energy in their legs to engage in further combat. Scar's practised eye swiftly found the weak point in the Othonian line that the Classica's retreat had created, and he raised his vine stick to point at the formations now clashing in the battle's centre, praetorian guard cohorts on the usurper's side of the fight under sustained assault by the famed six-foot-tall soldiers of the First Italica, both sides striving to their utmost to win the melee that would without doubt decide the battle, tearing into each other with swords and axes in a half-mile-long ribbon of gore-slathered slaughter that formed the battlefield's point of decision. Nudging Varus he pointed to the praetorians' open flank, left open and exposed by the marines' retreat to their left.

'There. The greatest opportunity any general can ever see laid out before him, an open flank. With even half our strength we could end this battle in less than half an hour. Do you still believe, Prefect, with the marines pushed back a hundred paces and in no condition to resist our advance, and with the Praetorians ripe for the taking, that it makes sense for your command to be sat here watching the river for—'

'*Scar!*'

He turned to follow the decurion's pointing hand, his face

splitting in a savage grin as he realised what it was that the man was trying to tell him.

'At last!'

'Fuck me but there's enough of them! I had no idea there were so many gladiators in Rome!'

Grimmaz stared at the men on the far bank with a look of evident disdain as they laboured to bring their assorted vessels to the water's edge, the Po's far bank suddenly crawling with armoured figures who had made their way through the vines that carpeted the land south of the river unseen, until the moment that the head of their column had emerged at the water's edge. Equipped like legionaries in their armour and weapons, they were nevertheless displaying little of the organisation that was evident in every action trained soldiers took, their activity a hectic tangle of bodies rather than the ordered work of centuries and tent parties led and cajoled by centurions and their officers.

'Just look at them. They've got all the discipline of a party of brothel bouncers.'

He stared at them for a moment longer, his lip curling in disgust.

'We're going to slaughter the bastards once they get themselves sorted out and try to cross this ditch.'

'And when is it that a man is at the most risk of making a fool of himself, eh Happy?'

The leading man answered without turning round, recognising the voice of the Second Century's centurion as the man tapped him on the shoulder with his vine stick.

'When he's pissed on cheap wine, Centurion Alcaeus sir?'

'When he gets overconfident, Leading Man Grimmaz. They might not be trained soldiers, but if we let them get ashore there's every risk that they'll prove themselves to be more than a little dangerous. Proficient with their weapons. Very good with them, in some cases. Capable of killing more than a few of us in their individual, showy ways even while we're reaping them in our usual, efficient manner. Oh we'll slaughter them alright, but we'll lose men, lose limbs, lose fingers that I'd rather we didn't lose. So we're not going to let them ashore, Leading Man Grimmaz, we're going to kill them in the river, quickly and without any fuss. Like the butchers we are. Aren't we, Banon?'

The watch officer nodded without taking his eyes off the enemy's preparations, his voice as relaxed as if the officer had enquired as to the fit of his new boots.

'We will do what is ordered and at every command we will be ready!'

'Good answer.'

Most of the tent party nodded at their centurion's words, watching as the enemy force dragged an assortment of improvised rafts and small boats that they had clearly commandeered and dragged across the farmland to the river's south, each small party manhandling its craft to the water's edge and standing alongside it ready to board, awaiting the command to commence the crossing. Egilhard watched in silence as the opposite bank's chaos gradually resolved itself, officers marching up and down the river's thin beach behind their hastily trained men and checking that all was ready for the assault on the northern bank.

Scar jumped from his horse in front of the Batavi line and started barking orders at the senior centurions of his eight cohorts.

'Leave the horses tethered, this is going to be a fight on foot! The seventh and eighth cohorts will move to line the riverbank and then lie prone! Stay low so as not to show yourselves to those animals, I don't want them to see our strength and decide not to cross or we'll be stuck here all fucking afternoon! The remaining cohorts will wheel to face the break in the enemy line and prepare to attack! *Do it!*'

Gesturing for Alcaeus to follow, he strode toward the river, pointing with his vine stick at a spot on the Po's bank and leading his men towards it without once looking back at them, Varus at his side.

'Seventh and eighth cohorts! Follow me!'

The other six cohorts watched as their comrades of the allied tribes surged forward in his wake, a ragged line hurrying to catch up to the man who ruled their entire world as he advanced into danger, the least soldierly of them simply advancing in response to his order, the natural warriors driven by their unreasoning love for the man and the martial pride he gave them by his simple example, and the remainder somewhere between the two extremes. Scar squatted down at the point where the land sloped down to meet the river's water, staring intently at the gladiators who were casting off from the southern bank and paddling furiously against the Po's strong current, reaching out a hand and gesturing to his men to keep low.

'Find your place and get down!'

Around him hundreds of men, bent double in crouches made awkward by their heavy equipment, hurried to reform their line close to the river's edge. Centurions and optios strode down their length tapping men briskly with their vine sticks and staffs, making sure that they lay full length on the soft soil, out of view from the water and then, with their soldiers concealed from the oncoming gladiators by the riverbank's slight lip, lay down themselves. Nodding to himself in satisfaction Scar looked behind him at the remainder of his command, as the six cohorts wheeled slowly from their position facing the river to point their spears squarely at the exhausted marines.

'Very well, Prefect, shall we see these slaves off?'

Beckoning to Alcaeus and the Roman to accompany him, he strolled along the line of the prone bodies of the two cohorts, bellowing orders as he watched the enemy boats draw nearer to the bank.

'In just a moment I'm going to tell you to stand up! When I do, you are to face the river and form a straight line in battle formation, four men deep! On the command "attack" you are to advance to the riverbank and fight! We will do this the old-fashioned way, like a Greek army of old, with spear and shield, because these men are professional swordsmen and if we fight them blade to blade then we fight on their terms! But they're not soldiers, they're arena fighters, trained to fight in an artful and showy fashion, but also to survive to fight another day like the expensive property that is all they are! We'll take the fight to them, and while they try to stand off and play at sword-fighting, we'll drive them back into the water and kill them there without offering them mercy. I want that river to run red with their blood! Priest, will you say the words our warriors wish to hear?'

Alcaeus raised his voice to be heard over the rhythmic chanting of the oncoming rowers.

'My brothers, this will be a brief fight, and a bloody one. These men will come at you dreaming of glory, and you will shatter their dreams with your shields and spears. You must reap them, hard-eyed and merciless, like Hercules reaped the life of his defeated foe Lityerses after beating him in the harvesting contest to which that bastard son of King Midas had unwisely challenged him. He threw Lityerses's body into the river Maeander, and so must you throw these men back into the river from which they seek to attack us, equally unwisely but equally murderous if we allow them to master us. There will be blood, a river of blood, but you must never allow pity or sorrow at their deaths to stay your hands. You men of the allied tribes, this is your time to show Hercules the depth of your anger at such a challenge, which you must punish to the fullest extent of your strength and valour!'

Scar nodded at him.

'I can always trust you to find the right words.'

He looked up again, gauging from the ramshackle fleet's proximity to the shore that the moment had come.

'*Batavi! On! Your! Feet!*'

Within half a dozen heartbeats the two cohorts were up and formed into an unbroken line, their sudden appearance throwing the oncoming gladiators into confusion just as they were stepping out of their boats into the Po's shallows. Some of the gladiators waded forward through the calf-deep water, eager to get into the fight, while others recognised the silent ranks of soldiers as the deadly threat they so clearly were, and looked about themselves for any means of escape from what was about to descend upon them.

'*Forward!*'

The German soldiers advanced toward their hapless enemies as one, a leather-lunged centurion bellowing the paean's first line, and as the two cohorts roared out the song the gladiators recoiled visibly, more than a few of them trying to climb back aboard their boats in order to flee, although their sodden clothing and the weight of their armour resulted in more than one of the improvised transports capsizing and adding to the overall air of panic. The remainder came forward, either more resolute than their fellows or simply realising that to retreat from the fight made them just as likely to die at the hands of their own officers, their advance still painfully slow as they waded ashore through knee-deep water, those few who had already reached the river's bank sprinting at the Batavi line with the courage of desperation. The Germans advanced down the bank's shallow beach in their usual cadenced step, remorselessly closing down on the amount of firm ground available to their enemies, two and three men at a time meeting the attacking gladiators with shields thrust out to repel their charges and spears flickering out to drop the enemy fighters writhing onto the muddy sand from the agony of their grievous wounds, to be finished off by the men behind the front rank.

The Romans' previous habituation to bloody violence seemed to protect a proportion of them from the horror erupting on all sides, continuing in their doomed attacks even as their comrades staggered back into the water with blood spurting from their bodies, some of them pierced through by so many spears that they were dead before they hit the mud. The dying men's cries of agony and the voiding of their bladders and bowels at the horrendous pain added to the nightmarish scene's horrific impact, and while some came forward regardless of the mayhem into which they were advancing others were immediately unmanned and threw their weapons aside, fleeing in all directions including that straight into the Batavi line, where they were despatched with ruthless efficiency by swift, merciless spear thrusts.

As they were herded into the river's shallows, retreating before the oncoming line of bloodied spears, the gladiators swiftly changed from a formed body of men, albeit one reeling under the shock of the Batavi assault, into a seething mass of individuals compressed into the few yards of water in which they could touch the river's muddy bottom, stripped of any instinct other than to survive. Those of them facing the Batavi, with no ability to retreat into the close-packed crowd of men behind them, stood and died, some railing against their killers in their last moments, others submitting meekly to the executioners' spear blades like sheep penned for slaughter, their deaths exposing the next rank of victims waiting behind them to the same fate. The men at the rear of the jumbled pack of desperate soldiers were fighting to divest themselves of their armour before they were forced out into water too deep for them to stand in, those who succeeded splashing away from the shore with no thought except for their own survival, most of them taken by the river's fast current and sent away downstream faster than a man could swim, while those less successful in shedding their dead weight of iron struggled briefly for their lives before sinking from view, pulled down beneath the water's blood-stained surface to drown unseen.

Scar and Alcaeus watched from the riverbank's crest, and as the gladiators' fate was sealed the Batavi prefect turned to Varus with a questioning expression.

'It seems to me, Prefect, that our orders have been fulfilled? Having removed their threat to the army's flank, are we free to act on our own initiative and make some form of counter-attack?'

The Roman nodded determinedly, watching with horrified fascination as the Batavi line advanced further into the shallows, displacing yet more men on the far side of the shrinking, ever more chaotic jumble of terrified men into the deeper water where they were doomed to drown under the weight of equipment that the press of their encirclement had prevented them from removing.

'I cannot argue with you, Germanicus. Our orders are satisfied, and now our honour can be addressed.'

The two men looked at each other for a moment before Scar replied.

'Spoken like a gentleman, Prefect. But when we get into the

fight you're to stay close to me. My boys will die before they let any of those usurper bastards get within a sword's length of me, and the same goes for you. These cohorts will need a live prefect to make sure they get their fair share of the medics once this is all done, not a dead man with a glorious name who's no use to them. Now let's go and show your former comrades in the Twenty-First Legion how warriors march to war, shall we?'

He strode across to the waiting cohorts, nodding approvingly at their crisp formation and evident readiness to fight.

'Your brothers of the Sturii, the Marsaci and the Frisavones have tasted blood already! Thin, weak blood, hardly worthy of our iron, but blood all the same! The threat to the army's flank is dealt with, so now it's your turn to go forward and earn the same honour for yourselves! Does any man here wish to march north knowing that he must greet his kin as a warrior who failed to wet his blade in this, the battle that must surely win our emperor Vitellius his throne?'

The men before him bellowed their answer, waving their spears and barking defiance at the enemy ranks.

'To our left are the men of the Twenty-First Legion! They have already fought themselves to a standstill attempting to recapture their lost eagle, and now they stand, exhausted and in need of our strength! On my command we will advance, my brothers, and take their enemy in the flank! We will break these marines, and in breaking them retake the Rapax's eagle on their behalf! And then, once those sailors are on the run, we will finish this fight by visiting the same terror upon those praetorian bastards beyond them, regaining the honour we lost when they schemed to have our palace guard sent home!'

He looked up and down the ranks before him, looking with a critical eye for any sign of weakness and finding none.

'Is every man here ready to go and take the glory in rescuing a legion's eagle? The glory that belongs to the Batavi!'

A chorus of shouts and imprecations greeted his challenge, warriors clashing their spear shafts and shields in a rapping thunder until Scar held up a hand to silence them.

'Are you all ready to take revenge on those praetorian traitors? The revenge that belongs to the Batavi?'

Another, louder chorus of shouts answered his question, as the tribe's soldiers clamoured to be unleashed on their enemy, and the rapping of spear on shield was loud enough to make normal speech impossible. Scar gestured to the Prefect beside him with an open palm, offering him the first step in the advance as was the prefect's right, then raised his voice to bellow over the racket.

'Our brother in blood Prefect Varus calls on you all to join him in regaining his legion's lost eagle! He has sworn to retake it by force, or to die in the effort! Will you join him, and fulfil our duty to Rome?'

Their invective against the waiting enemy was reaching fever pitch, and Scar could sense the mounting nervousness of the Classica's battered remnant, as they considered the sheer injustice of being assaulted by fresh enemies after all they had been through. It was time. Alcaeus looked at him questioningly, but his superior shook his head with a half-smile.

'Not on this occasion. These men need no tale of the divine to drive them forward, not when those poor bastards over there stand between us and the praetorians.'

He raised his voice to order his men forward.

'*Batavi! Glory and revenge! With me!*'

Striding forward, Varus at his side, Scar pushed his vine stick into his ornately decorated belt and drew the gladius from the scabbard in which it hung at his hip, raising the blade high and then pointing it at the waiting marines.

'*Forward!*'

The century behind him hurried to catch the two men, opening their ranks to admit them to the protection of their line as they overtook their officers, Alcaeus giving Scar a knowing look as he secured his own vine stick and drew his blade, shouting to be heard over the noise of their advance, the rattle of mail on wood as men hefted their shields, and the shouts and imprecations of men eager for combat.

'A nice speech, Scar! It looks like the boys of the Twenty-First don't want us to beat them to it though!'

Varus glanced to his left, seeing the legionaries moving towards their opponents at the braying command of their trumpeters.

'Their legatus doesn't want the shame of receiving his eagle back from a mere auxiliary prefect, that's all! Let's not allow them to beat us to it, eh!'

Sucking in a deep breath, Scar bellowed out the order his men had been waiting for.

'*Batavi! Ready spears and run!*'

The cohorts quickened their pace to a jog, accelerating towards the waiting marines whose line, pinned in place by the advancing Twenty-First, was bending round at its left-hand end in anticipation of the onslaught looming from the flank. The marines, knowing they had no choice other than to receive an attack in close to legion strength by fresh soldiers, were already wavering and it seemed to Scar that it was only their iron discipline and the violent remonstrations of their centurions that was keeping them in line as the Batavi bore down on them. Still running, he raised his sword and shouted the last command that would be possible before the carnage ensued.

'*Batavi! With spears! Attack!*'

Sprinting forward through the thick, blood-spattered mud, his men charged into the waiting enemy, their assault shattering the Classica's fragile line in a moment of swift, brutal combat and leaving the exhausted legionaries fighting for their lives as the Batavi cohorts stormed into them, punching with their shields to disrupt the enemy line before stabbing out with their spears, the warriors behind them steadying them in the battlefield's treacherous mud with hands gripping at their armoured collars. Scar and Varus went with them, the latter stabbing a momentarily disoriented marine through the throat as his victim, stunned by a crunching punch from an iron shield boss, fell to his knees and crawled beneath the Batavi shields. Kicking the dying man off his blade, Varus took guard as the legionary's comrade came at him with his sword raised, stepping neatly aside and tripping the man in mid-lunge, then hacking down into the back of his neck to sever his spine and drop him lifeless into the mud. Flashing him a savage grin of approval, Scar raised his shield to stop a spear-thrust that penetrated the layered wood and trapped the weapon's blade, wrenching the board down to tear the spear from its wielder's hands even as he stabbed up into the sprawling soldier's throat, punching the blade up into his skull.

In a final desperate effort, thrown forward by the screams and shouts of their centurions, the naval legionaries crowded in behind a massive figure wielding a two-handed boarding axe as he strode forward into the Batavi line, hewing first one man and then another out of his path as he forged a path towards the two senior officers, drawn to the crests that decorated their helmets.

Alcaeus's Second Century lurched back under the vicious attack, soldiers on either side of the axeman's charge into their line momentarily held in place by the legionaries' last desperate assault upon them as the desperately tired soldiers lurched exhaustedly onto their shields, hacking and stabbing with the last of their strength to either side of their champion's massive, whirling frame. Alcaeus himself stood aghast as a single soldier stepped forward into the blood-slathered weapon's lethal arc, raising his shield to meet the axe's deadly power and releasing his grip on the board's hand grip at the very moment the weapon's blade embedded itself in the softer iron of its rounded boss. Stepping swiftly back a pace the Batavi allowed the shield to fall into the mud, its weight dragging the big man's axe down with it and making him stoop in an attempt to wrench his weapon free, then advanced a pace and struck with his weapon held underarm, throwing his arm out to lance the spear's blade through the muscles of the giant's upper arm and tear it free with equal speed. Dancing back as quickly as he had attacked he took a two handed grip on the wooden shaft and wielded the spear over his head, lunging the point downwards to bury the weapon's long iron blade deep into the unarmoured gap beside the stooping giant's bull neck between collar bone and shoulder blade. The legionary staggered backwards, his lurching step wrenching the spear's shaft from the

Batavi warrior's grip to point skywards, his every movement a source of agony as the weapon's blade moved deep in his chest. Staring in horror at the blood pouring from the wound to soak his left side, numb fingers still tightly locked about his weapon's bloody haft dragging the shield-encumbered axe through the battlefield's viscous, clinging mud, he abruptly lurched forward as his senses began to fail, only the prop provided by the axe's blood-soaked handle keeping him upright.

'*Finish him! For Hercules!*'

Whether Egilhard heard his centurion's command or not he was already in the act of drawing his sword, Lightning's shining blade whipping up to hang in the air for an instant before he struck, hacking down at the hand still gripping the axe's handle and severing it at the wrist. With the only thing that had been keeping him upright gone, the big man fell face first into the mud and lay still. The warriors around Egilhard roared their approval as he raised the bloodied sword over his helmeted head.

'*BATAVI!*'

With a collective roar of blood-lust, the German line pounced forward, sensing that the moment had come in which their enemy would break, and the legionaries, bereft of their last focal point of resistance, shattered into a mass of terrified individuals intent only on escaping from the howling tribesmen, unable to hold their ground any longer in the face of the Batavis' bestial assault and the oncoming threat of the Twenty-First legion's incensed soldiery.

'*Batavi! Hold!*'

Varus pointed at the fleeing men with an expression of anguish.

'They're getting away!'

Scar shook his head.

'No, they're not.'

He pointed to their right, waiting for Varus to realise why it was he had failed to order a foot pursuit. Several hundred of the tribe's horsemen were cantering past their right flank, their spears held ready for the death strike they practised every day against straw targets, a spear blade punched through plate armour with all the force of a fast-moving horse, spearing deep into the organs around the base of a fleeing man's back.

'We don't only use the horses for swimming, and every man in the seventh and eighth cohorts can ride well enough to hunt down the remnants of a shattered legion. I told my cohort centurions to offer a gold aureus apiece to the tent party who retakes the Twenty-First's eagle, so I wouldn't imagine it'll be too long before you have the pleasure of handing it back to the man who was careless enough to lose it. And besides, we have a bigger fish to gut.'

He looked over Varus's shoulder at the units still fighting on in the battlefield's centre, nodding slowly with respect for the fact that neither had stepped back from their increasingly bloody struggle, as more and more dead and wounded men fell into the deeply churned mud beneath their feet, their spurting blood spraying the men still fighting, making them look more like abattoir slaughter men than soldiers.

'You wanted to look at those praetorians down the length of your sword, Prefect? Now's your chance, while they're locked in battle with "Alexander the Great's Phalanx".'

Varus turned to follow his pointing hand, a slow smile spreading across his face as he realised that the enemy he despised was at his mercy. The imperial bodyguard were still fighting doggedly, their once white tunics now soiled with the battlefield's fouled mud and the blood of friend and foe alike, barely resisting the onslaught of the First Italica's stalwart legionaries who, recruited by Nero only a few years before for a campaign in the east that had never come to fruition and with no man less than six feet tall being accepted to their ranks, both outnumbered and outmuscled them.

'They're fighting for their very lives, because they know that if we break them they're unlikely to be shown very much by way of mercy, the faithless, murdering scum.'

Scar pointed at them with his sword.

'So shall we go and show them the way to Hades' kingdom?'

Reforming under the lash of their centurions' and chosen men's tongues, boots and vine sticks, the Batavi had rejoined their formation for the most part, other than those men who had charged off in blood-crazed pursuit of the fleeing marines, and Scar stalked out in front of them to make one swift challenge.

'This time we win the battle! Are you with me?'

The answer was instant, a grumbling growl of readiness as men set themselves to charge into the enemy, and Varus raised his voice in command as he stepped out alongside the Batavi prefect.

'See the praetorians before us! The First Italica have them pinned! We will assault their flank and rear! Attack only men wearing white, and show no mercy! Revenge for a murdered emperor! Revenge for the lost pride of the German Bodyguard! Revenge!'

'*Revenge!*'

The Batavi surged forward, eager to take their iron to the hated praetorians, and Scar saw those men who stood at the rear of the guard's blood-soaked line glancing nervously at his cohorts as they advanced implacably across the two hundred pace gap between the spot where they had routed the Classica and the soldiers struggling over the point of the battle's decision.

'*Batavi! Swim the seas . . .*'

The soldiers to either side of Scar took up the song in a heartbeat, their voices swelling in a challenge that had both praetorians and legionaries staring at them as they strode across the battlefield's churned and fouled earth, their pace unaffected by the obstacles presented by dead and dying men other than the occasional stutter as a warrior broke step for a moment to deliver a swift mercy stroke.

'Batavi! Swim the seas!
Worship mighty Hercules!
Swords and spears!
Take their ears!
Never showing mercy!'

The praetorians on the left-hand side of their line were starting to edge away, every man already exhausted from two or three spells fighting for their lives against the Italica's giants with only their justified fear of the treatment that would be meted out to them in the event that they were to break and run to stop them from running, but as the oncoming Germans' song swelled to a full-throated roar it was clear they were at the limits of their desperate courage.

> *'Batavi, break your shield!*
> *Kill you even if you yield!*
> *Slash and hack!*
> *Stab your back!*
> *Never showing mercy!'*

They were close enough to see the individual expressions on the faces of both sides in the grim struggle now, the Italica's men shouting and beckoning their allies on, the praetorians now positively flinching from their remorseless advance, a few of quicker-witted men trying to pull their line back to the left to fend off the oncoming threat.

> *'Batavi, German spears!*
> *Best and bravest many years!*
> *Nail your balls!*
> *To our walls!*
> *Never showing mercy!'*

Scar raised his arm, bellowing to be heard over the tumult.

'Batavi! Halt!'

With twenty paces separating them from the cringing praetorian line, the command halted his advancing warriors in an instant. A hush fell across the battlefield, broken only by the weeping cries of the wounded and imprecations from the Italica's men, as they implored the Batavi to attack.

'Give them the last verse!'

The cohorts stared across the short space between themselves and the guardsmen in silence for a moment, and then a single voice roared out a new verse to the tribe's battle hymn, written with just such a moment in mind.

'Batavi, Bodyguard royal . . .'

Thousands of voices rang out, spitting out the words that summed up their outrage.

> *'Batavi, Bodyguard royal!*
> *To all seven emperors loyal!*
> *Guard disbanded!*
> *Emperor murdered!*
> *Never show you mercy!'*

Scar drew breath to bark out one last command as his men roared out the embittered last line, ready to shout the one order that he knew his men expected above all others, given their opponents.

'Batavi . . . No! Prisoners!'

Even as the cohorts lunged forward at the praetorians, the guardsmen were already in motion, running for their lives, recognising the Germans' deadly intent and fleeing to the last man, not one guardsman or officer willing to test the limits of what the incensed warriors might inflict upon any man who fell into their clutches.

'Typical. Not even enough class to accept their defeat and die like men.'

Scar nodded at Varus's bitter complaint.

'There'll be plenty of time for you to savour your revenge on them. Who knows, perhaps the emperor will make *you* their prefect, since you're so set on purging them?'

The prefect laughed at the thought, and made to reply, but their moment of humour was interrupted by the interjection of a man in the pristine armour and almost spotless boots of a legatus, his sword still sheathed as he picked his way through the blood-filled ruts that had been dug into the soft soil by thousands of feet.

'I see you arrived just in time to scare off the remnants of the usurper's army with your barbarian horde, Alfenus Varus?'

Varus stared at him blankly for a moment before wiping his sword blade on a dead praetorian's tunic, staining the off-white cloth scarlet, and sheathing it.

'Greetings Legatus.'

The newcomer looked around himself at the scene of devastation for a moment before speaking again, his voice bitter with disappointment.

'It seems to me, Varus, as if we've won the empire for Vitellius this day, with you and your Germans playing a pivotal part there at the end. Doubtless you'll be suitably rewarded.' He looked down at his blood-spotted boots. 'Whereas any legatus who manages to lose his legion's eagle can only expect the censure of his peers and superiors.'

'In which case, Legatus, it's a good thing that my command is so strong in mounted troops. They're combing the battlefield as we speak, with a generous reward offered to the man who presents himself to me with that lost symbol of your legion's imperial pride. And I saw the whole thing, how your leading cohorts insisted on driving into the enemy despite being ordered to pull back into line. You would seem to have been the victim of your legion's legendary eagerness for blood, a weakness with which I am only too well acquainted given my command of an equally bloodthirsty collection of savages. Isn't that right, Prefect Germanicus?'

'Quite so, Prefect! Bloodthirsty and almost impossible to control, once the enemy is unwise enough to turn their backs and run!'

The Twenty-First legion's commander stared at him for a moment, then nodded briskly.

'Indeed. I will of course be grateful for the return of the eagle, should your horsemen come up with it from that fleeing rabble.'

'And you'll pay the reward I've offered, I presume?'

'Whatever it is, send the man in question to me and I'll see him paid with a smile. There'll be a triumph when we reach Rome, and for the Twenty-First's eagle not to be carried through the city alongside those of her sisters would mark the end of my career, of that much I can be certain. Possibly even the end of the Twenty-First as well.'

He nodded and turned away, leaving Varus staring after him with a small smile. After a moment he looked round at Scar, whose face was still commendably straight.

'Well done, Prefect Germanicus. His career might be hanging on the latrine edge, but there was no need for him to have the slightest motivation to take you with him. And yes, before you ask, I do consider myself to be a politician. Who knows, perhaps I *will* end up commanding those faithless Praetorian scum. I might even ask the emperor for the opportunity to perform that purge you were speaking of.'

He stared after the fleeing guardsmen, nodding approvingly as the Batavi chased them away from the battlefield's ruined ground with whoops and shouts of savage glee as the slower runners were hunted down and finished off without mercy.

'If, that is, there any of them left to command after this rout. Oh, and I'd very much like to meet the soldier who took down that unfeasibly large marine with the axe, if he survives the day.'

Scar nodded, hooking a thumb at Alcaeus who was walking the battlefield with his sword drawn, delivering the mercy stroke to those wounded men who looked unlikely to survive.

'My wolf priest's new boy? I expect he'll have come through it unscathed. After all, heroes tend not to die quite so early in their ascent to greatness. Not until the weight of their fame becomes too heavy for them to bear.'

8

Castra Augusta Taurinorum, May AD 69

'We've only been here four days and I'm already sick to my back teeth of the fucking place!'

Grimmaz's tent mates nodded disconsolately at the truth in his growled opinion. While he was known to be one of the century's least cheerful individuals, when not distracted by the usual soldiers' pursuits that their centurion habitually referred to as 'feeding, fighting and fucking, and not necessarily in that order', the truth of his statement was indisputable, given the way in which the initial euphoria at their victory at Cremona had swiftly been followed by a post-battle hangover more severe by far than any of the Batavi had ever suffered after combat in Britannia. While the two armies' senior officers mused on the usual corrosive effects of Romans fighting Romans, with several rumoured cases of sons having killed fathers and men finding themselves face-to-face with their brothers at swordpoint, the concerns of the common soldiery, especially men who deemed themselves to be something other than Roman, were somewhat more basic.

'It wouldn't be so bad if we didn't have the "Fighting Fucking Fourteenth" sharing the town with us. Miserable cunts.'

More nodding greeted Grimmaz's gloomy statement. The six remaining Othonian legions, more than strong enough to have fought an attritional war across Northern Italy for months, and certain to have gained in strength as they moved to combine while the German legions would only have become weaker as the result of poor supply and unfamiliar diseases, had been ordered to surrender by their imperial master as a prelude to a needless suicide which, from the victors' perspective, only went to show how unsuitable he'd been for the role of emperor in the first place but which also, inevitably, provided his former followers with an excuse for their abrupt change of fortunes. His defeated legions had swiftly been ordered to disperse across the empire in order to nullify their remaining threat, with the sole exception of the Fourteenth, for decades the Batavis' parent legion, a relationship that had already been deeply riven even before the two had found themselves on opposite sides of the battle lines. Still truculent in the extreme in their reluctance to accept defeat, the legion had been deemed as insufficiently trustworthy to be sent away unsupervised, and had instead been posted to the fortress town of Taurinorum where a weather eye could be kept on its behaviour by a loyal unit of equivalent strength. The choice of the Batavi cohorts to provide that counterbalancing presence had been judged as inept by even the mildest opinions, and in the view of many men on both sides could only have resulted from a deliberately cruel sense of humour, the presence of so many battle-hardened and mutually inimical soldiers seemingly the perfect recipe for trouble. Attempts by the legionaries to convince the Batavi that Cremona would have been an entirely different battle had they reached the scene of the fighting in time to participate in legion strength, rather than the small advance party that had marched ahead of the main force, had already led in brief succession to mocking, vicious abuse of each other's perceived failings and then outright physical hostility. Now both Batavi and legionaries, under strict instructions to avoid any further conflict, walked the town's streets in search of entertainment with a variety of concealed weapons hidden about them just in case there was any repeat of a fight the previous day, a spontaneous brawl between two centuries of men who had found themselves occupying the same tavern and seen no good reason not to violently dispute its ownership, the legionaries driven to fight by wounded pride, their former allies by something far darker.

At length Wigbrand spoke, his voice more wistful than angry, and if any of the men around the table felt inclined to mock either his sentiment or the soft, almost feminine voice in which he expressed it, the fact that he was a head taller and half a chest wider than the biggest of them was a powerful deterrent to any mirth at his expense.

'I wouldn't mind it so much if there were women to talk to. Not necessarily whores, just some girls to joke with, you know.'

Grimmaz looked at his mate.

'You're getting soft, you daft cunt. Women are for fucking, Tiny, not for talking to.'

The big man looked across the table at him and shook his head slowly.

'How many men did you kill at Bedriacum?'

The soldier shrugged.

'Four? Five? Might have been half a dozen. I wasn't counting.'

'I killed three. And I can tell you how each of them died. I can tell you where I speared the first one, and the noise he made when the blade went through a gap in his armour. And the look on his face. I still remember how I cut the second one down with my gladius, after Achilles had tripped him and put him on his knees with his neck open for the blow. I can still see the colour of his spine. And the third . . .'

The man around him went quiet, knowing that he'd been having nightmares about the third man he'd killed ever since the battle, waking screaming among them every night and having to be calmed by the men to either side before they could resume their sleep, the curses of the tents to either side ringing in their ears.

'We know, the third was nothing more than a boy, and he begged you for mercy even as you were cutting his throat.'

Silence reigned for a moment before the big man spoke again.

'I miss my mother and my sisters. All I want a woman for is to talk to.'

'Just as well, since I doubt you could get it up anyway.'

Grimmaz's muttered comment was supposed to be sotto voce, but a momentary lull in the din from the tables around them allowed it to reach every man at the table, most of whom looked uneasily at the giant, whose big fist had tightened on the half-loaf in his hand until crushed bread oozed from between his knuckles. He started to his feet, only to find his rise obstructed by a powerful pair of hands on his shoulders.

'I don't know who said what, and I don't give a fuck. Sit down, drink your wine, eat your bread and all just concentrate on being friends, right?'

Wigbrand turned in his chair to find Alcaeus standing behind him. The centurion was dressed in his walking-out tunic with its ornately decorated and distinctly non-standard wide leather belt from which were suspended purse and dagger, while his vine stick was tucked between leather and tunic to free both hands for whatever it was he had in mind.

'Just as well I turned up, isn't it?'

He waited, looking pointedly at Grimmaz until the soldier muttered the expected response.

'Yes, Centurion.'

Alcaeus nodded his head at the abashed soldier in an exaggerated manner.

'Yes, Centurion, it is a fucking good thing you turned up and avoided me getting my face punched in. Isn't that what you meant to say, Happy? I am a clever centurion, knowing that with Banon on duty there'd be no-one to stop you from opening your big mouth and digging a hole with it, aren't I?'

'Yes, Centurion.'

'Perhaps you could take some notice of one of your men? Young Achilles here . . .' He gestured to Egilhard, who reddened at the unexpected attention. 'He doesn't seem to be bothered by anything much, does he?'

The younger man sank into his seat slightly, embarrassed not simply by being called out as an example by his centurion but by the glaring fact of his new nickname's swift replacement by the one his father had so carefully warned him not to court. Saving Lanzo from certain death had quickly earned him a reputation among the men of the Second Century, but the defeat of the axe-wielding legionary had made his name known among the Batavi cohorts overnight and suddenly the young man found soldiers twice his age favouring him with respectful nods, many of whom were unknown to him but who seemed as certain in their recognition of his battlefield exploits as his own tent mates, and none of whom seemed to harbour even the smallest hint of jealousy. Indeed they seemed to revel in his new-found fame, happily pointing out to all and sundry the deep notch cut into the boss of his shield by the legionary's axe at Cremona, marvelling that he had managed to stop such a powerful blow without any broken bones in his hand, the cloven iron one piece of equipment damage that Alcaeus flatly refused to see repaired, calling it a token of Hercules' favour too strong to be tossed needlessly away.

The centurion nodded, smiling beatifically at the men around the table.

'Good. Now I'll be around and about, mixing with the boys, having a cup of the overpriced piss that seems to be all that's left in town and generally making sure that none of my lads get themselves into any trouble. Which, given that those hysterical women from the Fourteenth are billeted on this desperate shithole, and still bitter that their side lost the war without most of them getting the chance to air their iron, might be harder than usual. So do yourselves a favour, spare me the arseache of having to have you all flogged tomorrow and just this *once* don't go starting any fights, right?'

The men around the table all nodded respectfully and voiced their wholehearted agreement, and after a moment more to make sure that Wigbrand had subsided back into his usual state of introspection, the officer gave them all one last hard stare and departed in search of more enlightened company.

'Scar's somewhere in town this afternoon, and he promised me a whole amphora of wine after the battle, for snuffing out the marines' counter-attack. And that's one debt I fully intend to collect.'

After a few moments desultory conversation Grimmaz stood, palming the coins that each man had placed on the table as his share of the pot. Striding up to the bar he eyeballed the man standing behind it confidently.

'We're moving on. Seven wines and a plate of bread. Four?'

'Ten.'

The soldier goggled in genuine amazement.

'*How* much? You *robbing* fucker!'

Clearly accustomed to having his prices challenged in such robust terms the tavern keeper betrayed only the smallest hint of irritation as he waved the Batavi soldier's protest away.

'The price is the price, soldier! If you want to eat my bread and drink my wine then you have to pay, same as everyone else! I have to pay more for the bread, and more for the wine, thanks to you lot doubling demand for even the poorest quality, which is pretty much all I can find on the market these days. So if you don't like my prices then go and find someone who'll sell to you cheaper, eh?'

He grunted abruptly as the soldier in question reached over the counter and dragged him across the counter by his tunic, punching him in the face and then dropping him gasping to the tavern's floor.

'You think I risked my fucking life to free you from tyranny so that you could ponce off me and my mates? I was putting better men than you to the sword while you were sat here sipping at your wine with a barmaid sucking your cock, and now you tell me to go and drink somewhere else, like I'm not good enough for your precious tavern? Well here's the news mate, your shit smells just like mine, and I ain't going to put up with you trying to have me over!'

'No! I was only trying to say—'

A boot in the ribs silenced the stricken innkeeper's protests, and the leading man's tent mates got to their feet, looking around the remaining clientele with the expressions of men hoping for a reason to unload their frustrations in a similar manner.

'Oi! Leave him alone!' A newcomer stood in the tavern's doorway, more men dressed in identical white tunics close behind him. 'I'm billeted here, so that's my man you're abusing. Pack it up and piss right off, unless you want to be dealing with the Fighting Fourteenth!'

To his obvious disgust the men gathered around the tavern owner turned to face him with barely restrained mirth, Grimmaz stepping forward with a look of derision on his face.

'Fighting Fourteenth? You can't mean the same Fourteenth Legion that minced around Britannia behind our cohorts, always sending us in first to make sure the enemy were nicely softened up before you came to give them a good kicking once they were on the floor?'

The legionary's eyes narrowed.

'Step outside and repeat that, and then we'll see where it gets you!'

'Right!'

Grimmaz strode purposefully towards the legion man, who stepped back into the street and looked to either side of him in a way that sounded an alarm in Egilhard's mind.

'This feels wrong.'

Grimmaz stepped up to the waiting legionary, so close that he was nose to nose with the other man, snarling the insult that he'd been challenged to repeat.

'What I said, you *ponce*, was that you pricks in the Fourteenth were always more than happy to hide behind the Batavi when the going got rough! And then always first to the front of the line when the hard work was done! You—'

He fell silent as he realised that half the men in the street were looking at him with expressions that boded poorly for his immediate future. Lanzo stepped through the door behind him with the rest of the tent party behind him, raising his left hand in apology.

'He's had a few, that's all! We'll take him away and you lads can all get back to your drinks!'

'No you fucking don't!' The soldier who had invited Grimmaz outside shook his head pugnaciously. 'This prick just pissed all over my legion's fucking pride, and he can suck it all back up if he wants to walk away!'

Lanzo shrugged good-naturedly, his smile untouched by the legionary's apparent unwillingness to let the matter go.

'In point of fact friend, nothing he said was all that inaccurate. We were always first into action when we marched with the Fourteenth, and that's the truth. There was a time when you boys loved us for that, but then you're probably too young to have seen the fighting in Britannia. So come on, for old times' sake, just let me take him for a drink somewhere a bit less heaving with you lads, eh, where he can't upset anyone? There's no need for anyone to get hurt, not so soon after fighting such a fucking horrible battle.'

He realised, the moment the words were out of his mouth, that he'd said the wrong thing. The soldier turned away, raising his arms to gesture to his comrades.

'Now they're having a fucking go because we didn't make it to Cremona in time! Are we going to have to listen to this shit for the rest of our fucking lives? I say we give them a good f—'

Turning back to the Batavi soldiers, he realised too late that the hand that Lanzo hadn't raised had contained a hidden threat, as the auxiliary revealed a brass-clad fist and swung a swift punch into the side of his head, dropping him senseless to the cobbles while the tent party stepped up alongside him, ready to fight. Andronicus looked up and down the silent street, knowing that an explosion of violence was almost inevitable, raising his voice to shout a warning he hoped would be audible across half the city.

'We only came out for a quiet drink! This doesn't have to end bloody, but if it does you *know* what we're capable of!'

A hulking bruiser broke the spell that Lanzo's swift disposal of the legionary had cast over them, bellowing at his fellow soldiers in a slurred voice that betrayed a long afternoon of drinking.

'He fuckin' decked Rufus! *Ged 'em!*'

Grimmaz nodded to himself, lowered his head and raised his fists, having retrieved a set of brass knuckles from his purse, barking a command at his men.

'*Ready!*'

The tent party took their places behind him with the speed of men whose afternoon had hardly begun, giving them a distinct advantage over the legionaries who were, for the most part, significantly more inebriated than them. As the last man stepped into place they snapped out a roared response to Grimmaz's challenge that raised hairs on the necks of every man within earshot.

'*READY!*'

The big man frowned at the Batavi as they moved quickly into a wedge-shaped formation on either side of their leader and Wigbrand bringing up the rear with the look of a man with a lot of frustration to unload on the unwary, a heavy wooden chair leg held in each hand.

'What the f—'

'*Go!*'

Stepping forward swiftly in perfect unison, they advanced into the street with a single purpose, Grimmaz at the point of their spearhead, closing with the big legionary whose alcohol intake had clearly sadly affected his cognitive abilities. Raising a hand to point incredulously at the auxiliaries, he went down spitting blood and teeth as the hard-faced soldier took him out with a single punch, bellowing the tribe's call to action for his comrades to echo an instant later.

'*Batavi!*'

'*BATAVI!*'

From either side the call was taken up, men scattered along the street's length tossing aside their wine cups and reaching into purses for the weaponry that they habitually carried when they walked out alongside any legion. In a moment the scene was transformed from uneasy truce to whirling melee, the single-minded auxiliaries snapping into action with vicious speed and purpose, grouping together to take on whoever was to hand. Grimmaz looked to his left, away from the route back to the gate through which they had entered the city, seeing a beleaguered knot of their fellows struggling against twice their number of legionaries.

'Second Century! Follow me!'

Pummelling any man that got in their way, hitting and moving before the legionaries between them and their comrades could mount an effective defence, the tent party battered their way through to their embattled brothers, who fell gratefully into their ranks, bloodied and bruised, as Grimmaz's men hammered their opponents into the gutter with brutal efficiency, Wigbrand laying into the hapless legion men two-handed and felling one after another with swift strokes of his improvised wooden clubs. Grimmaz stood panting next to Lanzo, his face twisted in a savage grin despite the blood trickling down his tunic from a split lip.

'*Fucking great . . . all we have to do now . . . is get all the way back . . . to the gate.*'

His comrade nodded sombrely, seeing legion reinforcements flooding into the street from the bars and taverns.

'This is turning into a goat fuck! We'll be lucky to get out of this shithole without getting our legs broken!'

The two men looked at each other for a moment and then simultaneously started laughing.

'What's so funny? We're going to get our arses handed to us!'

Lanzo looked down his nose at Egilhard, shaking his head.

'If you can't take a joke, you shouldn't have joined!' He sucked in a long breath, blowing the air out and rotating his head on a neck rippling with muscle. 'Come on then you bastards, let's show these cunts the honour of the Batavi!'

'Not so fucking fast!'

Lanzo snapped to attention.

'Centurion!'

Alcaeus stood before them, tunic immaculate and a cup of wine still held in one hand.

'What the fuck is going on?'

'We were challenged, Centurion, and you've always told us that a single step backwards—'

'—is a defeat? Yes, I did.' The officer shook his head in disbelief. 'So this is all my fault, is it?'

Grimmaz grinned, recognising the man's urge to fight.

'We'll cover for you, Centurion, you being a holy man and all. You just go back into that tav—'

Alcaeus drained his cup and tossed it into the gutter, pulling the vine stick from his belt.

'Like fuck. Let's show the Fourteenth how real men fight, shall we? *Hercules and the Batavi!*'

Castra Augusta Taurinorum, May AD 69

'Call Prefect Scar!'

The Praetorian centurion waiting beside Scar nodded and gestured to the door in front of them, which had swung open a moment before to allow the Fourteenth Gemina's legatus to leave the audience chamber. Pale-faced with evident fury, his glance across at the waiting Batavi officer had been poisonous, and even the guard officer had muttered a comment to the effect that it was a good thing a decent-sized party of Scar's biggest and nastiest men were waiting to escort him back to their barracks. Rules and seniority were one thing, but a dagger's blade tended not to have too many scruples as to whose blood it spilled. Marching forward into the audience chamber, he strode to the point where another of the praetorians recently enrolled from the victorious Vitellian legions was waiting with his vine stick pointing meaningfully at a point on the tiled floor, his other hand just as significantly resting on the handle of his dagger. Stamping to attention half a dozen paces from the throne on which Vitellius himself was waiting for him, the emperor tight lipped and evidently angry, he thrust a hand out in a salute so vigorous that the waiting guard officer visibly flinched, bellowing a greeting that made even the emperor blink.

'*Hail Caesar!*'

Waiting at attention, he fixed his gaze on a spot just above the emperor's head and allowed himself to relax into the momentary fantasy that he was a recruit again, avoiding eye contact with his new centurion for fear that the officer would wield his vine stick in anger at any implied insubordination. In reality he was the officer whose men were allegedly responsible for a fortress-wide altercation requiring the violent intervention of two full cohorts of praetorians to stop fighting that had threatened to result in mass casualties. An officer standing in front of a man who could, with a single word, end either his military career or his life.

'Prefect.'

Vitellius looked down at the scroll in his lap and Scar pounced, determined not to show any hint of weakness to the disapproving chorus of Roman officers gathered behind their ruler.

'*Tiberius Julius Germanicus, Caesar!*'

The emperor's gaze flicked back up to the scarred face of the man standing before him, but if he was looking for any hint of disrespect he was disappointed. Twenty-two years of soldiering had blessed Scar with the ability to wear a mask of such bland attentiveness, initially to avoid the ire of those above him and latterly to avoid betraying his disappointment with the vast majority of the men that Rome put in command of its armies, while silently working out how to work within their plans to the best effect and fewest casualties.

'There's no need to shout, Prefect, I can hear you perfectly well.'

'Thank you, Caesar!'

The older man stared at him for a moment longer, taking in the Batavi's lean figure and cruel, disfigured face, evidence of a life spent marching and fighting for Rome across the length and breadth of occupied Britannia, enduring months and even years of boredom interspersed by moments of sheer exhilaration when the men who held the Batavi's collar had unleashed the empire's favourite attack dogs. Nobody understood better than Vitellius the frequent necessity for the Janus headed coin of Roman diplomacy to spin and come down on its subtly weighted obverse, the application of swift and deadly force wielded by men regarded as little better than trained animals.

'So, Prefect Tiberius Julius Germanicus. Your tribal name is Scar, I believe. An interesting name. Did your father bless you with it, or have you earned it since joining our auxiliary forces?'

'Both are true, Caesar.'

Vitellius nodded, turning his attention back to the scroll.

'This altercation yesterday, Prefect. The details read poorly, from where I sit. Thirty-five legionaries hospitalised along with twenty-two of your own men. And even in the corridors of the fortress infirmary, with medicae working to mend broken limbs and heal stab wounds, my praetorian prefect has found it necessary to post his men to maintain the peace between your own casualties and those of the Fourteenth Gemina. Why do you think that is, Prefect?'

Scar hesitated for a moment, considering his response, and the emperor did some pouncing of his own, perhaps looking to restore balance to their conversation, perhaps simply from irritation at having to waste his time considering hostilities between a loyal tribal ally and a legion that until recently would have cheerfully have separated his head from his shoulders. And possibly still would, given the chance.

'Don't bother trying to work out what I want to hear, Prefect, just tell me what's on your mind . . . all of your minds. Tell me what it is that launches your Germans into a legion of defeated men like bolts from a ballista. And stand at ease, you're making my guardsmen nervous.' Scar relaxed his posture, shooting a swift glance at Varus who was standing at the emperor's shoulder resplendent in the magnificence of a praetorian prefect, and the emperor smiled at him without his eyes changing their gimlet-like regard of the man before him. 'Praetorian Prefect Varus has already pointed out to me your men's pivotal role at Cremona, and your own personal example of both discipline in holding firm to perform orders you found distasteful, and then undisguised martial prowess in defeating both the First Classica and the Praetorian cohorts in swift succession, so you can take it as read that I understand your value to my army. Just speak freely, man.'

Scar nodded.

'As you command, Caesar. The Batavi . . . Batavian cohorts and the Fourteenth Legion have a long history, much of it happy. They were our parent legion, and we served faithfully alongside them for twenty-five years in Britannia. They were the disciplined face of Roman order, their use against a tribe the last resort when the talking was done and a swift and savage war inevitable, while we were their weapon of choice when there was an example to be made, a village to be burned out or a rebel warband to be hunted down. We were first into battle, and often all that was needed to bring an enemy tribe to its knees, and for a long time the Fourteenth enjoyed the glory that reflected upon them, the relationship between us almost a meeting of equals despite the differences in our status.'

'Which rankled?'

'No, Caesar. We do not aspire to live like legionaries, we are Batavi and happy to be who we are. The truth is that a gap opened between my men and those of the Fourteenth after the defeat of the rebel Boudicca, for which the previous emperor named the Fourteenth Martia Victrix for defeating an army of sixty thousand with only their own strength and their Batavi and Tungrian cohorts. We were allowed no share of this glory, given no badge of honour for routing the enemy before the legion moved to make the kill, and when the legion's soldiers saw our unhappiness with this they started calling us barbarians and belittling our achievements. Rather than lauding us for our skills in battle they took to dismissing us as savages, while for our part it was a natural reaction to emphasise our own role as their shock troops, and compare it with their role as the weapon of last resort, which saw us do far more fighting than they were ever allowed. The relationship went sour, Caesar, for reasons I do not fully understand, and one thing led to another. When the legion was ordered to the east to take part in the planned invasion of Parthia it was a relief to my predecessor that we were not chosen to accompany them, he told me, given the state of hostility between us. And when the current sad state of affairs led us to this fortress, billeted alongside the Fourteenth, I went so far as to warn the praetorian prefect, a man I know to be both brave and honourable, of the risk that fighting would result.'

'This is true?'

Varus spoke from his place behind the throne.

'It is, Caesar. I spoke with the Fourteenth's legatus on the subject at some length, and advised him to counsel his men to behave in a manner appropriate for a legion that had been defeated on the field of battle, and which had erred so grievously in their choice of sides in the war you have now so conclusively won. I also had much the same conversation with the Prefect here, suggesting that his men should be ordered to demonstrate some magnanimity in victory, for the sake of their long association with the Fourteenth, and perhaps to prove themselves the equal to any legion.'

The emperor nodded.

'I see. It seems that your advice was ignored by both parties.'

'As was always likely to be the case, Caesar, which is why I had two cohorts of men waiting fully armed, in readiness for just such an outbreak of hostilities.'

'Wise, Alfenius Varus. You are to be commended for your foresight. And you, Prefect Germanicus, what do you believe I should do with your command for this utter disregard for the proprieties and discipline expected of any unit serving in my army, regular or auxiliary?'

Scar drew his body back to attention, sensing that the time for less formal discussion of the matter was at an end.

'The usual military discipline would be to have all participants in the matter punished according to their part in it. I have already conducted a thorough review of the matter and concluded that one tent party in particular was responsible for the initial outbreak of fighting, clearly provoked by a soldier of the Fourteenth but nevertheless guilty of a disproportionate response. They will all be flogged this evening in front of every man in my command, and their centurion has been reduced to the ranks for failing to keep a grip of his men. He will suffer the same punishment as the newest member of their party. As for myself, Caesar, I offer you my vine stick.' He held out his badge of office with both hands. 'Take it from me and I will do the only honourable thing under the circumstances.'

The emperor's eyes widened, and he turned to speak with Varus for a moment, watching as the prefect nodded in response to his question, then turned back to face the stony faced Batavi.

'I have considered your offer and am constrained by my need for good men on the frontiers of Germania to refuse it, especially as you have already demonstrated your willingness to seek out and punish those men guilty of starting the affray in question. Doubtless the Fourteenth's legatus will conduct a similarly robust investigation before following my orders and taking his command back to Britannia. Keep your vine stick, Prefect, your orders to march north will be with you before the day's end. Dismissed.'

The matter already dismissed from his mind, he turned to his praetorian prefect as Scar made for the door.

'Which reminds me, Alfenius Varus, we have still to discuss this Eighth Legion centurion, Aquillius, whom you have commended to me despite his naked refusal to refute his legion's oath of allegiance to Otho.'

'Quite so, Caesar. And to my mind it would seem a waste of a good man to simply throw away such an outstanding officer, even if his obduracy might tempt us to make an example of him.'

Their voices faded as he marched into the audience chamber's ante-room, where the praetorian officer put a hand on his arm.

'Wait here, Prefect. The praetorian prefect wishes to speak with you.'

After a short wait Varus walked into the room through the same door, waving a hand to dismiss his man and waiting until they were alone to speak, a small smile creasing his face.

'That's two good men saved from an ignominious end in one morning. I may have found my calling in life, it seems.' He shook his head at Scar with genuine amusement. 'Well now, Prefect Germanicus, it could never be said that you're a man lacking in bravado.'

Scar shrugged.

'The choice of taking the emperor at his word or playing the cringing subject was no choice, Prefect.'

'And you really intend to flog your warrior priest as punishment for a fight his men started?'

The Batavi shook his head.

'No, Prefect. I intend to flog a man I've reduced to the ranks as punishment for his making the mistake of being drawn into a fight the Fourteenth Legion started. You can take the man out of the tribe, Prefect, but you can't take the tribe out of the man. And it's time my men had it pointed out to them that we're not in any position to lay down the law to a legion, not even the pathetic collection of cry-babies that our former colleagues of the Fourteenth have become in the years since we last stood alongside them on a battlefield. An example is needed, and an example will be made. No matter how unhappy it might be for all concerned. Including me.'

Castra Augusta Taurinorum, May AD 69

'You all know what's expected of you. We put ourselves here, now we can accept the punishment that we've earned and repay Scar for saving us from worse by upholding the tradition of the tribe.'

Egilhard looked at his former centurion in puzzlement.

'I don't understand. What tradition of the tribe?'

Alcaeus looked at Grimmaz disparagingly.

'Looks like you have a little more education to impart, Leading Man . . . Sir.'

Grimmaz shook his head.

'Please don't call me *sir*. Not you.'

The older man shrugged.

'Deal with it, Happy. I've made peace with the fact that I'm paying the price for my own stupidity, so why can't you? I had the clear chance to walk away, but instead I stopped thinking and started punching. I asked for this punishment, and this is the point where I get what I asked for. So explain what's expected of him to young Achilles, before it's too late.'

Grimmaz sighed.

'What the cent– Alcaeus is trying to tell you, is that the pride of the tribe demands we take our stripes without showing any sign of weakness. When the moment comes we'll walk out in front of the cohorts like gladiators in the arena, not proud or haughty mind you, but strong. Walk to your whipping post without hesitation, put your arms round it and clasp your hands together.'

Egilhard frowned.

'I thought we'd be tied to the posts?'

The leading man shook his head.

'That's for criminals. Men of the tribe aren't tied for a beating, not unless they've done something so bad that the scourge is to be their punishment and then they have to be tied, and gagged, because no man can stand or remain silent under the scourge. We stand up and take our lashes, and we don't let out a sound. The first one's the hardest, after that there's a sort of numbness that takes over and it's over before you know it.'

Egilhard nodded.

'You've done this before.'

Grimmaz nodded solemnly, turning to show the young soldier his back, still bearing faint marks.

'Once, seven years ago. Three lashes for fighting in camp, and after that I swore I'd never put myself through the pain again, but it seems I'm not clever enough for the lesson to have—'

He sprang to attention as Scar walked into the tent.

'Attention!'

The Prefect looked around at the nine men awaiting punishment with a tired expression.

'Of all the things I need to get done today, having you fools beaten wouldn't even make it on to a list written in an extra-large tablet with a darning needle, except I've made a promise to an emperor to serve you idiots out for starting a fight that almost became all-out war between ourselves and an imperial legion. A beating is what I promised him, and a beating is what you're going to get, five strokes each, and you pricks are going to take your stripes without making a sound. Not a whimper.'

He walked down the line of men still speaking, his tone menacing.

'Did you know that in my entire time as the prefect of these cohorts, not one of the men who has received a punishment beating has made enough sound to be heard by anyone other than the man with the whip? And I don't intend for that to change today. So you're going to need these.'

He handed each of them a short piece of wooden dowel just large enough to fit inside a man's mouth.

'Bite on these,' he said quietly, 'it helps. I know.'

'Bring forward the men for punishment!'

Praetorian Prefect Varus and the Fourteenth Legion's legatus stood at the parade ground's edge watching as the Batavian cohorts stood in sullen silence.

'Not so clever now, are they?' The praetorian prefect turned his head to look at the legion's commander for a long moment before returning his gaze to the soldiers marching out into the open space at the heart of their comrades' formation. 'Perhaps after this they'll think twice about starting fights they can't finish.'

To Varus's eye the condemned men had more of a look of wounded pride about them than any hint of the shame that the man standing beside him was implying. Stripped to the waist, and wearing rough leggings that could be discarded after the floggings that they were about to undergo, they were marching towards the whipping posts that had been erected for the purpose of their punishment with the precision and pride of men parading before their emperor.

'I told Vitellius that this is what happens when barbarians like these animals get ideas above their st—'

Varus's patience snapped completely and irrevocably.

'You would be wise, Legatus, to hold your own counsel on the matter.'

He turned to stare at the legion commander.

'I—'

'There is nothing so irritating in life, I find, as an idiot that cannot recognise his own idiocy.'

The legatus bristled with indignation.

'I'll not stay here to be insulted, I'll—'

'Yes, you will. You'll shut your mouth and you'll stay here to watch this charade while I tell you the absolute truth about yourself, your legion, and your many and various shortcomings, if I choose to. Because if, Legatus, you choose to walk away, I promise you that there will be another man in command of "your" legion by this time tomorrow.'

'You couldn't . . .'

Varus smiled beatifically.

'Oh but I could. Haven't you heard? I'm the man who put both the First Classica and the praetorian cohorts to flight. I'm the man who tore your side's left flank to ribbons, and left the two strongest enemy formations on the battlefield running for their lives. I'm the man who retrieved the Twenty-First Rapax's lost eagle, so that it can be paraded through Rome in triumph, rather than lying at the bottom of some nameless well for the rest of eternity. And as a direct consequence of those exploits I'm now the Praetorian Prefect, with access to the emperor any time I like, and complete control over who gets to see Vitellius and who sits and cools their heels until they work out that they won't be gaining admission to the imperial presence. And do you know how I achieved those feats of outstanding valour that have seen me so richly rewarded?'

He pointed at the Batavi.

'With *them*. Through *their* efforts. *Their* bloodshed. Their simple, savage, *barbarian* bravery. And now, because your legion doesn't understand the fact that a fool like you chose to throw their weight behind an even greater fool than yourself, who murdered an honourable emperor to steal the throne, and then chose to end his own life when he realised just how far out of his depth he was swimming, and because you're not man enough to tell them that you made a mistake, they seek to take their frustration out on the very men who gifted them the victory in Britannia whose blood and courage led to them being named "*Martia Victrix*".'

Varus looked out over the parade ground, watching impassively as the last of the soldiers was led to his whipping post.

'Victorious and beloved by Mars?' He snorted dismissively.

'Those eight men out there have more courage than a cohort of yours. See how they're not tied to the posts? It's an item of faith for the Batavians that they take their punishments voluntarily, in silence, and so there they stand awaiting a punishment that they do not deserve, because you've allowed your men to mistake thin-skinned failure to accept a defeat as some kind of substitute for victory. I'd say the sooner you're on your way back to Britannia the better, wouldn't you?'

Alcaeus took his position at the last whipping post, turning his head to look down the line of his men. He grinned widely at Grimmaz, and Egilhard beyond him, provoking a baffled stare from the leading man.

'Where's your gag?'

The former centurion winked and waggled his right hand, waving the wooden dowel at them.

'If I can do this without the gag you can easily ride it with yours in place. This is my sacrifice to Hercules, not the death of some helpless animal, but my silence under the lash.'

Scar had walked out to address the gathered cohorts, his voice booming out over the parade ground.

'Men of the Batavi cohorts! Our brothers come before you for punishment, having been judged to have acted rashly in the face of an avoidable challenge in the town yesterday! They were the men who started the fight, for the most part, apart from Soldier Alcaeus who, as a centurion, failed to control his men when he had the chance to do so but instead chose to join the fight!'

He looked around at the cohorts standing in silence on all four sides.

'Batavi pride is one thing, but to seek to fight where no fight is needed is entirely another. All of these men have admitted to their misdeeds and have been sentenced to receive the standard punishment, five lashes to be delivered by their comrades who have been chosen by lot from each cohort.'

The selection process had been swift and transparent, the six centurions in each of the other seven cohorts than the First drawing lots to determine which of them would provide a soldier to wield the lash, then repeating the process to choose the tent party and finally the man who would have the misfortune of administering a punishment that was widely regarded as iniquitous. The men to whom the lots fell stepped forward, accepting their whips and taking their places behind each of the half-naked men awaiting their fate. Taking the last whip, Scar walked to the end of the line and took up his position behind Alcaeus, who looked around and smiled wryly at his former superior before bracing himself for the first blow.

'I'll be watching you as I deliver Soldier Alcaeus's punishment, all of you with the whips, and if any of you think you can go easy on these men then you'll soon enough find yourself in their place, with me showing you the error of your ways! Five lashes, delivered with the appropriate force, and if there isn't blood running down their backs by the time you're done then it'll be running down yours shortly afterwards. Got that?'

He leaned close to Alcaeus, affecting to prepare to deliver the first blow while he muttered quietly in his former centurion's ear.

'You palmed the gag, I presume?'

'How did you know?'

'Because I have eyes. And because your men seem to have the same rocks in their heads that seem to have taken the place of your brains.'

Alcaeus looked up at Grimmaz, finding the leading man's eyes fixed on his and his mouth spread in a wide grin. The wooden gag was at his feet, where he'd spat it out on realising that Alcaeus had elected to go without. The men beyond him had followed his example, their gags discarded on the parade ground's stony surface.

'You fucking *idiots*.'

Grimmaz chuckled back at him.

'For Hercules, eh? I'll have some of that. If it's good for you, Centurion, then it's—'

Scar laughed tersely.

'The time for chatter was past when you left the punishment

tent, ladies. Shut your mouths and keep them shut, if you know what's good for you.'

He raised his voice, swinging the whip back for the first blow. '*Commence the punishment!*'

Varus watched as Scar drew his arm back and then snapped the whip's tail across Alcaeus's back, the newly demoted soldier's body jerking with the white-hot bolt of pain as the leather's fierce impact raised a red weal across his muscular body.

'One!'

He drew the whip back again, taking careful aim before striking for a second time, the whip's blow landing an inch lower in almost perfect symmetry with the angry mark left by the first swing.

'Two!'

Along the line of whipping posts the unlucky soldiers who had been selected to exact punishment upon their comrades were doing the same, carefully considering each blow before they delivered it, and while each of the men being beaten shuddered with every impact, it was obvious to Varus that the lashes were being positioned to avoid them overlapping where possible. He looked at the Fourteenth Legion's legatus, daring the man to show any sign of approval.

'Remember, Legatus, just one word . . .'

Scar swung his whip for the last time, then threw it aside with an instruction to burn it and all the others that had been used to deliver his sentence.

'The punishment has been carried out, and accepted without a sound by the men receiving it! The Batavi have proven their honour and this matter is now closed!'

'And let's hope it really is closed, shall we?' Varus watched as the eight men who had been flogged walked away from their posts stiff-legged with the pain of their inflamed and cut flesh. 'Let's hope there's no repeat of yesterday's mayhem that can be tied to your command, Legatus, or you may find the emperor looking beyond the ranks of ordinary soldiers for men to blame. And to punish.'

He walked away, making for the Batavian headquarters where he found the tent party and their former centurion face down on the table having salve rubbed into their weals. Alcaeus looked up at him as he entered the tent, winked and put his head back onto the table with a grunt of pain. Varus looked at his back and whistled softly, as he realised that the angry weals, some of them deep enough to have cut the skin, were all more or less parallel to each other, rather than crisscrossed to deliver deeper wounds where they intersected.

'Neat work, Prefect. You and the other unfortunate men who drew the lots to deliver this punishment must have been practising for most of the day to get this sort of precision into their whip work.'

Scar turned to face him.

'I told Vitellius I was going to have them flogged. I didn't promise to wield the whips like butcher's cleavers.'

Varus raised his hands.

'You'll get no criticism from me, Germanicus. I've spent the last half-hour telling that senatorial oaf that commands the Fourteenth what I'm going to do to him if his men cause any more trouble.'

'What *you're* going to do to him?'

The prefect smiled wryly.

'Well, not so much what I'll do to him as a certain emperor of my recent acquaintance. I have the man's ear, and he's proving to be somewhat receptive to my ideas, for the time being at least. I've persuaded him to send the Fourteenth back to Lindum, their previous fortress in Britannia before they were moved in support of Nero's hare-brained idea to invade the east two years ago, so that should mollify their sense of injustice at not having made it to the party at Cremona in time to enjoy the fighting. No soldier can harbour very much of a feeling of resentment for very long towards the man who's just decided to send him to see his woman and children.'

Scar nodded.

'That's decent of you. And it'll allow us all to relax for a while without their constant wailing and rending of garments.'

'Not for all that long, I'm afraid. I've also persuaded the emperor that you need to be away from here, back to your own land. He's having orders written sending you back to Germania, the Winter Camp at Mogontiacum in the first instance. Hopefully that will put you close enough to your homeland that you can get some of your men away on leave.'

Scar looked at him for a moment before replying.

'Thank you, Prefect. And trust me, that's not something I had expected to be saying to a praetorian any time soon. Your generosity will be appreciated by my men, even if it does mean another four-hundred-mile march.'

Varus bowed slightly.

'I'll consider my debt to your men for putting me in such a good light with Vitellius paid. And as for my debt to your former centurion, perhaps this will go some way to clearing it from my account?'

He handed Scar a jar the size of a good-sized container of fish pickle, which the Batavi uncorked and sniffed carefully.

'Is that . . . *myrrh*?'

'Yes, and if you've never bought any then you'll have no idea how ridiculously expensive it is. I could have got every man in his century . . .' he waved a hand to the recumbent Alcaeus, '. . . blind drunk every day for a week for the sum of money that that little jar cost me.' Varus smiled at the memory of his purchase. 'The merchant would dearly have liked to have named a higher price, once he saw the weight of my purse. He started wailing that he was only selling at the price he'd agreed to because business was so poor, and that this was the best quality myrrh from the Arabian lands beyond Judea and Egypt, so I should expect you'll find it efficacious for those weals. It'll take the sting out them too, I expect. And if you apply it with a light touch, there ought to be enough for all of the centurion's tent party too.'

Alcaeus looked up at him from his recumbent position.

'My thanks, Prefect. Consider any debt between us to be paid, and myself in the position of debtor.'

Varus bowed.

'I shall consider us to be equal once more, Centurion, and myself to have the better part of the bargain.'

'Alas, those days are in my past, Prefect, I am now only a soldier.'

The Roman guffawed, giving Scar a hard stare that the Batavi returned with a look of complete innocence.

'There any many things I can be accused of, gentlemen, and with some justification, but stupidity is not one of them. And now I must return to my duties. There are rumours abroad that the hotheads of the Fourteenth plan to mark their departure from Taurinorum by leaving a few mementos for the townspeople in the form of burning buildings, and I'd dearly like to catch them in the act and make a few examples, just to demonstrate to them that they really did lose the war.'

He nodded to Scar and was gone, leaving the prefect staring after him.

'One decent Roman, and they make him the prefect of the fucking praetorians.'

Alcaeus looked up at him.

'Was he right?'

'About your demotion? Of course he was, you stupid wolf-headed bastard. You're reinstated as of the moment you took the last of those lashes. Although if you'd taken it badly and started shouting the odds about the punishment I was perfectly ready to leave you a soldier for a few months, just to teach you some manners.'

His friend raised a jaundiced eyebrow.

'I'm sorry to have been such a disappointment.'

'Not to worry, I'll keep myself happy by putting you in command of every night watch between here and the Winter Camp. You and the rest of these idiots. Now get your stripes dressed with the prefect's perfume and fuck off to bed. I'll need you bright-eyed in the morning to help me start planning the march north with the disappointingly small number of officers I can trust to think beyond the ends of their swords.'

Colonia Agrippina, Germania Inferior, June AD 69

'Very well, if that's all our other business complete?'

Legatus augusti Hordeonius Flaccus looked around at his officers, who to a man nodded their agreement and stood up to leave the legatus augusti's palatial office. As the last of them trooped through the door his secretary came in, his face creased with uncertainty.

'Legatus sir, there's . . .'

Flaccus waited for him to complete the sentence, but for once the urbane freedman seemed lost for words.

'Yes? Spit it out man.'

Drawing himself together, his former slave regained a little of his customary composure.

'There is an officer waiting to see you, Legatus. A centurion . . .'

Flaccus frowned, looking down at his list of the day's appointments which, as was the usual routine, had been waiting for him after he had breakfasted and taken a turn around the camp to clear his mind.

'There are no further meetings in my calendar, so I fail to see . . .'

He fell silent as a powerfully built figure loomed in the doorway behind the secretary. The newcomer's voice was gruff to the point of hoarseness, but the note of command was unmistakable.

'I have no appointment, Legatus. I was ordered to report to you at my first opportunity.'

Flaccus's curiosity overcame his initial concern at the big man's unexpected appearance, and he nodded to his freedman.

'You'd better come in and tell me your story then, hadn't you, Centurion?'

He waited as the other man came into the room and stamped to attention in front of the broad, polished wooden desk behind which Flaccus sat to do most of his business.

'Centurion Gaius Aquillius Proculus, Eighth Augustan legion, reporting for duty, sir!'

Flaccus looked up at him dumbfounded for a moment, then turned to his secretary.

'Are you sure we're not expecting a centurion to be posted to us from the Eighth Augustan?'

The freedman shook his head decisively.

'No, Legatus. I checked the messages and orders file carefully when the centurion arrived, and there's no sign of any formal notification.'

'Thank you. I think under the circumstances that will be all for now.'

The door closed again, and Flaccus looked up at the massive figure dominating his office with an uncertain expression.

'We're not expecting you. What was your name again?'

'Aquillius, Legatus.'

'Aquillius. I see. So, given we're not expecting you, and given I haven't asked for a centurion, might I ask . . .?'

'Emperor's orders, Legatus. I was ordered to report to you in person.'

'The *emperor*. You do mean Vitellius?' He looked up at the newcomer in bafflement, as the centurion nodded affirmatively. 'Why on earth should Vitellius take the slightest interest in my command structure, never mind the sort of detailed consideration that would lead him to have you ordered to join my army? Unless . . .'

His face went pale as he considered one very good reason why a centurion of such size and obvious martial prowess might have been sent to him.

'Has Vitellius ordered you to . . .'

Aquillius stared at him in bafflement.

'Ordered me to do what, Legatus?'

Flaccus stared at him for a moment and then breathed out a shaky breath of relief.

'You're not a killer, then?'

The big man shook his head in bafflement.

'A killer? I have killed men, Legatus, but I was given no orders regarding any killing to be done here.'

The legatus leaned back in his chair.

'Forgive me, Centurion. There is an old tradition, recently revived, for men of the centurionate to be used as convenient and highly effective assassins when men such as myself are deemed to be an irritation in need of removal.'

Aquillius shook his head.

'I was sent to you, legatus augusti, for reasons of loyalty.'

He fell silent, leaving Flaccus regarding him with bafflement.

'Loyalty, Centurion?'

'Loyalty, Legatus.'

Having restated what he saw as the simple facts the big man fell silent once more, and Flaccus shook his head in exasperation.

'This discussion will be a lot shorter if you just tell me why you're here, Centurion.'

Aquillius nodded.

'I was First Spear of the Eighth Legion, Legatus. The Eighth's legatus decided to throw in our lot with Otho, after the emperor Galba's murder, but we failed to reach the battlefield in time to turn the battle, and then Otho killed himself.'

'Leaving you without the emperor to whom you had sworn loyalty.'

'Exactly, Legatus.'

'But, and let me take a wild stab here, this loyalty you mention has resulted in you declining to swear allegiance to Vitellius?'

Aquillius nodded pugnaciously.

'That is correct, Legatus.'

'In the name of all the gods, why would you do anything so . . .'

Flaccus looked up at the man facing him, taking in his bearing, his glittering medal harness, his perfectly maintained weapons and armour and his chin, clearly recently shaved but already darkening with incipient stubble.

'I see. You're one of those rare men who considers his honour more important than his career. And so, having sworn to resist Vitellius, unlike most of your comrades, you refused to take the oath of loyalty to the new emperor as a point of principle. Is that right?'

The big man nodded, his face impassive.

'Yes, Legatus.'

'And it was pointed out to you that you couldn't retain your position if you weren't willing to swear the oath?'

'At length, Legatus.'

'At length. I can just imagine. And so Vitellius, not wishing to spark a mutiny in the Eighth Augustan, decided to have you sent away somewhere where you can do no harm. Somewhere so far from your legion that your influence will soon be forgotten. And so he sent you here. To me.'

'Yes, Legatus.'

Flaccus got up and walked around the desk, looking the other man in the eye, as best he could given the six-inch height difference.

'You know that I have little use for you? After all, none of my First Spears will accept you in their legions, given your refusal to swear loyalty to the man they put on the throne.'

Aquillius remained silent, and the older man laughed softly.

'You know, and yet you don't care. You are that rare and precious thing, Centurion, a man of principle in a world where every other man, myself included, is exercising morals so pliable that all the certainties we once depended on have been turned upside down. And I like that in a man. Given that you've been sent to me on the orders of a no less august man than the emperor himself, you will join my personal staff, and act as my bodyguard, my military advisor in matters of tactics, and will generally make yourself useful to me until the time comes that I can find something of greater value for you to do. How does that suit you?'

The big man nodded curtly.

'It will be an honour to serve you, Legatus. I expect that the experience will stand me in good stead once I have a legion under my vine stick again.'

'Ah.' Flaccus smiled, turning back to his desk. 'I see that I can add the crime of hopeless optimism to that of unconditional fealty to an oath sworn. The odds of you ever commanding fifty-nine other centurions again are probably so bad that even the most inveterate gambler in the camp would struggle to accept your coin.'

Aquillius shrugged.

'It is a time of war, Legatus, and that war may not yet be complete, from the rumours I hear. In times of war men like me have a tendency to prosper from the misfortunes of others.'

'If, that is, you don't suffer a misfortune yourself.'

The big head shook in denial.

'Mars will watch over me, Legatus, and reward my fealty to my oath as he sees fit. I will not fall to the swords of the enemy.'

Flaccus laughed.

'Given that the only fighting that's likely right now is a civil war, *if* another legatus augusti decides that his legions are strong enough to challenge the emperor, I'd be less worried about the enemy and more concerned with those wielded by our friends.'

The centurion shrugged.

'A man cannot always choose his enemies, Legatus. And in the absence of that choice, he must spend his energy not on bemoaning his fate, but working out the best ways to defeat whatever enemy is put before him. Defeat accomplished by the swiftest and most terrible of methods he can imagine.'

Flaccus looked up at him for a moment.

'And are you always this cheery, Centurion?'

The big man nodded without a hint of humour.

'If you wish to see me happy, Legatus, show me your enemy and release me upon them. Until then, I will tolerate what I have to do simply in order to enjoy that moment. Sir.'

9

Oppidum Batavorum, July AD 69

'No sign of anyone?'

The commander of the night watch, a former Bodyguard decurion whose men had been divided between the city's four gates and told to sound the alarm at the first sign of any approach to Batavodurum, shook his head at Hramn, his helmet crest a slash of white in the dim light of the torches that lit the eastern gateway.

'Nothing. If I wasn't so happy just to be back in armour and doing something useful, I'd be telling you what a waste of time this is.'

After their narrow escape from death at the hands of the Tungrians, Hramn and Draco had decided that it would be sensible to have the city's gates manned at all times, more to keep a watch for any Romans who might make an attempt on Kivilaz's life than to mount any meaningful defence against an attack nobody seriously expected to happen. At the prince's suggestion Hramn had also set his men to training the tribe's militia how to fight like professionals, as a means of bolstering their relatively meagre numbers. It was the closest that the guardsmen were likely to get to soldiering for some time to come, they expected, and so they had thrown themselves into the task with their customary efficiency, commencing the transformation of the militia from enthusiastic amateurs to something altogether harder. Hramn grinned happily back at his officer, tapping his own mail-clad chest.

'I know. It feels right, doesn't it, even if we're armed to defend the city against our own allies. And even if they could roll over us without too much trouble, if they were minded to.'

'Oh I'm not so sure about that. I suspect even a full cohort would find our boys an indigestible lump of gristle to chew on.'

Both men turned to find Kivilaz behind them, Hramn shaking his head at their tribune's unexpected appearance.

'One of these days you're going to have to teach me how you do that.'

The older man grinned lopsidedly at them, his one good eye twinkling in the torchlight.

'Just light on my feet, that's all there is to it. That, and telling myself that I'm not there.'

Hramn shook his head again.

'Whatever it is, don't do it to trained soldiers after dark unless you want to find four feet of spear shaft sticking out of your back.'

Kivilaz laughed softly.

'I'd be the man holding the spear, I think you'll find, with its previous owner looking down his own iron.'

He looked about him.

'All quiet then?'

'As quiet as the grave itself. And just as well. I was wondering how well we could defend the city, if the Romans ever sent their legions at us, and I came to the conclusion that we'd probably only manage to hold them off for an hour or two.'

The older man shook his head, his good eye glinting with grim humour.

'You're overestimating our neighbours, Hramn. With most of the Fifth and a good portion of the Fifteenth gone south to fight Otho's legions, they've been recruiting as hard as they can, which means that right now they're knee-deep in new recruits who still can't even beat a wooden training post in a duel yet. There's not one of your men hasn't wetted his blade with the blood of an enemy, so I'd say that if they came to confront us now our one cohort would give them a bloody nose they wouldn't forget in a month of Saturnalia, and that's before you consider the training you've given the militia and how much they've improved with their weapons lately. All they lack is iron armour to make them every bit as good as any legionary they might find themselves facing. And besides, the Romans won't come anywhere near us. Their legatus won't want to have to face Vitellius in the event that the actions of a couple of idiot centurions cause our eight cohorts to withdraw from his army, so I'd imagine that he'll make sure his men keep their heads down from now on. And besides, I don't think that we should be thinking so much about defence as—'

He would have elaborated on the thought, but a voice from behind him interrupted the conversation.

'There's a rider coming in from the east! I can hear his horse!'

The three men hurried to the gateway, stepping through the wicket gate and staring out into the darkness.

'Bring more torches! Call out the Guard!'

Men hurried to carry out Hramn's command, bathing the ground around the gateway with the soft light of a dozen freshly lit brands, and in the city behind them the street echoed with the sound of dozens of men's booted feet hurrying to their posts. After a moment's wait, during which the noise of Hramn's men died away to an almost perfect silence as they found their positions and stood ready to fight, every man strained eyes and ears for any clue as to what lay behind the slow clopping of an approaching horse.

'It can't be an attack, we'd be already deaf from the noise of men falling over in the dark and gagging on the smell of the shit running down their legs.'

The men around the gate laughed at Draco's loud observation, the veteran having walked up behind them during the Guard's rush to their posts, and Hramn turned back to look at him with a wry smile.

'Ever the diplomat, eh Prefect?'

'He's probably right though, judging from what I saw at the Old Camp.'

Hramn spun back to see the speaker leading a horse appear from out of the night's gloom into the circle of light. Dressed warmly, he was armed with a cavalry sword on his left hip, while the beast was laden with a pair of heavy saddlebags. The centurion of the guard looked at his superior expectantly.

'Want me to challenge him?'

'There's no need, Centurion. I know this man.'

Both officers looked at Kivilaz in surprise.

'You *know* him?'

'Indeed he does!'

The horseman came to a halt a dozen paces from the gate, holding up his hands to be clear that he intended them no harm.

'Apologies for disturbing your evening, gentlemen, I had hoped to arrive in daylight and cause a little less excitement, but I was delayed on the road. This blasted animal has gone lame, so I had to walk the last ten miles.'

Kivilaz walked forward and held out a hand.

'Gaius Plinius Secundus. Well met, even if it's taken you a month or so longer to make an appearance than I expected!'

Later, with the Guard dispersed back to their various lodgings and Plinius installed at Draco's table, warm, fed and with a cup of wine in front of him, the Roman cocked an interrogatory eyebrow at Kivilaz.

'So you expected me to arrive before now?'

The Batavi noble nodded.

'It seemed obvious to me that you would be the man chosen to carry the message from the east.'

Hramn shook his head in puzzlement, looking at each man in turn and frowning at their shared secret.

'Obvious that he would be the one to carry the message from the east? *What* message from the east? And how is it that you know each other, when I've never heard his name before?'

Kivilaz smiled knowingly.

'The dubious advantage I have over you, Decurion, is that I spent two months imprisoned in the palace on the Palatine Hill, waiting for Galba to complete his march in triumph from Hispania, and then, once he'd arrived in Rome, waiting some more for him to get around to pronouncing his judgement on the insignificant matter of a tribal noble accused of treason. Which took longer than you might imagine. For one thing, he had weightier matters to consider, such as the decision as to who he should appoint as his heir, and whether or not to not pay the praetorians the donative they had been promised in his name. And for another, there was a judgement to be made as to just how blatantly he could be seen to reward me for apparently having sided with Vindex in his ill-fated rebellion in Gaul. And during that time I received precious few visitors other than my jailers who, decent men though they were, were unlikely to be the source of either conversation or indeed information as to events in the outside world. One very welcome exception was a man by the name of Cerialis, who was kind enough to visit me on several occasions and bring a variety of books to keep me entertained throughout the long weeks of my captivity. I put it down to his regard for a brother at arms fallen on hard times, until he organised a dinner party to celebrate my acquittal. A dinner party at which I found myself seated next to this august gentleman . . .'

He gestured to Plinius.

'And that, pleasurable though it was, was the moment at which I realised that Cerialis's friendship was motivated by something more than his desire to do right by a former soldier who had fallen foul of Rome's jealousies. So tell me, Plinius Secundus, what is the nature of your message from Judea?'

The Roman smiled cheerfully.

'Vespasianus won't be in Judea by now, he'll be on his way to Egypt.'

Kivilaz nodded slowly.

'Egypt. Then the rumours are true. He means to claim the throne, and to hold Rome's Egyptian breadbasket as a lever with which to crowbar Vitellius out of power.'

Plinius took a sip of his wine.

'The message my friend Cerialis received implied that his father-in-law's mind was not yet entirely made up. If Otho had succeeded in defeating the German legions then I suspect he would have declared at once, given the man's total unsuitability and his murder of Galba, but Vitellius's victory and Otho's suicide have given him pause for thought. After all, a man would need to be very sure of his supporters before declaring war on the man who controls the military forces of Germania, Gaul, Hispania and Britannia. The eastern legions on their own are nowhere near strong enough to challenge that large an army.'

'That's a fact. But it's a simple enough piece of mathematics, isn't it? Without the Danubian legions any such attempt at power would be doomed to fail, especially as Vitellius's army is now blooded in battle and therefore a different proposition than it was a few months ago.'

Kivilaz fell silent and stared at Plinius for a long moment before speaking again.

'Let me put the pieces of this puzzle together for my brothers-in-arms, since I have the advantage of having had several months to ponder this question.'

He turned to Hramn and Draco.

'Plinius Secundus here carries a message from Gaius Petillius Cerialis, my unexpected friend during my captivity in Rome and, coincidentally, the son-in-law of Titus Flavius Vespasianus, Rome's general in the war with the Jews. And . . .' he paused, stressing the import of what he was about to say, 'quite possibly, the only man left alive in the whole empire with the stature to challenge Vitellius for the throne.'

'Which means that a message from Cerialis is in truth a message from Vespasianus?'

Kivilaz nodded at Draco.

'Exactly. And which means that even entertaining the idea of hearing what it is that Plinius has to say means that we are likely to become accessories to treason.' He laughed softly. 'That's not a problem for me, of course. I've been accused twice and escaped by the skin of my teeth on both occasions, and I am perfectly sure that once Vitellius has no further need for my support he'll bow to the vengeful urging of his centurions and give me my moment to savour the bitter taste of Roman justice. There's a tree somewhere not yet felled that will host my body's last hours, once the emperor no longer needs to placate our people. But it is a problem for you both. To listen to this request for our assistance is to countenance treason, and we all know where that path might lead. So think carefully before Plinius here continues, although you should be equally clear that to reject his message is to place yourself on the side of the Romans, and if you do so then by rights you should promptly denounce us both to Vitellius's legatus at the Old Camp.'

Draco shook his head angrily.

'A year ago I would have been troubled by the prospect of turning my back on an ally, but I have faced an armed officer of their army intent on murdering a prince of our tribe.' He looked levelly at Plinius. 'I will listen to what you have to say, sir.'

All eyes turned to Hramn, who looked back at each of them in turn.

'You need to ask? My command disgraced, my tribe dishonoured . . .'

He waved a hand in silent assent, and Kivilaz nodded to Plinius, who sipped at his wine again and then began to speak.

'Titus Flavius Vespasianus sends his regards to the tribe that fought alongside his men so bravely and effectively at the battle of the Medui, and throughout the long summer that followed. He remembers the Batavians with fondness, and says that never has he seen such skill or bravery before or since.' He paused, looking around at them. 'I can add some colour to those words, gentlemen, having enjoyed the man's hospitality on more than one occasion. His after-dinner remembrances of the campaign in Britannia still feature your auxiliary forces in pride of place. These words are genuinely meant from a man who still harbours the utmost respect for your people.'

Kivilaz nodded.

'And we thank him, through you, for these kind words.'

Another sip of wine.

'Flavius Vespasianus finds himself in a difficult position, gentlemen. He is, and always has been, a loyal servant of the emperor of the day, demonstrating his devotion to the empire throughout the reigns of three men whose imperium was not always exercised in the most responsible manner. There have been times when he has been forced to withdraw from public life as the result of misunderstandings, accidental and deliberate, but unlike many of his fellows he has never used public office for personal gain. Indeed, he managed to restore his personal fortune only by trading mules, with the result that his peers took to calling him "*mulio*" to his face, despite his having been the governor of North Africa, a position that could have made him rich had he chosen to abuse it in the customary fashion. Titus Flavius Vespasianus, gentlemen, is a good honest Roman at a time when such probity is in scare supply. And as a good Roman he is appalled at the state of affairs that he sees from the east. Nero hounded to the point of suicide. His successor cut down in the street by men sworn to his service in the pursuit of their own wealth, who then handed the empire to a fool with no more capacity to rule the world than any other man of his age, indeed a good deal less than some. Augustus may have ruled the empire from much the same age as Otho, but Otho was no Augustus. And now we are ruled by Vitellius, a man incapable of orderly rule, a man so cursed by the gods that when his father saw the infant's horoscope he tried to prevent his son from entering public service.'

Plinius looked around the table with a sober expression.

'A man whose legions spread chaos and debauchery wherever they go, victimising innocent Roman citizens for their own pleasure, or worse, profit. Can we really trust a man like that, a slave to his own gluttony and vice, a man infamous since his youth for surrendering to the sensual temptations of the flesh, to rule the empire with the necessary discipline and virtue?'

He paused, slowly shaking his head.

'I think not. Gaius Petillius Cerialis thinks not. And most importantly, Titus Flavius Vespasianus thinks not. He has the support of the legions of the east. He has the support of his colleague Mucianus, governor of Syria, and of Primus, who commands in Pannonia. And we believe that he will soon have the support of the Danubian legions as well, and thereby have sufficient strength to match Vitellius.'

Kivilaz nodded.

'And, if your friend Vespasianus does declare himself emperor, the empire will therefore be split neatly into two halves, east and west, and the stage set for a confrontation between the two. With Vitellius's main weapon being the legions from Germania.'

'Exactly.'

The two men exchanged a knowing glance.

'But then you knew most of this before my arrival, I expect?'

Kivilaz smiled slowly.

'I've made it my business to learn as much as I can as to the current state of affairs from the meagre sources I have available to me here at the edge of the empire. And I've looked into you, Gaius Plinius Secundus. My sources tell me that you were a decent enough man when you had command of the cavalry wing based in the Old Camp, neither too familiar nor too distant from your men, and that you were a dedicated and honourable soldier. And if I remember rightly from that night in Rome, you even wrote a book about horsemanship while you were there?'

Plinius smiled.

'Indeed. *On the Use of Missiles From Horseback.* A fond memory, of a time when I could immerse myself in the study of such an arcane subject.'

He shook his head wistfully.

'But when the trumpet calls all men must declare themselves as their conscience guides them. And my conscience calls me to the cause of Vespasianus.'

Draco leaned forward, locking stares with the Roman.

'So we know that you are a decent man, who follows the dictates of your ethics. And I see your small smile to hear such language from the mouth of a barbarian, so don't even think of patronising me for my skill with Latin. I spent the best years of my life listening to men spout just such words to the emperor Claudius, and for the most part it was clearly self-serving bullshit. But I do remember Vespasianus's time as a consul, and how he was forced to retire after falling foul of that poisonous bitch Agrippina. Why the emperor ever thought to marry her was beyond me, but a man can only sometimes go where his prick leads him, I suppose. Your friend Vespasianus seemed a decent enough man then.'

Plinius nodded.

'And he remembers you, Prefect Draco, and asked to be remembered to you, if the chance arose. He hasn't forgotten the favours you performed for him back in those dangerous days.'

Draco inclined his head in recognition of the point.

'And with all those nice things said, let us be very clear. You have come to ask the Batavi to rise up against Rome, I presume, and give Vitellius something more to worry about than dealing with a revolt from the east? You want to force him to fight on two fronts, and tie down the army on the Rhenus so that he can take no further reinforcement from here.'

'You have discerned my purpose with the utmost clarity.'

The veteran opened his hands questioningly.

'And what is it that you and your friends think is going to tempt the Batavi to destroy the fruit of a one-hundred-year-old relationship with Rome? Why should we risk the enmity of a people who, when the fighting is done and a single emperor rules, could grind *my* people flat with the greatest of ease? The centurions who command in the Old Camp already want my prince Kivilaz's head, and if we were to ally with Vespasianus they'd be baying for our blood even louder than before. Why shouldn't the Batavi simply ride out this storm, and let the coin land whichever side up fate decrees?'

Plinius leaned forward to match the older man's questioning posture.

'Titus Flavius Vespasianus recognises that your place in the empire might be uncomfortable, if the war that is almost certainly to come results in a Vitellian triumph. But he asks you to consider what you might achieve by being on the side of the victor in the event that his forces overcome those of Vitellius.'

'And what might that be?'

The Roman's smile was hard and businesslike.

'Ask yourself what you would like it to be, and, within the bounds of your own territory, you have your answer.'

Rome, August 3rd AD 69

'How is he?'

The duty praetorian tribune thought briefly before responding to his superior's question.

'Angry, Prefect. Hurt . . . And scared, I'd say.'

Varus nodded thoughtfully, looking at the door behind which the emperor was discussing the latest development with his closest council.

'I'd say he has good reason. This news puts the entire matter in the balance. Who's in there with him?'

'His brother Lucius. Celsus, Simplex, Atticus, and the two legati augusti, Prefect.'

'Oh, joy. Not just his idiot brother but the maniac Valens and his faithless colleague Caecina as well.'

He took a deep breath, remembering only too well the fact that it had been the combination of Valens and Caecina, the victorious generals at Cremona, and the emperor's hot-headed brother Lucius, who had driven through the decision to replace the twelve defeated praetorian cohorts he had inherited from Otho's guard commander with twenty new cohorts, all drawn from within the victorious army's legions. His advice that this would severely weaken the strength available to defend the empire, among rumours that the apparently undecided Vespasianus had decided to make a bid for the throne had been proven sound only weeks later, but now another body blow had been delivered to the emperor, and from the quarter it had been the least expected. He opened the door and stepped into Vitellius's council chamber, a relatively small space with room only for a table around which there were eight chairs. Guardsmen stood in every corner, men deemed worthy of such intimacy with the imperial person in order to provide him with constant protection, which less than a year before would have been provided by the German Bodyguard.

'Ah, Alfenus Varus, I'm glad you could join us.'

Varus bowed, ignoring the acid in the emperor's voice.

'My apologies, Caesar, I was inspecting the city's defences when the messenger from the Danubius arrived, and it took me a little time to return to the palace and make myself presentable.'

In truth he had spent a good portion of the time considering the implications of the latest news to rock the palace foundations, readying himself for his emperor's inevitable rage and apparent paranoia.

'I am informed correctly, I presume? The legions of Pannonia, Moesia and Dalmatia have *all* declared for Vespasianus?'

Valens looked up at him with a grim face.

'So it would seem. Which means that the pretender's army is swollen to thirty thousand legionaries, eighteen thousand from the east and another twelve from the Danubius. And that's *before* we consider their auxiliary cohorts.'

The emperor spoke again, his voice, Varus noted, remarkably calm for a man so badly betrayed by legion commanders who had sworn oaths to follow his commands unquestioningly less than three months before.

'He'll field fifty thousand men. As many, more or less, as our own strength.' Vitellius looked up at his praetorian prefect with a determined expression. 'I've decided that we need to gather as many men as possible, including those Batavians of yours.'

Varus raised an eyebrow.

'Hardly mine, Caesar. And might they not be better employed guarding the northern border?'

The emperor shook his head, and the other men around the table turned to face Varus with a variety of expressions ranging from irritation on the part of Lucius to open curiosity on the part of Caecina, the more malleable of the two generals.

'Four thousand men, Prefect. Hardly weakened by their part in the battle at Cremona, and all of them veterans. The equivalent of a legion, no less, and some of our bravest and most adaptable soldiers. How many other units do we have that are capable of swimming a river in their armour and then giving battle when they reach the far side, eh? I won't leave them standing idle when the entire army of the Danubius will be marching south to join with Vespasianus's legions from Syria and Judea. And besides . . .'

He gestured to his brother and sat back in his chair with a brooding expression. Lucius looked up at Varus for a moment before speaking.

'You are a friend of Quintus Petillius Cerialis, are you not?'

Varus frowned at the unexpected direction the conversation had taken.

'What? Yes, of sorts. I know him well enough, although I couldn't be considered a close friend, and just as well given he's Vespasianus's son-in-law. Presumably he's been arrested?'

Lucius snorted.

'By the time the urban cohorts had woken up to his family relationship with the pretender he was gone. Apparently he was last seen leaving the city by one of the northern gates, presumably in hopes of meeting his father-in-law's army, dressed as a peasant and in the company of two rough types who would appear to be ex-soldiers who protect him wherever he goes.'

Varus shrugged.

'That's hardly surprising, is it? After all, Vespasianus's brother is still the Urban Prefect. You could hardly expect him to hurry to have the man arrested, and let's face it, one sadly failed legion commander isn't exactly going to tilt the scales of power, is he?'

Vitellius looked up and spoke in a weary tone, rubbing a hand across his face.

'It's not Cerialis that worries me. It's the *Batavians*.'

He raised a hand to forestall Varus's baffled question.

'Who was it who visited the Batavian prince Civilis when he was imprisoned in this very palace accused of treason? Cerialis, that's who. And who hosted him to a lavish dinner the very night that he was freed by Galba? Cerialis. And who among Cerialis's friends, the informers tell me, spent the most time talking to Civilis while he was Cerialis's guest? Gaius Plinius Secundus.'

Varus waited in silence for the emperor's chain of apparently unrelated facts to gain clarity, and Vitellius continued with the thread of his thinking.

'And who rode north from Rome a month ago, all on his own,

for a nostalgic tour of his former military postings in Germania? At just about the same time that, as we know now, Vespasianus was declaring himself emperor in the east? The self-same Gaius Plinius Secundus. For all we know his trip north had one aim, and one aim only – to solicit his friend Civilis to raise the Batavians in revolt against us in support of Vespasianus, and just at the moment when our northern frontier is at its weakest! We will be forced to fight on two fronts, and at no cost in men to the pretender. As a military strategy it's little short of perfect.'

Varus nodded slowly.

'I can only bow to Caesar's insight. And again, to your eminently sensible decision to recall the Batavian cohorts before Civilis has a chance to embroil them in whatever it is that he's planning.'

Vitellius sat back, mollified by his prefect's words.

'Very well. Get them back over the Alps as soon as you can, Prefect. Send one of those bright young tribunes you've appointed to command my new guard, just to make sure that your man Germanicus, or Scar, or whatever his name is today, completely understands that to disobey the command to return would be treason. Yes?'

Varus bowed again.

'As you command, Caesar.'

'Good. Now take a seat. We have a good deal to discuss, starting with how we're going to put more troops into the field in time to deal with Vespasianus's Danubian legions. Your colleagues . . .' he waved a hand to Caecina and Valens, the former smirking while the latter's expression eloquently bespoke his usual ill-temper, 'are of the opinion that Legatus Augusti Flaccus should provide at least another five thousand men from the German garrisons, which should easily be replaced by the men he'll have recruited since our forces marched south. I'm going to order him to start conscripting men from the allied tribes as well, so he'll have no excuse not to release the forces we need.'

'Conscription?' Varus nodded. 'A sound decision, Caesar. Let Rome's subjects take some of the pressure that we're under. Presumably not the Batavians though, given their treaty exemption?'

Valens scoffed across the table at him, leaning forward to stab a meaty finger at the table.

'Especially the fucking Batavians, Alfenus Varus! Rome needs men, and under the circumstances they should be proud to make their contribution. And besides, pulling a couple of thousand of their men of fighting age out of the tribe will serve to blunt any ambitions this man Civilis might have for a revolt. It's hard to stage a successful uprising when all you have to fight for you are old men and children!'

The Winter Camp, Mogontiacum, August AD 69

'There's an officer to see you, Prefect!'

Scar nodded curtly at the centurion who had knocked on the door of his office and saluted punctiliously.

'Bring him in.'

The Batavi stepped back, and another man replaced him in the doorway. Scar was already halfway round his desk, coming to attention and saluting once he had room to do so, while Alcaeus, who had been sitting on a chair facing his superior, was already standing in the brace position.

'Greetings Tribune! Prefect Germanicus reporting for duty! This is my deputy, and the cohorts' chief priest, Centurion Alcaeus.'

The newcomer, a young man fully equipped in armour of the usual high quality, looked him up and down before replying. Scar was wearing his best tunic, his dress boots and belt, and had shaved less than an hour before, looking every inch the legion senior centurion even if his command was of a lower status. He returned the salute and looked about him at the office, painfully clean and tidy with only a sword and a sharpening stone on the desk as evidence that it was in use, although a flask and three cups had been placed on a small table flanked by a pair of wooden chairs.

'At ease, Prefect, Centurion. My name is Marcus Aelius Varus, and I am indeed a tribune, although you seemed to know as much before I arrived. How *did* you know my rank, by the way?'

Scar's imperturbable face didn't display even a scintilla of satisfaction as he answered.

'We've had time to get to know the local legionaries, Tribune Varus, and some of our lads played them in a game of harpastum and made friends with them in the bath house afterwards a few days ago. So when you arrived in the fortress last night it didn't take long for us to hear about it.'

The younger man nodded his understanding, waving a hand at the wine.

'Military intelligence at its best, eh? But why does this office look like it's been prepared for my arrival?'

'Intelligence plus deduction, Tribune.'

'Which means . . . ?'

'It wasn't hard to work out, Tribune. The only battle-proven units in this great big half-empty two-legion fortress are the eight cohorts I command. So when a man arrives and declares himself to be here on behalf of the new praetorian prefect, a man we fought with at Cremona, having come from the south on a horse that was just about on its last legs, it wasn't hard to make an informed guess as to what your purpose here might be.'

Varus smiled.

'And the wine?'

'This is your office now, Tribune, I've already moved my effects to the senior centurion's quarters, I simply thought you might appreciate a moving-in gift.'

The Roman nodded cheerfully.

'You're remarkably subtle, Prefect. I was expecting someone a little more . . .'

'Rough-edged, Tribune? There are a few of us with the ability to soak up the lessons that we learn in a lifetime of service to the empire. And besides, I'm fond of a cup of wine myself.'

Taking the hint, Varus gestured to the table.

'In which case join me, and I'll tell you why I'm here. If, that is, you haven't already read my orders?'

Scar poured the wine while the tribune placed his helmet on

the desk alongside his dagger and then took a seat. The two Batavi officers sat, Scar raising his cup in salute.

'There was no need, Tribune. A man doesn't have to be blessed with the skills of an augur to know why you're here.'

'Oh really?' Varus took a sip. 'Decent wine too. I could get to like you, Prefect. Go on then, tell me what you've deduced with regard to my purpose in being here then.'

Scar sipped his wine.

'There's a new pretender, Tribune, a legatus augusti called Vespasianus who has declared himself emperor in the east. When Vitellius sent us away up here he thought that his position was safe, and that he could disperse the legions that had opposed him, to prevent an unscrupulous rival from taking advantage of their combined strength. He believed that it was therefore safe to do as his praetorian prefect was suggesting, and so he sent us back north to guard the frontier.'

The tribune nodded.

'Not forgetting that it was also deemed a good move to stop you from picking any more fights with certain legions. Tribune Varus sends his regards to you, Centurion Alcaeus, along with the hope that your back is now completely healed.'

Scar conceded the point with a raised wine cup.

'But now Vespasianus has declared that he'll fight for the throne. Which means that all those defeated legions will need to be rehabilitated, where possible. And that our eight cohorts of battle-hardened, mad-eyed barbarians are suddenly no longer surplus to requirements. Vitellius ordered our former colleague Alfenus Varus to recall his former command, and Varus chose you to come and get us. Although that in itself is making me wonder if it's just the legions from the east that Vespasianus has on his side. After all, even if the eastern legions are more experienced than those declared for Vitellius, even that many legions aren't going to be enough to let Vespasianus take the throne by force, not with a good dozen on the other side, and most of them recently blooded. Unless there's something that we've not been told?'

Varus stared at him for a moment.

'Such as?'

Scar shrugged.

'Not for me to speculate, Tribune. But it does occur to me that while Vitellius has the legions from Britannia and Germania sewn up tightly, he might or might not inspire the same loyalty in the men posted along the Danubius?'

The tribune nodded slowly.

'An astute surmise, Prefect. It seems that the legions of Pannonia, Moesia and Dalmatia are not proving as loyal to the emperor as he might have wished. Every man available is being recalled to Italy in readiness to face an attack from the north-east, including your command.'

Scar nodded cheerfully.

'Very good. In which case it's a good thing that Alfenus Varus thought to send you along to collect us, Tribune. Our equipment has seen better days, and some of the men are wearing boots that have been worn to ribbons, more or less. We're going to need you to perform that trick you senior officers are so good at when it comes to persuading reluctant stores officers to produce the necessary equipment to make soldiers battle-worthy.'

'Ah, you mean the one where I manage to squeeze blood out of a stone?'

Scar nodded sombrely.

'That's the one.'

The Old Camp, Germania Inferior, August AD 69

'Conscription. You're certain about that, Legatus?'

Munius Lupercus looked up from the scroll before him and nodded soberly.

'There's no doubt about it, Marius, and no room in these orders for interpretation or attempting to skate around the issue, especially as these instructions have come direct from Rome and not via Hordeonius Flaccus's headquarters in Colonia Agrippina. I am hereby directly ordered to commence conscription of all the local tribes, with particular attention to the Batavians. The emperor is expecting me to recruit and train a full legion of new soldiers from the German tribes by this method, and to send the equivalent strength south to join his army as soon as they're in barracks and ready for training.'

He read from the order's text.

'"You are to recruit five thousand men from the Batavians and their allied tribes, the Ubians, the Chattians."'

He looked up at Marius.

'He goes on to name numerous other tribes just in case I've forgotten them, and then tells me to release ten cohorts to march south under my broad-stripe tribune just as soon as their replacements have been recruited. Need I continue, or do you see the thrust of the emperor's instructions?'

His First Spear shook his head in amazement.

'Has the emperor . . .'

Marius choked on the words that were forming in his mind, unwilling to voice them even to a man with whom his relationship was as good as it could be given the social gulf between them. Lupercus smiled sadly.

'Has he failed to appreciate the realities of this frontier, and of the time it takes to make fighting men of willing volunteers, never mind sullen conscripts? Undoubtedly. Has he lost his mind? Quite possibly.'

The words hung in the air between them for a moment.

'The emperor, Marius, is a worried man. Vespasianus has enough legions committed to his cause, if he can bring them to the battlefield at the same time, to match or even better what's available from the western provinces. In that state of fear Vitellius will cling on to whatever sources of manpower he believes are available, and in the short term that means Germania. Taking a lenient approach to Hordeonius Flaccus's understandable reluctance to volunteer any more men was an easier decision to make when he only faced a callow youth like Otho, and had unleashed some of the most dangerous legions in the empire on him, but now that he's faced with the most powerful man in the world apart from himself, an enemy with battlefield experience going back twenty-five years, he's probably feeling a good deal less affable on the subject. Hence this . . .'

He waved the scroll at Marius with a wry grimace.

'You can be sure I'll be taking very good care of this, if only to make sure my family aren't implicated by the whole sorry mess that must result when the tribes react in the way I believe to be inevitable.'

'But can't he see . . . ?'

The legatus shook his head.

'No. He really can't see what we can. Vitellius isn't a soldier, Marius. To him a man is just a man, and once you have that man you have a legionary. And if you don't, then you'd better make him into one quickly, hadn't you? So we're going to have to do as we're told, I'm afraid.'

Marius thought quickly.

'The Batavians . . .'

'Yes?'

'They're not going to be easy to intimidate. They have the emperor's former Bodyguard, for a start, five hundred battle-hardened cavalrymen. And our spies tell us that they're drilling their militia every day, making them into soldiers. If we march in there proclaiming that we're conscripting their men of fighting age I expect that their reaction is going to be unhappy to say the least. And if it came to a straight fight I have my doubts as to whether our new boys could stand up to them.'

Lupercus looked down at the order in front of him.

'Well, in point of fact this doesn't tell me exactly how many men I'm expected to levy from them specifically, just that I have to perform the levy. So I suggest that we think a little creatively around that aspect of what we're being told to do. How many men do you think you could get away with if you sent recruiting parties into the villages closest to the edge of their tribal territory, and used the distraction of a centurion going into Batavodurum at the same time to hold their attention long enough for those parties to bring out anyone they could conscript?'

Marius frowned.

'Not many at all. Half a dozen villages, say ten men apiece, since most of them would be in the fields. If we grabbed men on the march in as well, perhaps twenty, because most of them will see us coming and run for it just on instinct. Two centuries' worth at best.'

Lupercus nodded.

'Then that may well have to be the best that we can do for the emperor from the Batavians. We'll focus our recruiting on the other tribes who are less well placed to resist and satisfy Vitellius with the overall number we take from the area around the old camp. If I omit to detail the numbers by tribe in my dispatch informing him of the result of this conscription, and simply detail the tribes involved it might just be enough to satisfy the man.'

'But—'

The legatus raised a hand.

'I know. How are we going to release ten cohorts to Vitellius when we barely have that number ourselves? What if the Batavians choose to open hostilities with us over this matter, given we'll be breaking the terms of their treaty with Rome? And what if they chose to take that momentous step *after* we've sent the cohorts he wants south, and there's nothing in the fortress but rebellious conscripts? Perhaps the position of First Spear isn't turning out to be quite as attractive as it once sounded, eh? The gods know I still reminisce fondly about the time I was a military tribune in Britannia, during the year of Claudius's invasion, serving under a fire-eating legatus called Hosidius Geta with nothing more to worry about than how I'd perform if I ever saw action. Vespasianus was his colleague as it happens.'

He stared out of the office's window for a moment, then tapped the table hard with his finger.

'Simpler times, eh Marius? I'm sure you've happy memories of a time when there was nothing much to worry you. But that was then and this is now, and this is what we have to deal with. So I suggest you gather our centurions and get them ready for a conscription effort. We'll have to hit all of the tribes at the same time, because once word gets out about this it'll spread like a forest fire, and all the men we want to pluck from their homes will be away to hide in the woods for a while. And make sure that the Batavians are the first tribe we visit, because if they get so much as a hint of this we might find our reception somewhat warmer than we'd like.'

Oppidum Batavorum, August AD 69

'By the order of the Emperor, Aulus Vitellius Germanicus Augustus, High Priest and Father of the Fatherland!'

The centurion paused and looked about him imperiously, as if he were pronouncing his own ascension to the godlike height of the Roman throne, drawing more than one amused titter from the Batavi civilians who had gathered dutifully around him to hear the proclamation he had for them. Momentarily nonplussed by their evident lack of respect he bridled, and in doing so lost track of where he was in the scroll that he had unrolled a moment before stepping up onto the small wooden platform that had been respectfully placed before him.

'By the order of the emperor, it is decreed that the people of the tribe known to us as the Batavians will at this time provide men and whatever other support may be requested of them by the emperor's appointed representatives, in order to allow the army of Germania to make their full and rightful contribution in the war to defeat the pretender Vespasianus!'

'He did it then.'

Kivilaz nodded brusquely at Hramn's musing.

'Of course he did it. Didn't Plinius tell us he would? He's a cornered rat, and we all know what cornered rats do. Now listen to what the man has to say for himself.'

'You are hereby *ordered* . . .' he paused to savour the word, looking around the gathered crowd with a look that oozed satisfaction, 'to provide all men of an age to serve in the imperial Roman forces, promptly and without discussion. I will wait here for one hour.' He raised an hourglass, and ostentatiously tipped it over to start the sand running. 'And at the end of that hour I expect every man in this settlement between the ages of fifteen and forty to come forward and swear the military oath, promising to serve our emperor to the fullest extent of their abilities, and if need be to sacrifice their lives to his cause!'

After a moment's sullen silence, the people gathered around him did as they had been carefully instructed by Hramn and his men, who had gone from house to house over the previous few days telling their kinsmen what to expect, and how they should react. Dispersing in perfect silence, they emptied the town's forum and left the centurion and his eight-man escort standing alone, slightly baffled by the lack of any reaction. Kivilaz turned to Hramn, nodding decisively.

'Go on then. As we agreed it.'

The decurion nodded, striding out into the open space and walking up to the centurion.

'I'm Hramn, Decurion, former commander of the Imperial German Bodyguard and current commander of the Batavian Guard, imperial Roman army. Can I offer you some refreshment, Centurion, while you wait for the men of the tribe to consider your request?'

The Roman looked down his nose for a moment, considering the man before him as if he were assessing the worth of a hunting dog.

'The imperial decree is not a request. It is an order, from the emperor to this piss-pot little tribe of yours. You *will* surrender every man of military age, or—'

Hramn raised a hand.

'I'll stop you there, Centurion. The Batavi enjoy a special relationship with Rome, one that we thought all Romans and their servants were aware of, but in the absence of your having been appropriately briefed, allow me to educate you. We serve Rome voluntarily, under a treaty agreed with Gaius Julius Caesar and ratified every emperor, with the guarantee from Rome of complete freedom from the usual taxes and conscriptions. We have eight whole cohorts of men serving under your banner—'

'Not my problem.' The officer stepped forward, putting his face so close to Hramn's that the decurion could smell the fried onions that he'd eaten for breakfast. '*Your* problem. My orders are to take your men to serve in the Fifth Legion, and if you or anybody else tries to get in my way I'll have you, or them, beaten, stripped and flogged. I'll—'

He looked over Draco's shoulder as something at the forum's edge caught his eye. A single man, dressed in the white tunic and heavy mail shirt of the renamed Batavi Guard had stepped into the open space, a long spear held upright in his right hand and an oval shield at his left side.

'What the *fuck*?'

He fell silent as another guardsman appeared from behind a building to his right, his head swivelling as a third Batavi stepped out of the concealment of a house to his left. Watching in continued silence, his eyes narrowed as more armed and armoured men revealed themselves, until there were enough to match his distinctly nervous-looking escort.

'What you see here, Centurion, is a small number of men of the Batavi Guard. Each of them could take down three of these children standing behind you, even if they had the balls to stand and face us, which I doubt. And as for punishment, I'm happy to promise that just as long as you turn about and make your way out of the city, away to the east and out of our land, no harm will come to you or any of your men.'

He drew breath to continue, but the officer nodded dourly.

'I can see we've been misled. I was told that you people were obliged to provide more men if they were required, whereas it's clear to me that you have a case. I'll take my men and be on my way.'

Hramn allowed himself a smile at the Roman's sudden discomfiture.

'I thought you might. Leave any time you like, Centur . . .'

The word died on his lips as a boy of no more than twelve darted into the forum, eyes wide and lungs heaving for breath. The officer shot him a glance and turned on his heel, gesturing to his men.

'Detachment, form up! Quick march!'

He strode away with the look of a man who was likely to start running the moment he knew he was unobserved, slapping one of his men with the end of his vine stick more, it seemed, from a desire to encourage the same sense of urgency in his men than because of any lack of effort on their part. Hramn watched as the child, having staggered the last few dozen paces to Kivilaz, stood in front of the prince fighting for breath and gabbling out the message he had been sent to deliver. Having already guessed what it was, the veteran turned to Hramn with angry urgency.

'The boy's from the closest village, and he's trying to tell me something about Romans. So I suggest you get your men saddled and send every century you have to the villages nearest to our border with Roman territory. That centurion had the look of a man who'd been caught out, and I'm willing to bet that his presence here was meant to distract us while other men like him drag our boys away to the Old Camp.'

The decurion called for his officers and started barking orders.

'Mount, take a village apiece and ride as hard as you can. If you find Romans trying to conscript our people you disarm them, at spear's length if need be, and then you kick their arses and send them back to where they came from.'

'Where are you going?'

The big man turned to Kivilaz with a tight smile.

'If those fuckers have already done what they intended by the river then they could be halfway to our border with the empire with every man of military age in his village by now. So I'm going to ride out that way and see if I can flush out any game.'

'I'll come with you.'

The prince had his horse saddled and mounted before Hramn's century was assembled. They rode out of the city's east gate at a canter, overtaking the recruiting party two miles later. Hramn reined his horse in alongside the trotting soldiers, shouting over the din of eighty sets of hoofs as his century passed.

'You'd *better* run! And if I catch any of your men conscripting my people I'll send them home with their arses kicked in.'

The centurion looked up at him and raised a hand to halt his men, unable to reply and continue running. Putting a hand on his hips he threw his head back to gulp down the warm summer air, sweat already staining his padded subarmalis black beneath his armour.

'*Are you fucking mad? You stupid bastards are auxiliaries! The emperor will have the lot of you crucified!*'

Hramn shook his head and laughed mirthlessly.

'I don't see your emperor, or a soldier worthy of the name to nail me up! All I see is my spear, my sword, my shield, and *my* people in need of protection from *you* people! Now get off our fucking land and don't come back unless you want to leave as naked as the day you were born!'

He rode on, overtaking his men and calling them to a halt a mile further east.

'If these bastards have tried to get in and out without being seen then they've not used the roads, but sneaked through our fields like the deceitful scum they are! We'll make a sweep to the north and see what we can find! I want an eight-hundred pace front, one man every ten paces! If you see something out of the ordinary you shout, and if you hear a shout, you shout too, and ride for the point where the shout came from! And nobody dies today, not us and most definitely not them, not unless you want to be thigh-deep in legionaries while Batavodurum burns inside the week!'

Leaving his chosen man to shake the century out into a line, he stared out across the farmland to the north with an expert eye.

'What are you looking for?'

He turned to find Kivilaz at his side, the veteran as comfortable in the saddle as any of his guardsmen.

'If you're a recruiting officer, probably with no more than a dozen men, and you hear us approaching, what do you do? We've ten times as many spears as you and we're faster than you are, so you can't fight us off and you can't outrun us.'

'In which case all I can do is hide. And the only place to hide out here is in the hedgerows.'

'My thoughts exactly.' Hramn looked up and down the century's line, nodding approvingly at the speed with which his men were spreading out to either side of him. 'Forward! Scour the ground for Romans, and keep your spears ready! Pay special attention to the hedges!'

It took less than half a mile of progress to flush out the men they were looking for, shouts and horn calls summoning Hramn and Kivilaz to a spot where half a dozen soldiers and another centurion stood defiantly in a semi-circle of spear points with their swords drawn, twice their number of Batavi civilians huddled deep in the shelter of a thick hedge where the soldiers had presumably pushed them in an attempt to avoid detection.

'You have no business to be threatening us! Stand aside and allow me to go about my legitimate business, as I am duly authorised by Legatus Munius Lupercus and the emp—'

Hramn dismounted, landing so close to the officer that he involuntarily stepped back, raising his sword's point at the Batavi's face. Kivilaz stepped down from his own beast, shaking his head at the Roman.

'Put your sword back in its scabbard, Centurion, or I'll be forced to take it off you! There will be no blood shed here, not unless you're foolish enough to start something I'll have to finish for you!' He waited for the Roman to lower his weapon, looking across the crop of manhood that the legionaries had gathered. 'Firstly, your legatus has no jurisdiction on this land. The Batavi are an allied tribe, not a subject people of Rome, and our military service is freely given in return for taxation privileges. You are not permitted to conscript our men, and I will not tolerate this invasion of our territory.'

The centurion shook his head in amazement.

'*Your* fucking territory? The emperor has ordered our legatus to gather recruits for the fight against the pretender Vespasianus, and he specifically ordered your shithole little tribe to be included! So you have no choice, you stupid bastard, because when an emperor gives an ord—'

'Decurion!'

Hramn turned from his brooding consideration of the Roman officer to find one of his men at his elbow.

'What is it?'

The guardsman's face was dark with anger, and he beckoned Hramn without speaking. Half-hidden behind a pair of soldiers a child of no more than twelve was weeping silently, using one hand to stop his torn tunic from falling off his body. His throat was bruised, and one of his eyes was starting to blacken, but is wasn't the obvious physical damage that had caught the guardsman's attention, but rather the way in which his eyes were fixed on the ground before him, and he was refusing to look up at the men around him. Sliding his sword slowly from its scabbard, Hramn eyeballed the legionaries standing in front of him with the dead-eyed expression his men had come to recognise as the precursor to violence, speaking slowly through gritted teeth.

'Get out of my *fucking* way!'

He stared at the closer of the two until the man's nerve broke and he stood aside, then pushed the other out of his path as he stepped closer to the child.

'Look at me.'

Slowly, reluctantly, the boy raised his gaze to look into the centurion's eyes, and the fear that Hramn saw there kindled the flame of anger burning in him. He looked around, finding a villager nodding at him.

'It is exactly what it looks like. Those two took him into my barn, and after a short time he stopped shouting and started screaming.'

The guardsmen looked at each other in horrified anger, and Hramn knew that a single word from him would see every one of the legionaries dead within a dozen heartbeats. He looked at Kivilaz, but the older man shook his head impassively.

'If we kill these men we will pay for it a hundred times over. The Romans will have no choice but to attack in force. And I have a better alternative.'

He turned to the legion centurion, whose grip on his sword's hilt was white-knuckled.

'It seems to me, Centurion, that you've made something of a mistake. A mistake which, were I not here to assist you, would have resulted in your untimely death.'

He stared levelly at the officer's clenched jaw and white face, knowing that the Roman was close to doing something foolish despite the forty guardsmen surrounding his party and the remainder of the century flooding in from either side.

'I suggest you sheathe your sword, before someone does something unwise.'

The centurion shook his head curtly.

'Tell your men to sheathe theirs first.'

Kivilaz stared at him for a moment before replying.

'You want to die here then, I presume? I promised my people that I wouldn't shed blood today, wouldn't invite the revenge of your legion, but that was before I discovered that your men have been abusing our *children*!'

The last word was a shout, and the Roman flinched visibly. Kivilaz took a breath, evidently struggling for self-control.

'So here's what's going to happen. You're going to put up your swords. *All* of you. Then you're going to take off your equipment. *All* of it.' He raised a hand to forestall the centurion's protest. 'Wait until you've heard me out. *All* your equipment, *and* your belts. And you're going to walk away with your lives, which is something you'll look back on in old age, when you've lived those lives, fathered children, raised the children you already have, and on that day you'll thank me for disregarding all my instincts. Because my instinct, Centurion, is to have you all beaten senseless, stripped, flogged half to death and then crucified in the village where this crime was committed. All of you, not just the men that committed the act. And it'll be me doing the flogging, and me hammering the nails in. So you can choose. Talk it over with your men while I have my people escorted away from here.'

He looked over the terrified soldiers, now surrounded by a ring of horsemen with their spears pointing inwards.

'Run if you like, but you won't make twenty paces before we put you down.'

At his signal the dismounted guardsmen shepherded the villagers away, ignoring the legionaries who stood helpless, their swords lowered. Hramn looked down at the centurion from his horse.

'Well? You heard my prefect. How do you want to do this?'

The centurion's tone was bitter.

'You'll pay for this! All of you barbarian f—'

Hramn shook his head.

'Time's up, Centurion, and I don't need an hourglass to tell me that. So make your mind up. What will it be? A little embarrassment or the hardest death imaginable?'

One of the legionaries made the decision for him, dropping his shield to the ground and then sheathing his sword. Unbuckling his belt, he dumped his weapons on the ground beside the shield, then started unlacing his plate armour. His comrades followed suit, and after a moment's stare about him the officer reluctantly dropped his sword point first into the grass, dropping his belt and then struggling out of his scale armour while his men looked numbly on.

'And the tunic belts. Let's not let there be any doubt that you're being punished.'

The Romans glumly complied, allowing the hems of their tunics, usually belted above the knee in the military style, to fall to their upper calves. The centurion shook his head in red-faced anger, his scowl murderous.

'You will regret this. Rome's arm is long.'

Kivilaz shook his head with a chuckle.

'Centurion, I was serving as Rome's long arm before you'd even learned how to piss in your potty. I was the Prefect of the Batavian cohorts, the leader of four thousand men famous throughout the army as the best and bravest. That was before you men of the legions got jealous of us, of course, and decided you could live without us once the Britons had been beaten into submission. So yes, Rome's arm is long, but Rome needs to be careful not to overreach itself and get its fingers lopped off. And you can tell Legatus Munius Lupercus this: if Rome's legions come to the Batavi in peace, as allies bound by a treaty whose terms will be respected by both sides, and not just by the junior partner, then the Batavi will greet those legions as comrades in arms, and will do all that can be done to assist Rome in its cause.'

He paused significantly.

'Once Rome has decided who rules, that is. Our cohorts in the service of Vitellius can look after themselves, they're all veterans and they'll fight for each other, but the idea of allowing you to take our young men and drop them into legion cohorts where no man cares for his comrades?' He shook his head emphatically. 'Is simply not acceptable, and will not happen.'

He pointed east.

'The Old Camp is that way. Tell Munius Lupercus that he's welcome to visit Batavodurum any time he pleases, as long as he comes in peace. If he comes to fight he will find the Batavi a harder nut to crack than he might have expected. And while you're at it you can remind him that he still owes me his life. On your way.'

The Old Camp, Germania Inferior, August AD 69

'They did *what*?'

Marius had never seen his legatus really angry, he realised. Irritated, occasionally irascible when confronted with some unfathomable aspect of military bureaucracy, but incandescent rage had never been a facet of the legatus's behaviour before that moment. His superior leaned forward across his desk with the look of a man who intended visiting violence on someone in the very near future and wasn't overly concerned with who that person might be, and even as the centurion started to explain his shocking news it occurred to him that the only person present on whom that ire could be vented was himself.

'One of the recruiting centurions lost control of his men. They raped a Batavi youth, and the detachment in question was intercepted by the tribe's new guardsmen before they could make it off their land. The fact that they were allowed to live is probably a testament to the discipline of the men who uncovered the truth of what they'd done. Civilis and his decurion Hramn stripped them of their armour and weapons and sent them on their way with a warning not to come back if they valued their skins, then hunted down every other recruiting party and did the same to them. They came back through the gate half an hour ago, just after dark, with nothing more than their boots and tunics.'

Lupercus stared at him for a moment, one hand on the hilt of his pugio, and for a moment Marius saw the naked urge in his eyes to unsheathe the weapon and allow its blade to taste blood, but after a long moment staring at his First Spear the legatus shook his head in amazement. Stabbing a finger at the desk for emphasis, he grated out his orders in a tone that brooked no argument.

'The centurion commanding that detachment is to be reduced to the ranks immediately, with a note on his record that he should never be promoted above the rank of soldier again. He's clearly proved himself incapable of controlling his men.'

Marius nodded, but as he opened his mouth to speak Lupercus raised a hand.

'Not yet, First Spear, I'm not done. Get the rest of the officers involved re-equipped, then take them out onto the parade ground before dawn tomorrow morning, and tell them all to consider their actions very, *very* carefully. Any man who confesses to a crime committed by himself or his men in the course of this abortive mission will receive the same treatment, permanent reduction to the ranks, while any man who declares his conscience to be clear will receive my full backing as an unfortunate victim of circumstances and their colleagues' stupidity. But should any of the latter be proved to have carried out or permitted any such act of despoilment, or theft, or murder, both they and any perpetrator will be crucified without any prospect of mercy. And that sentence will be carried out in front of the entire legion, and the legion will remain paraded until they are dead. Is that understood?'

Marius saluted.

'We will do what is ordered and at every command we will be ready, Legatus!'

He turned to leave the office, only to be frozen in place by the legatus's softly spoken rejoinder.

'I'm not finished, First Spear.'

Turning back, he drew himself up to attention.

'Legatus.'

Lupercus stared at him for a moment across the desk before sinking back into his chair.

'No, Marius, I don't want your vine stick. That was your expectation, I take it?'

The centurion nodded, and Lupercus laughed bitterly.

'What earthly good would it do me to be deprived of my senior centurion at a time like this? Do you think I want to face the consequences of this act of idiocy on my *own*? I'm going to need all of your skill and determination over the next few weeks, I suspect. But we have to recognise what's brought us to where we are, given that we may very well just have given the Batavians all the cause they need to go to war with us.'

He looked up at the office's roof for a moment before speaking again.

'Let's be clear about this, First Spear. You and I are in a very lonely place at this point in time. The emperor issued us with an instruction, which was only ever going to end in failure and repercussion, no matter how reasonable it will have seemed when viewed from the perspective of a non-military man with an empire at stake, not to mention his own life. After all, the throne has already killed three men in the last year, and with Vespasianus in open revolt it looks likely that there'll be a fourth victim before this year is done with. And I know who my money would be on as the more likely of the two to come out on top.

'And so, in attempting to carry out his orders to the best degree possible given the circumstances, we've run headlong into the consequences of previous decisions that were made at a level neither of us could influence. Tell me, this centurion who failed to keep his men in check, was he a chosen man six months ago?'

Marius nodded.

'And there's the proof. We were forced to promote men who weren't ready, who perhaps might never have been ready in normal times, and as a consequence one of those men has permitted his men to do something that has given Civilis all the excuse he needs to switch his role from that of a willing, if misused, servant of the empire to tribal warlord. So organise the punishments I've ordered, First Spear, and redouble your efforts to get our men ready to fight. Dismissed.'

Marius saluted again, but before he could turn for the door Lupercus raised a hand.

'Oh, and one more thought. Make sure your men are as practised at retreating as they are going forward, eh? I suspect we may have need of that under-regarded piece of military skill. Call it advancing to the rear if you like, but make sure that when the time comes your men aren't falling over their own feet, because I doubt we'll get a second chance to get it right.'

10

Oppidum Batavorum, August AD 69

'Tell me, Kivilaz, what is it that you want from us? And why have you chosen to bring us here, of all places?'

Tiberius Claudius Labeo had been the first man to approach the Batavi prince on his appearance in the grove, voicing the question that was on the lips of every one of the dozen men Kivilaz had invited to meet in that place and at that time. Dressed in a military tunic of fine wool, his boots and belt waxed and buffed to a shine, he was every inch an officer in the service of Rome, whereas Kivilaz was dressed more simply, having seemingly chosen to eschew the uniform he was entitled to wear. Hramn, discreetly standing at the clearing's edge, was dressed equally finely in his own uniform, with a silver and gold decorated dagger hanging from his belt.

'Why here? What better place could there be to discuss the matters I wish to raise with the tribal council? Until a century ago the tribe worshipped in groves like this, sending our prayers to Magusanus, greatest of the gods. And then Caesar came, and in our haste to ally with Rome we allowed the suggestion that their god Hercules and Magusanus are one and the same to result in our abandoning the groves, and moved our places of worship into Batavodurum itself, alongside temples to Rome's emperors who, they tell us, are deities in their own right. This place sums up our relationship with Rome, I'd say, and provides the perfect setting for the questions I wish to raise with you all.'

He grinned at Labeo, reaching for a cup.

'And besides, given that this grove is nicely hidden from prying eyes, what better place to take a cup of wine and discuss the world around us?'

Pouring himself a measure of wine, he gestured to his guests to join him and waited until they were seated at the rough table he had bidden Hramn to erect in front of the grove's ancient altar.

'Long life!'

He drank the cup dry and refilled it.

'So, brother, what do I want from you?'

The prince shook his head briskly.

'In truth I don't want anything from you. I simply thought that an opportunity to discuss the tribe's situation, without the risk of that discussion being communicated back to the Romans, might be . . . wise? You know as well as I do that they do not trust any of their allies, and always pay men among each of the German tribes to report back to them the doings of those men with influence. Why else would I have suggested that we meet here?'

He waved a hand at the trees around them, illuminated by the light of a dozen torches. Labeo nodded, but still looked far from convinced. Standing, he gestured to the men around him, the most influential members of the tribe, without whom no major decision could be made.

'Before we hear what you have to say, you should be very clear that the feeling among the tribe's citizens is that you have already brought the Batavis' good name with our allies into disrepute. We consider it unlikely that a man can be imprisoned for the alleged crime of treason twice without the distinct possibility that there are some genuine questions for him to answer. Perhaps the new emperor's dismissal of the German Bodyguard was not entirely disconnected from your own imprisonment in Rome at the same time? And now he has ordered conscription of our men, a clear signal that he intends to tear up our treaty with Rome.'

He looked around his audience.

'Can we truly believe that this is entirely without just cause? Perhaps Rome has decided not to trust the Batavi as a consequence of your association with this man Vindex?'

Kivilaz drew breath to respond, but Labeo raised a hand to silence him.

'And further, brother, many of the men who have recently achieved citizenship, or whose fathers were the first of their line to achieve that status, like myself, for example, harbour suspicions that you have been manoeuvring, and continue those efforts, to have yourself proclaimed leader of the tribe. You men of the Julii, Augusti and Tiberii, those of our tribe's noble families that were granted citizen status in the reigns of the first emperors, you have enjoyed a monopoly on power within the tribe until recently, using the votes of your families and the men allied with you to elect magistrates within your own ranks. For this reason little has changed from the days where your ancestors were kings, but with each successive generation more and more men from the tribe's ordinary families have earned citizenship through their service, to the point where they outnumber the men from the old nobility. It is only our division, our failure to vote together, that has prevented a change in this situation. But then you're a clever man, aren't you Kivilaz, you know all this to be true without having to be told. Perhaps you feel threatened?'

He stared at Kivilaz in silence for a moment.

'And perhaps you should. There are many men, men like me, men who gained their citizenship under Claudius and Nero, who resent the fact that the older, *greater* families seem reluctant to relinquish their control over our people's doings. And there is a time not far off now, when we will band together and vote for a magistrate who will fairly represent our interests, and argue as strongly for them as the current office holder does for yours. And now you bring us together, not in our town hall where more rational opinions can hold sway, but in a sacred grove where all that is missing to return us to the time before the Romans came with the gift of civilisation is a priest sacrificing to Magusanus on that altar. Or is that also part of your plan for the tribe?'

He sat down, leaning back in his chair with the look of a man who was pleased with his work, gesturing for Kivilaz to take his turn. The prince took another drink from his cup and wiped his lips with the back of his hand before getting to his feet, looking around the brightly lit grove.

'As I say, I requested you all to come here as my guests in order that we might discuss the current crisis . . .' He raised a hand to forestall any comment from the man who had spoken before. 'Claudius Labeo would have you believe that nothing has changed in the last year, and that Rome remains just as beneficent a master as it ever was. That the recent upheavals will resolve themselves, one way or another, with an eventual return to stability and prosperity, whether under Vitellius or Vespasianus. And there is much within me that would dearly like this to be true, and yet . . .'

He looked at Labeo for a moment before continuing.

'If I have brought the Batavi into disrepute, it has been through no conscious act of rebellion against Rome. I met with Vindex, when the fool was trumpeting himself as "the saviour of humanity" and busily minting coinage rather than taking any practical steps to defend his revolt from the inevitable backlash, but only to counsel him to make peace with the men sent to deal with him. Counsel that he accepted. There would have been peace in Gaul, my brothers, but for the officers of the legions who came south against him, proud men who desired conflict, hate-filled men who would not allow that peace agreement to bear fruit!'

He clenched a fist in frustration.

'They ordered their legionaries to attack, a pack of wolves unleashed on sheep, and when Vindex's meagre forces had been scattered they implicated me in the uprising as a means of diverting the blame for such a one-sided massacre from themselves. It was the centurions who dragged our tribe's name into the dirt, brothers, and it was they who were responsible for my brother Paulus's execution, ordered by a legatus who was unable to resist their demands for blood. They would have had my blood too, had he not been compelled to send me to Rome for an imperial judgement. A judgement, brothers, that exonerated me completely. And then, not content with that, these same upstart soldiers, the best of them worse than the meanest man of the tribe in their single-minded lust to see me dead, persuaded this new emperor, this Vitellius, a man more dedicated to the pleasures of the flesh than the rule of the civilised world, to arrest me once again. It was only his calculation that he would be better with the Batavi as allies than enemies that saw me released a second time. But the third time I am accused – and trust me in this, my brothers, there most assuredly will be a third time, if these same centurions have their way, when this war is over and Vitellius has no further need for my influence on the tribe – there will be no reprieve. There is an executioner waiting in my future, I know that. And if it were just me, well . . .'

He bowed his head wearily.

'If it were only me the Romans wanted to see dead then I would take my own life, both to frustrate the centurions' desire to see me suffer and to give the rest of you peace. But it isn't only me, brothers, it is *every* last one of us. These same centurions, these bloody-handed animals who slaughtered Vindex's men, they want to see the Batavi bent to their will, and our men conscripted into their legions to feed their civil war. A war that will consume the empire, and see our men lying dead on battlefields we neither know nor care about by the thousand. It's not me they want, it's *us*.'

He paused, looking around him.

'*All* of us. They would see every man in this grove dead, given the opportunity, and the Batavi reduced to no better status than the slave peoples of their provinces, rather than the free men we are now.'

He looked at Labeo with a sad smile.

'Can you deny my words, Claudius Labeo? Can you deny that Rome's urge to expand and enslave is as strong as it ever was? Before you answer, allow me to remind you of our time in Britannia.'

The other man nodded slowly, pursing his lips in reluctant agreement, and Kivilaz smiled sadly at him.

'Will you tell them, or should I spare you that pain?'

Labeo waved a hand in silence, and Kivilaz picked up his cup and drank, milking the tension that held every man in the room.

'We served together in Britannia, Tiberius Claudius Labeo and I, and we saw at first hand the way that the Romans do business. Their foreign wars are sponsored by men of such wealth that they could buy and sell the Batavi and think nothing of it, donating huge fortunes to equip and transport the legions to the scene of their next conquest. A thousand ships were built to carry the army of the man whose name our brother Labeo proudly uses to Britannia, an island populated by a dozen noble tribes much like our own. One thousand ships, as many as sailed to assault ancient Troy, built with money provided by rich and clever men who fully intended to profit from what they saw as nothing more than a business venture. Of course we were young, and wanted nothing more than glory for the tribe, so we fought battles for them that tore the heart out of the Britons' resistance, assisting the Romans to conquer a swathe of territory big enough for these money men to go to work, loaning funds to the newly conquered peoples to build temples and baths, to copy their new masters' image of civilisation. And when those loans came due and could not be paid, or when the men who had incurred the debt died, then the bankers would cry foul and call in the centurions to do the dirty work of extorting what they were due. Why do you imagine Boudicca rose against Rome? Because of the violent annexation of her dead husband's kingdom when he tried to leave his daughters some part of his fortune. Daughters who were raped by men just like those who came here looking for conscripts and victims for their urge to sully our youth, while his wife was flogged for her temerity. And now we find ourselves faced with the same choice that confronted Boudicca, I fear.'

He took another drink, peering over the rim of his cup as if waiting for an interjection, and one of the men facing him spoke up, his tongue loosened by the wine.

'But what would you have us do, Kivilaz? Even Boudicca discovered the futility of defying an empire. Do you intend for the Batavi to defy Rome in the same way, and risk the same wholesale destruction and enslavement that overtook the Iceni once *we* were done with them?'

Lowering the cup, Kivilaz nodded his acknowledgement of the point.

'Well pointed out, Nero Claudius Ariston. But there is one crucial difference between our position and that of the Iceni tribe.'

He took another sip, smiling at the unspoken question on every face.

'What is that difference? I will tell you, brothers. The Iceni rose against a united Rome, they insulted Rome in ways that Rome never forgets and never forgives, and they paid the full and bitter price for doing so. Whereas we?'

Another sip, another pause.

'We, brothers, have an emperor on our side.'

Labeo sat forward, his eyes wide with amazement.

'You mean?'

'Yes. Vespasianus. The emperor in the east. The man against whom Vitellius now turns his entire army, recklessly leaving the Rhenus unguarded by legions little better than no legions at all, forcing him to show his true intentions toward the Batavi in this attempt to conscript our young men. Making those same centurions who dream of our enslavement bold enough to insult our children's honour. I tell you this, brothers, if Vitellius defeats Vespasianus then the return of his victorious legions to the Old Camp will be the death knell of our way of life. Our independence will be torn from us as roughly as a maiden's virtue in a time of conquest, our cohorts will be posted to the other side of the empire to prevent them from coming to our aid, and we will be no better than the Ubii, or the Tungri, enslaved in all but word. Whereas . . .'

He sipped again.

'Whereas if Vespasianus wins, and we are seen to have been instrumental in that victory, our current way of life will continue.'

'How can you know that? Unless . . .' Labeo shook his head in disbelief. 'You've been colluding with an enemy of the state?'

Kivilaz smiled at him.

'There's that question of where a man views the question from again. Your "enemy of the state" is another man's "rightful emperor"'. And I have hardly colluded with the man, although *we* have received certain encouragements from him of late.'

'I'm sure you have!' Labeo's voice was heavy with irony. 'I'm sure he'd say whatever was needed to have an uprising in Vitellius's rear distracting his attention at just the right time!'

Kivilaz shrugged.

'As you will know, I have recently received a visitor, a scholar I met in Rome after my trial and release. Gaius Plinius Secundus, a friend of Vespasianus's son-in-law and secretly his agent in Rome. He told me that his patron has been watching events closely, waiting to see how the eventual victor behaved, and, when Vespasianus decided to make his claim for the throne, Plinius already knew what was expected of him as a result of previous instructions from Egypt. He told me that he has delivered a similar message to the commander of the German army, Hordeonius Flaccus, and that Flaccus was sympathetic to Vespasianus's cause. And the message?'

He looked around the table.

'He asked me to consider bringing the Batavi to his cause, as you say, Labeo, to distract our mutual enemy's forces and make his own victory more likely.'

The other man shook his head in disbelief.

'And what was your answer?'

Kivilaz shrugged.

'What answer could I give? For one thing the situation had not yet arisen, and to speak of it publicly would have been to condemn a good few of us to death, in all likelihood. And, more importantly, how could I answer without the authority of the tribe? I do not mistake myself for a prince in anything but name. And so . . .'

He opened his arms to encompass the silent gathering.

'I throw the discussion open to you, my brothers. On the one hand, we have a man who might well become emperor who is asking for our support to help make him victorious, and who promises to restore balance to the relationship between Rome and the Batavi. A simple, straightforward soldier known to many of us from our days in Britannia, an honest man who shares many of the virtues that we ourselves hold so dear. And on the other, Vitellius, unable and most likely unwilling to control the depredations of his centurions, men who have assumed power beyond that of their role. An emperor who, once victory has been secured, will allow his men to go about destroying our previous harmonious coexistence with Rome, no matter what support we provide him in the coming struggle, and despite the unassailable fact that, to judge from the reports I've received, without our cohorts at Cremona that battle might have ended very differently. An emperor happy to unleash his dogs to conscript and abuse our men, and who doubtless will extend that treatment to the women of the tribe, given the opportunity. I have no doubt where my lot would go, were we to vote on the matter.'

He sat back in his chair and took a deep drink of his wine, waiting while the men gathered around his table erupted into a tumult of discussion. After a moment he drained the wine and banged it down hard on the table. The men around him started, and in that instant of silence he spoke again with a knowing smile.

'Of course there is one more reason why I believe the time has come to rise against the Romans. A reason some of you may have heard about. Which is why I chose to meet with you all here, in the cradle of the religion we *used* to hold dear. A religion still very much alive on the other side of the river.'

He looked about him with a smile, waiting to see who would be the first man to ask the question.

Oppidum Cananefates, August AD 69

'Revolt? Against the Romans?'

The de facto leader of the Cananefates tribe looked at Kivilaz solemnly for a moment before bursting into laughter, shaking his head and then looking around the tribe's clan chiefs with a look of amazement that invited them to join in with his amusement.

'You hear this, my brothers? This prince of the Batavi, a man who has fought alongside the Romans for twenty-five years and more, invites the Cananefates to join him in a rebellion against the very empire his people has served so faithfully since the days of his great-grandfather's father. Even your Roman name, Gaius Julius Civilis, tells us how long it has been since the Batavi, and by means of our alliance with the Batavi, the Cananefates too, have been anything other than faithful servants of Rome!'

Kivilaz nodded equably.

'I cannot deny anything you say, Brinno. Your people and mine have served Rome together for longer than any man can claim to remember. Two cohorts of your warriors accompany the Batavi into battle, and have won honour with Rome on more battlefields than either of us could name. And yet . . .'

The Cananefates leader leaned forward.

'And yet? And yet *what*? My people have followed your tribe's lead all these years, fought, and bled, and died for Rome. And now you stroll into my hall and tell me that you plan to betray the Romans? Have you lost your *wits*, brother?'

The Batavi prince grinned at him, laughing softly.

'Some within my own tribe made the same challenge, if not quite as bluntly. You are the son of your father, Brinno, clearly descended from the man who told Caligula that his military schemes were idiocy and walked away with his head still attached to his body because the emperor saw a man cast from the same metal as himself, walking that fine line between frank counsel and suicidal honesty.'

Brinno raised an eyebrow.

'Your flattery is welcome, Kivilaz, but hardly likely to influence me.'

'Not flattery. A blunt statement of the facts. My own people were just as sceptical as you, to begin with, and I relish your disbelief as an opportunity to rework the arguments I used to convince them that we, Batavi and Cananefates both, yes, and the Marsaci, and the Frisavones, we all stand on the edge of a moment of decision that will determine whether we remain as proud and independent peoples allied to a mighty empire, or become just subject peoples, ground underfoot by Rome simply because that is the nature of empire. Any empire.'

The Cananefates prince looked at him flatly.

'Go on then. Persuade me. And more than that, persuade these men that I have come to trust for their honest and sensible counsel.'

Kivilaz leaned back in his chair, weighing his words.

'I could tell you that the empire is tottering, on the edge of falling into an abyss after a century of rule which, while no man could ever describe as enlightened, has at least provided its people, and our tribes too, with stability and, for the most part, prosperity. Nero's suicide has allowed the dogs who played at the emperor's feet to become bold, and to sink their teeth into the juicy meat on the table rather than the bones they were previously accustomed to receiving. First there was an old man, a throwback to the days of Augustus but lacking in that great man's intellect and sure touch. Now dead, murdered by his own praetorians after having dismissed the very men of our tribes who, still loyal to the throne, might have saved him from that treachery. His murderer was a young fool, who grabbed for the ultimate prize and then, having captured it, found himself unequal to the task of imperium. Now dead, and by his own hand, like the callow boy he was. Which leaves the empire in the hands of a man not fit to clean the shoes of the leader after whom I am named. If there were a Gaius Julius Caesar to follow in this world I would throw my entire strength behind him, but there is not, which means that the emperor who has risen in the east, this man Vespasianus, is the best hope that civilisation will survive this cataclysm.'

Brinno nodded.

'We know this man, having fought alongside him in Britannia. And as you say, he is a man of common sense and decency. But what if we stand for him, and do as you suggest, and he then loses his fight for the throne? If that comes to pass, then surely that which you profess to fear, the destruction of our independence, must inevitably follow.'

The Batavi noble smiled wanly.

'Such an unwelcome state of affairs is inevitable under Vitellius, whether we rise and strike his armies at this moment of their maximum weakness or not. If we sink the dagger into them their revenge will doubtless be bloody, with fire and slavery, but if we sit here meekly and wait for the struggle to play out, to whatever result, our days as independent tribes will be numbered.'

He leaned forward, fixing the Cananefates with a level stare.

'If Vitellius wins then his centurions will return to their fortresses ready to conclude their unfinished business with the Batavi, and where the Batavi are seen as the enemy you can be sure that the Cananefates will be eggs in the same basket. But if Vespasianus wins without our assistance he will hardly be minded to hold out the hand of friendship that will protect us from those same officers, embittered by defeat and looking for a dog to kick.'

'But if we rise?'

'I have assurances from a man who is close to Vespasianus, a man who seeks our help to topple this gluttonous, idle emperor who will embody the worst possible combination of sloth and venality in his rule. Assurances that our intervention in the struggle between these two will be rewarded with guarantees of our independence, and the appointment of a legatus augusti to command the army of Germania Inferior who will serve as their guarantor. More than that, he has suggested that such loyal service to our former comrade in arms will be rewarded with the establishment of a truly independent Batavi homeland, with the Cananefates equally free to govern themselves as our allies.'

Brinno stroked his beard.

'So your reward is to become the new king of the Batavi?'

'Hah! Not likely! I have suffered too much in the last year at the hands of Rome's servants to harbour any such ambition! My brother Paulus was killed for a crime that he did not commit. I myself was imprisoned under sentence of death twice for the same crime, of which I was never guilty, and freed both times not because Rome recognised my innocence but for reasons of mere expediency. I wish for nothing more than the chance to see my people stay free, and for the threat posed to our independence by the legions that eye us balefully from the Old Camp to be stamped flat once and for all. Let other men worry about how the Batavi should be governed, I will serve the tribe in whatever capacity is granted to me.'

The Cananefates leader pulled a disbelieving face.

'For a man to be granted the power of a war leader, and then to step away from that golden cup and return to his plough like the Roman generals of the old days are supposed to have done – that I would enjoy watching. For my part, I would seek the leadership of my tribe under this new treaty, and I can be sure that my people would grant me that role, for I love them and they love me.'

Heads nodded around the table at the unassailable truth in his words.

'But I care little what you do or do not hope for as a result of sinking your sword deep into Rome's back, only for the chances of such a bold step resulting in anything other than the destruction of this hall, and the end of my ancestors' line. I presume that you have a plan to put the Romans in the position of the most disadvantage, before you strike the blow that will put them on their knees?'

Kivilaz's face creased into a smile.

'I have a plan, Brinno, that will have the Romans confident in their victory over our meagre forces until the moment that the realities of the day become clear to them. A plan, it seems, that has the favour not only of my tribe but of the gods themselves, if reports from the tribes across the river are to be believed.'

The Old Camp, August AD 69

'Very well, Legatus, your message certainly succeeded in getting my attention. I suggest that you brief me on the latest situation.'

General Flaccus had arrived at the fortress in the Rhenus fleet's flagship less than an hour before, and under normal conditions would have enjoyed a sweat in the commanding officer's bathhouse before getting down to business. Instead he had immediately been led to the headquarters building, where the two legions' remaining military tribunes and the centurions commanding their cohorts were already gathered, awaiting his arrival. Munius Lupercus stood, pointing to a map of the area to the east of the fortress.

'As my message told you, Legatus, we have reason to believe that the Batavians are planning an uprising, and our information is that their allies the Cananefates will attack our forts at the eastern end of their territory any time now. We also have very good reason to believe that their leader Civilis will then use this as a pretext to gather all of the Batavian troops he can muster into one force, which he will then turn against us in a further act of betrayal. All in the name of Vespasianus's rebellion against the throne, but secretly for his own ends, and the re-establishment of the Batavian kingdom.'

Flaccus shook his head in disbelief.

'I've been turning this over in my mind all the way downriver, and I still find it difficult to believe this intelligence you claim to have come by. Gods below man, Civilis is a veteran of every battle fought in Britannia since the invasion! And the Batavians are a loyal ally of Rome, for all that there's been some unhappiness between us of late. They were instrumental to the defeat of Otho's army at the Po, and no more faithful auxiliaries exist in all of the . . .'

He fell silent as a man stepped forward from behind Lupercus, saluting smartly and waiting to be addressed.

'And you are?'

'Tiberius Claudius Labeo, Legatus.'

'You're . . . Batavian?'

'Commander of the Batavian cavalry wing, Legatus, based at Ridge Fort, close to Batavodurum.'

Flaccus stared at Labeo for a moment.

'But you're not in Batavodurum, are you, Prefect? You're here . . .' He thought for a moment. 'With your unit? I presume that you're the source of this most recent intelligence on their hostile intentions?'

The Batavian nodded.

'Yes, Legatus. When the mood among our people hardened to the point that rebellion was being discussed, I thought it best to relocate my command before the men became prey to the sedition that was being proposed.'

'I see.' The general looked at his colleague. 'Very well, Munius Lupercus, you can consider your point made. But before I permit this man to tell his story I'll be needing a strong chair and a large cup of wine. And not necessarily in that order.'

Seated, and having graciously commanded that the gathered officers should follow his example, he regarded the Batavian officer over the rim of his cup while taking a first sip at its contents.

'Good wine, Lupercus. As usual you are to be commended on the quality of your estate's vintage. It's rare to find anything this good so close to the edge of the world. Now then, Tiberius Claudius Labeo, let's have your story. And be sure not to spare any of those little details that might convince me that I haven't been dragged all this way just to listen to some alarmist nonsense with a tribal feud at the heart of the matter, rather than a revolt that could be a disaster for the empire.'

Labeo stood and pointed at the painted map of the area governed by the Old Camp's legions that covered half a wall.

'When you look at that map, Legatus, you see a tribal territory that provides the empire with eight cohorts of part-mounted infantry, one cavalry wing to police the tribe's territory, and of late, a five-hundred-strong unit of men who were formerly the emperor's bodyguard, who have further been training two cohorts of militia to a reasonable standard of competence. I've seen them drilling, Legatus, and what they lack in equipment they compensate for in discipline and fighting spirit. The former soldiers of the German Bodyguard have turned them into an effective force, given the right circumstances.'

He pointed at the map again.

'What you see is an allied territory, supplier of some of the finest shock troops in the empire. What you *should* be seeing is a pugio pointed squarely at Rome's back. A knife wielded by my compatriot Gaius Julius Civilis. In recent days he has taken to meeting with the tribes' citizens, one family at a time, building a base of support for his plan to strike at Rome when the empire is at its most preoccupied with matters elsewhere.'

'And you know this how, exactly?'

'I know this, Legatus, because I was invited to a gathering in our most sacred holy place three nights ago, a meeting of all the senior men of the tribe, mainly those qualified as citizens of the empire, the men who elect our magistrate, plus a few others of high standing who for whatever reason have not achieved citizen status. This gathering was called by Civilis, a man with whom I have personal differences.'

Flaccus nodded his understanding.

'No less than I expected. He's a Gaius Julius, which means that his family achieved citizenship a century ago when Caesar first conquered this country, whereas you are a Tiberius Claudius, the son of a man granted citizenship by the emperor Claudius. Am I right?' Labeo nodded in silence. 'Which means in turn that Civilis and the other men of the tribe like him, members of the families used to controlling your affairs in a tight little clique, now find themselves beset on all sides by men who see no reason why the initial cosy set-up whereby they elected one of their own to the magistracy should be allowed to continue. After all, whoever leads their faction is in truth the de facto king of the tribe. And there are more than enough men like you to challenge their oligarchy, if you act together. Although that has been a big "*if*" in the past, hasn't it?'

Labeo nodded slowly.

'You are surprisingly well informed, Legatus.'

Flaccus snorted his amusement.

'What I am, gentlemen, appearances to the contrary, is not entirely *fucking* stupid.'

The gathered officers stared back at him in barely concealed disbelief, and he laughed tersely at their collective discomfiture.

'I know you all look at me and see a fat, gout-ridden old man, chosen by Vitellius to command the legions of Germania because the odds of my being offered the purple by those legions is somewhere between scant and none. But my father didn't raise an idiot, and nor did he stint on my education as a younger man. I'd wager I've a better political brain than any man here, and I know very well what's motivating your compatriot Civilis, and you, for that matter. He wants to rule your tribe, like an old-fashioned king, and you want to break his grip on the reins of power and avoid him becoming a tyrant. Right?'

Labeo nodded slowly.

'Your view of the matter is well informed, Legatus.'

'Good. Now we're being honest with each other. So what happened at this gathering?'

'Civilis told the men of the tribe that we were being exploited by the emperor's decision to allow the legions to recruit directly from our people by force. He argued that this decision, whilst lawful, makes a mockery of our long-standing treaty with Rome to be exempt from taxes and conscription, especially given the way in which your centurions have been going about it. I think you know what I mean?'

He shot a hard glance at Marius, who stared back at him expressionlessly.

'Civilis is telling our people that we're on a slippery slope to being just another subject people, rather than a valued ally.'

Flaccus nodded with a knowing expression.

'A good choice of argument, I'd say, given the sorry details that Legatus Lupercus and his First Spear have already shared with me as to what happened when our recruiting parties, shall we say, exceeded their brief somewhat. Presumably this man Civilis told your elders that that Flavius Vespasianus is their best hope of maintaining their independence, and coincidentally keeping his head attached to his neck?'

'He did. But there's one thing he made great play of that I'm willing to bet good money you haven't heard yet.'

Flaccus's eyes narrowed.

'Really? I do love a challenge. But I'll warn you, Prefect, that I see every single intelligence report before they go off to Rome for the men who advise the emperor to fret over. Still want to take that bet?'

Labeo looked at him for a moment, then shook his head.

'No, Legatus. I don't think I will.'

The senior officer smiled tightly.

'A wise choice.'

He turned to address the legion's officers.

'The most persuasive argument that this man Civilis could have brought to this meeting our ally has described would be one based not on logic, but on religion. Your people, Claudius Labeo, are still effectively wedded to the old ways, are they not? Rome's gods are tolerated alongside the imperial cult, but when you pray, you pray to firstly Magusanus, and then to Hercules. And there is a woman hidden deep in the forest beyond the Rhenus who exercises a good deal more influence on the tribes on this side of the river than Rome finds comfortable. Did Civilis mention her, by any chance?'

The Batavi officer nodded ruefully.

'Yes.'

Flaccus addressed the room.

'Our biggest problem here is not that the Batavians feel slighted by the emperor's decision to recruit from their ranks, or that this man Civilis wishes to be king of his tribe, or even that he is looking for a way to avoid the emperor having him executed, once the war against Vespasianus is done with. No, gentlemen, our biggest problem is that there is a priestess in the tribal lands beyond the Rhenus who has accumulated more power than any chieftain in a remarkably short amount of time. Her name is Veleda, and whole tribes bend the knee at even the mention of that name, it seems. Her reach is so long that she has even brokered agreement in a territorial dispute between the *Roman* inhabitants of Colonia Agrippina and the Tencteri tribe on the other side of the river. They believe she sees the future, like a Germanic version of the oracle at Delphi, and her proclamations are brought to those who ask for them by her acolytes, allowing the woman herself to maintain a remoteness that only feeds her myth.'

He took a drink of wine, savouring the taste for a moment.

'This really is *very* good wine, Munius Lupercus. So, why should this woman's auguries be such a problem now?'

As the question hung in the air, he gestured to the Batavi officer.

'Claudius Labeo here knows, which might give us a clue.'

Labeo bowed his head fractionally in recognition of Flaccus's point.

'Nobody else? Very well, gentlemen, the reason why this woman is now no longer simply a curiosity but a deadly enemy of Rome, is two-fold. Firstly, she has recently predicted that the Batavians will rise up against their Roman "overlords" and defeat them, freeing the German peoples who are not yet their subjects from the threat of their yoke and liberating the tribes to the west of the Rhenus to enjoy fresh independence. And that, although significant enough in its own right, is the smaller of the two issues that we have with this priestess and her prophecies. Would any of you care to guess what the bigger of them is?'

He looked around him at the legion's officers, inviting anyone to comment, but they stared back at him to a man, baffled as to what it was that could be worse than the seditious words they were hearing.

'The major reason why this Veleda represents the biggest threat to the empire on the entire northern frontier is the simple fact that the Germans *believe* her prophecy. Not just the Batavians, but *all* of them. In and of itself her prediction of Batavian victory is simply an incitement for them to rise against us, one of many that have been hurled across the Rhenus since the days when we stood on the brink of subduing Germania Magna only to have that prize torn from our fingers by the disaster of the Teutoburg Forest. But invested with the power of that belief it becomes deadly, a casus belli that has the potential to ignite every damned tribe on both sides of the river all the way down the frontier to the Winter Camp in the far south. If the Batavians make war on Rome, then Civilis and his men won't stand alone for long, that seems certain enough from the intelligence reports I've been reading of late.'

He turned back to Labeo.

'This gathering of your tribe's elders took place in one of your holy places, did it not?'

'Yes Legatus, a grove formerly used by our priests for the worship of Magusanus.'

'And did Civilis order a ritual to be held?'

'He did.'

'There it is.'

Flaccus gestured to the Batavi officer with a grim smile.

'This man Civilis plans to use the priestess's prophecy as the spark to light the dry tinder of his people's frustrations with Rome. And that fire will blaze across Germania with a speed that would have represented enough of a challenge to our authority even if Vitellius hadn't emptied out the frontier fortresses to spearhead his march on Rome. As it is, we are already perilously close to defeat before the first spear is thrown. And make no mistake, gentlemen, if we lose so much as a single battle to whatever force the Batavians can put into the field then the tribes that surround us on both sides of the river will be at our throats in days, as the news reaches them and proves this woman's claim that Rome's northern frontier is vulnerable, ripe for the taking.'

He fell silent, and every man in the room pondered on the sudden, terrifying nature of the abyss that had opened beneath their feet. Munius Lupercus cleared his throat, looking at Flaccus questioningly, and the general nodded his assent to whatever it was the legatus had to say.

'So, Claudius Labeo, tell us of Civilis's intentions, as much as you know them.'

The Batavi nodded.

'I know them well enough, Legatus Lupercus. He plans a ruse, to allow him to gather his forces into one powerful army under the disguise of what he hopes you will order him to do, when the tribe's allies rise up and lay waste to the Roman fort on their territory along the north-west frontier, which will happen at any time now. He will send word of this apparently minor rebellion to you, and seek your permission to take my cavalry wing, his own German guard and the tribe's militia west to put down the revolt, whereas in reality he will swiftly join with their leader Brinno and his men, trapping the Roman forces that remain between his army and the sea, destroy them one fort at a time and then turn back to face us with the threat at his back neutralised and the German tribes flocking to the banner of a man who has defied Rome and won. Your remaining legion strength will face an army that becomes stronger with every day, and most of your legionaries are still as green as fresh-cut wood.'

Flaccus played a penetrating stare on him before replying.

'You realise that your people will see what you're doing in revealing Civilis's plan as treason, pure and simple? When we've defeated them, as we surely will in the long run, you will be a man without a homeland?'

Labeo shrugged, his eyes hard with certainty.

'I am a faithful servant of the empire, Legatus. I hold no allegiance for Civilis, a man I believe to be motivated by dreams of becoming king of my tribe but who will instead lead us to disaster. When, as you say, Rome has stirred itself to stamp this rebellion flat and restored the rule of law to my people, I will see what state of mind they have with regard to my behaviour in alerting you to this threat. If they will have me back I will be glad to serve the tribe, and if they are hostile I am sure that Rome will find some small place for me to live out my days in the happy knowledge that I did the right thing by my oath of allegiance to the empire. A man must always follow the dictates of his conscience, and my conscience will not allow me any other path than that of honour, and to attempt to save my people from this disaster.'

The general nodded.

'And well said. It would be ideal if we could avert the need for you and your horsemen to take up arms against your comrades, but I fear we will need your spears if we are to snuff out this embryonic rebellion before the fire takes hold and sends the whole of the north up in flames. What's our strength in the land of the Cananefates and the Batavians?'

Lupercus pointed to the wall map.

'On paper we have the men needed to deal with whatever manpower the tribes can muster. The tribe is thirty thousand strong, and four thousand of their fighting age men are away with the army in Italy.'

Flaccus shook his head dismissively.

'In point of fact, Munius Lupercus, their cohorts were at the Winter Camp in Mogontiacum until a few days ago, but Vitellius has ordered them south again to rejoin his army in preparation for Vespasianus's attack. There'll be no help for Civilis from that quarter.'

Lupercus continued his briefing, pointing to a point close to the coast.

'We usually have an infantry cohort here at Praetorium Agrippina, but the fort's current real strength is a small fraction of that. There's normally another cohort here . . .' He pointed at a spot on the map five miles from the first. 'But it's the same story, just token centuries left to make sure the locals don't rob the place while the rest of them are away. Further to the east there are another three forts guarding the frontier and the bridge across it, but once again they've no more than caretaker strength. With all the men who've been withdrawn to satisfy the emperor's demands for more units to be sent south, we've only got a single cohort guarding the frontier from Bridge Fort to the sea.'

Flaccus eyed the map sourly.

'When do you believe the Cananefates will attack, Decurion Labeo?'

'In the next day or so, Legatus. No later.'

'Then the forts closest to the coast are as good as lost, and the men manning them too, unless they see the attack coming and manage to make a run for it.'

'I . . .'

The general's gaze snapped back round to the Batavian cavalryman.

'You what?'

'I took the precaution of sending one of my men west to warn them, Legatus.'

Flaccus stared at the Batavi with a new light of respect in his eyes.

'Gods below, you might just have saved them. What did you tell them?'

'That they were about to be overwhelmed, and that they should abandon their positions and fall back on Bridge Fort where they were to await further orders. The fort being close to the river, Legatus.'

A smile crept across Flaccus's face.

'And thereby convenient for the fleet.'

'That was very much what I had in mind.'

'I see. And while you're suggesting strategy, do you have any more ideas you'd like to share?'

Labeo smiled weakly.

'I may already have over-reached myself.'

'Not at all. We're all strangers here, but you know this land intimately. So come along, out with it.'

The Batavi nodded, walking to the map and pointing at the river Rhenus north of Batavodurum.

'The banks of the river are shallow here, which means that it'd be easy enough to get a decent-sized force ashore from our naval vessels. And less than fifteen miles from our tribal capital. Which means that if several cohorts of trained and well-armed soldiers came ashore there, to meet with my five hundred horsemen, the resulting force would be enough to ensure that Civilis would have to bring his full strength to meet it or risk losing the war before it begins.'

'I see.' Flaccus pondered the suggestion for a moment. 'But would your men fight their own people? Surely there's a risk they'd refuse to spill their brothers' blood?'

Labeo shook his head emphatically.

'They fear Rome's retribution on our people if this rebellion succeeds. They'll fight, if only to safeguard their families from the wrath that will descend on them if Civilis gets his way and declares a Batavi kingdom. If you can put an army up against the rebels my men will join them, and do their duty to the empire, in the hope of a swift resolution to this potential crisis.'

Flaccus looked at Lupercus questioningly.

'What do you think, colleague? Should we wait until your legionaries can get forward to join the fight, or chance the decurion's plan and seek to put this fire out before it has the time and space to take hold?'

The legatus looked in turn at his senior centurion.

'How long will it take us to put the legion in fighting order and march to Batavodurum, First Spear?'

Marius, who had been expecting the question, answered crisply.

'I can put nine cohorts on the road in a day, with the Tungrian auxiliaries camped here, Legatus, and we can be within striking distance of the capital inside four days, if we advance with sufficient caution to avoid the potential for an ambush.'

Flaccus thought for a moment.

'So we can either strike now, with whatever auxiliary forces are available plus your cavalry, Claudius Labeo, using the fleet to bring forward the auxiliary cohorts that can be detached from their current deployments, like your Tungrians, or we can wait several days to have legionaries available to strengthen the battle line.'

He nodded decisively.

'I'm approving your plan, Decurion, with certain conditions. We'll pull the auxiliary cohorts on the north-west frontier back from their forward positions by means of the Rhenus fleet, and concentrate them close to Batavodurum, while your cavalrymen move forward to join them, then use the fleet to take more auxiliaries down the river to join them. The combined force will then move to threaten the Batavi city, and we'll see if we can't flush out this man Civilis and his fellow rebels. My orders will be for the auxiliary forces to engage, if the circumstances of that engagement look favourable. And if not, the force can simply fall back and join Munius Lupercus's men as they advance down the Rhenus. So either we beat them quickly, and with the minimum fuss, with the job done by Rome's loyal allies, or we beat them later, with the full force of Rome's iron fist. But either way, gentlemen, we must beat them, so the prime factor for the auxiliary force's commander will be the preservation of his force to fight at the right time.'

Labeo nodded his understanding.

'And who will command, Legatus?'

The general considered the question for a moment.

'It must be a legion officer, and it must be a man I can trust both to follow my orders to the letter and act with the necessary aggression. It can't be any of Legatus Lupercus's officers, since not only are they going to be busy enough getting their men moving, but none of them apart from the legatus himself has any combat experience.'

He turned and looked at the hulking man standing behind him.

'And it will need to be someone with sufficient experience of war and martial vigour to ensure that the auxiliary cohorts do as instructed. In short, Centurion Aquillius, given your previous legion's extensive war record against the Dacians and Roxolani, it must be *you*.'

Praetorium Agrippina, August AD 69

'You're sure this will work?'

Solon turned slowly to face Brinno, leaning closer to his tribal chief to whisper in his ear.

'If you manage not to alert the Romans with your shouting, Brinno, then yes, I am sure that this will work. Remember that a man's voice will carry twice as far in fog as on a clear night.'

The younger man stared at him for a moment, then spoke again with his voice lowered to a whisper. They were nestled in a dip in the ground less than a hundred paces from the Roman fort that guarded the lowest reaches of the Rhenus before it joined the sea, a wooden walled encampment that usually housed a cohort of five hundred auxiliaries but was now manned by little more than a hundred men of one of the few remaining cohorts on the frontier between Batavodurum.

'You are not a centurion in their army now, Solon, with an inexhaustible supply of men to be tapped if you should lose a few of your soldiers. Every man waiting in that wood is precious to the tribe, a son, or a father, needed by their dependants. So are you sure that we can do this without half of them being killed by the ironclads?'

Solon opened his mouth to reply, but a faint rustle from the grass in front of them caught both men's attention and stiffened their bodies, both readying themselves to leap to their feet and either fight or run. A soft whistle, barely audible, reached their ears, and both of them relaxed, sinking back onto the ground as a man crawled out of the mist.

'It is done?'

The newcomer, another former soldier whom Solon had chosen for his steady demeanour, nodded in reply to his question.

'I poured it onto the gate timbers, and the wall to either side of the southern gate.'

'And there was no sign of the Romans being alarmed, or just more alert than usual?'

A shake of the head.

'No. The men on the wall were talking about which of the women in the village they would like to fuck, and about home.'

The older man turned back to his prince.

'It will work, Brinno, because I know these men, or at least their like. The Romans recruit men from across the river, dress them in their iron armour and expect them to think and act like legionaries. But these men are not like the men of the legions, or our own. They are not warriors. They still think like the men of their tribes do, like cattle thieves rather than soldiers. They should have listening patrols out looking for an enemy approaching in the darkness. There should be lilies, pits of spiked sticks, dug into the ground around the fort to tear into the feet of the unwary, and stakes dug into the ground beneath the walls to impale an attacker in the darkness. Instead, there is only a wooden box with some frightened soldiers inside who would rather be at home, and most of whose comrades have gone to war. They see no threat, and thereby make their defeat a hundred times more likely.'

Another man whistled and crawled into their hiding place, confirming that he too had managed to empty his jar of pitch onto the fort's western wall, and that he too had not been seen by sentries who might as well have been asleep at their posts.

'The fools cannot believe that there is any threat, not even after Rome's failed attempts to conscript the Batavi into their legions. They believe that because the Cananefates and the Batavi have been allies of Rome for the last hundred years this can never change. They are about to learn that this is a mistaken belief, and to learn this lesson the hard way.'

Brinno regarded his military leader levelly.

'And you, Solon. After so long in their service, can *you* do this?'

'You asked me that once before, if you remember?'

'I did. But that was when you were fresh from their service, and all I was asking you to do was train our young men in readiness to serve in the cohorts of the Batavi, and drill our men in the use of weapons in order to make them capable of seeing off raids across the river. Now I am asking you to lead our men *against* Rome.'

The older man shrugged eloquently.

'And I can do this. Not because of this story of the priestess in the tower who has seen our victory. Not because I am disgusted with the way that Rome has treated our allies, and will soon enough attempt the same cruelty with ourselves. But because, Brinno, the men of our tribe have raised you on the war shield and declared that you will be our king, when the Romans have been removed from our land. So now, with your permission, lord, I will lead our men to their first victory over Rome.'

Brinno nodded with a smile, extending an arm towards the fort, a dark outline in the darkness and mist.

'Very well.'

Solon backed away until he was sure that he would be invisible from the fort, with Brinno close behind him, leaving the other two men to watch the fort for any signs of alarm.

'Will they smell the pitch?'

Solon considered his king's question, answering with a fierce grin.

'I think not. Not until it's alight, that is.'

Making their way through a stand of trees, they found the space behind them thick with men, each of whom was armed with a spear and a small shield, and carrying a torch to be lit when the time was right. Brinno stepped out before them, calling for them to gather close round him.

'No shouting, my brothers, not until we have the Roman fort alight. After that you can shout all you like. Listen to Solon now, he's going to tell you what we're going to do.'

The former centurion stepped forward.

'When I've finished speaking, light your torches. Our plan of attack is simple. We march on the fort, as quickly as we can to avoid them having time to work out what's happening. You will recall I have told you of the small bolt throwers that the Romans call scorpions, and how these weapons can spit a bolt so hard that it will pierce through a warrior and still have enough power to kill the man behind him. So we will run out to the fort, and surround it on three sides, in *silence,* because if we do not threaten them they may not realise what we intend until it is too late. Centuries one to three . . .'

He paused, enjoying as he always did the novelty of referring to his tribe's militia in Roman terms. Solon no longer served Rome, but twenty-five years as a soldier had left him convinced him that Roman organisation and tactics, combined with their lavish iron weapons and armour, had been what had enabled them to conquer so much of Germany so quickly. And as he had told Brinno earlier that evening, when Cananefates courage was married to the enemy's way of war, all of their men would be ironclad with captured war gear soon enough.

'Centuries one to three will move round to the western side, four to six take the southern side, and seven to ten the east. Get as close as you can without having a spear thrown at you and then throw your torch at the fort walls. Not into the fort, they might just be ready for that, but against the walls. Some of those torches will catch light to the wooden beams and set the place alight, and we've poured pitch on the wood at the places where their bolt throwers should be mounted to make them impossible to use from the heat of the fire. And then . . . ?'

A man in the front of the press surrounding Brinno and his general spoke up.

'We wait.'

'Exactly. We back away to reduce the chance of anyone being hit by a bolt, and wait for the fire to do its work. The Romans will either burn with their fort or try to escape. And if they come out, we kill them. Do it quickly, and cleanly. No torture, no gut stabbing a man and waiting to see him bleed out, just get it over with. I catch any man disobeying that command and I'll do the same to him. We're not barbarians, no matter what they might think, and we'll not behave as if we are. Remember what you've been taught, ironclad they may be, but you put a spear blade in here,' he pointed to his throat, 'or here,' he pointed to his thighs, 'And he'll be dead before you can count to fifty, and good for nothing but dying a good deal before that. Now, are we ready?'

A chorus of growled assent answered him, and he looked at Brinno, who nodded and stepped forward.

'Brothers, I thought long and hard before committing us to this war. Only when it became clear to me that if we hold back from choosing a side in this fight then whichever side wins will punish us for doing so, did I agree to commit us to the support of Vespasianus. Solon has told you that we must fight like the Romans to defeat them, and as my war leader, as my . . .'

He looked at Solon.

'First Spear, my Lord.'

'Yes, as my First Spear, he is right to lead you in this way. We will fight with honour, as he suggests, and so I command you to make only clean kills. There can be no prisoners, no wounded to be spared, and not one Roman can escape. We must finish them to the last man! And when this place is destroyed we will march east and do the same at Matilo, and again as we work our way east, killing all Romans we meet by chance upon the way, the traders and merchants who live on our wealth like ticks on a fat cow. This will be a war we can only win by terrifying Rome so much that they will leave this land and never seek to return. We must convince them that every footstep on Cananefates soil will leave only a footprint filled with the blood of the man whose boot made the mark!'

He looked around him at men whose families had traded across the river with the tribes to the north from which the soldiers inside the fort were recruited.

'I know that under different circumstances we would consider those ironclads as something close to kin, long known to us in our dealings with them and the other tribes to our north. Some of them may carry Cananefates blood.'

He looked at his feet for a moment.

'And that is a thing of sadness.'

His voice hardened.

'But necessary nonetheless. Is there any man here that cannot kill such a man?'

He looked about his tribesmen for a long moment, but if any man present harboured such a qualm, not one of them was willing to admit to it.

'Very well! Then come my brothers, let us do what no man of the Cananefates has done for a hundred years, and in doing it restore the manhood Rome stole from us all those years ago, forcing us to play the vassal to their empire! Allied with our brothers the Batavi, and with Rome's soldiers all so very far from here, fighting one another for the right to rule their empire, this is the time when we must strike, and aim the killing blow at Rome's rule over these lands! Come, my brothers, join me in this fight, a fight for freedom that will be remembered in the songs of our sons and grandsons, and make this day a day to remember for all time. For we go to make war! War on Rome!'

II

River Rhenus, August AD 69

'He's a fucking strange one, and no doubt about it.'

The warship's captain nodded at his helmsman's opinion, staring forward at the silhouette of the big centurion who had come aboard the flagship the previous evening, standing in the vessel's bow as he had done for most of the night.

'I don't think the prefect would be quite as gentle with his opinion.'

The fleet's commander had retired to the privacy of his tiny cabin and was presumably still fuming at having been ordered to take his ships downriver in the darkness, an unorthodox if relatively low-risk course of action to skilled sailors with an intimate knowledge of the Rhenus's twisting course. His short-lived attempt to resist the legion officer's command to get his ships underway so late in the day, understandable in a man used to looking down on the rank of centurion from the lofty height of the equestrian class, had rapidly turned from outrage to startled submission with the drawing of the big man's sword, coupled with the straight-faced question as to whether the naval officer was aware of the penalty that insubordination in time of war usually carried.

The helmsman nudged the steersman standing next to him.

'Come left another point, aim for the centre of the river. I've never seen a prefect threatened with an immediate death sentence before.'

The captain turned his head away and grinned into the darkness.

'Nor have I. Nor do I ever expect to again. And if you know what's good for you we'll not speak of it again, eh?'

He paced down the raised walkway between the oarsmen's benches.

'Come on you barbarian bastards, put your backs into it! Our orders are to put the fleet alongside at Bridge Fort before dawn, not just in time for dinner tomorrow night!'

Pacing back down to the master's usual place on the command deck he muttered a quiet curse.

'Is it me, or are these German layabouts even surlier than usual?'

The other man shrugged.

'What do you expect? Rousted from their mess at no notice to row all night against the tide for the most part? Not what most of them joined for.'

'Hah!' The captain snorted derisively. 'What most of them joined for was the chance to earn some coin, and not to end up stuck in the same shithole village looking at the same raddled collection of their close female relatives for the rest of their lives. If the price of that's having to pull an oar for a night at least it'll make a change from pulling each other's pricks. How far now?'

The other man spat over the ship's side into the Rhenus's black water.

'Five miles, no more.'

His superior nodded decisively.

'Right. We'd better get the marines on deck then, and get the scorpions ready for action. Sounded to me like that big bastard was expecting to be walking into some sort of trouble when he gets off, and given he doesn't look the nervous type, I think we'll take him at his word.'

Fort Traiectum, August AD 69

'There!'

The men standing watch on the fort's eastern gate were the first to see him, pointing at the distant figure marching purposefully through the fort's vicus from the direction of the river, the masts of a good dozen warships looming out of the mist above the vicus's riverside houses. Their watch officer strode down the wooden wall's fighting platform and stared out at the oncoming soldier, his centurion's crest evident even in the morning murk.

'A fleet turns up and one fucking man comes ashore? What's the point of that?'

Turning back to look down into the fort, he barked an order at the men posted at the gate to fetch the senior centurion, who arrived with the cohort's prefect at his side just as a hammering announced the newcomer's arrival at the gate. Prefect and centurion looked at each other in mystification for a moment before the cohort commander nodded at his junior.

'Open the gates, Centurion, and let's see what this man has to say for himself.'

Unbarring a small, man-sized entrance, the soldiers stepped back as a massive figure bent his head and ducked through the opening, straightening up and looking around him with sharp, alert eyes before turning back to the prefect just as he started speaking.

'Greetings, Centurion. We've heard rumours that the Cananefates and their allies are planning some sort of revolt, so naturally we were expecting some reinforcement . . . But it seems that you're alone?'

The newcomer shook his head, reaching to the message container hanging from his belt as he spoke.

'There will be no reinforcement of your outpost forts this far to the west, Prefect. To do so would be to spread the available forces too thinly, and make what remains of our strength easier to pick off one or two centuries at a time. The legatus augusti plans to concentrate the available men instead, and offer the enemy battle in force. Your orders.'

He handed over the message scroll, continuing to speak as the prefect unrolled it.

'I am Gaius Aquillius Proculus, centurion, Eighth Augustan legion, detached to duty with the headquarters of Legatus Augusti Flaccus, commanding general of the army of Germania.' He paused for a moment, looking about him at the expectant faces that surrounded him. 'And I am temporarily appointed to command all auxiliary cohorts to the east of the Batavi city of Batavodurum.'

The prefect looked up from the orders with a frown, staring at him in disbelief.

'But that would make you my—'

'Your superior. Yes, Prefect, it does, at least temporarily. Please read my orders. They contain your own.'

The prefect's eyes widened as he absorbed Flaccus's instructions. His senior centurion, recognising that whatever trouble they were already in was about to get a good deal deeper, stared at Aquillius with hard eyes for long enough that the legion officer, even though his own gaze remained fixed on the prefect before him, felt the heat of his indignation. Without diverting his attention from the officer's perusal of his orders, the big man spoke, his tone matter of fact and his stance relaxed.

'Stare all you like, Centurion. I'd be doing the same in your place. These are troubled times indeed, when a man of my station can be placed in a position that requires him to issue orders to men of higher rank. So for as long as it takes your prefect here to read my orders you can stare, and look as pissed off as you like. But when those orders are read, and your prefect has acknowledged that, until I'm relieved of these unexpected responsibilities I am effectively his commanding officer, then I only want to hear two words from you, Centurion. Can you guess what they are?'

The auxiliary centurion regarded him in amazement, and after a moment's silence Aquillius turned to look at him, flicking a glance up and down his body, as if assessing the amount of effort that would be required to deal with the man if their trial of wills became physical.

'Those two words, Centurion, are "Yes, Centurion". Your prefect here won't have a problem with them, because he is a Roman, and will obey the orders of his superior without question. But you, you're a different matter, aren't you? You might be tempted to question my instructions, and that, Centurion, would be unwise, given that we're at war and I really don't have either the time or the patience to argue with you. So, do as I tell you, quickly and without question, and there won't be a problem between us.'

He turned back to the prefect, who had forgotten the scroll in his amazement at the big man's swift and ruthless manner with his subordinate.

'You've read my orders, Prefect?'

'Yes, Centurion.'

'Do you consider them to be a valid order from your superior?

'The Roman looked down at the message scroll again, examining the wax seal carefully.

'Yes.'

'And you'll follow my instructions to the letter?'

The prefect nodded slowly, looking up from the written order that left him absolutely no latitude for anything other than complete subordination to the man before him.

'Yes, Centurion.'

Aquillius nodded, his expression unchanged from the emotionless, professional mask that he had worn since stepping through the fort's gate.

'And you, Centurion? Will you and I have a problem?' He turned back to his colleague, permitting a small smile to twitch his lips momentarily. 'On *this* occasion only, the word "no" will be acceptable to me.'

The other man looked at him for a moment longer and then shook his head.

'There'll be no problem, Centurion. If my prefect will follow your orders, then it's my duty to do the same.'

'You may find others who are less willing to accommodate your assumption of command.'

Aquillius nodded at the prefect's baldly stated opinion, his hard-eyed mask back in place.

'We'll have to hope they see sense then, won't we, Prefect? The military code is very clear as to the punishment for failing to obey orders. And now I'm going to need a horse—'

'*Smoke! Smoke on the horizon!*'

All three men spun to face the source of the shout, Aquillius reacting first and sprinting for the fort's western gate. Taking the steps up onto the wall's parapet three at a time, he stared out over the flat landscape. On the distant mist-shrouded horizon a thin line of black smoke was rising in the dawn light.

'That's Praetorium Agrippina.'

Aquillius turned to look at the centurion, who was staring out over the empty landscape.

'You've already evacuated the fort, I presume?'

'Evacuated it?' The other man turned to look at his new commander in confusion. 'Why would we have evacuated? It's a perfectly—'

'When you received the warning? Decurion Labeo's messenger?'

The centurion stared up at the hulking legion officer in confusion.

'There's been no messenger from anybody, Centurion.'

Aquillius thought for a moment, then shook his head dismissively.

'What strength was based there?'

The other man grimaced.

'*Was?* Ah, you mean . . . a century.'

The centurion nodded solemnly.

'Those men are already dead. Hopefully they died quickly, but that century is already lost. Where are the rest?'

The other man thought for a moment.

'Another century at Matilo, two more at White Water, two at Black Soil, one at Laurel Fort and three here in reserve.'

The legion man nodded.

'Show me a map. And get some men ready to ride with messages. You have horses?'

Staring at the map in the fort's small praetorium, he thought for a moment.

'Your men at Matilo are also probably already as good as dead unless their centurion is astute enough to pull his men out and make a run for it before the tribesmen get there when he sees the smoke. Is he . . . ?'

He looked at the senior centurion, who shook his head with pursed lips.

'Then we forget them.'

He waved away the prefect's feeble attempt to protest at the abandonment of his men.

'They'll be under attack inside the hour and dead less than an hour after that, unless they get out before the tribesmen surround their fort. As for the rest, send messengers to them as fast as they can ride, and tell them to march east, as fast as they can. We've got enough ships to get everyone away, but I can't risk sending them any further downriver, so we'll evacuate from here. My plan is to head back upriver and consolidate with the Ubian cohort that's holding the forts further to the east, and a Tungrian cohort will be shipped downriver from the Old Camp. With your Frisians and the Batavian cavalry cohort we're going to form a new line of defence close to the river, with the warships to provide artillery support, and then we'll see what these rebels do next, once they're done with burning out empty forts and find they have a real battle on their hands.'

Batavodurum, August AD 69

'Your ruse hasn't worked, Kivilaz.'

Hramn dropped his helmet on the desk, running a hand through his hair. He had dismounted a moment before and was sweating heavily from his exertions in the saddle. 'You hoped they'd leave the border garrisons in place and trust you to hunt down the raiders who are burning them out, but they clearly didn't believe you when you made the suggestion. The Romans used their fleet to pull them out, and left the forts for Brinno and his men to burn. Satisfying for him, but meaningless for us when they've rescued most of their strength and denied us the victory that would have drawn the tribes to join us.'

The prince looked up from his study of the map before him.

'It was always a gamble, hoping that they would leave the border forts manned so that we could pick them off one at a time.' He grinned at the cavalryman's sweat-stained tunic. 'You look as if you've had an interesting time of it.'

The guardsman laughed curtly.

'If you call being chased for five miles by Labeo's cavalrymen interesting, then I suppose it was.'

'And did you get close enough to see anything worth seeing?'

The decurion shook his head.

'I didn't. They saw me and the rest of my century coming and chased us straight back down the road in force, pretty much all the way to the city gates. I thought you said our brother and his cavalry wing were with us?'

Kivilaz looked up.

'Not every plan goes as we might like, Decurion. Tiberius Claudius Labeo has clearly decided which side of the line he stands, and at least he had the decency not to make his intentions clear in the middle of a battle. I presume your century weren't the only men we had scouting the enemy force?'

'No, I sent a pair of my best men round to the west nice and quietly, and they got close enough to see what's going on at the river. It seems we face three cohorts of auxiliary infantry and Labeo's cavalry, that and the ships they used to transport the Tungrians here from the Old Camp so quickly, all lined up with their bolt throwers ready to shoot on the flanks.'

Kivilaz nodded.

'As I expected. The Frisians from the forts to the west, the Tungrians from the Old Camp, probably the Ubians from further down the river and our erstwhile brother in arms and his horsemen. I'd imagine they shipped the Tungrian cohort in on the way to pull the Frisians out, while more ships went to get the Ubians. On their own the infantry wouldn't worry me, but Labeo's decision to turn against his own people means that your guardsmen will have their work cut out keeping them honest on the battlefield, rather than being free to terrorise the auxiliaries' flanks and rear.'

'You plan to fight them then?'

The older man nodded briskly.

'As soon as Brinno and the allied tribes are done with burning out empty forts and get themselves across the river, yes. If we wait any longer the legion that was left behind in the Old Camp when the rest marched off to fight Otho will get their men into the field, and even raw recruits have some value in battle if they outnumber experienced soldiers by enough of a margin and are sensibly led. If we had our cohorts with us I'd be happy to wait until the legions arrive, because our boys would go through them like a sword through silk, but without them we'll have to chew the enemy up one mouthful at a time. And speaking of the cohorts . . .'

He walked to the wall map, pointing at a spot far to the south-east.

'Fresh word has reached me from Scar. His original message from the Winter Camp was that they'd been sent back north by Vitellius, to stop them from bickering with the Fourteenth Gemina again. But this morning another messenger arrived with fresh news that's not half as much to my taste. It seems that with Vespasianus having challenged him for the throne, Vitellius has thought better of having banished our men back to Germania, and has ordered them back south again. I need a man to ride and warn them what's happening here, get them turned around and heading back north as quickly as possible. Someone I can trust to get round the enemy forces coming downriver and get the message through, because without their strength we'll be a lot weaker than I'm comfortable with, even if the tribes do rise up and join us. So pick your best and brightest decurion and tell him to have his men ready to ride south at dawn when we march north.'

Hramn stared at him for a moment, and when he spoke his voice was devoid of any emotion.

'You want me to send a whole century of my men away, quite possibly never to be seen again if they run into serious opposition?'

Kivilaz nodded.

'Yes. This is one message I have to know will get through, so whoever takes it has to have enough strength at his back to fight his way through anything short of a full cohort. And enough men to scout the roads in front of him to avoid anything he can't overwhelm.'

'You miss my point. You're asking me to send men on what might turn out to be nothing better than suicide?'

Kivilaz shrugged, fixing the guardsman with his one eyed stare.

'I can see your point, Hramn. Now you see mine. Without the cohorts the best we can ever be is a tribal army, a loose alliance of armed mobs capable of overrunning a single legion on its own, under the right conditions, but you were at the battle of High Hills when we tore the guts out of the Iceni, so you know what happens when a tribal army runs into even one well-led legion and its auxiliaries. Slaughter.' He allowed the word to hang in the air for a moment before continuing. 'We need the cohorts to give the army an iron core. Ironclad. Iron disciplined. Without them we won't last more than a few months, but with them we've a chance of building an effective defence, and tying down the local garrison for long enough that Vespasianus has a better chance of winning. And if that's not enough to convince you, consider this question. What do you think will happen when the news of this revolt reaches Vitellius?'

He paused briefly, allowing time for Hramn to ponder the question, but continued before the other man could answer.

'I don't have to think, because I know exactly what I'd do if I were him. I'd order our cohorts to be separated into three or four groups, and marched to legion garrisons where they could be broken up and used as casualty replacements. Our men will end their days as hated traitors in a sea of enemies, always under suspicion, handed every dirty job going, and cursing our names to the day they die.'

'And it has to be my men that bear this news?'

The older man looked up at him in silence for a moment.

'You tell me, Hramn. Tell me who's cleverer than your men, tougher than your men, more bloody-minded than your men? Tell me their names, and look me in the eye as you're doing it, and I'll send them instead. But in the absence of anyone else who can demonstrate those qualities then yes, it has to be your men. The future of this tribe depends on those cohorts marching in from the east before the Romans can muster some real legions to come and knock on our doors, which means we only get one chance at this.'

Hramn nodded tiredly.

'Very well. I'll brief your cousin Bairaz tonight and have him ready to march at daybreak. But if he ends up on a cross you can expect your eventual arrival in Hades to be greeted with a fair amount of derision.'

Kivilaz snorted.

'My arrival in Hades is going to be noisy enough, with or without your being there to greet me. This war is going to claim a good few spirits before we get done.'

River Rhenus, August AD 69

'They're ready, Kivilaz.'

The prince nodded, accepting Hramn's assessment of what he could see with his own eyes as he scanned the line of his make-shift rebel army. Drawn up on the right wing in an impeccable formation were his horse guards, the former imperial bodyguards who were gimlet-eyed in the presence of the enemy, eager for the opportunity to avenge the injustice that had been done to them. Next to them, and in boisterous good spirits after their rout of the Roman border forces, were the Cananefates, hundreds of newly blooded warriors eager to fight again. He smiled, knowing that men who had not yet tasted defeat would always clamour for another opportunity to drink the heady wine of victory, never believing that the taste might prove unexpectedly bitter. And there, on the army's left, were his own people, the two five-hundred-man strong Batavi militia cohorts that had been trained by Hramn's men to the point where, whilst they lacked the Roman troops' lavish equipment, they were likely to prove the auxiliaries' match in discipline. More would come from the German tribes across the Rhenus by the thousand, always eager to strike out at their hated oppressor given the chance to do so, but only if he managed to beat the enemy waiting for them along the river's southern bank.

'They knew we were coming.'

Kivilaz nodded, looking out from the vantage point of his horse's saddle across the half-mile of open ground that separated the Batavi and their allies from the Roman force waiting for them close to the Rhenus. The river's bank to either side of the compact enemy formation was lined with moored warships, clearly positioned to give clear arcs for their bolt throwers and doubtless ready to unleash a murderous storm of iron-tipped bolts as soon as his men advanced into their effective range.

'Of course they knew we were coming. They have some of the most experienced cavalry scouts in the empire in their service, thanks to our former brother Labeo. And besides, he was careful to make sure he knew our plans, before he took his men east to join Vitellius's general. Which means that they know we plan to defeat them here, before the legions from the Old Camp can intervene, and that we have to take the initiative to do so. While they can win simply by holding their positions and resisting us.'

Hramn shook his head in disgust.

'Labeo. Of all the men I would have expected to desert the tribe in its hour of need, I would never have picked him.'

The prince smiled wryly.

'If it's of any consolation, Decurion, neither would I. Why else would I have made him privy to our designs for throwing the Romans out of our territory? Not that he knows everything.'

The guardsman turned in his saddle to look at him with narrowed eyes.

'You kept something back from him that you intend to use to our advantage today?'

'It's not so much that I didn't tell him, more something that only ripened in the last few hours.'

'And do you intend to share this with the rest of us?'

Kivilaz returned his stare.

'Not for the time being, Decurion. Let's see what our opponent chooses to do first, shall we? Although I'd say his choices are limited. He can bring his three cohorts forward, of course, and take us on at close quarters, but I'm not sure his Frisians will be up to the job, not after having been pulled out of their frontier forts having abandoned their comrades to their fate.'

'They might be raving for revenge.'

The prince shook his head.

'Do they *look* like they're raving for revenge? They look sullen, pissed off, scared, but raving? Not from where I'm sitting. The man leading on the other side knows they're brittle, so he's put his Tungrian cohort on their left flank and his Ubians on the right, to make sure they don't shuffle off in either direction when the blood starts flying.'

He stared across the gap between the two armies, seeing the armoured figure of a big man on horseback with a centurion's crest riding along the Roman army's rear.

'Novel of them to have given command to a centurion. Whoever he is, he doesn't look like the soft touch I was hoping for. I wonder who he is?'

River Rhenus, August AD 69

Aquillius climbed down from his horse, his back and legs already aching from the unfamiliar posture, walking briskly across to Labeo's Batavian cavalry on his small army's left wing and looking up at their commander with a stare which was, if not overtly hostile, then certainly sceptical as to the man's trustworthiness. Labeo dismounted, a move clearly intended to placate the rugged centurion's concerns, and saluted neatly.

'Centurion Aquillius. My men are ready for action.'

The big man looked past him at his horsemen, well equipped, stern-faced and waiting for the battle with the look of men ready to do their duty.

'I believe they are. I still wonder on which side though.'

The Batavi officer's face didn't change from its grave professional expression.

'I understand your suspicion, Centurion. After all, the rest of my tribe has decided to arm against Rome. My men and I will just have to convince you of our loyalty with our spears, when the time comes.'

Aquillius stared at him for a long moment, one hand resting on the pommel of his gladius.

'You told Legatus Augusti Flaccus that you had sent a messenger to the Frisian cohort's commander, warning him of the rebel attack. And yet no such message was ever received by the prefect.'

Labeo nodded, meeting his stare with eyes empty of any guile or evidence of deceit.

'So I gather. I expect my man didn't survive his journey across the Island to deliver my warning.'

The Roman held the gaze a moment longer, then shook his head and turned away to look across the space between his men and the Batavi army. He had spoken privately with Flaccus after the conclusion of the conference at which he had been handed the poisoned cup of commanding the Frisian cohort's rescue, and the planned subsequent attack on Batavodurum, his words blunt and uncompromising.

'I agreed with everything you said in there, Legatus, because to do otherwise would have demeaned you in the eyes of that barbarian. But I do not agree with your plan to attack the Batavian city, not with only a cohort of Tungrians, some Ubians if you can get them up the river in time and the remnants of the Frisians. That, and of course these Batavian horsemen who would have us believe that they have turned their backs on their tribe. It would be all too easy for me to find my command trapped between this man Civilis's barbarians and their cavalry, should Decurion Labeo's change of allegiance prove to be only temporary.'

Flaccus had shrugged, his eyes bright with calculation.

'That will be your decision to make, Centurion Aquillius, once you are clear as to the conditions on the ground. As to Labeo and his men, you are of course empowered to take whatever measures you see fit to ensure that they remain loyal to Rome. Or, if that proves impossible, to neutralise any threat they might pose. With the responsibility I am giving you comes authority, Centurion. Absolute authority. Wield it wisely, but above all else, wield it.'

He looked back at the Batavi prefect.

'What is your assessment?'

Labeo looked across the battlefield at his tribe's forces.

'I'd say that this fight will be finely balanced, Centurion, if my old adversary Kivilaz doesn't have some advantage that we can't see yet.'

'An advantage?'

The Batavi looked at his commander with a hint of exasperation.

'Spare me the feigned innocence, Centurion, it doesn't sit well with your otherwise brutal approach to everyone and everything.'

Aquillius stared back at him levelly.

'It was a question. One you'd do well to answer.'

'When you've known Kivilaz as long as I have, you get a measure of the man. He's not like you and I, Aquillius, he's . . .' He groped for the right word. 'Sly? Duplicitous? Capable of saying one thing in a way that inspires complete trust in his words and then, just when you think you have his measure, doing something completely different to what you were led to expect. You should take nothing you see here for granted.'

'So what am I seeing here?' Aquillius bent to speak quietly in the Batavi's ear. 'Talk me through it, Decurion, and be assured I will apply the same rules to everything you say that you suggest for your countryman's skills at misleading his listener.'

Labeo smiled grimly back at him.

'How very wise of you. And what do I see?'

He looked at the Batavi battle line for a moment.

'I see the German Bodyguard, looking a little short on their usual numbers it has to be said. I wonder why that might be?'

He shrugged.

'At their full strength they are five hundred very well trained and very highly motivated men with a grudge the size of a temple column to exercise, shamed and looking for revenge after being dismissed from the emperor's service. At some point Kivilaz's going to send them at your men, or quite possibly at mine, but probably not until he's broken your army, since we both know that cavalry is at its deadliest in the pursuit. Now, what else . . .'

He stared at the warriors gathered in rough ranks next to the guardsmen.

'I see the Cananefates, fresh from butchering every soldier and Roman civilian they could find on the eastern side of the Island, wound up like a bolt thrower and ready to come at us like mad dogs. And I see the Batavi militia . . .' He stared at his own tribe's men for a moment. 'Don't be deceived by their lack of equipment, they've been training under the men of the Bodyguard for the last nine months. They'll be just as dangerous as the Cananefates, but calmer and more deliberate. Better trained too. So what are your intentions?'

Aquillius spoke without taking his eyes off the waiting tribesmen.

'My intentions? I *intend* to kill as many of those barbarians as possible. Indeed, I intend to tear that collection of tribal idiots, snot-nosed youths and tired old men to tatters, and send the survivors home in such a state that every other man, woman and child on this Island of yours will cower in fear at the sight of us. But you were asking how I plan to do that?'

Labeo nodded, and Aquillius waved a hand at him, as if offering the Batavi the opportunity to comment.

'You tell me, Decurion. After all, you've probably seen more combat than almost any other man in this piss-poor pretence at an army.'

The Batavi officer nodded.

'It's not a hard one to work out. Our infantry needs to stay exactly where it is, with the Frisians kept in place by the Tungrians to their left and the Ubians on their right. Kivilaz might try some of the usual old tricks, having his men feign a retreat after a short period of fighting to tempt the Ubians or the Tungrians to chase them, so I hope your prefects and first spears were listening when you told them not to be fooled, and to warn their men of the likelihood of such a ruse. My horsemen will be enough to keep the Bodyguard from trying to get at the flanks, because Kivilaz will have given orders not to waste their strength in open combat unless there's no choice.'

The Roman shrugged.

'I don't think they'll even get to spear-throwing distance. Look behind you and tell me what you see.'

Labeo turned and stared at the riverbank.

'Warships.'

'How many warships?'

'Twenty-four.'

'Twenty-four. And every one of them is armed with a pair of scorpions. Every scorpion can throw a bolt three hundred paces every time you can count to fifteen, and even at that distance the missile will pierce a shield and kill the man behind it, and sometimes the man behind him, if the first man is unarmoured. While the Batavi are advancing to attack, my sailors will kill at least a hundred of them in the most terrifying manner, spraying their comrades with blood and fragments of bone. Once the battle has begun they'll pour bolts into the enemy flanks and tear the poor bastards to shreds. And if this famous mounted bodyguard comes forward they'll focus their shooting on the horses, and then we'll see how long the bravest and best can stand up to that sort of killing power.'

'I doubt they'll stand up to that sort of pounding for very long.'

Labeo's response was little more than a horrified whisper, and Aquillius turned to look at him with a pitying stare.

'Still harbouring sympathies for your fellow barbarians? If you're wondering if it's not too late to change sides again I've got some bad news for you.' He pointed to the closest ships. 'The crews of those vessels have all got orders that override any other considerations, orders I personally delivered to every captain in the fleet last night. Under those orders, if you or any of your men act against any other unit in this army, they are to commence shooting at your horsemen, and not to stop until you're out of range or they run out of bolts. I'm taking quite a risk just standing here next to you, knowing how light those boys can be on the trigger.'

Labeo shook his head resignedly.

'They won't have cause to turn their weapons on us, Centurion. My men and I know which side we're fighting with, and we won't be changing sides any time soon. Perhaps when we've taken casualties and spilled rebel blood you'll find it possible to trust us.'

Aquillius regarded him steadily for a moment.

'Perhaps.'

River Rhenus, August AD 69

'Cananefates, are you ready?!'

Brinno raised his hand in response to Kivilaz's shouted question, and his warriors roared their approval, the men in their loose formation's front rank capering and waving their spears at the distant Romans, one or two of them waving grisly trophies of their swift and merciless triumphs over the hopelessly outnumbered Frisian soldiers who had attempted to escape the burning forts at Praetorium Agrippina and Matilo, and of the random and brutal acts of slaughter they had inflicted on those Romans unfortunate enough to have been caught on the Island when the fire of their war against the empire had been ignited at Kivilaz's command. A few of them were clad in armour taken from the corpses of their victims, but most of the auxiliary troops had died in the flames of their forts, first overcome by the smoke as dry wooden walls and roofs went up in flames fuelled by jars of pitch and lit by burning brands, then cooked to charred, log-like corpses with their armour welded to their skin by the incandescent fury of their defences' immolation.

'Batavi, are you ready?!'

The militia cohort's twelve centuries' response was more disciplined but no less impressive, a succession of three barked cheers at the command of their senior centurion that marked them out as trained soldiers. At the shouted command to make ready they set themselves to advance, a wall of shields held up with their spears gripped underhand, the long blades protruding by a foot or so.

Hramn nodded approvingly.

'They have learned their lessons well. Will you ask the same question of the men who trained them?'

His prince smiled slowly.

'The Guard? Your men have been ready for this moment for nine months. They were ready the moment they left Rome.'

He turned to the trumpeter mounted alongside him.

'Sound the call to advance.'

At the horn's mournful note the army stepped forward, the Batavi at a slow, careful pace, each man chanting the paean to help regulate the speed of their progress, the Cananefates at an easy walk, some men running ahead with spears and swords held aloft in threat, while the Bodyguard walked their horses towards the enemy in impeccable formation at their officers' silent hand signals. Kivilaz rode forward alongside the militia, Hramn beside him, and after a moment the prince addressed a question to his companion, raising his voice to be heard over the soldiers' chanting.

'What worries you most in their army, Decurion?'

Hramn answered swiftly.

'In their army? Nothing. Their men of the Frisii will run at the first sight of blood, I'd imagine, and the other auxiliary cohorts are no better trained than our own, even if they are better equipped. And the Guard will keep the traitor horsemen from attacking us, or else tear them apart if they do. No, what really scares me is their naval artillery. We've both seen the damage that a legion's scorpions can do to unarmoured men at this sort of distance.'

Kivilaz grinned at him, and the younger man narrowed his eyes in question.

'What is it that you're not telling me, Kivilaz?'

River Rhenus, August AD 69

'Give the signal.'

Aquillius gestured curtly to the signifier he had taken from the Tungrian cohort to act as his signaller, and the soldier raised the standard high above his bearskin-covered head and pumped it up and down three times.

'Now we'll see how well that rabble stands up to artillery, shall we?'

With a volley of muffled thumps as their slides shot forward, the warships' bolt throwers discharged their first shots, missiles arcing out across the battlefield to fall in steep trajectories onto the advancing rebels. Shooting at the maximum extent of their range, the majority of the shots fell short, studding the ground before the advancing Batavi with iron-fletched bolts, but more than one missile fell into the oncoming mass of troops, and men staggered and then fell with horrific wounds as the heavy iron arrows ripped through their flimsy wooden shields and sprayed blood across their comrades. Closing their ranks the rebels continued their steady advance, and Aquillius frowned at their apparent composure under the sudden onslaught.

'They should be running forward, not marching, it's the first rule of crossing ground contested by torsion artillery. Why wouldn't this man Civilis have ordered them to—'

Shouting from the river caught his attention, and he turned in his saddle to stare back at the ships moored along the bank to either side of his formation. The usually tidily ordered decks of his warships were suddenly boiling with violent activity, and where a moment before the weapons' crews had been busy re-tensioning their scorpions for their next shots there was only a chaotic melee, the few uniformed men aboard the closest ships lost in a mass of bodies as more and more of the vessels' rowers seemingly abandoned their benches and joined the fight. Labeo was the first to speak, pointing in disbelief as a marine centurion aboard the nearest ship ran an oarsman through with his gladius, and was promptly set upon by half a dozen more swinging hand spikes and bailing buckets, falling back in the face of their thrashing assault.

'It's a mutiny!'

The centurion stared aghast at the scene for a moment and then shook his head.

'I can't spare any men, not with an attack imminent! They'll have to sort it out themselves!'

Without the threat of the ships' artillery to deter them the oncoming rebels were closing the distance between them and the Roman line in a slow but inexorable human tide, and Aquillius rose up in his saddle to bellow his orders.

'All cohorts! Ready . . . spears!'

His men hefted their shields and raised their iron-shanked spears ready to throw, staring at the advancing Batavi with an evident combination of anticipation and fear. At thirty paces distance, just outside effective spear throw, the rebels halted at their leaders' command, the militia dressing their ranks while continuing to chant their defiance at the Romans before them. The tribal warriors to their right were howling their own ritual challenges with the exaggerated facial expressions intended to strike fear into the opposing army, something no Roman army in Germania had seen in any man's memory, other than picturesque demonstrations by allied forces on campaign or at major celebratory parades. Stamping from foot to foot, they stabbed out and then down with their spears, slamming their shields into the turf and then stabbing their long spear blades forward again, all the while howling their war cries as one man, their voices booming low and then soaring high, the threat all too evident even to men who had never seen the ritual performed before. They fell silent, and Aquillius took a look backwards to find the scene on the warships calmer, the fighting apparently having burned itself out, although his hurried glance failed to reveal the mutiny's outcome beyond the unavoidable fact that bolt throwers that should have been pouring missiles into the enemy were unmanned, their threat negated by the unexpected struggle for control.

'Now comes the barritus.'

He turned back to Labeo.

'The *what*?'

'Listen and you'll understand. Kivilaz will let them do it for a while, I'd imagine, to tempt you to come forward at him. Perhaps I should be with my cohort?'

Aquillius nodded.

'Perhaps you should.'

The Batavi officer saluted and turned his horse away, riding back to his men who were standing where they had been ordered to await further instructions, the horsemen still seemingly untroubled by the likelihood of battle against their own people. The situation on the warships seemed to be under control, men wearing the armour and helmets of centurions directing the sailors to throw bodies over the vessels' side, presumably the detritus resulting from the short-lived mutiny. Taking a breath, he bellowed a command loudly enough to be heard over the growing noise the rebels were making.

'*Get those scorpions back into action!*'

More than one of the officers raised a hand in acknowledgement, and Aquillius nodded to himself in satisfaction. Once one or two of them started shooting again the remainder would follow their example quickly enough, and that would soon put Civilis's forces onto their back feet, caught under a pitiless sleet of iron-tipped bolts that would rip holes in their formation and shatter their morale in the usual way.

And then the rebels started making a noise unlike anything he'd heard before, a low, muttering susurration of voices, their shields if they had them pulled close to their mouths, cupped hands serving the same purpose if not, the sound slowly swelling as they increased the volume of their chant, until it was all he could do to think with the barritus's infernal din. They fell silent for a moment, and the Roman readied himself to order his men to throw their spears as the enemy began their advance, only for them to start again, their voices swiftly building to a peak and then dying away again. The chant continued, ebbing and flowing like waves on a beach, and with a moment of insight Aquillius realised that there was a part of him willing the Germans not to stop, because when they did so it would mean the battle's descent from shouting and posturing to the bloody mayhem he knew was inevitable. Shaking his head angrily, he looked across the ranks of his men, taking stock of their postures and apparent readiness to fight and seeing nothing to trouble him, each cohort's prefect looking to him for their orders in readiness to do whatever it was that he determined was required.

'Fuck this.'

The decision was instant, almost instinctive, a sudden moment of realisation that to stand and wait for the Germans to complete their preparations was to hand them an advantage that might be too much for his men's shaky morale. He took a breath, ready to roar the command that would send his cohorts forward the ten paces required to put them in spear range, ready to shower the unarmoured Batavi with sharp iron and disrupt their leisurely build up to an attack, when the first thumps of the scorpions re-engaging rang out, immediately followed by the screams of men whose bodies had been ruined by the heavy arrows' impacts. On the verge of making another, equally instant decision not to attack, but to allow the artillery time to soften up the enemy, he started as a man staggered out of the rear of the Ubian cohort in a fine mist of blood, a metal-finned bolt protruding from his armoured back.

'Jupiter!'

More scorpions discharged their loads, each shot spitting an iron-tipped bolt into the rear of his defenceless infantrymen and dropping soldiers kicking and screaming onto the grass. He turned in amazement, staring aghast at the warships and realising that the men wearing the armour of the military crews were unkempt and dishevelled, their equipment hastily donned and unfastened, helmets askew on their heads as they hurried to reload the bolt throwers that were tearing into his army's defenceless rear. Again his decision was instant, the only possible course of action. The rear rank would have to about-face and charge the moored warships, overrun their mutinous crews and stop the treacherous assault before it broke his men's resolve, but even as the thought solidified in his mind, he realised that he was looking straight down the slides of the nearest warship's weapons. With twin thumps both scorpions unleashed their bolts, and the unforgiving ground came up to meet him with enough force to knock him senseless as his horse keeled over.

River Rhenus, August AD 69

One moment the Roman commander was looming over his battle line, his head turned to stare at the warships whose crews seemed to have taken leave of their senses, the next he was gone, his horse shot out from beneath him.

'There! *That's* what I was waiting for!'

Draco watched as Kivilaz touched his heels to the horse's side, walking the beast out into the gap between his men and the Tungrian cohort facing them. Bracing his thighs he stood up in the saddle, pulling his cloak away from the soiled tunic beneath. A handprint was clearly visible on the white wool, its original deep red now almost black but still recognisable as blood, arching his back to present it to them as clearly as possible and shouting a challenge to the enemy soldiers before him.

'*Who will avenge him?*'

The reply was almost instant.

'*We will avenge him!*'

He repeated the question, pointing to the bloody handprint on his chest.

'*Who will avenge him?*'

'*We will avenge him!*'

Clenching the pointing hand into a fist, he raised it over his head and bellowed the words that they were waiting for.

'*Proud men of the Tungri! Join us, and reclaim your lost pride!*'

Centurions stepped out of the auxiliary cohort's ranks where they stood on the left of the terrified Frisians, raising their swords and blowing signal whistles. Their prefect started forward, only to find himself facing his own first spear, sword drawn and grim-faced.

'No, Prefect. This cohort no longer serves Rome. On your knees.'

The Tungrian cohort was suddenly moving, wheeling the four-deep lines that had faced the Batavi a moment before through ninety degrees so that their spears and shields were aimed at the left flank of the Frisian cohort, whose men were shrinking away from them in amazement, unable to believe what they were seeing. The manoeuvre completed, the soldiers paused momentarily, waiting for the command they were expecting as their senior centurion, having handed his astonished prefect over to the custody of a hard-faced officer, swept his sword down to point at their hapless neighbours, whose soldiers were backing away from his men's presented spear points with disbelieving stares, their tidy line fragmenting as the trickle of men turning to flee swelled with their terror.

'Tungriii! Spears . . . *throw!*'

The Germans stamped forward a pace at their senior centurion's command, hurling their spears into the men who remained in the Frisian left flank, wide open to the assault, their own officers still dithering at this most unexpected development. Unprepared for the attack, the rain of iron focused on that end of the hapless cohort's line effectively destroyed it, spear heads thrown at such close range either finding the unarmoured points on their targets' bodies, necks, arms and legs, or simply punching through the auxiliaries' mail armour into the flesh beneath. The air was rent by the screams and imprecations of scores of wounded and dying men, sobbing howls of pain and anger, and what order remained in their disintegrating was suddenly no more than a mob of panicking, terrified, individuals, all thought save that of survival gone from their heads.

'*Tungriii! Attack!*'

The waiting soldiers, swords already drawn, marched forward in the manner that had been drilled into them a thousand times and began the harvest of those men who, already wounded, were unable to escape, or who either disdained the chance to run or were unable to find a way through the mass of their comrades quickly enough.

Kivilaz grinned at Hramn, his eyes alive with delight as he turned to the waiting Batavi militia.

'Batavi! *Attack!*'

The tribesmen lurched into motion, not throwing their spears as they closed with the Ubian cohort but hefting them underhand, ready to begin the remorseless grinding advance in which they had been drilled so assiduously over the preceding months, and roaring the paean that they had been taught as they had practised the advance. Those men of the enemy cohort who were still standing their ground, already shocked and reeling at the discharge of dozens of scorpion bolts into their rear, and the unexpected onslaught on the neighbouring cohort, were unable to absorb this further threat and retain their cohesion. Disintegrating before their prefect's startled eyes they too literally burst in all directions, one moment still formed despite the cruel attack on their rear from the warships, the next no better than a frenzied mob of men running in all directions with survival their only aim. Those soldiers who ran at the Batavi died on their spears, as the militia's warriors instinctively obeyed their training and the muscle memory of long months of drill, punching with their shields to stop the running men and then spearing them, punching again to smash their wounded and dying victims from their spear blades before setting themselves to advance again, held upright by the firm grip on their collars of the men behind them.

Amid the battlefield's sudden chaos, Hramn sat watching the mayhem from his saddle, nodding grimly as he spotted Labeo leading his cavalry cohort away to the east, clearly seeking to escape the battle's abrupt debacle before they too were embroiled in the spreading, bloody chaos.

'Let me go after them!'

Kivilaz shook his head without taking his eyes off the chaotic scene before him.

'No, Decurion. Today is not the day.'

Unable to contain his anger, Hramn rose up in the saddle and drew breath to roar a leather-lunged challenge at the fleeing traitor.

'*Labeo!*'

The Batavi officer seemed to hear his name, reining his horse in and looking across the battlefield's bloody carnage. Hramn drew his sword and raised it over his head in an angry gesture.

'*You'd better run, traitor! We'll hang you up by your guts for this! Run! Run to your Roman masters! We'll see you soon enough!*'

If he even heard the threat over the screams and howls of the battle, Labeo showed no sign of it, simply raising his hand in salute and then spurring his horse on, away to the east. Hramn sank back into his saddle, shaking his head in disgust.

'There's nowhere for you to run but the Old Camp, traitor. And we'll see you there soon enough.'

River Rhenus, August AD 69

Aquillius came to his senses after what could only have been a few seconds, finding that he had mercifully been thrown clear of his dying horse, the animal kicking and screaming on the ground a few feet away as its blood-spattered body convulsed at the pain of a pair of scorpion bolts buried deep in its side. Staggering to his feet, he fumbled his sword out of its scabbard and groggily stared around him at the scene of horror into which his ordered battle plan had descended in the moments while he had been unconscious. The Frisian cohort was now only recognisable as a military formation by their red tunics but was little more than a seething mob of men fighting to escape their former allies' spears and swords. The Ubian cohort had also disintegrated, the ground at their rear littered with the corpses of men killed by scorpion bolts that protruded from their sides and backs. He could hear rather than see the Batavi militia that he knew would be advancing into their disordered ranks, a gift from the gods for Civilis, the chance to blood his men against an enemy who was already beaten and needed only the mercy stroke. Looking to his left he saw that the Batavian cavalry cohort were riding away at a brisk canter, clearly recognising a lost situation when they saw one, and he watched as Labeo, recognisable by his crested helmet and ornate armour, reined his horse in momentarily, looking out over the battle's chaos as someone shouted something in the guttural German language away behind the Batavi line. Their eyes locked, and the Batavian prefect shrugged resignedly before saluting and spurring his beast away, leaving Aquillius standing alone in the middle of the battle's carnage. Looking at the scene of chaos before him, he saw the Roman prefect who had been in command of the Tungrians being stripped of his magnificent armour and weapons at sword point by a pair of his own centurions, while the Frisian and Ubian officers were being led away from their surrendering soldiers and herded together under the threat of dozens of raised spears.

Shaking his head he came to his senses, the wits seeming to snap back into his body from wherever they had been wandering while he'd staggered upright and gazed glassy-eyed about him, the potential victim of any man with a spear.

'*Fuck . . .*'

The battle was already lost, and he had been reduced from commander to foot soldier in the moments while he had been unconscious. Pulling off his helmet, he ripped away the crest that stood above its iron bowl and which marked him as a target for every enemy warrior who saw him, snapping the leather cords that held it tautly in place and pulling the brass mount loose from its sleeve. Tossing it away he pulled the helmet back on and laced the cheek guards tight, then discarded his silver decorated scabbard and medal harness, cutting at the straps with his dagger rather than wasting time with the buckles. Cutting away the leather ties that held on his greaves, he completed his transformation from officer to soldier, looking around for the best route out of the battle's swirling chaos. His army was surrendering in ever greater numbers, throwing down their weapons and pleading for their lives with an enemy who, whilst not treating their capitulation with any subtlety, was refraining from the massacre that might have been expected. Knowing that he would be captured within minutes if he failed to act, and swiftly betrayed by his former soldiers in hope of some sort of favour from their captors, he made a decision and turned to his left, running hard in pursuit of Labeo's fleeing Batavian horsemen in the only direction that held any prospect of safety.

A Tungrian soldier blundered into his path, staggering away from a fight with his helmet dented and his wits momentarily absent, and Aquillius put the gladius's blade through his neck without a second thought, stripping the shield from his lifeless fingers and shouldering the corpse aside. Another Tungrian came at him with a spear, his own shield lost, thrusting in with the weapon so inexpertly that it was all that Aquillius could do not to bellow a correction at him, as he pushed the lunge aside with the shield and stabbed deep into the hapless soldier's thigh with the gladius before ripping the blade free, nodding to himself as the man stared helplessly at the rope of blood running down his leg.

Moving on, weaving around the knots of men fighting forlorn, doomed actions, he saw a horse, still saddled, standing over the body of a mail-shirted man with a scorpion bolt protruding from his back, lying face down on top of a vivid yellow shield. The shield's colour made the man one of Labeo's men, whose mutinous comrades had evidently found the cavalryman too appealing a target to ignore. Moving quickly, knowing that a beast of such quality would be a prize beyond the dreams of most of the men on the battlefield, he tossed aside the Tungrian infantryman's shield, shoved his gladius into his belt and snatched up the dead rider's long spear and rolled him off the shield, tugging the brass-bound yellow oval onto his back. As he pulled the horse's reins from the corpse's unresisting fingers and prepared to mount, something made him look over his shoulder, barely in time to duck beneath a swinging hack of a gladius's blade, the sword's owner lunging in with a triumphant snarl that became a cry of agony as Aquillius swayed to one side and kicked him in the kneecap with brutal speed and power, snapping the joint. Snapping a punch into the reeling man's face that broke his nose and shot blood across his armour, he followed up with a sweeping boot hook that dumped the stunned soldier onto the ground, then stamped down with his hobnails into the helpless man's unprotected crotch, wrenching a high-pitched scream from his lips. Startled, the horse shied away from him, pulling him bodily away from the crippled soldier before he could finish the tottering man off.

'Get him!'

The battle was almost done, most of the auxiliary troops now either face down or kneeling, terrified, under rebel swords and spears, and Aquillius's rage-fuelled battering of the hapless soldier had been enough to attract the attention of more than one of his victim's comrades. Dragging the horse back to him with a vicious wrench at its reins he vaulted into the saddle as the closest of the Tungrians turned with their swords raised, pulling the animal's head round to the east and digging his boots into its flanks. Galloping away from the Tungrians Aquillius looked to his right, at the full cohort of Batavi horsemen standing in a formation so neat that it would have graced any parade ground, and he quailed, knowing that they could ride him down with ease. But the luck that had deserted him a moment before now shone brightly again, the enemy guardsmen looking across the battlefield at him without any intention of giving chase, as if the capture of a single beaten soldier were beneath their dignity. Following the path that Labeo's men had taken moments earlier the fugitive centurion rode away to the east, leaving behind him the scene of an abject defeat while he plotted the ways in which he would take his revenge for the betrayal and dismemberment of his army.

'It seems you have been a busy man these past few months.'

Kivilaz acknowledged Hramn's barbed comment with a nod of his head, as the two men watched in silence for a moment while the last corpses that were all that remained of the Roman cohorts were dragged away by their defeated brothers-in-arms to the pyre, while their men feasted on the supplies that had been intended for the defeated army. One of the guardsmen walked up with a flask and two cups, bowing to Kivilaz and handing him the wine. Pouring a cup for his comrade, he took one for himself and turned back to address Hramn's unspoken question.

'The Tungri have been mine from that moment on the road back from the Old Camp, with a little prompting from my messengers. After all, that fortress has been wide open for any man to enter, since they emptied the place out and sent most of its strength south.'

'And the fleet? How did you manage that?'

'I had divine assistance.'

Hramn frowned.

'I don't understand.'

Kivilaz grinned, draining his wine and pouring another cupful, gesturing for the decurion to do the same.

'You will recall what I told the elders, at our meeting in the grove? About the Bructeri seer Veleda?'

'Yes. But one priestess?'

'One priestess with a following the length and breadth of the great river's valley. One priestess worshipped so fervently that she can bring about peace between a German tribe and a Roman subject people with a simple pronouncement. One priestess revered so strongly that a simple message from her to the fleet's German oarsmen, telling them that they held the destiny of their people in their hands, was enough to put them on our side overnight.'

'Clever.'

Kivilaz shrugged.

'Oh I'm clever alright, but I'm more than that, Hramn. Clever is never enough against Rome. To defeat Rome you need luck, and stealth, and guile . . . and one thing more. You need burning hatred. When that bastard Capito had my brother murdered for the crime of accompanying me south to meet with Vindex, I swore a blood oath over his corpse, in the moment they gave me to say goodbye before they buried him, expecting that the sight of my dead brother would unman me. But it didn't. It lit a blazing fire in me, a fire I have kindled until it is hotter than a smith's forge. Hot enough to burn Rome out of our lives for ever.'

Hramn looked into his prince's face, and saw the hard implacable lines of a man who was at war.

'And Vespasianus? What will you do when he triumphs over Vitellius, as you believe he will? Will that be the moment when we make peace with Rome?'

'Vespasianus? Vespasianus entreated me to bring revolt and chaos to Rome's northern border. And revolt and chaos he shall have. I will launch an onslaught against Rome that will shake the stones on the Palatine Hill.'

He emptied the cup again and set it down, turning to look at the fire that was being kindled to consume the dead auxiliaries' bodies.

'Vespasianus wanted a revolt? I'll give him everything he asked for. And more. Much, *much* more.'

Historical Note

Researching the *Centurions* trilogy was a fresh challenge for a writer who has, over the course of writing nine previous stories in the *Empire* series, become a little blasé about the historical background, events, military units and tactics, weapons and armour and just about anything else you could care to name about the late second century. To find oneself suddenly over a hundred years adrift of one's chosen period of history was in one respect easy enough – after all, not that much changed over the period in many ways – and yet a bit of a head-scratcher from several other perspectives. The revolt of the Batavi tribe is on the face of it a simple thing – Romans upset tribal mercenaries, who then rise up and teach them an almighty lesson as to how to manage subject peoples and their armies – and yet the history, and the story that can be teased out of those dry pages left to us by the primary sources Tacitus and Cassius, is far more complex than anything I could have predicted.

To start at the beginning, the Batagwi (and we'll get to the source of that name in a moment) – Batavians to the Romans – were one of the German tribes subjugated by Caesar in the wake of his rampage through the Gauls, and quickly became a firm ally of what was to become the empire. Having originated from the Chatti tribe, and migrated away from that part of Germany for whatever reason, they settled on a piece of pleasingly fertile land in the riverine delta in a location we currently know as Nijmegen. It seems likely that this land, surrounded by rivers on two sides and marshy ground to the west, would have effectively have been an island in those days before the reclamation of so much land by the Dutch, and it is termed as 'the island' in the contemporary accounts of the war. They called this new homeland Bat-agwjo, 'the better land' for the very reason of its fertility, the first element *bat* effectively the same as the *bet* in our modern day better, while the second part of the name, *agwjo* refers to meadows surrounded by water, in modern German aue and in Old-English *īeg.* Or in other words an island, and that's how the Romans translated it. It is likely that the tribe called themselves Batagwi or something close to it, but to make life a little easier for the reader, however, and since the tribe are these days routinely described as *Batavi,* I have chosen to use that term, rather than anything more authentic but harder to get the tongue around.

Providing Rome with a military contingent that sounds like it would have been the match of any legion – eight part-mounted five-hundred-man infantry cohorts and a cavalry wing – they were a powerful blend of German ferocity in battle with Roman equipment and, to some degree, Rome's military ethos and tactics. In return for this disproportionate contribution to the imperial forces, they paid no taxes to Rome, an indication of just how valuable their contribution was deemed to be. Their role, to judge from the relatively scant sources, was in the long tradition of shock troops that has continued into the modern era in formations like the Parachute Regiment and the US Marines, hard men trained to high levels of physical competency and tactical aggression and, by consequence of both that conditioning and their collective underlying social backgrounds, lacking some of the instincts to self-preservation that can hamper soldiers from risking everything in pursuit of victory in the moment of decision that occurs on all battlefields. The best equivalent for us to consider with regard to the Batavi tribe's contribution might well be the Gurkhas, Nepalese soldiers who have fought with great honour and bravery for the British empire and its post-colonial army, and whose bloody reputation has resulted in their mere presence in the order of battle proving fearsomely intimidating to Britain's enemies on many occasions.

Parented for decades by the Fourteenth Gemina Legion, it

seems that the Batavi cohorts did a good deal of the initial dirty work on one battlefield after another, as at the battle of the Medway in AD 43. Their sneak attack at dawn across the seemingly unfordable river seems to have destroyed the British tribes' chariot threat before the battle commenced, and allowed the Fourteenth, under the improbably young Hosidius Geta, and the Second Augustan under the future emperor Vespasian, to establish the bridgehead from which victory would eventually result. Incidentally, for those readers with an interest in the cursus honorum and its age restrictions, the historical record is a little confused with regard to Geta, and the legatus in question might have been an older brother, although age restrictions on command tended to be relaxed by a year for each child born to a family – so we can consider legion command at the age of twenty-four (it was usually no younger than thirty) as improbable but eminently possible, under the right circumstances. The most startling aspect of all this is that on more than one occasion the Batavi used an organic amphibious capability – and by organic I mean without the assistance of any third party such as a naval unit – to cross rivers and narrow coastal straits and turn an enemy flank by appearing where they were least expected. How did they do this, swimming while wearing their equipment which, weighing around twenty-five kilos, would obviously overwhelm even the strongest of swimmers in short order even before the encumbrances of having to carry a shield and spear are taken into account? It's possible that the latter were carried by means of some kind of improvised flotation device, but we cannot discount the possibility that fully equipped infantrymen were carried across the water obstacle and straight into battle by means of the cohort's horses being used to literally tow them across. This seems to have been what Dio Cassius is describing in *The History of Rome:*

> *The barbarians thought the Romans would not be able to cross this* [the River Medway] *without a bridge, and as a result had pitched camp in a rather careless fashion on the opposite bank. Plautius, however, sent across some Celts who were practised in*

swimming with ease fully armed across even the fastest of rivers. These fell unexpectedly on the enemy . . .

This was probably as innovative and disruptive to an unprepared enemy as massed parachute drops were (under the right circumstances) in the twentieth century, and the Batavi seem to have been viewed as Rome's best and bravest shock troops, capable of doing the impossible and turning a battle to Rome's advantage by their unexpected abilities. For a long time this guaranteed them the highest possible status as an allied people, ruled not by a governor but instead by a magistrate voted into office by the tribe's most exalted citizens, the *noblissimi popularium* (the ruling class, literally 'noble countrymen'). This tended to mean, one suspects, that they were pretty much guaranteed to take a Roman perspective on the behalf of a self-interested ruling class of families, themselves granted citizenship in perpetuity by the early emperors, in the pursuit of a Roman foreign policy that sought to ensure an alignment of the empire's ambitions with those of the tribe's rulers.

This relationship went even further than the battlefield, for in 30 BCE Augustus recruited an imperial bodyguard from the Batavi and the other tribes that dwelt in the same area, Ubii, Frisii, Baetasii and so on. Where the Praetorians guarded the city and in particular its palaces, the *corporis custodes* protected the emperor himself, and were trusted for their impartial devotion to the task of ensuring his safety and deterring assassination attempts that might otherwise have been considered by the praetorians themselves (and for which they later gained an unenviable reputation). Disbanded briefly at the time of the Varus disaster in AD 9, they were swiftly reinstated when it became clear that the tribe had taken no part in Arminius's act of outright war, and the Batavi played a full role in the suppression of the tribes to the north and east of the Rhine that was to follow. They remained at the side of a succession of emperors until late AD 68, when the new emperor Galba made what appears to have been the fatal mistake of dismissing them for their loyalty to Nero, thereby leaving himself open to assassination by an improbably small number of praetorians.

It is important to understand just what this meant to the Batavi, and why they took the dismissal quite as badly as they undoubtedly did. The Bodyguard were, of course, a source of enormous kudos to the tribe and their local neighbours, and a significant source of income to boot, but the importance of their place in Rome went deeper than simple national pride – the influence of their position close to the throne on the tribe itself cannot be ignored. Exposed to Rome, the hub of empire and meeting point for dozens of nationalities and cultures, it was inevitable that the guardsmen would have had the blinkers of their previous existence removed to some degree, and that they would have been eager to share their new experiences and learning with friends and families. Anthony Birley argues in *Germania Inferior* (in an article entitled 'The Names of the Batavians and the Tungrians') that many guardsmen would have been likely to have been given new Latin or Greek names on their entry into service, as their own names might be unpronounceable for a Roman, and the perpetuation of these names into the Batavi mainstream as proud parents sought to rub a little of a brother or an uncle's fame off on their new offspring must have been inevitable, which is the reason why some Batavi characters in *Betrayal* have apparently anachronistic Greek names that are in fact entirely valid for their time and place. The guard effectively came to define the Batavi's significant status within the empire, a source of enormous prestige at least within the tribe itself. This in turn justified the degree to which they had subjugated their culture to that of Rome, including the incorporation of their religion into the Roman framework, their god Magusanus, as was so often the case with local deities, being deftly spliced with the Roman version of Heracles/Hercules to create a new and mutually acceptable deity. The Bodyguard had come to define the Batavi to a large degree, and when they came home for good late in AD 68 it must have seemed as if the tribe had been cast aside by the previously doting parent regime, with immense impacts on both the Batavi's own self-esteem and indeed their relationships with the other local tribes who were equally impacted by this inexplicably sudden and shocking change of fortunes.

Of course the split with Rome was more complex than just the overnight loss of their prestige. It went far deeper than the sudden thunderbolt of late AD 68, and had been growing ever more obvious to those with eyes to see it over the previous years. The Batavi and their allies the Cananefates, the Marsacii and the Frisavones had to some degree, if the Roman commentators are to be believed, simply got too big for their own boots. In effect, it seems, they had made the age-old mistake of believing their own propaganda (or at least that of their Roman allies who called them the 'best and bravest', in itself possibly a play on the Germanic origins of the tribe's name, Batavi, which might well have meant 'the best'). They had taken, we are told, to strutting around telling anyone who would listen how important they were to Rome, had fallen out with their former parent legion the Fourteenth Gemina – possibly because the legion was lauded by Nero as his most effective after the Battle of Watling Street and the defeat of the Iceni, while the Batavi had presumably gone relatively unrecognised – and had thereby contributed to the increasing disenchantment with what was later portrayed as their overbearing behaviour. Rescued from internal exile of a sort by the onset of war between the German army of Vitellius and Otho's loyalist legions – having previously been posted to garrison duty standing guard on the Lingones in eastern Gaul ostensibly to prevent a recurrence of the Vindex revolt – they had immediately (if we believe the primary sources who were of course propagandists with their own agenda) taken up where they had left off, telling all and sundry how they had mastered their former parent legion and how critical they were to the success of the war against Otho. It is doubtful if they were much loved by either legions or generals, but rather tolerated for their ability to turn a battle given the chance to do so.

In late AD 68, and at about the same time as the returning men of the Bodyguard, Gaius Julius Civilis ('Kivilaz' in the book, this being entirely my own invention, with a little learned help, and in no way attested by any source) returned from captivity, trial and acquittal in Rome. Civilis's Roman name identifies him as the son of one of the tribe's original noble families – a prince and successful military commander, but he was a man with an unhappy recent past. Charged with treason for having allegedly participated in the Vindex revolt, a failed uprising that had ultimately led to Nero's suicide, his brother had been summarily executed and Civilis himself sent to Rome to face the same charge. Freed by Galba – who had after all benefited hugely from Vindex's apparent folly in rising up without an army worthy of the name – he went home and was promptly rearrested by the army of Germania Inferior under the emperor-to-be, Aulus Vitellius, on the same charge. Freed once more, by a canny emperor who realised the risk posed by potentially hostile tribes in his own backyard while his armies were for the most part far distant in Italy, Civilis seems likely to have discerned the inevitability of a third attempt to make the charge stick, once Vitellius had no further need to tread softly around the Batavi at the war's end.

And if the quasi-judicial murder of his brother and the threat hanging over his own head weren't enough to motivate him to revolt against Rome, the opportunity to seize power in a political system that must have seemed to be sliding away from the *noblissimi popularium*'s control, as more and more men of common rank achieved citizen status through their military service, may also have been too strong a temptation to be passed up. Whatever the reason, Civilis roused his people to revolt and the bloody events that will play out in *Onslaught* and *Retribution* came to pass.

There are some other smaller subjects to discuss while we're looking at the historical backdrop to *Betrayal*.

As you'll have read (and if you've not read the book yet, be warned that this is a spoiler of sorts), it's fairly clear that the man with the most to gain from a Batavi revolt was actually not Civilis, given that Rome was always going to stamp the rebellion flat eventually, but rather Titus Flavius Vespasianus, Vespasian as we know him. When the Batavi and their allies rose up and started killing Roman soldiers, the effect was to plant a dagger in Vitellius's back at the worst possible time, dragging his attention away from Vespasian's army as it advanced on Rome and preventing him from drawing any further reinforcements south from Germany to bolster his cause. It's worth making the point that there's no evidence that (another spoiler) Pliny the Elder was Vespasian's emissary to the Batavi, but rather my invention based both on his previous military service in Germania Inferior and the fact that he was a friend of the emperor-to-be who rose to a position of significant responsibility after the latter's victory. Perhaps I'm taking two and two and adding them up to make seventeen, but given Civilis's time in Rome it's far from impossible that Pliny and Vespasian's son-in-law, Cerialis – a man we're going to be seeing a lot more of – found an opportunity to make mutual cause, or at least to form the friendships that later translated to that alliance of convenience.

Perhaps my favourite character in *Betrayal* is Gaius Aquillius Proculus (more spoilers here), blue-chinned dead-eyed warrior of Rome – at least in this fictional version of the revolt. What a gift for a historical novelist looking for a charismatic protagonist. All we know about him is that a phalerae – a medal, worn with several others on a chest harness – with his name and legion engraved onto its reverse, was discovered in the remains of the cavalry fort close to Batavodurum, and that, as Tacitus tells us, he was a centurion of the first rank – presumably a *primus pilus* – of the Eighth Augustan who led the initial resistance to Civilis's uprising (another spoiler: which failed in the face of treachery from both Tungrian auxiliaries and the fleet). He then disappears from the historical record, but not from this story! Gaius Aquillius Proculus will return . . .

And on to Claudius Labeo. To be frank, if Labeo hadn't existed I would have invented him because – as we're going to see in *Onslaught* – he's a complex character who's going to bring out the very worst in Julius Civilis. I can't say much about him now, as his major part in the story is yet to begin, but I think it's safe to say that he represents everything in his tribe's ruling class that

Civilis disdained and revolted to overthrow, and which must have been one of his major motivations in making his bid for independence from Rome.

And lastly, that name Kivilaz. When I started out writing this trilogy I sought the assistance of a world renowned scholar of Rome and the Batavians, Jona Lendering, owner of the justly praised *Livius* website. If you've never used it then I heartily recommended a visit. In the course of working with him, a collaboration which has paid off massively for me due to his knowledge and generosity in sharing it, we speculated as to Julius Civilis's real name, which is not contained within the surviving historical record. His first suggestion was Kivil, and that in itself was a brilliant extrapolation of the Romanised version that I then used it all the way through writing the manuscript of *Betrayal* with a very good feeling that we were close to the truth. Imagine my excitement, both for the book and for Jona himself, to receive the following a few days ago:

"I have news that will make you happy: *Kivil* may be related to Dutch *kiven*, "to fight", with a suffix that indicates the agent. If this is correct, *Kivil* means "fighter". Now here's the beautiful part: that suffix was, in Anglo Saxon times, *el*, and in reconstructed ProtoGerman *ilaz*. We might therefore also reconstruct a name *Kivilaz*, which is even closer to "*Civilis*".

Which, as you can imagine, works for me and just feels like it fits. So *Kivilaz* it is. You won't find it in any textbooks I'm aware of. Or at least not yet.

So there it is, my partial understanding of the period and the help I've had in filling the inevitable gaps laid bare for your consideration. The assistance has been considerable, and as ever any errors are mine and mine alone. Your comments and criticisms are very welcome, whether via my website's comments page or social media. I endeavour to answer all posts quickly, but writing and work sometimes get in the way, so please continue to show the usual patience and don't be afraid to nudge me if I'm slow responding. And now I'm off to start writing *Onslaught*.

Anthony Riches

A CHANCE TO WIN A PIECE OF ROMAN HISTORY . . .

For your chance to win a mint condition silver denarius from AD74, go to Anthony Riches' website

WWW.ANTHONYRICHES.COM/COMPETITIONS

and answer the following question:

Q: IN WHICH YEAR DID THE EMPEROR VESPASIAN TAKE THE THRONE?

PLUS, for the unique opportunity to win a solid gold Vespasian aureus, answer the first of three questions to be found in the pages of each book in *The Centurions* trilogy.

Q: FIND A SOLDIER IN THE YEAR OF JULIUS CAESAR'S ASSASSINATION

Look out for the next two questions – and answers – in the following books in the trilogy, *Onslaught: The Centurions II* (October 2017) and *Retribution: The Centurions III* (April 2018), for your chance to win.

UK only. For full competition terms and conditions please go to www.anthonyriches.com/competitions